STEP CLOSER

STEP CLOSER

TESSA McWATT

HarperCollins Publishers Ltd

Step Closer
Copyright © 2009 by Tessa McWatt.
All rights reserved.

Published by HarperCollins Publishers Ltd.

First edition

No part of this book may be used or reproduced in any manner whatsoever without written permission except in the case of brief quotations embodied in reviews.

HarperCollins books may be purchased for educational, business, or sales promotional use through our Special Markets Department.

HarperCollins Publishers Ltd
2 Bloor Street East, 20th Floor
Toronto, Ontario, Canada
M4W 1A8

www.harpercollins.ca

Library and Archives Canada Cataloguing in Publication

McWatt, Tessa, 1959–
Step closer : a novel / Tessa McWatt.

ISBN 978-0-00-200566-1

I. Title.

PS8575.W37S74 2009   C813'.54   C2008-907926-4

Printed and bound in the United States
RRD 9 8 7 6 5 4 3 2 1

Andrew,
Natalie,
friends on the long road.

"We little know the things for which we pray."
Geoffrey Chaucer, "Knight's Tale," *The Canterbury Tales*

" . . . mere flim-flam stories, and nothing but shams and lies."
Cervantes, *Don Quixote*

At 11:05 am November 3, 1968 (a Sunday), five different magnitude 5.4 earthquakes were registered around the globe. One in Connecticut, near the Moodus River Falls, where stones of several tons were thrown from the top of the cliff into the foaming river below; another shook Oaxaca, Mexico, where one farmer's donkey was found on the roof of a shed; the third was registered in Bartin, Turkey, where two women were trapped under the rubble of a fallen clock tower; a fourth in Papua New Guinea, with still unmeasured damage; and the final one was felt only by my mother, in Flinton, Ontario, as I came through her and into the world.

I think seismic is a relative term. You can never say for sure what force is needed for change to take place.

Perhaps the seismic events on that day were purely coincidental, but if they were, would that make everything else that happens on the planet coincidental as well? The hunger for a meal, the preparation of a meal, the eating of a meal? Coincidence goes against our experience of events, doesn't it? It denies our desire and what we feel to be true: that life is not random. There is an order here, awkward and quiet, even now, if you look carefully. And gazed at from beyond, today's events might appear to have a shape as graceful and loud as the shifting of tectonic plates.

I was born, rocks fell. Do I convince you of cause and effect? If I order the past just so—the flickers, moans, bruises—will I assemble my own pardon? Words skid off the tongue, language can be so slippery, but perhaps you will stay the course with me if I begin with Once upon a time . . .

One

Dawn. He teetered now, the limp from a childhood mishap was more pronounced in the urgent, wide strides. His toe clipped the edge of a boulder and sent him stumbling forward, his hands circling like propellers to keep him upright. *Whooaa.* He continued away from the lighthouse, his eyes focused on the cliff edge in the distance. *This cliff,* he thought, but pushed back thoughts. Thoughts were torture. He wobbled among rocks, sneaking up to the coast as though in an ambush.

Panting.

He kept clear of anything that looked like the footpath that had brought him north from Santiago de Compostela. To the end. Finisterre. He stopped. To his left was a sculpture of bronze walking boots. He veered right towards higher ground, the sharp edges of the mortal coast, and then out over the goatgrass that sprouted among the cliff rocks.

He slowed down, looked up as if to sniff the air . . . *this air* . . . and then down again at his brogues. He could smell the stench rising from them. He waved it off. Walking even more quickly now, he made a last dash towards the edge. He found himself looking out over the coast just as the sun made its presence felt on his neck.

This skin, he thought and slapped his neck. He couldn't bear the prick of heat that held promise, or the sky before him whose very molecules were forming a blue net that might catch him.

Rain. At least there should be rain.

Gavin sat on the edge of the cliff and considered what was certainly below—the jutting rocks, the fractured boulders. He didn't look down yet. Screaming, he heard. Tearing, he felt. Ribs, legs, face on the sharp edge, stumps, and bramble down the slope. Yes, it would have been like that then, on that other cliff. He placed his fists behind his buttocks and pushed himself forward until his legs dangled over the edge. He hesitated. This edge was so different from the one back then, the one in the Scottish Highlands. The tufts of heather, the brassy air, and the slanted rain were missing. As was the watching face. If this was to work, the face beyond the heather would have to come into focus. Drawing down the rain or triggering a gust of wind to hide it would not do now. He slapped his neck again. *This cliff.*

He pushed himself farther forward . . . *watch me now . . .* the knuckles of his right hand inching his buttocks towards the sharpest of the rocks. He raised his legs and looked at his shoes. The dread wafted up. Beyond his feet he could see the heady surf of the Atlantic gobbling boulders and spitting them out again. He wanted mist, not the sea. This calm was unexpected. He thought of the sounds of that other raining cliff. Closed his eyes and pictured the face. He inched forward. And again. He felt the land's end on the back of his thighs and then on his backside. He pushed himself forward.

And he fell.

Words have built up over the years, repeating themselves in a loop as I sleep. In attempts over the last five years to write the beginning, middle, and end of Gavin's story, some words settle, like those you've just read, but others grow in vertical piles so high they regularly tumble. When I first met Gavin the words that came to me had to do with hope, and possibility, because I couldn't understand how a man could have run out of those. I once wrote the story's opening like this: *The coastline at dawn is a shiver of hope. That yellow moment when the sun cracks itself open on the surface of the sea is drenched in possibility. But sometimes hope is the last thing a man needs.* But those words were not about what needed to be told.

Last year the words were walnut, primordial, and salt. Walnut. Primordial. Salt. They did a kind of möbius strip loop around images that have no bearing on their meaning or on the story that remains untold. I had begun to wonder if I could really tell it at all, given the long passage of time, my absence from defining moments during the course of events, and the impossibility of knowing a simple word like *why*. Since watching the television news with Sam this morning, I am inclined to think it's important to focus on the events themselves, and on moving through them. Perhaps the words are as simple as *step on*.

My name is Alexandra, but people have called me by my middle name since I was very young. I can feel it now, the chill of a February morning in Canada when the light was flat and orange. A park near my grandmother's home in Tweed, Ontario, where my mother had taken refuge for the weekend while my father hosted his French cousins at our house, one of whom was the Alexandra I had been named after. I had been outside all afternoon. The snow sparkled. I remember being on my hands and knees, rolling a ball of hard packing snow to build a sphere big enough for a body. My snow goose. It was time to go home, and my mother had been calling me for several minutes, with the quiver in her voice that meant she was serious. But I had to make that goose. I worked harder. "Emily! Emily!" she called, again. I rolled snow into a cylindrical shape for a neck. "Emily!" I gathered more handfuls in order to fatten my goose. I thought about how Alexandra hadn't liked the wallpaper in the guest room and had told my mother so. "Emily!" I sculpted a head. "Emily!" I smoothed out the oval of my snow goose and realized my name had changed. I wasn't Alexandra anymore. I was Emily forever now, severed from Europe, and claimed by my mother in one of her small territorial victories over my father.

Step on.

That short sentence moves me out from under the day that began under water.

"Today has begun under water," Sam said as he left for the market looking troubled. Sometimes I think he should be the writer instead of me; my attempts never seem to nail a thought so precisely. Today began under water.

A tsunami struck southern Asia this morning.

The images of the disaster have been replaying on the television news, and all day long I have been grateful for Sam's presence. He is the love of my life. When he's here, everything is fine. As I watched the broadcast of home-video footage and heard the whoops of disbelief as water, in a reversal of roles, swallowed people, I felt just how much he was the man above all others who could make me feel safe. During a clip taken from a hotel balcony, as the wave swept over deck chairs and the pool, the cameraman's *whoooaaaa* reminded me of the perilous days of Gavin's presence in my life. Those whoops nudged me forward into reattempting his story, to understand just who he was, and perhaps to shed light on who I had been.

How does a life get saved?

I feel the need to do something that will make a difference, make meaning—or just make something.

Gavin has come back to me like an echo sounding, measuring the distance between now and then, when we'd met, and culminating with a moment that took place on water. It is a moment through which I am trying to understand actions and their consequences: cause and effect. Although we seemed like opposites, Gavin and me, what eventually happened between us makes me think there's more to the events of that day than I have allowed. Sounds and smells have stayed with me, but I have pushed away the images just as Gavin had pushed the haunting face of David Williams aside for years.

It's time we both looked.

As I wait for Sam to return, I sit in my room that overlooks the city of Santiago de Compostela, and I can almost taste the sea salt on my lips that final day.

Whoooaaaa . . .

But I'm jumping ahead. First I must focus on Gavin himself.

He appeared in April 1999.

I know that he arrived in Spain by air. I believe he didn't initially choose Finisterre, but that this last resort chose him in a confusion of airports—Luton? Stansted?—as he left his own engagement party and hailed a taxi. Arriving at Stansted, he would have found that the only available flight that would take him close enough to Pamplona was to Santiago. Was it on the plane that his search would have seemed impossible? The sudden foreignness of everything upon arrival, his distance from where he needed to be, the impossibility of finding his feet, let alone one man in a city of thousands—these would have made the cliff seem like an answer. The cliff that would replicate the one that had haunted him must have seemed like the fastest way of getting what he thought he deserved.

There are reports of him leaving the airport in Santiago and taking a coach to Finisterre. I see him walking feverishly, with that familiar limp, rushing along the Costa da Morte on a bright April morning. In agony. It's this agony that I have been trying to translate to the page, in order to piece together what came later, but I can only conjecture the nature of Gavin's emotions.

I know some of the concrete details. Others have been garnered from the story as Marcus told it to me. The Chinese whispers of those who saw him along the pilgrim's trail corroborate my guesswork. But what's important to me is how I tell it here, to understand *why*, and to finally shake the feelings that have haunted me.

In 1999 I was living with Marcus in Pamplona. There we both met Gavin, both fell for him, and both lost him. But in truth he's still with me. That April in Pamplona, the spore of Gavin Lake was lodged in me.

He was a tall, attractive man of forty-one. His marbled blue eyes were as intense as a determined train in a dark tunnel. These I experienced, but from facts gathered during and after our acquaintance I try to create an omniscience that suits my narration. I am implicated, so I must construct him meticulously:

Born in London, middle-class upbringing. He was oddly distinguished by both grace and grittiness. His tastes and gestures spoke of privilege, perhaps even aristocracy, so I give him Eastern European heritage. In another era he might have been a fallen prince. His mother was Polish, from the noble class of Szlachta, but in England she had married a Jew, so Gavin's aura of entitlement was not pure-bred. This hybridity gave him an odd elegance that was evident even in the way cloth loved his body. His cashmere sweater fell over broad shoulders the way fine silk perfectly pleats at each of the four corners of a table. I imagine that height ran in his family, a dominant gene from an age of shorter men, but I also sense that Gavin belonged not so much to his family but to an idea of life he believed they'd been spawned from—a vintage sensibility inherited from the continent. He seemed distinct from the England that raised him, the England he loved the way a deer loves trees. England surrounded him, but Eastern Europe was in his blood.

Judging from what happened to him as a teenager, and who he became as an adult, I imagine that as a child he hated being the outsider, made excuses for his odd parents, and would have kept them away from his English friends, who demanded his compliance—in exchange for acceptance—in their small acts of defiance at the very Englishness he sought to achieve. They must have had specific targets: Marks & Spencer's, Sainsbury's, and any shop in which lifting the odd item meant two fingers up in the face of the establishment their families belonged to. Meanwhile, Gavin's family must have been oblivious to his uneasiness, wanting their first-generation English boy to have all the opportunities they had emigrated for. Wanting him to be Happy Gavin, Known Gavin, Loved Gavin.

I do know how he got his limp, but is this the place to start?

Chronologically? Perhaps not. Perhaps I need to get back inside his thoughts, to begin at the cliffs. And with Porter.

But not yet. Sam is home.

❧

When Sam arrived home this afternoon from the Praza de Abastos market, I felt it again: that whoop of disbelief over the tsunami, which makes my telling urgent. He brought home with him the feeling of *saudade*. It's not Spanish, but a Portuguese word. No other like it, and no translatable meaning I can find, except for what I feel below my ribs that is also out there in the dusk of Santiago. *Saudade*. Longing. A place in between birth and happiness. Sam had it in his face when I met him at the door.

I was anxious for him after a few hours of being lost to my reconstruction of Gavin Lake. Having heard Sam searching for his keys, I opened the door and there he was—a man the right size for me, unlike the tall, august, and wholly unreachable Gavin. I hugged Sam and felt our fit: I am barely average height, so his below-average frame suits me fine. Given that after I left Pamplona in 1999 I vowed to stop trying so hard and so gave up wearing high heels, I am grateful that Sam stopped growing at seventeen.

He handed me a full bag of vegetables, but it took him a moment before he stepped through the door into the warmth of the apartment. I asked him what was wrong, knowing that the market is our favourite place in the city—his for the fish, mine for the greens—and the simple yet sumptuous displays of bounty always filled us with giddy pleasure. He told me that the farmer he bought his olives from had fallen from a rafter in his barn and broken his neck. Sam described how the farmer's son had spoken sadly as he scooped the black *arbequinas* from his barrel. "Not because his father is dead, but because he now has to sell olives in the market," he said. His long lashes fatigued his eyelids; his eyes nearly closed.

But two seconds later he looked up at me with a playful face. "How many Dadaists does it take to screw in a lightbulb?" he asked, his cheeks dimpling.

"Oh no!" I said, turning away. He followed me into the apartment.

"Come on, the olive vendor's son told me," he pleaded.

"How many?" I asked, turning back towards him.

"Potato."

His expression didn't change. He held his breath, and the moment I laughed he exhaled.

"Wait a minute, he's telling jokes and his father has just died?"

"Why not?" Sam replied defensively as he took off his coat. "*He*'s not dead."

"But in mourning," I pleaded, wanting to hold the *saudade* and paint the day with it.

"Na, he's cool." Sam said, his step light as he retreated to the kitchen.

I had to readjust and catch up with him, to make sure he wasn't covering for his own sadness. Sam is a rigorous scientist, but also very sensitive. He is not by nature a sad man, although he can lapse into *saudade* easier than anyone I know. His family thrived on humour, his brother a comedian, whose jokes would cause their father to collapse in laughter. "A tough audience," Sam calls his father, still in awe of the effect his brother had on the man. Sam tries his jokes out on me, but wouldn't dare crack one in front of his dad. After his brother left, the idea of making a joke in front of his parents was distasteful. And sometimes a cloud descends that makes all humour taboo. But I know how to reach him. I leave him to himself for a while and then rescue with everything I've got—he likes it when I challenge him with factual questions, and also when I rub his back. It works every time.

After ensuring that he was in good spirits, I retreated to my room. Once this story is complete, I can focus again on Sam, his work, and a happy future together. He's preparing our dinner now, and, as I return to Gavin—the swoosh and gasp as he falls towards rock and sea—the radio news is announcing the rising death toll in Indonesia. Sam chops onions, underscoring the reporter's stupefied statistics with a steady, executioner's knell against the chopping board.

And I imagine what it feels like to land.

❧

Not a sound. He had been expecting the same sounds, again, as on that day in the Highlands in 1973. The *Aaaaaaah* of the long, blood-curdling scream as the figure plunged before him, down the side of that other, slanted-rain cliff. This time he heard nothing but his own intake of air like a vacuum seal closing.

He was so tired of air.

Next was the crack of something that must have been the branch that broke his fall. He had fallen only a few metres to the next ridge and had landed on his side, his cheek planted into hard dirt near a shrub.

A shot of pain pierced his shoulder, spread to his neck, just behind his ear. He waited for thought. It didn't come. Nor did memory. Not even mocking laughter. There was some relief in that.

He might still die.

He waited. Slowly he raised his hand to his chest, pulled away the neck of his T-shirt and felt for the coarse hair. He searched for the particular one he'd fingered on the flight from London to Santiago a week ago. The pimply Ryanair steward had raised his voice, and he had been forced to take his seat. It had been the click of his seatbelt that had made words meaningless. *Click*, and they were feeble, like this spiral of grey hair he now twirled with his forefinger. This hair, he thought, and shuddered to realize that he was alive. This hair had appeared first, years ago, then another and another until his chest had become speckled with grey. These little bleached questions had multiplied over the years as had the flashes of that moment on the other cliff. They marked the years like scratches on a prison wall, for locked up he'd been, privately, until Porter had invaded his purgatory.

A tear slid from his eye. He'd have thoughts again, and the flashes, which had multiplied, split apart, and then taken on a separate life.

"Dad," he said angrily to the dirt. His voice even sounded like Martin's. Martin the refugee. Martin, who had always told him that hope was all there was. He moved his leg to see if it was injured. Rage arrived like laughter and he hollered, "Help!"

The silence that answered was the joke of existence.

He touched the injured leg. He listened. The screaming was right in his ear. Again.

"Aaaaaah!" he screamed for real to drown out the sound. His voice returned in an echo, shuddering. He pounded the earth, but even this arm was weak. He felt along his other arm to where it had hit the branch.

He'd failed.

As he touched his ribs and bruised hip, he realized he was unbearably thirsty. His throat felt like dried tar. Breathing came with its demands, so he sat up stiffly, then stood. He scrambled up onto the fallen tree, grabbed the roots protruding from the cliff face, and slowly hoisted himself back on the ledge, pulling himself up with his good arm, throwing his leg up onto the rough grass of the ridge. His arm throbbed as he put weight on it to roll himself onto his back.

The sun pitched its rays. At first he raised his hand to block them, but then let the rays bowl over his resistance to life. *This life.*

And this is what you call a man? As he lay there, he strained his lust, brought the image of Kate's backside and legs into his mind, and willed the erection that for weeks had been denied him. He still felt nothing.

He hollered again. He longed to be . . . safe . . . in bed with her, but he knew that sooner or later the screams would have escaped him and he would have had to tell her. And he couldn't.

So here he was. Not even man enough to accomplish death. Men did certain things in the face of truth—men like Porter, or the heroes in movies. They would pick their weapons. A choice few: guns, swords, fists. Porter would have chosen a gun for its speed. But what did Gavin have? The truth had come in floods of sound: the scream that had drowned out all else. If he had a weapon it was these piercing, gouging thoughts. To turn them on someone else would mean taking responsibility for them and to turn them into action. This was the reasonable, manly thing—to obey the call to do the right thing. But what was that now?

The first solution had been to attempt to ease his conscience by seeing the other boy's face again, to know he was alive. And free. But not for a moment had he considered what he would say when they met. Then when the anguish took hold on the Ryanair flight, all reason had been lost to a black hole of sound.

Haaaaa, haaa, he exhaled, now becoming his own joke.

If he was doomed to stay alive, he would have to do it with brawn. Men did what they had to do. This he had to remember.

Porter had found him, after twenty-six years, and over the telephone, while Gavin shuffled paper on the desk of his Canary Wharf office, he reminded him of the details of their acquaintance in Scotland. Gavin fingered the mock-up of the engagement party invitations that Kate had wanted his decision on, and tried to keep calm, despite the slow realization that people were so easily traceable. "It's me, yer old mate from Dundee," Porter had said, and Gavin's chest clenched. He was reminded of the refugee echo of his father's voice: "There's no room to put a foot wrong. You're lucky you were born in this country." And right then, as Porter wheezed down the line about what he knew—"The bastards'll never find out . . . It's between you and me and the mountain, probably . . . and I'm nearly gone"—the decades-old bolt shot up into his throat again. After years of swallowing it back, it spat itself loose in that moment. Tempted to hang up and deny the existence of Scotland itself, there was an intense relief at sharing the memory of those moments with another human. As Porter coughed out what seemed like uncertainty about whether or not there had been a witness—"you'll wanna just make sure"—a surge of bile pushed up into Gavin's mouth. He agreed to visit Porter in the hospital.

Lying in his bed at St. Mary's Hospital near Paddington Station, Porter hadn't seemed much changed. The weight he'd lost in the battle with the emphysema that was a few weeks from killing him made him look a boy of sixteen again, although a thinner, paler version of the Porter he'd been in Dundee, the Porter who had carried flesh like a weapon.

"What do you mean 'make sure'?" Gavin asked upon seeing him.

"What?" Porter asked, wheezing into the mask.

"Make sure of what?" It was the only thing Gavin wanted to know as he arrived at the man's bedside. Porter gestured to Gavin to help him remove the oxygen mask so that he could speak. Gavin's fingers brushed the man's face as he obeyed. He was surprised how little it repulsed him.

"Fuck, you're still useless," Porter spewed and pointed towards the bedside table. "Take that with you," he gasped, indicating a file folder with pieces of newsprint jutting out from it. "It's some shit I been collecting on who was there. The one who they took away and a couple of the others. They're the only ones who would say anything . . . and they haven't so far . . . You keep an eye. Like a' said, the bastards'll probably never know, but you'll wanna see to it . . . one way or another," and his eyebrows slid closer together in a code for something between men, something Gavin was meant to understand. "It's up to you now, Lord help us. You're probably as useless now as you were then, city boy. But I got a wife, and don't want her to suffer . . . after," and then he motioned for the mask to be replaced.

The accusation felt true. Gavin was useless, and he realized that he would never be able to hide his past from Kate, to atone for his mistakes, or to make the screaming go away; and then he'd lose her too, along with everything he'd gained in the years since Scotland.

Leaving the hospital, he had opened the file. The face of

the young boy looked out right at him from the yellowed newsprint. He quickly crumpled up the clipping and threw it into the nearby bin. There were two other photos taken at the school, before the arrest. These he kept in the file, which he hid in his flat like the trace of a secret lover. That night, when he and Kate made love, he wasn't able to penetrate her. And every day since then had been torture, as his guilt dripped from him as though from a slit in his wrists.

Finding the boy was now the only rational option. Porter had insinuated a particular action Gavin could barely fathom, but he'd think of the right thing to do when the time came.

He rolled over on his side and put weight on his good arm to push himself up. As he stood he was dizzy and again flashed to the Borstal known as Spiers Residential List D School in Dundee.

He's fifteen, sweating and cold. A don has pointed him towards the pale plaster-wall dormitory room and left him in the hallway. Other boys, some scrawny and agitated, others sturdy and pocked, are going about small tasks in their corners, their Saturday afternoon freedoms from the regimented instruction on how to be better citizens. Gavin picks up a comb he has spotted on the floor, wondering how to give it back to its owner, but suddenly his skin feels like it's being crawled on—a hundred tiny spiders whose legs pinprick his back, bottom, and thighs—so he places it gently back on the floor before moving over to the bed he's been designated.

On a lower bunk in the far corner of the room, one boy is masturbating, in full view of everyone, with only the bedsheet to hide the hand furiously stroking his cock towards climax. The boy's face is unspeakably determined. This is Gavin's first and lasting impression of Porter.

But it wasn't Porter's face he was trying to focus on as he began to walk again, it was the other boy's. After twenty-six years he would have to bring it out of the shadow. He tried hard to remember if the comb had been an Afro pick. And why had it been on the floor? Had the boy dropped it there or had one of the others stolen the comb and tossed it aside? Gavin forced himself to picture the boy's back as he had seen it one afternoon, hunched over on the dorm cot, shivering, racked with sobs. He thought about the boy's hands and his skin. He wondered if a brown man's skin would spot with age. For a moment—which put his breath and stride at odds—Gavin wondered what the boy had smelled like.

Retracing his way back to the footpath, Gavin worked out the kink in his calf muscle. He circled the air with his stiff arm. By the time he reached the Camino his thirst was suffocating. He swallowed continuously to push back the sticky dam in his throat. He knelt down and pulled at the leaf of a shrub, tearing it from its branch, flinging it onto his tongue to suck out moisture. None. He spat it out and walked on.

❦

The night is black. Sam is asleep, and I have begun to write once more. Gavin's story has surfaced as the day that began under water comes to an end. The sounds in the apartment tick over like pages turning. I see Gavin as a speck on the cliff, a hairline fracture on a perfect April horizon. April stirs people, with its particular tilt of the earth, the ribbon-like quality of light. It brings the season of thaw, of rebirth, of pilgrimage. He doesn't walk like someone would on a pilgrimage, when meditation on the register of a step or a particular moment's slant of the sun might be appropriate. When I zoom in, I see that he's walking away from the rugged coastline of what was long thought to be the westernmost tip of Spain—away from Finisterre from where the Romans had watched the sea engulf the sun each night and had prayed that it would release it again the next morning.

The Camino de Santiago de Compostela is a path dedicated to meaning; as you travel along it you can ask St. James to change your life. Walking the route in reverse, with no knowledge of its significance, and yet with a hope of release not unlike a pilgrim's, Gavin Lake was engaged in one of the simplest of human acts: he was on the move.

Sam recently told me that evolutionary biologists believe that diet affects the way animals have historically moved about the planet and the kinds of social groups they form. Horses, for example, are creatures of open space. Big and mobile, they are able to traverse a continent in a few decades. They are also slow breeders, like humans. Both human and horse are, evolutionarily speaking, extremely successful in spreading their kind around the world. They adapt well. Bands of creatures racing hither and thither, continent hopping, back and forth, to and from places, changing them, being changed by them.

Some cultures demand movement, I observed: there were medieval mandates for every devout Christian to travel at least once to Rome, Jerusalem, or Santiago; there is the obligatory hajj to Mecca; the crystallizing trek of the Wild West frontiersman. Sam countered that some migrations are forced: hejira, holocaust, famine, persecution. In any case, migration is the norm, not the exception. We are born, therefore we move. A step gives order to movement and gives the body rhythm. I remember how Gavin swayed, side to side like a vessel in waves. I want to copy him, to feel the precarious movement and to determine any similarity between us, in order to understand my responsibility for the events of that summer.

I used to fall in love with a man for this precarious sense of a place wilder than myself: beyond the known, on the other side of proper, out of bounds. As though making love to a man would confer some sort of a key. With dark men I could go beyond my pale-skinned limitations. With an artist I would discover myself in his work—a painted smile or a loaded lyric—until I realized that what I wanted was to be out of bounds myself. To be wild. *Whooooaaa!*

But that summer of 1999 I paid a price. Wild is dangerous, the territory of foothold traps and bounty hunters. Wild is the tsunami that struck like the lashing tail of a hungry beast disturbed. I can't sleep. Not now, as the dead become countless and this story that I have been trying to tell for five years has started to take shape.

The wave is urgent. Time is precious. But if I follow Gavin's spoor across the top of Spain I will reach . . . something. The end is always near.

I fell for Gavin Lake's off-balance step, the blue tunnel of his eyes. I followed him then, as I am compelled to follow him now.

What did I want to belong to? I don't know yet.

I must write him.

Walk in his step.

And retrace my own.

There's a way forward that isn't frightening, stepping in line with a path towards meaning like the Camino de Santiago. The idea is to keep moving, do something.

Do. Something.

Two

Three days later Gavin woke to gauze. The room was blurry; the light was jaundiced with dawn. His head spun as he grabbed for the bottle of water at his bedside. "How?" he asked into the mouth of the bottle, before gulping some water. He looked at his surroundings. A bare light bulb, an overly sprung bed. He had spent the night in a cheap hotel on Rúa das Hortas at the edge of Santiago de Compostela, near the entrance to the city from the Camino.

Haaaaa, haaaa, haaaa, he exhaled just above the bottle's opening, trying to raise the pathetic laughter. The previous days had been like blackouts of mania, as the blood-curdling Highland scream pursued him as though shouted through a megaphone. He had walked without break, without thought. The nights had brought some calm, but there had been nowhere to stop and rest, so he had slept in the cradle of bushes and rocks on the way to the city.

And now last night's near-death sleep was wearing off, and that sound was rising again. He slapped his knee, and somehow that assured him that will and action were still connected. He didn't want to lose his mind.

In the dark of night he had imagined falling into the arms of the monk who had opened the refugio door to his poundings. The plump man had turned him away, saying they were full, but he had whispered, before closing the door, that Christ too had thirsted for many weeks in the desert. Gavin had slept on the monk's words, but this morning as the raging panic took hold of him again, he wished he'd told the monk that he stank like a goat. He raised his arm and sniffed his armpit.

He left the hotel and made his way slowly through the city, his feet heavy, his head throbbing. He barely looked up. Focusing on his shoes he tried to turn them into that face, and he mouthed words as they formed in his thoughts, "I . . . we . . . him . . . sorry, sorry, sorry."

He touched his trouser pocket and felt the photographs tucked in beside his mobile phone. The file from Porter had also contained an original *Scotsman* article from the incident in 1973, a Dundee paper's announcement from 1980, when the case had been briefly reopened, the names and addresses of three men, two of them crossed off, and a list of addresses and phone numbers attached to the remaining name, the one belonging to the boy in the mug shot. He now regretted having thrown that clipping away; it marked a change on the boy's face that he was sure he'd be able to trace in the man.

He took the phone out and turned it on. It still worked, despite the blows from the fall, and it indicated messages. He quickly turned it off again, as the dry humiliation shot into his throat. He wanted to be safe again, but he'd gone too far now. She'd never forgive him. But she was not the point now. What mattered was all that remained of his reason.

He took one photograph from his pocket and looked at it again. Porter had been thorough, but research was fallible. What if he was on a path to nothing and the man had left

Pamplona? There was always the unexpected to take into account in any plan, like the click of the seatbelt that had unhinged the conviction with which he had left London and turned up the pitch on the scream so that it threatened to crack his skull. Then the damn ledge that kept him alive. The madness that had led him there was almost easier than all of this. Dad, he thought, like a curse for the man whose righteousness could do nothing for him now.

He walked through the tourist quarter, trying to find his way out. He was moving now, momentum in his legs, so he couldn't stop. How far could he walk? Pamplona was probably weeks away on foot, but as he moved the scream's pitch dropped and death's hold loosened. The walking gave him time to sharpen the weapon of his reason. He would try to find the boy, along with the right and reasonable act. He had to behave in a way opposite to what Porter had expected . . . *the bastards'll probably never know* . . . And make sure to act like a man. He looked down at his trousers torn at the knee, at the dirt and blood on his elbow. He touched his face, still caked in dirt and blood. *This*, he thought, and walked on.

Crossing the city took no time. Under the trees surrounding the chapel of San Marcos, the air felt cool for the first time in days. As the path narrowed again, he came face to face with a barefoot man with long, matted hair, wearing a cotton robe and carrying a loaf-sized stone. Following him, a better-groomed, younger man was carrying a similar stone. His look was strained, while the man in front looked peaceful and was smiling. Gavin waited for the wild-haired man to pass, but when the second one approached he dared, in English, "What are you doing?" The man nodded and pointed ahead with his chin. "Santiago de Compostela, St. James," he said, and continued on his way. Gavin touched his temple, then his hair.

Purgatory crossed his mind: had he died and was now doomed to wander in a shadow world of madmen? He picked up his pace, continuing away from the city and out towards the airport. He considered taking a flight to Pamplona, with the idea that the rush of a takeoff might subdue these internal sounds.

An hour later he was soaked with sweat. The fever had returned, and in his distracted pace he saw the far end of a runway and realized he'd missed the airport.

Rain began. He ran, taking shelter in the woods, hunching over his breath as though in prayer. Life was forcing itself upon him. Rain thrummed the eucalyptus trees. As he shunted closer to the trunk of a tree, an elderly woman appeared. Her grey-streaked hair was woven into a coronet, her clothes unevenly hand-sewn and worn. The woman was also carrying a stone the size of an infant that she cradled in her arms. Her baking apron protruded from the hem of her light coat, which rode up and gathered at her thighs with the weight of her burden. As the rain lightened and she neared Gavin, he could hear her breathing. He stared at the large St. Christopher's medal around her neck.

"Pamplona?" he asked.

The woman stopped and held the stone out for him to take from her. He obliged, and wondered at her strength as the stone announced its weight in his hands.

"English?" she asked him.

"Yes."

"You follow, here," she pointed back in the direction she had come. "A long way. Signs, but some very bad, no sense." She shook her head.

He looked up and saw a sign that said Melide. "Why the stone?" he asked, nodding towards it with the appropriate reverence.

"Road . . . all of this . . . ," she waved, "built by us, pilgrims: we come, we put, we walk," she said and then smiled. "We sing," she added, with a shrug. "We make game . . . rock is bread. But bread is easier," she said in the rumble of a laugh.

Gavin looked down at the stone as if it was a gurgling infant, and he nodded, not sure he had understood, but the idea that he was following a pilgrimage route unsettled rather than calmed him. The woman raised her arms high in the air and clasped her hands together, stretched up high, and bent to the right, then to the left. Her apron was shredded near the knee—as though a cat had clawed through while clambering up to her lap. His throat tightened. *I will . . .* he thought, swallowing back a sob. She lowered her arms, held her hands out, and readied herself for the infant stone. She nodded at Gavin, and he placed it in her arms, gently. More gently, he felt, than he'd ever done anything in his life.

"*Gracias*," he said. She nodded again and walked off.

Gavin continued in the direction the woman had indicated, walking steadily now. There was no going back, and there would be nothing left for him there if he did. He tried not to think about the apron and the cat. He hummed to drown out his buzzing brain, digging down and drawing up the conviction he had left London with. Reason was asking for one last chance, and he had no choice now but to let it try.

❧

As Gavin walks, I take a break from writing to wash my hands. In order to accurately recreate Galicia in April I have to remind myself that it is lush. The farmers' plots that quilt the region are distinctively green in summer—a contrast to the lizardy dryness of southern Spain. The weather must have forced him onto the bus by which he eventually arrived in Pamplona. Rain would have been a constant companion on Gavin's trek, as the verdancy of the summer in this area is due to the highest seasonal rainfall in all of Spain. I have to get it right.

But I take too many breaks. I have washed my hands five times today, and it's not yet noon. My writing is slow, distracted by the television news in the background that is noisy with talk of plagues. The new threat to the tsunami-hit areas is water-borne illness from the rotting carcasses that have been abandoned by the retreating Indian Ocean. Limbs and heads hang in trees. All human. The animals knew; they had retreated to higher ground before the wave hit. The undertow dragged the dead through the streets, and the bodies were caught and twisted on boards and broken glass, mangled among the wreckage. The breeze that blows over the flesh like breath from a leper asks the rest of us if we really live. I pace here in my small room that looks out over the Cathedral of Santiago, and I wonder if I have provided Gavin with the right questions that will lead him to an understanding of how life decides things.

Could he actually have been weighing up what being a man really meant, or am I highlighting that part of his dilemma to make sense of what happened between us that first night? What do I want to blame him for in order to assuage my own guilt for what happened on water?

I know about bodies on water. I know that a live human body sinks in water, while a dead body eventually floats. Does that mean that life has weight? When the heart stops, blood stops circulating, and gravity makes it settle. The area where the blood settles turns dark blue or purple.

Life leaves a colour when it goes.

One drawback of my daily writing routine is that I have neglected the promise I made to myself—and to Sam as well—to learn more about viruses so that I can better understand his work and help translate his research into Spanish when it is required. My Spanish is better than his, and there are moments he looks so lost when speaking to a colleague at the university that my heart lurches forward and I speak for him. He likes it if I jump in and give him the words. But I need to better understand biochemistry, and that has been my project since we arrived here. Science, Sam, and Santiago; it's all that has mattered for nearly two years. But learning is invisible and hard to account for, and since December 26 I have needed something to show for my days. Now that the story is beginning to write itself, I need to continue, and my view of the city's great cathedral encourages it.

We have the best view in town. Our apartment on 65 Rúa de Teo is at the top of the city, on a short street on a steep hill overlooking the Parque do Monte Almáciga, which was once the general cemetery. White-washed walls now enclose the deserted mausoleums, and the park has been turned into a recreational area, as though enough people have died by this point. The spare room where I work is just above the spot where Galicia Radio broadcast its first signals in 1933. In the last few sunny days I have moved my writing outside and have gone to sit on the stones that mark this milestone.

The lawn of the park flows down the hill, and becomes the Parque San Domingos de Bonaval, which leads into the grounds of the Convento é Igrexa de San Domingos de Bonaval, a seminary with a spectacular triple-spiral staircase that now houses the Museo do Pobo Galego, the Museum of the Galician people.

Beside the seminary, in contrast, is the chic contemporary art gallery, and just across the road are the pilgrim's gates into the old city. Some days I wander into the old town, but mostly I stay up here, these days washing my hands in a conscious exercise to see if what Sam says is true: wash your hands a lot and you'll never get sick. Apparently you can outsmart viruses.

The old and new of Santiago are mine to contemplate from this window. When I moved back to Spain, I didn't want to live there in the old town and be trapped by history, as I had felt in Pamplona before Gavin's arrival. I had mixed feelings about this entire northern region carved by the Camino, which I had tripped along that summer. But I didn't want to live without Sam, so I agreed to move here with him when he was offered a research post at the university.

We had left Kenya once Sam's term researching retroviruses in Nairobi had finished, and we had both been job hunting in London when the Spanish job offer came through. We arrived here from London to look for an apartment during Semana Santa, or Holy Week, between Palm Sunday and Easter. We stayed in a hotel near the cathedral while we searched for something clean and affordable. Towards dusk each night, a religious procession of barefoot men and women, robed in purple, green, or red silk hoods evocative of the Ku Klux Klan, marched through the streets before floats depicting scenes from Christ's passion and the crucifixion. The drumbeats resonated deep in my chest; the trumpet calls made my hair stand on end. The thrill I felt spoke to the mystery of my European namesake—the fussy cousin Alexandra—and to the richness of my father's Catholicism in contrast to my mother's literal Puritanism. Santiago's Easter was incomparable. In Canada I had grown up with bunnies, eggs, and Sunday school; Santiago's processions gave a whole new meaning to *Easter parade*. By the end of the week, though, after the nightly drumming, horns, and even more elaborate floats, I found myself trying to avoid the sounds of the city. They reminded me too much of life in Pamplona, and I wanted to live up above the cathedral, to keep an eye on Santiago, rather than be shadowed by it. So we moved up here, to the top of the city, and I can visit the old town merely by walking straight downhill.

Sam is beautiful as he soars, feet off the pedals of his bicycle, down the hill to the university each day. He is free of the Old World's weight, his simple perspective a pointed contrast to the Gavin I am reconstructing, and my attempt to understand if where we're from determines what we become.

Samuel Gorjan Lawrence—his middle name from his mother's Macedonian father—wanted to be a pilot when he was a boy, but events during his adolescence changed all that. While lesser men might have been derailed by the disappearance of a brother, Sam became devoted to a life of achievement and the study of the mystery of matter. He is a man of integrity, with a passion for the virology lab, where each day he endeavours to unlock the chemical puzzles of the universe. It's one of his most attractive features. As I gaze out to the wide horizon, my Sam looks down through microscopes, tracking the molecules that compose the minutest elements of life.

His talent has not gone unrecognized, as a week ago he was awarded a Spanish Research Council grant for the largest sum the department has ever seen. He is now in charge of the budget, the new researchers, and the direction of the retroviral research that is his specialty. Yet when I encouraged him to celebrate, he refused to let me throw a party, saying, "It's nothing; it's nothing," humbly, and even looked annoyed at me for suggesting it. So I will help in other ways.

Despite his Macedonian and Irish parents, Sam is an American through and through. While politically opposed to America's current ethos, he is a man who, having lived in Europe for years, still requires potato chips and a Coke with his lunch. I watch in amazement as he layers the most refined chorizo, peppers, olives and Idiazábal cheese on *pan de horno*, then arranges the plate so that it has space for the cheap crisps he buys from the corner shop. The Coke or Pepsi—he doesn't discriminate—is the last thing he downs, as if it was a dessert. Other Americanisms—grumbling at poor water pressure, the price of gas, and poor service—surface from time to time, but it's the small details that stick out for me.

This man—Sam—I know. He's as familiar as every television show I watched growing up in Ontario. Whereas, Gavin I have to work to understand and as I build his character to fit my story, I ask not only about where he was from and what made him, but about how I let myself ignore the natural boundaries between us.

Other facts I have learned about Gavin's background: His father, Martin, arrived in Dover from Poland in 1938, surname Laski, which he changed to Lake. He was a man who struggled to be upright and professional, a man who married the beautiful Polish Catholic woman who had read him poetry on the steps of St. Martin-in-the-Fields—his favourite church because it shared his name. He was a man who sired a daughter he could eventually afford to send to riding lessons, and a perfect son who was to fulfill the father's dreams of belonging in this new country, but it was not to be. The pressure to belong confused his sensitive son, and at the age of fourteen, Gavin would be coerced by schoolmates to take part in a series of petty crimes.

Gavin's pressures were from the Old World; mine are from the New.

I am a Canadian by birth, many generations on my mother's side, and I am proud of the land and what it gave me. Her family plants a tree on their property in Flinton, Ontario, whenever someone close dies, a kind of life-for-death repayment to the earth. These people are from the Land O'Lakes region, north of Belleville, and my mother's father planted all the trees on his land along the Skootamatta River, from where, as a child, I would watch canoeists and kayakers navigate the rapids for summer thrills.

I wanted to live in a canoe. I learned how to canoe when I was eight, refining my skills as I grew stronger, learning to lift the canoe up from an overturned position on the lake, find the air pocket that would pop it off the water, and then flip the vessel right side up. I'd make my way in from the stern without tipping it again. That was mandatory summer training on Mazinaw Lake, where my grandfather had built a cabin he took my grandmother to for their honeymoon and where my mother, aunt, and uncle were conceived.

Not long before I met Gavin, however, I had become interested in my father's side of the family. My father is an adventurer; my mother likes roots. My father is a French man who ducked the Nouvelle Vague of Truffaut-Godard-Chabrol in 1960s Paris, and at twenty-four left to find the mythical *cabane au Canada*. He had loved the tales of *coureurs de bois*, and while his friends made fun of the Québécois—with the Belgians coming a close second for ridicule—he championed them, and brought his love of art to Montreal, where he studied sculpture and met my mother, who was a history student at McGill University. Their differences attracted and then destroyed them.

My mother plays a lot of bridge now.

I owe her a call, so will break for a few minutes, as she has probably had her first cup of coffee and won't be morning-grumpy.

She was in uncommonly good spirits. Until, of course, I ruined it all towards the end of our conversation.

"Mom," I said, still fixated on my writing, "why did you stop calling me Alexandra?"

There was a hiss of long-distance silence.

"What do you mean?"

"I mean, was it because of something between you and Dad?"

"She was a snob."

"Aunt Alexandra?"

"You didn't look anything like her. Emily suits you. I named you after someone I loved very much," she concluded and I felt her sadness return. I wondered if her Emily had been a favourite teacher or a girlfriend who had moved away. I didn't ask, because I had done it once more, toppled the delicate balance of our conversation and changed the tenor of the moment completely. Trying too hard again. I realized suddenly that this is what I have done my entire life with my parents: back and forth, balance and topple. And it might have been what I did with Gavin as well. The thought made my stomach churn. Suddenly I wanted to cry on her shoulder, but that had never been our way.

"You should visit, Mom. In the spring. You'd love the colours here," I said, needing her good spirits.

We said an awkward goodbye and by the time I put the phone down I missed Sam with a burning. Sam doesn't lock any part of me out. He is neither Old World nor purely New; neither my mother nor my father. We are not my parents.

My parents live completely different lives. While my mother mews in my grandfather's lakeside cabin, watching the autumn rain spittle down windowpanes, my father, well into his sixties, lives an exciting life, not doing much sculpture anymore, but still teaching philosophy and art at the École nationale supérieure des beaux arts in Paris.

I had been with my mother at the cabin on Mazinaw Lake, after my grandfather's funeral, when I'd felt the final tug of my father's Europe. I'd spent a week watching her mouth carefully, the way it curled over the *O*'s and as her slight lips formed sounds. I had tuned out, but I knew the sounds were well-meaning missives about the dangers of being unattached over the age of thirty. I compared myself physically to each of my parents, checking off the list: height, hers, check; dimpled thighs, wide bottom, hers; muscular arms, his; long fingers, his; green eyes, his; small breasts, hers; wavy brown hair, his; smile like a baguette flute, his, check. They came out pretty even.

My mother continued her warnings, but I wasn't yet thirty, and she was ignoring her own single status. She had divorced in her late twenties, raised her only daughter on a part-time basis, and shared me with my father, who had moved back to France when I was a teenager.

It was as I watched her mouth and felt the damp of the cabin invade me that I understood that being unattached for her was a consequence, rather than an opportunity, which it was for my father, who treated being single the same way he treated time—succumbing to it, revelling in it, losing it. He lives with one of his students now.

My father once explained to me that babies understand time and their movement within it better than anyone else. Babies are born to keep moving, my father told me.

One New Year's Eve when I was seventeen, in Flinton with nothing to do, I volunteered to babysit our neighbour's three-month-old, so that his parents could enjoy their first night out since his birth. It was close to midnight when he woke and started to wail. He wouldn't stop crying. I fed him, changed him, but cry was all he did. I looked into his wide-open mouth, felt his despair, and was helpless. I walked with him, I made faces, I sang, and I even opened my own mouth wide and wailed back at him, but nothing worked. I phoned his parents at the party they were attending.

"Put him in his car seat and put it on top of the dryer and turn the dryer on for twenty minutes." His mother quickly hung up. I stared at the receiver, stunned, then did as she told me.

It worked. The boy cooed at the simulated drive. The seat, the sound, the hum beneath him. He was moving again. He was safe.

I observed this time and again when I was a teenager as I babysat to make pocket money. My charges were happier when they were in motion. In a car they relaxed from the sensation of being trapped in the forward momentum, stopped crying, and fell asleep content. If I jiggled them up and down, or put them in a pram or stroller, that which had been upsetting them vanished. Even the imitation of movement worked.

In my grandfather's cabin on Mazinaw Lake, I sneezed as my mother's *O*'s turned over on themselves and her lips seemed to grow thinner. I lit a fire and donned a cardigan, but I continued to sneeze as though I had contracted the virus of her discontent. It was something that would remain in my system, mutate, and resurface from time to time over the next few years. Was it this discontent that led me to Gavin? Can that moment in Spain be understood in the light of how we infect one another?

I left the cottage as soon as the sneezing stopped. I fled to Paris to visit my father, who was living with a different student then on the boulevard Barbès in the eighteenth arrondissement. I turned twenty-nine on November 3, 1997, on the Pont des Arts. Alone. Wondering how I would become a writer, not how to find a husband.

A few weeks later, I left on a tour of Europe—the south of France, Italy, Greece, Portugal—and ended up in Spain, catching the fever of the bull run in Pamplona that July. Holding the fever there. Fuelling it each night in a bar called the Mesón de la Nabarreria. Ending up staying. Ending up with Gavin's story to write.

Gavin and I have both been on the move.

Step. On.

Three

I distinctly remember the moment I really saw him. He was standing in front of the neoclassical fountain in Pamplona's Plaza Nabarreria, staring at the tumbling water as though it contained a miraculous apparition. I remember thinking that the sharp sun must have carved out a rainbow in the droplets of fountain spray and that he was seeing something beautiful. I was making my way across the Calle del Carmen towards the Mesón bar, where I worked the afternoon and early evening shift. Gavin seemed different from the other Anglos and Australians who usually visited this quarter, and they came only during the bull run, San Fermin.

The moment I spotted him I wondered where Marcus was. Marcus and I shared a boredom with everyday tourists and were always waiting for a little spice in our bartending lives. Gavin seemed like just the kind of oddity about whom we could both make up stories. Of course, seeing Marcus was unlikely; he would return to our apartment in Plazueta de San José after the market and would sleep away the afternoon before taking over from me on the night shift. He had been out most of the night, and had arrived home early in the morning with his girlfriend, Constanza. They had banged and clattered into the apartment, arguing about his flirtation with two French women at the bar and, a few minutes later, their reconciliation was just as noisy as the jealous confrontation. I had found it difficult to get back to sleep. When I'd finally dozed off, I was awakened by Constanza slamming the door as she left. I decided to get an early start on my writing.

At that time I had constructed a project for myself that would keep me busy and allow me to believe I was a writer. I'd called it *Emily's Tales*, an adaptation of Chaucer to the modern Camino de Santiago, where Chaucer's Prioress had transformed into her modern equivalent—my Dietician—a pristine woman schooled in the latest theories of health, with perfect manners and obsessed with cleanliness. It had been that morning, I remember well, before glimpsing the commanding yet pathetic form of Gavin Lake by the fountain, that I had wanted to close the gap between Marcus and me, and to stop being intimidated by him.

Marcus is key to my search for the whys of who we are. Early on in our friendship, I gave up trying to learn about his past and respected his desire to start anew. I knew only that he had been born on an island—I assumed it was a Spanish-speaking one, and had surmised that the family had disintegrated from adultery and migration. He had one relative living in Spain. No childhood anecdotes ever leaked out in conversation, but there was a theme-park-roller-coaster anger about him that must have been bred early in life. I guessed that it had been his father who was white, his mother black, but I never knew, and I don't know why it was this combination that made sense to me, but it seemed that the feminine side of him had a river of slave work and rebellion running under it. Marcus was soft but furious.

When we'd first met at the bar and I had told him with pride about my grandparents and their tradition of planting trees for the dead, his face had changed. He looked at me seriously then broke into a wide, could-enclose-the-world smile. *"Mi cielo,"* he'd said, but from his tone I didn't feel like his darling. When he laughed, I tried to believe it wasn't at me. He'd continued with a flurried phrase that roughly translates as *what you're from is not what you are.*

I had been interested in Marcus at first, but never brave enough to show it, and by the time we became roommates, I was convinced that a man as attractive as Marcus would not be interested in me. I learned to suppress my feelings, and I treated him like the sibling I'd never had. Still I got jealous of the attention he got, so that morning, resentful of his loud cavorting, I decided to rouse him for my own amusement, and tell him about my writing. We had learned an easy interplay and never locked our doors, so I burst into his room and sat on the side of his bed. The sheet was pulled up over his head, only his arm poked out from beneath it.

"My dietician," I began in Spanish, "she's writing her own character traits. I've lost control of her. I think I told you before, she's a woman who is overly compassionate towards animals; she weeps if she sees a mouse caught in a trap; she feeds her pets with the finest cuts from the butcher." I paused, watching how Marcus's body had become alert at my story, the curve of his upper arm bulging ever so slightly with awakening. I was encouraged, so on I went to test the power of a story on my mysterious roommate.

"I was thinking . . . well maybe the thing that . . . um . . ." I wanted to say wrong-foots her, but I didn't know the expression in Spanish, so in English I said, "trips her up," and then continued, "is that she likes her dog just a bit more than she should . . . you know . . ." Although my Spanish was getting better, it faltered as I tried to explain the special petting that could take place between woman and dog. I had overreached in a language I was not fluent in, and my once-upon-a-time hold over him was broken. The sheet covering Marcus began to shiver, then vibrate. He was giggling. He pulled the sheet down from over his head, squinted, smiled, and touched my thigh: "Your mind is a dangerous place. I'm worried about your fantasy life," he said, his Spanish as thick as marmalade.

"It's fiction!" I protested.

"So you say," he said, grinning, as he threw off the sheet. His naked brown body glided out of bed towards the chair, where his clothes hung carelessly over the back. I examined his sleek, muscular legs, his buttocks like a hard plum, and the V-shape of his back. He would be thirty-nine that summer, and I was in awe of the body's tricks, its perseverance, its determination to be a state of mind. Marcus was beautiful. His skull was like a piece of fine pottery: his hair shaved close, but not bald, accented the curve towards the base of his skull that demanded a hand—a hand to stroke it like the hand that could have moulded it from the raw material of bone spun on a potter's wheel. The shaved look suited the sense of danger in his eyes, but the moment you talked to him you knew there was nothing to fear. His voice wasn't exactly soft—it had a grainy chafing like someone with a cold—but it was full of air and seemed to ring out easily from his diaphragm.

"Manners and writing don't mix," he said, as he lifted his jeans off the chair. I was taken aback, as I was sure I'd never told him that my character had been obsessed with manners. "And Spanish men don't care about stories," he continued, with one foot raised, ready to slip into the jeans. "They love ass . . . and you do very well in that department." He twisted around and gave me a cheeky-bastard wink, before he slipped the jeans on and tucked himself in.

"What? You've read it when I wasn't here?" I asked, unable to contain my suspicion.

He turned towards me. "What are you saying?" Silence. He stared at me, angry, yet closer to tears than I'd ever seen him. "That's what you think of me?" My breath caught in my throat and I wasn't sure I'd understood the emphasis in his Spanish. Neither of us could help the other in that moment. Avoiding his eyes I looked at the painting on the wall behind him, a recently finished work, crazy with blue and orange angles. It hung beside an older piece he'd painted in a more figurative style. I too was all angles and not a proper human form.

"*Vacía, vacía, querida, vacía,*" he chimed.

I looked into my lap. He had called me his empty darling. I felt sick at the thought that he would think less of me now. This kind of lyrical, rhythmic self-defence was something I'd noticed in him before. It was a rap of endearment combined with insult. I felt ashamed.

He picked up his shirt and left the bedroom. I was left alone with my humiliation, and was no closer to knowing him. But Marcus was good at hiding. And charm. The way he'd chided me and loved me in one comment was typical of his ability to cut through my defences. Not only did I trust him completely, but it was most unlikely that he'd spend time trying to translate my English scribbles. He must have been referring to my own manners. He could feel that I didn't know how to find my place in Spain. There was some element of European aloofness I just wasn't pulling off, and I didn't want him to see me as a homely Canadian. I wanted to be exotic and sophisticated; classy and yet unrestrained, like him. I should have apologized, but I had missed my chance to speak. I followed him out of the room.

"I'm off to the market . . . starving," he said as he pulled the lime green T-shirt over his head. "If you want vegetables again, you're on your own. I need meat." He slipped into his sandals. I tried not to love him.

"You'll be late for work," he said, tapping my forehead and its short fringe gently on his way to the door. In that moment I wished I had flowing, molten Latin hair like Constanza's, which he could run his hand through instead of pat fondly.

He held the door open for me. We both fled down the stairs and parted at the bottom.

I made my way the short distance from our sheltered square behind Pamplona's cathedral towards Estafeta, the main route of the bull run. In Pamplona I had chosen history. I had wanted to be at the centre of an old world where there would be no traces of the North American virus of progress: the suburban sprawl of malls, retail chains, and so-called security. I wanted something old and dangerous. And here, tradition had made even bulls holy. So it was as I made my way towards the St. Cecilia Fountain that I was accompanied by the cobbled-stone ghosts of those who had walked the same streets for centuries before me. This made seeing Gavin akin to getting a glimpse of the fabled Don Quixote. With that glimmer I must have felt compensated for Marcus's "empty darling" comment. Emboldened, not homely, I stopped in my tracks and stared at this strange man and wondered if Marcus would approve of him for me.

A few seconds later, Gavin turned from the fountain and caught his reflection in a butcher-shop window. He looked at himself as though taking in his appearance for the first time. His cashmere cardigan was in tatters, and the shirt under it was also shredded. He looked like someone in the process of dismantling himself. This reflection was of the raw materials, the pieces rather than the whole of what it was to be Gavin Lake, and I realized that his gazing into the fountain had had little to do with beauty, peace, or even hope. I was intrigued.

He ran his palm along the growth of brown and grey-speckled beard along his cheek. I could see his eyes flicker. I wondered then what it was he was seeing. I can now conjure what I couldn't have imagined then.

❧

The film of his life jump-cuts back to the dormitory in Scotland twenty-six years ago. He has started to unpack, and the other boys are going about their business. A voice from a dorm cot in the corner suddenly breaks free of its heavy breath and moans: *Shit! Shit! Shit!* Gavin turns in alarm, while the other boys seem oblivious. They keep their attention on their games and tasks. He traces the cursing to the figure on the farthest bed, the boy with the old face, who is hunched over, in the last shivers of orgasm. The posture of the boy repulses him, and Gavin returns to his unpacking.

"Porter, you're a complete arsehole," says one of the older Highland boys to the gasping figure, who has now collapsed on his back. Gavin tosses his underpants and socks into the drawer under his bed and slides it shut. He braces himself for the rest of the day.

❧

As Gavin stared into the butcher-shop window, I was struck by a recognition that made no sense. I had never seen him before, yet he was familiar. He fingered a slit in his shirt and tore it further, exposing the skin near his nipple. Suddenly, he spun around to catch my eye as though he'd sensed me spying on him. In that moment, like the sneeze in my grandfather's cabin, I'd caught him. He was attractive, yes, but in his state of dishevelment I would normally have walked right past him. Instead he reminded me of a tortured wolf without a limb, missing the very essence of what made him capable of survival in the wild. The look of the haunted beast that I'd conjured on a day on the frozen lake as a child with my father—an image that stayed with me like creatures from fairy tales do. I put my head down and quickly walked to the taverna.

As the afternoon sun softened, he came into the Mesón. I spotted him out of the corner of my eye but didn't look up and kept wiping the glasses that I had taken out of the dishwasher. He came up to the bar. I arranged the dry glasses in a tidy row. We both stood silently waiting for something from the other.

"*Por favor,*" he muttered. I didn't look up. I was testing him. He was a man whose appearance suggested two very opposite possibilities, depending on the angle at which he was viewed. Was he a man who had tilted at one too many windmills or was he about to discover something glorious? Was he on the edge of destitution or freedom?

"*Por favor,*" he repeated, desperately. I looked up. "Whiskey." Ah, destitution, the little voice in me muttered. But then he raised his hand and shook his head, "No, sorry . . . *agua*, mineral, no gas." No, freedom, I said to myself. Absentmindedly, he touched his tummy, which protruded slightly over his waistband, even though the rest of him was lanky, as though he had never really outgrown the awkwardness of adolescence. His shoulders, however, were broad and assured, and these spoke to my sense of him as more than he seemed. His hands were those of a pampered man.

I brought him the water and asked for payment, keeping the Canadianness out of my accent. He took a euro from his pocket and dropped it on the bar. I went back to wiping glasses, watching him out of the corner of my eye, waiting for his next move. I thought of my writing, the Dietician's character as it was evolving: her exacting manners, each passion controlled like medicinal drops of vitamins. I wanted to shake her off. I put the dishcloth down suddenly and moved forward.

"Which part of the UK?" I asked, looking him in the eye for the first time. Surprise fluttered from his eyebrow to his cheek, where it stayed, stored like a squirrel's autumn booty.

"London," he said quietly, and I could see he was taking me in with the lens reserved for women, a way of looking that is tinted with possibility. But possibility is too much like hope, and his face darkened, as if acknowledging that he had no interest in even the oddest beauty at the moment. I didn't mind that he hadn't come on to me as many Camino pilgrims of his kind had done—those men in their forties searching for themselves, and mistaking me for what they were looking for. It seemed right that Gavin should not care for me, but that only spurred my interest in being drawn out of my comfort zone, hoping too that it would be something Marcus might approve of.

Gavin drank water from the bottle, then put his hand in his trouser pocket and drew out a plastic package of white tablets. He pushed two out of the foil backing and popped them into his mouth. Aspirin. He took another swig of water. He touched his hair, then his shoulder, then the nipple that was exposed through the tears in cashmere and cotton. He popped out another two tablets and put these too in his mouth, without water, and it looked like he chewed them before swallowing.

"A bed. A good bed, any chance next door?" he asked, and I deciphered that he was looking for a place to stay. He must have had some rough nights to look so dishevelled. His lip curled, his eyes wandered, and he touched his hair again.

"It's a *refugio*, for pilgrims on the Camino," I said, unaware of the draw of his helplessness. He looked to his left, then right, adjusted the collar of his shirt. He was not the kind of person that the state of his clothing suggested.

"You a pilgrim?" I asked.

"No," he mumbled and fingered the packet again.

"It's not bull season, yet," I joked. He looked at me as though I was suggesting an insult associated with bulls. His big, vulnerable aquamarine eyes were rheumy—from the tablets I thought—but they still had light, while the rest of his body seemed dull, yet unpredictable.

"I mean," I corrected, not wanting to lose his attention, "there are hotels with vacancies; we're not full outside of San Fermin. Even in the old quarter, or the Barrio de San Juan, or near the Plaza de los Burgos . . . or just across the street from here." I noticed he wasn't wearing a ring on his marriage finger. It wasn't my vanity that took over then—I'm neither vain nor particularly confident—but I felt drawn to Gavin as one might be to a lost boy in the street. My writer's curiosity was already at work. I knew that it was something wild that had brought Gavin here, and my life was in need of something unruly at that time. I turned away and left him alone, but kept my antennae alert for everything he did. After five minutes of what looked like confusion, he left.

And now I can put into order what he did when I wasn't watching.

The screaming again. Just above his neck, behind his ear. Not one voice but many. A chorus of screams. It had grown as he walked from the bar to the Plaza del Castillo. He spotted a hotel with a name, La Perla, that meant nothing to him, yet didn't seem as foreign as the others. The lobby wasn't clean, but he didn't care. The young woman at the reception desk asked him what kind of room he needed. He stared at her, while inside him the raging chorus was begging her for mercy. "Just a bed," he managed eventually. He put his credit card carefully on the counter, as though it might shatter on impact.

The room, the crystal chandelier, the bed. Bygone glory now a teetering wreckage. He went into the bathroom, took off his cashmere cardigan, and tossed it in the small bin beside the sink. He pulled his shirt over his head without unbuttoning it, feeling it tear further. He took his passport, credit cards, and euros from his back pocket, the mobile phone and Aspirin from a front pocket, and undid his trousers. He reached into the other front pocket and slid out one of the photographs from Porter's file, now crumpled and creased. He smoothed it out and put it on the edge of the sink. He dipped in again and took out another. This too he placed on the porcelain edge, careful not to get it wet. A third photograph came from the other back pocket.

The hotel was quiet. For a moment he was grateful. He stared at the three photographs and chose the first, most crumpled one. He picked it up and examined it closely. He had selected it because the face had a softness that had been absent in the newspaper mug shot. When was the exact moment he'd excused himself from the hair, skin, scent of this face and what had happened to it since the camera took this shot? When had he let himself be lulled into believing he'd never again have to look back at the Highland ridge? Had it been the conversation between his parents?

"He's nothing to do with that now," his father had said to his mother the day they brought him back to London from Dundee.

"But, Martin—" The complaining, nasal vowels of his mother's accent grated. "He told them he thought he'd seen something; these things are traumatic." In her characteristic way, she talked about Gavin while he was in the room, as though he were still at an age when he might not understand.

"It was an accident, these things happen, and he's old enough to know that. He gave his statement. What more? He has to get past that whole place and make something of himself. There's no other choice. He's damn lucky it did happen, or he'd have been doomed to his full term there. Who knows the damage—"

"He was sent there for a reason—"

"There's no other choice!" Martin shouted.

That was it—that tone—that moment told him all he had to do was feel relieved and not to think about the past. The never-look-back chime of hope.

The photograph portrayed a group of teenaged boys gathered at the end of a football pitch, their clothes soiled, hair ruffled, faces triumphant and giddy with exertion. They crowd around the football as though it is a flame. The smile on his own face is twisted, bent in a question of how he'd landed up here with these Borstal boys who possessed the same kind of assurance as Martin, the kind reserved for adults. He'd stopped the questioning when he was released, and had believed in Martin's tone, held on to the words: no other choice.

But now he knew much more: the *other choice* had been an impossible and yet simple decision to tell the truth; the past could not be silenced the way his father or Porter had wanted it to be. And he understood that all he had wanted from following the other boys was to make his mother's accent disappear.

He focused on Porter's face. This time the film jumped to the front of the school.

The grounds at Spiers Residential List D School are a paltry attempt at a recreational area—scrubby dirt patches eat up the lawn, where the angry feet of captive boys continuously trample any new seedlings that have been planted. Gavin crouches next to Porter near the bleak, imposing school building. The brick walls are mossed over and cloudy with neglect. He has been here for six of the enforced twelve-month residence that is meant to reform him of the "jitters." That's what he calls the feeling that came on at thirteen, when all he wanted to do was run, see things fall, hear them smash. The small thefts, the vandalism, and finally a joyride in a car he didn't know how to drive, have brought him here, but the jitters had started it all. Squatting close to the ground he feels safer than when he is standing up, and he's beginning to see things move more slowly. He is learning the real lessons of survival now, the kind even his father would think are useful. He takes his lead from Porter, who knows how to get along. Gavin takes note of Porter's every move.

Porter shows him the weapon he has smuggled into the school—a switchblade with an edge so fine and sharp that it has easily sliced off the tail of a field mouse that is now wriggling in agony in Porter's hands. Gavin picks up the tail and swivels it between his fingers, amazed but stymied by what's expected of him now that he is Porter's best mate at the school. Porter has chosen him: he confides in him, gets him cigarettes, protects him. Porter trusts him. That's the part that makes Gavin most uncomfortable, because he knows that trust needs to be mutual. With the other jittery boys in London, not one trusted another, and he thinks now that must be why they were eventually caught. But since becoming Porter's friend, Gavin feels protected, and his only choice is to do as Porter does. He has learned to curve his mouth in imitation of Porter's snarl. He tosses the mouse's tail towards the patchy grass and looks up to catch the eye of a younger boy watching the two of them from the distance. The boy's eyes are wide set with wonder, his cheeks full like a doll's. He turns and walks off but Gavin has had enough of a glimpse to be able to freeze it in frame, to memorize it.

He dashed the school photo onto the bathroom floor, remembering the comb he'd come across that first day, and later, the boy curled up, sobbing. All the others had targeted this boy, so why should he have been any different when the authorities had asked *Who?* But this glimpse of cheeks and eyes, with pain and promise behind them—this face should have stopped him.

From the sink's edge he picked up the one photo not given to him by Porter. She was still the woman who seemed to be the best decision he'd ever made. Still the most beautiful, still the elegant blonde English rose, who could stand on Westminster Bridge with the Houses of Parliament behind her, and still overwhelm the skyline. Martin had called her ravishingly appropriate, and Gavin had agreed. He'd confirmed his father's certainty by telling him of his plans for marriage . . . *there's no room to put a foot wrong.* The flashes, which had appeared sporadically since the ridge, arriving randomly like belches of his undigested guilt, had turned faint with this plan for commitment. But then they'd increased the moment he actually proposed to Kate, as though voicing a promise to her meant asking her to share in his secret. While he wanted to believe that this marriage would be enough, that it would eventually set him free, his body revolted, failed him, and turned his kisses sour and self-conscious, made his caresses awkward and clawing. When Porter's call came two months later, it seemed inevitable, and it brought the loud rain and the piercing scream front and centre. If Gavin was to have any chance of winning back even a portion of the life he'd invented for himself, one that allowed a woman like Kate to love him, he'd have to be a different kind of man from Porter, or even from his father, who had made a covenant with denial itself.

He placed the photo gently back on the sink. His calves and thighs ached, but his foot, crushed and repaired in childhood, felt oddly stronger than ever. He tried to count the days he had been walking before succumbing to the bus, ten? More.

Over a fortnight ago he had disappeared out the back door of the E+O restaurant in Notting Hill, where he and Kate and their parents had been hosting the engagement party. But the walking seemed to have been happening much longer than that, this trundling towards . . . release.

He slipped out of his brogues for the first time since London and vaguely caught the scent that had, for some unknown reason, accompanied the repeating scream. He stripped off his socks and examined his feet, the blisters, the red blotches like stains. He had to keep his reason.

The third, a blanched photo, had been taken at a later point than the first, and featured a few of the younger boys, including the one who had watched him and Porter with the field mouse. Gavin let the face come to him and held it there beyond the heather and behind the gust of rain on the ridge.

He slapped his neck again. That cliff, he thought, but felt the uselessness return. What if the man was no longer in Pamplona, or in Spain, or even alive? After all these years, would anything he had to say matter? He tossed the photo to the bathroom floor and picked up the one of Kate. He returned to the bedroom, lay on top of the bed, and held himself between his legs as he stared at her.

For several cold minutes he thought of only her mouth on his cock, but in fatigue flung the photo back towards the bathroom with the others. He sat up and from the bedside table he took up a pen and a sheet of paper bearing the hotel's modest letterhead.

YOU MUST HELP ME ... I AM IN HELL, he wrote, paused, and continued.

IT WAS ME, IN 1973. ME ... WHEN ... but he stopped. Fingering the edge of the paper, he realized this would not be the route his heart needed. He slipped the page under a pillow. The night closed in; the hills surrounding the city trapped him. He shivered, rubbing his bare chest and arms with his hands.

❧

I was leaving the Mesón at closing time, having stopped by to make sure Marcus wasn't still cross with me for my silly accusation that morning. There was Gavin, back by the fountain, without his cashmere cardigan, but wearing the same torn shirt. There were few people out on the street. Perhaps, I thought, he had needed to retrace his steps to find out where he was going next, or maybe he was interested in me after all. I could not know then that the highlighted address in Porter's file had been that of Mesón de la Nabarreria.

I tapped him on the shoulder.

"You lost?" I asked. He looked up at me with an ironic smile, as though I'd asked an absurd question.

"I'm trying . . ." he started, then stopped.

I sat down beside him. "Maybe you shouldn't try so hard." He didn't seem to get my humour, and I was blind to the irony of my own efforts.

"Have hit a bit of a wall," he said, and I took this to mean that he hadn't found a place to stay for the night.

"There are cheap places in the Barrio," I said, rushing in to be useful, the way I'd learned to do as a child when my father would look at me as if to ask how on earth he would survive my mother's dullness. Gavin looked tired, but less crazed than when I'd first seen him, and more attractive.

"I have a hotel," he said, "but I don't know what to do." He needed to talk but didn't know how to open up.

"You want to go for a walk?" I asked. I was stepping out of bounds and the danger felt exhilarating. He thought about it for what seemed like far too long, so I stood up and motioned him forward. We walked.

I led him through the historic quarter out towards Parque de la Taconera, its rows of maple and strolling boulevards like a city within the city. Among the ruins below the old walled battlements, the city maintained a makeshift eccentric zoo— goats, deer, chickens, geese, peacocks and, rumour had it, a wild pig that few had ever seen but which many had heard squealing at night. At the entrance to the park I stopped and pointed to the yellow scallop shell marker.

"If you want the Camino, it's this way," I said, trying to find out at least why he was in Pamplona. For a man who looked like he'd run out of hope, the Camino was always an option. But he made no response except to stare at the marker and frown as though remembering something, so we continued towards the park's centre. The peacocks shrieked and I could hear birds scuffling about below. No sign of the deer or the pig. Gavin stopped and listened. I thought he might crack a smile, but he walked on, his galumphing gait like a slow metronome.

"What happened to your leg?" I asked.

He seemed to consider the answer with care. "Accident, when I was a kid."

For some reason I felt this was a way to draw him out, so I pushed on. "What kind of accident. What happened?"

"I crawled under a car to get a ball," he began.

"Go on."

"I tossed it back to the kids I was playing with on the street, but stayed there, under the car, hiding from them—so long that they forgot about me."

"And what? Don't tell me, you fell asleep."

"Someone started the car and backed up. I was still under it."

"My god, but where were your parents?"

He didn't answer me; but that didn't matter. The fact was that he'd told me something about himself. Deep within he was a gentle soul.

We circled the park and headed back to the old town, which was still, like sleep itself. We talked only when I made further attempts to draw out the details of how he came to be in Pamplona. "The town's not exactly Club Med," I stated, hoping for a hook, but also merely grateful to have someone in the off-season with whom I could be sarcastic in English. He rubbed his elbow, looking cold. I noticed that beneath the torn shirt there were massive, dried scrapes on his skin.

"What have you done to yourself?" I asked and pointed to his chest. He looked down at his body and shook his head. The abrasions saddened me, and underlined the sense of hopelessness in him that I refused to accept. I walked him towards our apartment, wondering what to do with him. As we entered the Plazueta de San José the darkness seemed more intense. No light could be seen from our third-floor apartment. Marcus, I was sure, was there with a woman.

Then I had an idea. "Wait here," I said, knowing he would. I took the stairs in twos and made it to our apartment quickly. I listened and opened the door quietly, but there was no need. Marcus was not yet home; the door to his room was wide open. I turned on lights and opened his closet. The rainbow array of designer shirts both plain and patterned would soothe any eye. I took the striped one. I didn't know why it seemed to me that Gavin should wear stripes, but I went with my instinct.

When I arrived back in the plazueta Gavin was standing in exactly the same position in which I'd left him. "Here," I said, handing him the shirt, pleased with myself.

He touched the sleeve tentatively at first, then pulled the shirt out of my hands. A sob escaped his lips and his spit sprayed me. I liked the feel of it on my cheek, but I wiped it off. He lunged towards me and drew me close to him, holding me tighter and tighter.

"I thought it had gone away," he sputtered. For a brief second I wondered if there had been a cosmic joke and that I had handed him a shirt that once belonged to him—could Marcus have stolen it?—until I realized he was referring to something quite different. What "it" was I would only learn much later and never from him. Nevertheless, I felt that he'd chosen me to say those words to, to let me in on a secret. Instead of hearing alarm bells, I felt a thrill.

Briefly, I thought about taking him upstairs to our apartment, but worried that Marcus might soon return and I didn't want to have to explain Gavin.

"I can't sleep," he moaned as he held me. "Please help."

I pulled away purposefully and led him back through the Calle del Mercado to the Calle Estafeta.

"Emily." I liked the way he said my name. "You don't know me, but you're being kind," he continued. I liked the comment too. I was kind. My father had always said kindness was the greatest virtue, and I had always wondered if he thought I was kind enough. Was there a particular kindness—like a school of thought—that he had been referring to? I stopped and turned to listen to Gavin.

"I've done some things . . . and yet you're just here. I wish . . . ," he paused. I was drawn in. I wanted to become that wish. A part of me vowed I would.

"Where are you staying?" I asked in a nurse's whisper.

"Perla," he muttered.

I headed there.

I had in mind my grandmother's trick: it was something she'd performed on me throughout my childhood when I thought the scary monsters would make me their plaything. She'd gently rub a particular spot behind my ear with two fingers, and down along the muscle in my neck. Her featherlike strokes eased my breathing and sent me flying towards dreams. I'd tried it on a bird I once found outside the cottage on Mazinaw Lake. It had flown into the window, believing our living room to be a new land. I had stroked and stroked it, but the sun had set and my grandmother insisted it was bedtime, so I had to abandon my care. When I leapt out of bed at dawn, the bird was gone. I was sure it had flown away.

Gavin's room had a musty smell, as though poultry had been cooped in there previously. The Perla still pretended it was a class act, milking its *Sun Also Rises* legacy, but the faded walls and furnishings gave it the air of a brothel. He sat down on the bed. My eyes shot to the illuminated bathroom and the photographs strewn on the floor. Gavin tucked something further under a pillow and looked up at me. He stared for a long while until I couldn't bear it. He seemed so complicated, and I believed I had the power to streamline him.

I moved towards the bed and touched his head. He grabbed hold of my hand and put it to his cheek. Then his chest. Uneasy, I felt myself watching it all as though in a film. I bent down and hugged him. He grabbed me fiercely. I put my face to his, now more willing, but he wouldn't kiss me. He held me tighter until I was worried about breathing. When I released myself I saw that he was crying. I pulled him back towards me.

I kissed his head and put my two fingers behind his ear, preparing to perform my grandmother's magic, but suddenly I felt his hands on my head. Pushing me down. I was frightened, but not enough to pull back. I had to continue, the way I'd always continued across the frozen lake in my snowshoes. The image of the creature in the ice from my childhood came back to me. Gavin wasn't the bird after all; he was that beastly lupine creature that my father had forced me to observe carefully.

But I didn't dare look up. I went lower. Onto my knees. Before him on the floor. I undid the belt on his jeans. The clasp. The zipper. He helped me to slide him out of his underpants and to draw his jeans down to his ankles.

His cock lay still and soft.

I took it into my mouth nevertheless, convinced of some power to revitalize him. After several minutes of emboldened effort he remained limp. I tried little tricks I'd thought I'd learned. Nothing. When my jaw was stiff, I lifted up my head to find him staring blankly.

"Sleep beside me, please," he said. He pulled off his shoes, slid his feet out of his jeans, and took off his shirt. He pulled back the crocheted bedspread and got in. I took off my shoes, my trousers, and T-shirt and slid in beside him. He touched my hand with his, not patting it exactly, just making sure. We lay still. I watched the ceiling for what seemed like hours, listening to breathing patterns, hoping that he had fallen asleep.

Morning took ages to arrive.

Four

As a child I told a lot of lies. I wasn't trying to get out of anything, or fool anyone; I was simply adjusting reality to the life of my mind. Words were easily misunderstood; everything was vague, so I had to shape it.

But lies take a lot of energy.

Tales are easier to tell than lies. Lies catch up with you, whereas tales get passed along like secrets, and they leave you, changed by you. And usually the secret is revealed. This fact keeps me writing, after my modest beginning of Gavin's story. It makes the April light he walked in less slanted. Since the night five years ago, I've wanted to shape that picture of myself on my knees before his flaccid cock. In finally writing it, I have understood it as the first act with consequences that took place that year. It set off a chain reaction of emotions in me, and there was no turning back after that. In a way I had begun to explore Marcus's edict: *What I am from is not what I am.* I didn't know what I wanted from that night, but I chose to play a part in Gavin's story, and everything else that summer is linked to that decision. But as I shape the rest, I have to include the others around whom the story will pivot. While I didn't know it then, these others are crucial to understanding any pattern. There is Marcus and his chiming, rhyming riposte; there will be Christophe and the bull; and eventually there will be Claire and her innocence, which gave me something to steal.

Gavin's quest, the flashes of memory that accompany it- these are a beginning, but, in the end, I will have to find the threads that will help me piece together my part in all of it. Even so, there is no end; it seems to be the telling that matters. The rising pattern and its ordering is what creates meaning. There is no other peace.

If what I'm from is not who I am, then the same is true for Gavin, and I must look deeper.

"I don't want to eat alone again," Sam said, earlier, interrupting me as I began to explore Gavin's feelings. I wasn't able to continue writing because I went into the kitchen to eat the lunch he had prepared. But there was something eating him as well. I wondered if it was the fact that his lab had been colonized by technicians seconded by tsunami relief. I asked him what the matter was, several times, but his responses were curt or cryptic. "Nothing, just the olive vendor's son." "Have some chorizo." "You're writing a lot these days." I let it pass. Sam has rituals and strict habits for food, drink, and daily exercise. He watches the clock, is early for appointments, and always remembers the small things, like the day of the week we met (Wednesday), my favourite number (four), and the things not to say to my mother when she calls (many and various). I didn't get back to work after lunch. I spent the rest of the day with him, and we took a long walk.

Down the hill, through the cemetery, we passed the modernist stone sculpture of a coffin. I've always admired the stairs on top of it that lead to nowhere, an appropriate metaphor for the mystery of death, but today I noticed the new graffiti marking the piece.

"Oh, damn them," I said, not knowing who them was.

"It's normal, Em," Sam said.

"Normal? Vandalism is normal now?" My voice was raised. Sam slowed down and looked at me. Then shook his head.

"What?" I asked.

"Who are you really angry with, Em?" That shut me up. I didn't have an answer. It might have been that the size of the graffiti somehow overwhelmed the size of the sculpture, because it suddenly became obvious that the coffin wasn't big enough to be realistic, to hold a human body. I pictured Gavin's arm through a tear in his shirt and heard again the sound of the peacocks in Pamplona's Parque de la Taconera. I shook the image of Gavin from my mind, and reached for Sam's hand, but missed it as it swung forward with his stride. I reached again, and he let me take it.

We continued to the Praza da Universidade, talking about his morning. His colleagues are speculating on the diseases that are likely to sprout up in tsunami-hit areas. Water-borne viruses are the obvious threat. I listened intently, taking note of any viral names I could manage. I felt soothed by his steady, knowing tone—an obvious contrast to Gavin's anguish—and I asked him questions based on what I'd learned about viruses on my own. There was no greater pleasure than to give him a sounding board for his ideas. The viruses were dangerously beautiful as he described them.

He talked about the measures being taken, the low-cost solutions springing up, in particular, one pioneered by the epidemiologist Sam had worked with in Kenya. Contaminated water collected in a plastic water bottle, left in direct sunlight for more than thirty minutes, becomes completely safe to drink—despite any fecal matter or other impurities. The water is free of viruses. This simple process works because of a chemical reaction between plastic and water, facilitated by UV rays.

Sam was excited by the fact that he knew the discoverer of the cure. "He didn't know it when we were there," he said, smiling at the miracle of discovery. "It must have been an accident. Someone must have drunk fecal-infected water from a bottle and not become sick. How else would they have known? Damn!" he said, shaking his head with respect.

"Shit!" I said, trying to be funny. He didn't take me on. Sam is a purist when it comes to research; his brother's territory of humour was not allowed here.

When we reached the square, he wanted to stop for a drink.

"Oh no," I protested; it was much too early to stop. "Let's go there," and I pointed to the small baroque church where an exhibition by a German artist was featured. I wanted to savour Sam's animated mood. He agreed to go in. I felt excited as we entered the historic space now exhibiting art that was made only yesterday.

One video installation featured a man burning crops in a field—the shadow and light of a farmer's day. Another showed a young man jumping up over and over again, trying to overcome gravity. "Take me up" read the caption. I felt a small thrill, the kind that came from talks with my father, who can speak about shadow and light in a way that you know it's about more than art—and it was something my mother always hated. My parents told each other lies, not tales. What they said to one another got stuck, did not get passed along. Each held the other's words, took them personally, and resented the other, so I am careful not to do this with Sam.

"It's the coyote from the Roadrunner cartoons, trying the ACME anti-gravity device," Sam said, his curls swaying as he shook his head up and down, faking the seriousness of a connoisseur.

I bristled at the irreverence and, inside, called him pedestrian in my father's tone of voice, and wondered why we could make jokes about my interests and not his.

"I like it," I said, trying not to sound offended, but for a rare, brief moment I hated him.

He took me by the shoulders and said, "I know, and I like you for liking it."

"But you don't."

"I could, if I tried," he said, standing back.

I watched his forefinger curl over his top lip and was reminded of my grandfather's honest surrender before the ancient trees in the forest. I felt Sam's beautiful effort to see what could be seen in everything, and I was grateful for the clarity of that moment—a relief from Gavin's wretchedness.

"Let's go for a drink and you can tell me more about the lab," I said, and put my arm through his.

We left the church and crossed the plaza to a small bar. Sam started to talk about his new colleague in the virology lab, whose work involves vectors related to HIV. But at one point his voice trailed off and he mumbled into his Cinzano. I asked him to speak up.

"Beyond the lab's scope," he said.

"How so?" I felt there was something he wasn't revealing. He stared into his drink and then looked up at the far wall. One, two, three. I counted to myself, knowing he often needs time to respond. He shuffled the five cardboard beer coasters that were on our table.

"Her husband seems a nice man . . . ," he said, dealing the coasters to imaginary players at the table. I looked at the empty chairs and wondered whether Sam was dealing to the husband, who, obviously overshadowed by his formidable virologist wife and her dubious research, would need a good hand. "He's better off here than there," he said as he gathered up the coasters again. And from that I thought I understood. His colleague must have triggered Sam's enduring antipathy to the America he had left as a young man.

"You rarely say a good thing about the States," I ventured, accepting that the discussion about the lab was over. In over four years with him I'd never before asked him why.

"What's there to say?" he asked without sarcasm.

I waited, not satisfied. "People run away in Europe too," I blurted out—a reference to Thomas, who had disappeared when they were teenagers and the reason, I had assumed, that Sam felt bitter about his homeland. He looked agitated; I'd hit a nerve I hadn't targeted. The subject of Thomas was out of bounds. I didn't want him to have to go there. "Sorry," I said. "Never mind . . . what's your new colleague's name?"

"What's her name?" he asked drifting off like he does. "Marianne," he said, with an exhalation floating beneath the syllables of the name. I felt my stomach go into motion.

So I pursued a familiar track, asking questions related to his work. I know the difference between bacteria and viruses, the distinction in size, complexity, and the way they reproduce. Bacteria contain the genetic blueprint and all the tools they need in order to reproduce themselves, whereas viruses are moochers. They need to invade other cells and hijack the cellular machinery in order to reproduce. They attach themselves to a cell and inject their genes, making themselves indispensable to the host. Viruses and bacteria are as different as frogs and leopards.

When Sam and I were first together, I didn't like not having access to his thoughts, so I would surf the Web to know him through what he was studying. I scoured Web pages about viruses and became friendly with the International Committee on Taxonomy of Viruses database. I would spend hours reading the descriptions and working through the Latin construction of each name. I grew to love the logic and beauty of the language. I felt that, if I tried, I could learn Latin from this Web site alone. I liked the sound of the Togavirus, draped in white. Civilized.

"So, the togavirus," I said, trying to get his full attention, which seemed to have veered off towards the Americans, "I can't remember—which animals?"

Through his distraction I didn't get much: Each virus has a code, and the *togoviridae*'s code is 73, its virus accession number is 73000000. It infects vertebrates and plants. But this is not the area that Marianne was pursuing, he added. With support from the grant, she was bringing a whole new angle on retroviruses to his lab. I could tell that this disturbed him.

We left the bar and headed back up the hill to our apartment. "Are you going to the convent today?" he asked, referring to my volunteer work at the hospice run by the sisters of the convent adjacent to the Monasterio de San Martin Pinario.

"I did already, this morning."

"Some days you go more than once," he said, as though encouraging me to go again. I felt dismissed, and could feel him retreating into himself as he sometimes does. I wanted to write, but perhaps I should have been researching retroviruses. Suddenly I did feel the need for the company of the ailing yet fiery Señora Ormaza, a Basque woman, alone in the world after the death of her husband. Her care was paid for by the Pinario Order, thanks to a lifetime of pious devotion to the church. It was my job to take her meals on my visits.

As we reached the top of the park, at the site of the first radio broadcast, I put my hand through Sam's hair. We kissed, a tender, deep kiss, and I felt his shoulders sink, his pelvis inch towards me, and his breath drop lower into his belly. I felt our perfect fit. Sam is beautiful. His brown curly hair reaches his shoulders and bounces up just below his chin, giving him a youthful look. His eyes are hazel; his pectorals are like an athlete's. I held on. I love Sam's kisses. They are creatures: determined, seeking. Once satisfied, they don't retreat but seem spurred on to give back the very thing they needed. Sam can kiss for hours.

We stood like that on the hill, the cycloning December vendavales picking up force. As the year wrapped its shroud around us, I felt safe from the drowning waves and from infection.

But Sam pulled back.

"It's cold, and I have to get back to the lab. Paolo will be waiting for me."

"He can do his own thing, can't he?"

"I'm running the grant, Em. It's big."

We released one another and walked back to our apartment.

Unsettled over Sam's shifts of mood, I decided to return to the convent. As I walked there I mulled over what was missing: the optimism that had first attracted me to him. Sam's not a man to dwell on misfortune, despite the pains of his past. When I first met him in London, the same year I'd met Gavin and then fled Pamplona, I thought that being American explained his optimism.

"People I know who are happy were born that way. Some people will never be happy," he had said in response to my description of Gavin, told to him during the long first night and following day that we spent together in his flatshare in Maida Vale. We lay in bed memorizing one another, before either of us got up, and even then only out of necessity. I didn't want to be away from the haven of his optimism for even a minute.

"Look," he said when I'd returned quickly from the bathroom. He'd taken a deck of cards from his shelf and was shuffling them in front of me. He made cards appear where there had been nothing; cards disappeared and turned up under my pillow; he guessed the card I had chosen each time. He was magic. Later that night he described himself as lucky to have been born positive; otherwise he would certainly have caved in by then.

By the time I arrived at Señora Ormaza's small room in the convent, I was agitated. Writing about that night with Gavin had me wrenched from the present. I needed Señora's calming nature.

"How's the man?" she asked me, in Castilian—knowing there was no Catalan in my vocabulary—as I fluffed her pillow and poured her a glass of water.

I told her that one man, someone I'd been trying to write about, was causing me pain.

"Oh, no, no!" she protested, "Do not settle for pain. See other men." She hadn't understood me, or my Spanish had been so badly phrased that she thought Gavin was my lover.

"No, but . . . you mean Sam. Sam is distracted."

"Why?"

I told her how there were times I worried about him, when he was remote and hard to reach.

"*Hijo prodigo*," she said, referring to Sam's brother as the prodigal son. I'd told her about Thomas when I first started to visit her a year ago, and our conversation had veered towards the death of her teenage son in a car accident. I had sought to comfort her and told her that Sam had experienced a similar loss. Thomas had been born just fifteen months after Sam and had been Sam's playmate. They played out their teenage years at an average school in Brooklyn, with average parents, and an average life of basketball and girls. They had their roles: Sam was the achiever, Thomas the clown who offered tricks at every occasion.

My son is a natural comic, Sam had often heard his father say. But at the height of puberty, things became tricky indeed. Thomas started to defy average and began hanging out with the unusual kids at school. He ran away in late December at the age of sixteen.

"How long ago?" Señora had asked when I'd first told her.

"Nineteen, no, maybe twenty years ago," I calculated.

I could see Señora doing her own calculations, about teenage boys and the passage of time. Since then she has always referred to Thomas as *hijo prodigo*.

This afternoon, as I picked up the broadside pages of *El País*, dropped to the floor as soon as the headlines were read, she seemed deep in thought.

"He lives life for two," she said bluntly.

"What?" I asked, distracted, having just read an *El País* headline that read, *"miles de cadáveres para enterrar"* and wondering where they would bury those thousands of drowned bodies. I stood up and turned to her.

"He lives for his brother; he lives sideways in time, not just forward," she said and I wondered if I was understanding the Spanish correctly. "Breadth for breath," she concluded with an exhalation that made me understand that her lost son took up space in her with every continuing breath of her own. Señora reached for the glass of water and sipped from it. She coughed, replacing the glass on the table, and looked about for the cookies I'd brought for her. I folded up the newspaper and retrieved the tin from the side table. I wondered about what she'd said. Sam's optimism had always seemed oddly paired with guilt. Perhaps living life for two meant weighing up first what the other might also do. Sam is hesitant, has a way of staring off when asked a question, taking a breath, then repeating the question, which allows him a moment to consider before answering with a compromised version of what he really feels. Perhaps all that breadth, according to Señora, explains why Sam stopped growing at seventeen. Although he is relatively slim, he has a wide chest and a full face.

I couldn't stay still. I fussed about Señora's room, doing unnecessary things until I couldn't stand being there to no purpose. I kissed her on the forehead before I left.

Sam has this way of saying things that make me double-take, look to him for meaning, though usually I don't pursue them. "The brain is eighty percent water. Thomas swam like a dolphin, won all the medals at school," he'd said when we first met. Sam himself had starred on the track team, in shot put and sprinting. It occurred to me, as I wound down the long, tree-lined drive of the monastery, that since we'd left Kenya two years ago and moved to Santiago Sam had started to swim regularly too. But surely that's just a way to keep fit, and the sailing off of his thoughts is due to the complexity of his work.

As I reached the foot of our street and began the climb to our apartment, I wondered if the reason he researches viruses and bacteria is because he wants to get to the bottom of life, to the essentials of his existence in order to be able to create a place for Thomas to exist even while living without him.

Perhaps he is doing exactly what I am. By writing Gavin, I am able to have him here.

No, Señora is wrong, and doesn't know my Sam. He is devoted to his work and has room for only science and me.

In the autumn of 1999, after the summer with Gavin, I had run away from Spain like someone fleeing from a swarm of biting insects. Its sting was all over me, in air, light, water, and I was confused. Guilty. I needed to find somewhere familiar. I was going home, but had made a stopover in England and visited my mother's cousin in Croydon. Her overprotectiveness was so similar to my mother's that I must have felt safe there. I stayed. I looked for jobs to support myself and allow me to travel into central London, where a tiny part of my remaining free spirit still found sustenance.

I walked the streets during the day and spoke to no one, but developed a conversation with myself that took no prisoners. I slaughtered the voices in me that had said that wild was true and real. I laid to rest the illusion that I could live on the edge like those artists and dark men that I had always fallen for. I became convinced that the cause of the events that summer had been linked to my fascination with my father's wanderlust. I began to enjoy the cramped, damp flat where my mother's cousin cooked me kippers for breakfast every morning. Slowly I felt my head and emotions clear.

My mother's cousin set me up with someone who handled market research, and I soon went from being on the phone in a call centre to finding a niche being paid to be a part of focus groups.

As one of a group of seven or eight people invited to share their opinions, I would sit in a room with a two-way mirror along one wall to discuss my so-called consumer needs for soap, children's clothing, detergent, cars, or even wine and speciality products like designer water. I quickly became a professional market research focus-group attendee, which seemed to me an unnecessarily long title. I called myself a Professional Opinion.

"And how do you like your cheese?" I asked one marketing manager in response to the same question from her. She glared at me, sure I was a fake, but I had used the trick of turning the question back on the questioner in order to gain time—the trick I recognized in Sam when we finally met. I quickly came up with an appropriate response: "I don't care for the mouldy kind, my children won't touch it, but I like a bit of tang," and the woman backed down. I don't eat much cheese, but during my career as a Professional Opinion my self-image expanded exponentially with each product I was called upon to judge, and in this way I became prismatically distanced from the desperate woman I'd been in Spain. I was capable now, and didn't need a man to reflect back to me who I might become.

I had thought the handler for the client wouldn't have invited me back after the cheese episode, but she did, and this time the topic was household cleaning products—disinfectants, bleaches, and toilet cleaners. I felt confident when I arrived in the room with the plastic bottles of thick bleach, the cylinders of powder, and the spray bottles with brightly coloured liquid. Thanks to my mother, I was at least very clean.

I took my seat, looking about at my co-Opinions, scanning them to see if I would be outclassed in my knowledge of cleanliness or shamed by my ignorance of the latest trends in cleaning a toilet—a brush and some bleach was what my mother had always sworn by.

A woman in her forties with brightly hennaed hair sat

next to me. She smelled of rose, but not the rose of a rose, or even the rose of the essential oil of a rose, but a rose that could easily have perfumed a toilet cleaner. Next to her was an older woman who looked worried. Beside her was a man with glasses and a string of hair swept over a bald patch. My friends at university would have called him pathetic, but I was beyond such judgments by then. As my eyes scanned the next group member I felt a distinct blow, like a jolt of electricity or a piercing sound, but it was neither. It was merely a bold certainty below my ribs. This man was focused on the cleaning products in front of him. His curly hair fell over his eyes, but it was his jawline that attracted me—rugged and yet formed as though from papier mâché—a crooked, uneven, and bulky line. Sam looked up and caught my eye. I held it for a brief moment, and then continued to scan the circle of Opinions while my heart raced.

During the session Sam was the most reserved, the quietest among us, and yet his opinion was solicited regularly by the facilitator, as though he had higher status or was the special needs student in a classroom. All the Opinions had their say, including me, and we made our points adamantly, with feigned or appropriate authority. Sam's answers were precise and technical.

"What do I think of limescale removers?" he asked, taking that necessary breath in the repetition of the question. "Products with cationic and nonionic surfactants seem to be effective in removing limescale. Bacteria breed in limescale. Bleach whitens it but doesn't remove it."

His answers stopped the rest of us short every time. The room would go quiet until the facilitator asked another simple question, like what smells we preferred, citrus or floral? Citrus for me. Sam just repeated the end of the question,

"Citrus? Or floral?" then smiled and passed on it, with a shake of his head.

After the session, while we waited to collect our cash, I went up to him. This was the moment I noticed his height and it made me instantly comfortable.

"Hello."

He smiled at me.

"You seem to know what you're talking about," I said.

"They told me it was a group of specialists—biochemists. I wanted to sound like I could contribute positively."

"Scientists?"

"My friend knows the facilitator, who was desperate for another person, so she lied to me, I see now. But that's okay; you can talk about germs in lots of ways. And I need the cash." He laughed.

I loved him.

"I like the idea of germs," I said, wanting to keep him engaged, and feeling that the man before me was as familiar as my changed name had become. "They're determined. Good technology. I've always been intrigued by killer bugs, that sort of thing. *Love in the Time of Cholera* is my favourite book title."

Sam and I left the building together and proceeded to spend our earnings in the nearby pub. He told me about his post-doctoral work in virology and I told him about my writing, the poems and stories that had been rejected by every journal and magazine or sunk without a trace with every literary competition I'd submitted them to.

"Why didn't you answer the question about which smells you prefer?" I asked.

"Because the scents in cleaners are not real scents. They're chemical compounds—like benzyl alcohol for rose-scented things or limonene for lemon or orange, or pinene for pine. All I could think of was how they can cause skin tumours, so I kept my mouth shut."

Since that moment I have felt the need to keep up with him. We laughed easily that entire evening, but we also turned to serious topics, like his interest in visiting Kenya, and actions and their associated responsibilities, which, at the time—with Gavin's story so recently lodged in me—was an idea I was obsessed with.

"Here, take this," I said, handing him a pepper shaker. He did as he was told, holding it in his palm, turning it over with his other hand.

"Now, what do you do with it?" I asked.

"What do you want me to do with it?"

"Not what I want, what do you do with it?"

"Nothing."

"But you can't do nothing; you have to do something," I said, holding my breath a little, hoping he'd get my point.

"Why?"

"Because it's in your hand."

"So, I can put it down."

"Yes," I said, and took in a gulp of air, holding on to my fledgling sense of self. He waited, not seeing why I could be so animated about salt and pepper.

"That's something, don't you think? There's responsibility attached to the action—where do you place it on the table, upright or on its side?" I couldn't tell him about Gavin yet, so I tried to make it relevant. "If I go to a market research focus group just for the money—it's how I'm surviving at the moment—I have to decide how to be there. Mostly I don't really know the products, so I lie, but I also get to challenge the manufacturers on just why they do what they do; why I don't use their products; and how their system keeps me and others like me out. Do you see?"

"No, not at all," he said, putting the pepper shaker back in my hand, his forefinger lingering on my palm. "I'd prefer salt, thanks," he said with a smile. That was good enough for me. But suddenly he stopped and looked serious again.

"Microbes have evolved so as to be able to kill us, and yet a microbe that kills its host kills itself."

This was my first exposure to his talent for non-sequiturs. I was stumped then, but I'm used to them now. Most of the non-sequitur blurts are about germs.

I waited.

"Some microbes don't wait for the host to die," he told me. "Viruses hop rides on saliva, mosquitoes, flies, or in the case of some serious viruses, like rubella, are passed along in childbirth." And that's when he told me about how bacteria are different. They require no hosting. Party animals all on their own. Cholera, quite beautifully and responsibly for its own survival, induces a massive diarrhea in its victim, which spreads the bacteria into the water supplies of potential new victims.

"Brilliant," I said.

"Hackers have invented computer cholera. Less stinky."

I laughed and touched his leg under the table with my hand. He blushed and stared into his beer.

"What's your blood type?" he asked two days later, on the bed after sex.

"O," I said.

"Positive or negative?"

"Negative."

He smiled; I didn't know why, yet I didn't ask. I nuzzled in, and we explored each other. It was during these dizzy hours that Sam first told me about Thomas. And he was the first person since Spain that I told about Gavin. It was the first inkling of relief, like the short answer to my own question about the salt shaker. What do you do with it? You can't do nothing because it's in your hand. Gavin has been in my hand. And now I'm finally putting him down. Here, not there, and right side up.

After that night, and the next, and the next, I had to return to work. A well-established French chateau was considering marketing a kind of working-person's champagne, so we sat about less formally this time, tasting and giving our views on vintage and bouquet, sipping from multiple bottles, being treated like people who could really afford the stuff. I became tipsy and told them it was splendid—a word I had never used before. I was thrumming with happiness that my work life and romantic life seemed, for just a few precious hours, to be perfectly in tune. Sam deserved celebration.

In those early days we were a couple who dined out when we had no money, bought each other gifts weekly, and laughed at Sam's bad jokes.

Recently, his dives into himself have been more difficult to rescue. It may have been Kenya that might have changed us. The intensity, the no-joke nature of pervasive viruses and bacteria. In our three months in Kenya before we moved to Santiago, Sam and I learned a lot about microbes.

More on Kenya later. Sam is back from the lab. I can hear his key in the door. I am glad I've had time to write this evening. Although Señora Ormaza is wrong about Sam, she has given me a path to understanding Gavin—the idea that in losing someone we begin to live life sideways, breadth for breath. Is this what I too have done? More will have to wait; I am eager for my Sam. I hadn't imagined he would be so late. He is still my reason for celebration.

Five

YOU MUST HELP ME . . . is, in my opinion, not a particularly graceful way to reach out to someone, but since I first wrote that line three weeks ago, I've begun to appreciate Gavin's clumsy technique. Sam has remained moody, pushing me away as he did on the hill after we kissed. This hunger I feel to be let in makes me think I might be living sideways too. Maybe living sideways, as Señora Ormaza meant it, comes from feeling abandoned.

Since Christmas, Sam is often grumpy and he has snapped at me on occasion. He quickly apologizes, but when I ask him to explain he tells me everything is fine, that he is just overwhelmed by the responsibilities that come with the grant.

"My father's the one who works in retail; I never learned the trade or how to bargain with wholesalers," he grumbled after describing the new equipment he had ordered for the lab. He takes any advances I make towards him as a threat. A barrier is growing between us. It is like a glass beaker in which his life continues as an experiment that I am watching. I can see him there, but I can't touch him. Every effort I make to penetrate the glass just seems to make it thicker.

I haven't been able to write a word of Gavin's story because of Sam's mood, but now that he has left for a conference in Paris I have a week to do nothing else. I'll begin with Gavin's words and ignore their relevance to me.

※

You must help me.

Gavin rolled over and I heard paper crunch under his head—it would have been that letter. I opened my eyes and remembered where I was. The room and its smell of damp and dirty feathers descended upon me, and I had trouble breathing from the smell and a feeling of shame. I looked over at Gavin who had rescued the letter from beneath the pillow and was folding it carefully. He placed it in the bedside drawer. He didn't look at me.

He got up and went to the shower. I listened to the sound of the water as I slowly put on my clothes. When Gavin came out of the bathroom he was clean but wearing his soiled trousers. He put on the striped shirt I had taken from Marcus's closet.

"Did you sleep?" I asked. He didn't answer, his eyes went small, his elegant eyebrows slid together slightly to say "badly."

"Do you know of any Brits living in Pamplona?" he asked, out of nowhere.

"Probably hundreds," I said, "but I don't know them. The only person I really know here is Marcus." For a second he became alert. "He's Spanish." Gavin's shoulders slumped as though I'd said something disappointing.

"You'd like him, though," I said quickly. "Everybody likes Marcus . . . mostly women. Can't tell exactly who he likes, though. Keeps to himself, but he's a good friend; we share shifts at the bar." I couldn't tell if his expression was of surprise, disgust, or pain.

"He works at the Mesón?"

"Yes."

"Marcus," he repeated, "is not a Brit?"

"No, why?"

"The name . . ."

"Why are you looking for a Brit?"

He paused, searching for the right answer. "Someone I know is dying."

His shoulder twitched. He was like a racehorse in harness, ready to run, straining against the harness. His appeal was not unlike Marcus's. He turned and looked about the room.

"Look, I'll catch you later," he said, hinting that I should go. I quickly put on my shoes, grabbed my bag, and turned to see him nod at me before I darted out of the room.

That nod. It was like the answer to a question as wide as who I was. It kept me hooked and, despite everything, wondering who it was I'd spent the night with.

⚜

The name had been spoken and the man had become real. "Marcus," he said aloud as he crossed the Plaza del Castillo during midday. He entered the post office. He picked up the local phone book and scoured its pages . . . Garcia, Lopez, Ramirez, Sanchez . . . until the end of the alphabet. Of course there were no Williams, let alone the name Marcus Williams. *How, how?* "Aagh" he groaned, louder than he'd intended, and people around him turned to look. He looked up at the chipped paint on the ceiling. "Aaghh," this time more of a whisper. He would lose his mind if he didn't act quickly.

Porter's file and the discarded mug shot had borne the name Williams, but the boy's name had been David, not Marcus. "Help," he said, and wished that David could hear him. Facts were supposed to be reliable. Like reason. Action was to be taken on the basis of fact. He slammed the book shut. Yes, David had probably changed his name, as he himself would have done if he could. Javier, he thought. It would have been a name that suited him, if he could be rid of Gavin, stop here, retreat from any act of deliverance, and automatically be a different man. He hurried out of the post office.

Siesta was beginning. Shops had begun to close for the afternoon. The sunshine hurt his eyes, his skin, his hair.

Kate had wanted him to grow his hair, to stop looking like a Tory banker and to join her in a Notting Hill life that—for a reason he could only take on faith—included longer hair. She had replaced his pinstriped Ralph Lauren polos and black cords—the clothes he had used to cultivate respectability after Scotland—with cashmere sweaters, raw silk shirts, baggy, low-hanging jeans and Camper shoes. He had worn precisely that combination to the engagement party at the E+O, except for the Campers. Wearing his brogues in the trendy Portobello restaurant felt tamely unorthodox.

His hair was now much longer. Would Kate love him more? He touched the spot where his scalp hurt. He'd seen his reflection in mirrors and windows, but he couldn't tell what he now looked like. He had spent weeks preparing himself to propose to Kate by asking the question of himself in the mirror. He had looked good—young, modern, successful—who could refuse? *This face*, he thought as he touched his straggly beard. For months he had been readying himself for a change, something that would commit him, engage him, rid him of the dread of others and the terror of being found out. But Porter's timing had been perfectly stealthy. For twenty-six years Gavin had lived quietly with his secret, but just as he was ready to share his life with Kate, he found himself avoiding sleeping at her flat for fear she'd hear the sounds escaping from his skull. With every wedding band he'd examined, the scream had become louder. Each jeweller had suggested something different, and in each of their diamond voices he'd heard the screech from the cliff. To stall Kate, he'd told her he wanted to share the moment of the ring with family and friends, but the night of the engagement party arrived and he'd bought nothing. Just before the announcement, which was to be made by his father, with champagne in hand, Gavin slipped out the back door and kept walking, unable to do anything else but find a way to make it all go quiet.

Now, noticing an antique shop across the street that was still open, he walked towards it. The shop was filled with military paraphernalia, bull-fighting gear, and vintage clothing. The shopkeeper was pulling down the blinds, preparing to close for siesta. Gavin entered and saw the man's frown, but continued towards the rear of the shop. The shopkeeper cleared his throat—an interruption also ignored by Gavin.

"Señor," the shopkeeper said, and Gavin finally looked up from the row of antique knives in a cabinet to see the man's shoulders rising in a question, his head cocked to one side. He gestured to the man to open the cabinet. The shopkeeper moaned, "*No, no, Señor . . .*" Gavin kept his eyes fixed on the weapon—*what I deserve is . . .* He heard the surrendering groan from the owner, who took down the cabinet keys from a hook beside the cash register. He unlocked the cabinet and handed the indicated knife to Gavin.

The feel of the knife was perfect: smooth pearl handle, cold blade, a smidgen of roughness that would widen the entry point and make it quick. This would be his backup if talk was not enough. *You must help me* . . . He touched his hair. *Haa, haaa* . . . He fingered the knife tip then held it against his palm. He tilted it towards his torso. Slowly, slowly he brought it towards him, then quickly jerked his hand up and back—

"*Señor! Espere! Loco!*"

The shopkeeper grabbed the knife from Gavin's hand. He quickly placed it back inside the cabinet and locked the glass door, shaking his head, repeating over and over, "*Loco, loco.*"

"Sorry, sorry, I didn't mean to . . . I wasn't going to . . . Is it sharp enough to kill someone?"

The shopkeeper grumbled again and waved Gavin towards the door, but Gavin refused to budge. He took out of his pocket a Gold credit card, and then cash, and held it all in front of the shopkeeper, who continued shaking his head.

"I'm sorry . . . ," he searched for a good lie. "I'm a collector . . . I would like to have it." He stared at the man, wondering if he'd understood. Trying to stop his hand from shaking, he found himself pointing randomly at a delicate lace object in the cabinet. It had a price tag he registered only as outrageous, but to divert suspicion, he told the shopkeeper he'd like to buy that too.

The man gave in, opened the cabinet door, and took out both objects, holding up the knife and sermonizing in Spanish. Gavin nodded, careful not to annoy the man further. When the sermon was finished, the man wrapped up the knife and lace fan in separate packages and charged several hundred euros to Gavin's credit card.

Outside in the sun, he unwrapped the first package and slid the knife into his back pocket. Holding the folded fan in his hand, he walked quickly across the plaza to the shade of the historic quarter, and headed back to the Mesón. When he arrived at the alley that would take him to the bar, he stopped and shook his head. The sounds rattled; he took a deep breath.

"Do . . . you . . . fancy . . . a . . . sssag?" The woman's accent was molasses as she effortlessly pronounced the English words. Her voice was liquid, like sherry, and came from the alley, just inches away. If he peeked around the corner he would almost meet her lips. He held his breath and listened.

"A shhhag," a male voice clarified for pronunciation. Gavin took a step back along the wall, away from the corner. "Fffancy a shag," the man repeated, his English meticulously eked out, his voice just as liquid as the woman's. He repeated "shag" slowly. "Shag," the woman copied, in a catlike whisper, and then burst into giggles. Gavin listened and imagined that the man then took her face in his hands and kissed her. A few seconds later the man said something in Spanish. Gavin lowered his eyes to the ground to concentrate. He could recognize the word for statue and a few others. He thought he understood that the man was telling the woman she looked like a statue. "*Pareces una estatua.*"

His heart raced as he stood with his back flat against the wall. The stone felt hot, like the flint between the man and woman just inches away. Clothing rustled. Ambergris and musk wafted by. The man and woman moved off from the wall and left the alley. Gavin watched the back of the man's close-cropped head as he walked away with the woman under his arm. It must have been him, he thought. The head was different from the photos, but this man could speak English and was here, next to the Mesón. *Haa, haaa,* the madness said. He turned around quickly and headed back to La Perla.

That evening the Mesón de la Naberreria was unusually crowded for the season. Normally it's only during San Fermin that you can't move about, but it was packed with university students and a loud group of young Basques who had been drinking all afternoon, on my shift. Before I left I had worried about violence erupting, but now, as the sun set and the men were drunk and sad, they seemed harmless as they poured out of the bar and loitered around the fountain. I was returning to the Mesón to look for Marcus, hoping he might help me make light of the previous night's fumblings with Gavin. The air was humid. As I passed the fountain I saw Gavin seated on the curb, a bottle of water in one hand and in the other another plastic packet of Aspirin.

"Hey," I said, pretending nonchalance.

"Hi," he said, looking up, and at the expression in his eyes I was drawn in again.

"Coming in?"

"I'm sorry," he began, but I couldn't bear to hear him explain why it hadn't worked between us.

"You look like you've had some rest, at least," I said quickly.

He shrugged, got up, and a thin wrapped object the size of a ruler fell from his lap. He picked it up and looked at it as though remembering he had it. He absently handed it to me. "Unwrap it," he said. I did, and in my hands the object opened up like a waking creature and expanded into a black-and-red lace antique fan trimmed in gold thread. I'd never seen anything like it. It was the most beautiful thing I'd ever held.

"What's this for?"

"Please take it," he said, and I saw that it was difficult for him to make this offer. I guessed that he was asking for forgiveness. Although my pride had been ruffled, I pushed it aside and thought about how Marcus had accused me of being empty. I looked hard at Gavin, wanting to sculpt him, or paint him the way Marcus could, but he still eluded me.

"Come in with me. There's someone I want you to meet," I said, as I took his arm. We walked into the bar together.

Marcus had the music up loud. He swayed and cha-cha'd to Dominican salsa as he poured drinks. He was more beautiful than ever in his intractable feline aloofness. He wore a parrot-green T-shirt that accentuated his physique and the muscles in his arms as he poured a draft. When he looked up and saw me approach with the limping Gavin, he didn't take his eyes off us, except to quickly check that the draft was not overflowing. More precisely, he kept his eyes on Gavin, who was undeterred by the exacting attention. Something between them made me start to perspire. When I introduced them, I did so with tight lips. Here were two beautiful, odd men—the kind I always fancied. I had desired them both, but with Marcus I'd accepted our friendship and his exotic distance. Gavin was new, while the territory—that edge—was old.

"*Me esta pareciendo conocido,*" Marcus said to me, meaning that he'd recognized the shirt Gavin was wearing. I cringed, realizing that I hadn't told him I'd borrowed it.

"He needed something. All he had was rags," I said, a small plea. Marcus's look didn't change. He wiped the counter in front of us and asked us what we were having. I looked at Gavin.

"*Agua,*" he muttered. I ordered a beer.

"I thought you wouldn't mind," I said guiltily when Marcus brought me my San Miguel. He shook his head and moved on to serve another customer.

He looked back our way a few times. He came over to where Gavin and I stood not talking to each other, now that we had an awkward past between us. "Tourists are arriving a bit early this year," he said in Spanish, sounding suspicious. Gavin simply stared at Marcus, his face rippling through a range of emotions that seemed to settle at pain.

"That's Marcus," I told him after Marcus had moved off to serve a woman at the other end of the bar. He nodded, and kept his eyes on him. I wondered if I'd just discovered why things had not worked out between us. Gavin's top lip curved down with what looked to me like desire.

When Marcus returned to us, he stood still in front of Gavin, boldly examining him.

"Shirt suits him. You chose well," he said glibly in Spanish.

I scrambled to repair the moment. "This is Gavin," I said in my most cheerful Spanish pronunciation. Marcus nodded in Gavin's direction. Gavin rubbed his arm with his hand, warming it or scratching it, I wasn't sure. He looked like he wanted to speak, but still he said nothing. "He's looking for a Brit," I said to bridge the gap, at which point Marcus stepped back, then moved away again quickly.

"You said he was Spanish," Gavin muttered as he turned to me.

"Yes, he is."

"African-Spanish?"

"I don't know."

"But he speaks English."

"No, he doesn't." Gavin looked like he was about to smile. When Marcus came back again he seemed agitated.

"Gavin," he asked, emphasizing the man's name, "*como te ganas la vida?*" He poured another drink.

This time it was Gavin who stepped back from the bar and looked about the room in discomfort. Marcus waited, looking at me and down again at the bar, but I noticed his eyes return to examine Gavin's face.

"I'm in business," Gavin parried. His use of English was intended to control the conversation.

Marcus leaned onto the bar. "Business is a big category," he said in Spanish. "You a builder? A banker? A music producer? A pornographer?" His face gave away nothing, but I was uncomfortable enough for both of them.

Gavin stepped up to the bar again. "I fix companies that need help," he mustered in Spanish.

"A corporate healer," Marcus said abruptly in English, which caught me off-guard. I did a double take. Gavin rubbed his arm again. Marcus didn't miss a beat, seemingly relieved at the idea of business, and continued so quickly in Spanish that I thought I might have imagined the English. The suspicion in his voice did not change, though, as he went on about illness being a problem for governments and that most people in business drank too much and ate too much sugar. Sugar is angry food, he concluded and turned away in that instant to serve a grizzled regular at the far corner of the bar. I listened and watched in confusion.

Marcus went about his job, flinging lids off bottles of Estrella and San Miguel, and chatting up two young women who had asked for cocktails. He pressed a button on the blender. Tequila and fruit swirled up. With one hand holding down the lid of the blender, he reached for the stereo with his other and cranked up the volume even more on the system. The dance beat thrummed up as though from the floor itself. Those at the bar could feel it in their feet. I watched them start to move, the beat building up inside them until a few women were compelled to dance. I felt hot and dizzy, the beat rattling me. I opened up Gavin's gift and began to fan myself. *A thing of beauty*, I said to myself, over and over, willing myself to be worthy of the fan. I dared not to look up in case someone might be watching, and yet I desperately wanted to be noticed.

Marcus had spoken English; Gavin was fixated on him. And I needed to erase the previous night's humiliation. If only Gavin would hold me, I thought, he'd know that I could help him. I finally looked up at him and moved my hips from side to side as I fanned myself. He looked about the room, oblivious to my signals. I caught Marcus's eye and invited him to the dance floor with a gesture, but he shrugged and raised his eyebrows, cracking off another lid from a beer bottle. I took off my cardigan, revealing my spaghetti-strapped silk top, and left it and the fan on the bar. I meandered through the crowd, until I came across a group of women and a few men. I asked a short man with a large nose to dance. He put down his drink and joined me in a salsa.

At the bar, Marcus offered Gavin a drink, but he declined, and I know, from what Marcus told me later, the shape of the conversation between them.

"Just water, thanks."

"How long are you staying in Pamplona?" Marcus asked, in Spanish again.

"I don't know," he replied, and touched his side. "No Brits live in Pamplona," he said, with an implied accusation.

Marcus looked down, wiped the counter, and cleared away some empty glasses and bottles.

A woman at the other end of the bar had been staring at Gavin. Marcus noticed and nudged him, chinning in the woman's direction.

"Maybe she's a Brit," he said. "*Tal vez sea Britanica,*" he said. "*Ella tambien te quiere conocer.*"

Marcus beckoned the woman over. When the young local made her way to Gavin's side she looked like a doll beside a beast. She had large front teeth divided by a gap. He was sour; she was sweet. She took him by the hand and dragged him to the dance floor.

"*Quién eres?*" she flirted. Gavin grimaced, about to burst, and looked back at the bar. I watched from my spot on the dance floor. He managed to nod at the woman, then waved off, moving back to the bar.

"You don't like women, no?" she called after him loudly.

He'd had enough torture. He gulped back a shot of vodka that Marcus had poured for another customer. The song finished and I returned to the bar. I watched the vein along Gavin's neck swell and, for the first time, felt frightened that I had underestimated him.

Marcus filled another vodka shot and passed it to his customer. I gestured for him to pour me one; he did. Gavin braced himself against the bar and stared at Marcus, making us all uncomfortable, until Marcus offered him another vodka. Gavin declined. As the next hour wore on, Marcus continued to offer him shots; each was declined. Gavin drank water, twice popping out a couple of Aspirin from their small plastic bubbles.

Finally, Marcus broke the barrier between them. "Things aren't fixed so easily, you know, and you're a long way from 'right' yourself. Lost your touch, have you? You've come to the right place to mend what's broken," he said, the Spanish rolling like thunder off his tongue. He knew Gavin had not understood, and yet it seemed so personal.

"You married?" he asked slowly, and this Gavin understood.

"No."

"Ah, and the Brit you want is a man."

Gavin missed or ignored the implied insult; instead he took out another Aspirin.

"If you've come to find yourself, the Camino will help. Just keep walking."

I couldn't understand why Marcus insisted on being so odd, drawing Gavin out, yet so insistently rude. This was not the Marcus I knew, the man who was a gentle, hospitable host to all the pilgrims that came into the bar, a man who affirmed the essence of themselves they thought they might find in Spain.

"A little bit of what ails you, aired to the Spanish sun. 'A little flesh, a little breath and a Reason to rule all—that is myself.' It's something I learned from a priest," he said—all in English.

I froze. Gavin stiffened. Marcus moved to the other end of the bar to serve a customer.

His English had been perfect, a kind of East-End London accent I'd heard in TV shows. In the next suspended moments, I thought he'd turn and laugh, and reveal he had been putting us on, teasing us with a memorized phrase from a movie he'd watched over and over, but as the seconds passed I realized it was no act. The act had been everything else. My mind swam to find the surface of reality.

Gavin downed the rest of his water and quickly left the bar. I stayed, standing in the same spot for the rest of the night, not talking, not drinking, merely staring blankly as the life of the bar and that of its bartender went on around me. Everything I had believed I'd known about Marcus and Pamplona in the last eighteen months was false. The kaleidoscope was shifting.

❧

A little bit of what ails you, the man had said. In his room, Gavin hunted for the photos he had left under the pillow. He arranged them on the bed. He picked up the photo of the younger boys. *This*, he thought and put his finger on the face he'd seen just a few minutes ago in the bar. He tore down the centre of the photograph and then around the face of the thirteen-year-old mixed-race boy with black hair in a bowl cut. The flash of memory played again, faithfully, but this time with a different spotlight.

Top of the ridge. The first holler is angry, close by, clear. There is movement to his right. Porter is there. Struggling. Mud. Rain like a whip. The ground is wet as Gavin is thrown onto it. He tries to stand, slips, tries to reach out. Two sets of legs are before him. His hand touches a chest, then an arm that slips from his grip, then nothing. More tussling beside him. Then a short sharp scream. The whoosh of wet clothing near his ear. Then one long scream like a coyote's howl.

Over and over, this scene repeats, and he tries to slow it down, hold it. The next time, in the corner of the frame, as he is slipping in the mud, he catches the movement of something beyond the scree, on the other side of the rain. The scream is fading, into the valley. He is on his knees now but looks up in time to see the back of a boy, his spongy hair, as he retreats down towards the Dryas below the scree. Voices below shout up to this boy. Just before he disappears from sight, he turns, for a split second to look. Freeze this, there. *Flash.*

The face in the bar had been more like the mug shot he'd discarded—the eyes sunken and twitchy; the chin, a man's before its time. But still, the guileless glint he'd remembered from the day with the mouse's tail behind the school—the very openness that had made him choose that boy when asked to pick one—was there. It was that openness that had driven him here, to shake the *haa, haaa* madness.

Men did certain things, he reminded himself, but they often had to enlist the help of others. He sat down on the bed. There was still the knife if relief wasn't forthcoming. He took the letter he had started the previous day from the bedside table, along with the Bible, which he used as a hard surface to write on. At the top of the letter, his hand trembling, he wrote the Spanish words as he thought he had understood them:

Pareces una estatua.

He read what followed: *You must help me . . . I am in Hell.* He scratched out the demand for help and wrote: *You don't remember me . . . I have to tell you . . . this hell has been my price . . . and now . . . Please.*

Six

As for me, my reality had been hijacked. I was still standing in the Mesón long after the pilgrims had retreated to their refugios for the ten o'clock curfew. The regulars were hitting their stride, sipping their sleeping potions or talking into their glasses as though to loved ones.

I eventually picked up the fan from the bar and opened it again; it felt like a prop from a costume drama. I closed it and nodded goodnight to Marcus as he swept up litter and cigarette butts from the floor. He said nothing, but we both knew something had been permanently altered.

The next morning I couldn't get out of bed; my mind had been racing even through sleep. It had been tricked, and now it was vulnerable.

Because a virus contains genetic material and yet is incapable of metabolic functions like taking in food or getting rid of wastes, when it attacks a body all it can do is reproduce itself. In a campaign of solipsistic nihilism of unimaginable proportions for something so minute, a virus vigorously attaches its tail to the outside of a host cell, and quickly injects its hereditary material. The virus's protein outer shell is left behind, discarded, like a coat left at the door permanently. Once inside the cell, the virus's genetic material takes control of all of the host's activities. The host is no longer able to function properly and begins to produce only viruses. Soon it is so filled with these new viruses that it bursts open. The new viruses are released and they infect nearby cells. This pattern continues until all living cells have been infected. The host and its environment are fundamentally changed.

I had been invaded. My understanding of life no longer matched what I was experiencing, and Gavin's arrival in Pamplona had forever changed the three of us. I stayed in bed listening to the modalities of sound. Marcus's usually slow meandering through the ablutions of a new day was hasty, and he left with a slam of the front door. I rolled onto my stomach and lay with my face on the sheet for a few uncomfortable breaths, then turned to face the wall. Gavin's legs, the hair, the small bumps near his groin, the pelvic bone, all came to mind in slashes of textures that seemed somehow narrated by the sound of Marcus speaking English.

I called in sick at the bar that day and stayed home to write, but the knight I was creating for my *Tales* became violent as I wrote him. His delicate maiden seemed unbelievable as a character, so I began to rewrite her. The story started to unravel, and ridiculous phrases like, "a creature so foul it pains me," poured out. I sat in front of the notebook and doodled. I took a walk through Parque de la Media Luna, came home, and doodled some more. My imagination was letting me down.

I never returned to that story. Instead I took on Marcus. Who was he? Why hadn't I known him at all for the past year and a half? Despite Gavin's gift to me, it was obvious that I had been a convenient link to Marcus. I had missed out details and hard facts, but every good storyteller is also a keen observer. I would watch and listen, I vowed. I would turn my attention to Marcus, and know him. I left the apartment to seek him out.

I headed towards Plaza del Castillo, to a café I knew he frequented, particularly because of its afternoon waitress. *A little flesh, a little breath, and a Reason to rule all—that is myself.* It was what Marcus had said to Gavin in the bar, and I had read it weeks previously on the cover of a book beside his bed—of course, a fact I should have paid attention to. The *Meditations* of the Roman philosopher-emperor Marcus Aurelius, in the trendy paperback edition, had been beside Marcus's bed for weeks. When I had asked him if he was reading it, he'd replied in Spanish that he couldn't read English. He had claimed that a pilgrim at the bar had insisted on giving it to him, and he'd been too fed up to argue with her. But the truth is that he had been reading it.

When I saw him sitting outside at the Café Iruña, with the book beside his espresso on the table, I felt ridiculous. I stood and watched him as he sipped his coffee, unaware of me. I tried to see him differently, to see him as he really was. A Brit? A Spaniard who spoke perfect English with a London accent?

Our relationship had been based on teasing and my respect for his privacy. We had barely spoken of his background, though he once told me he was not a Catholic when I had accused him of sleeping with Camino pilgrims as a way of saving his own soul. He had done another of his Spanish raps and assured me that he believed only in material goods and sex, and although I knew he was covering up something, I had no idea the cover had been a complete disguise.

I waited until Marcus finished his espresso to walk over to the café, and stand silently beside his table waiting for him to look up at me.

"Sleep well?" he asked in Spanish when he finally looked up.

"Who are you?"

"Who do you want me to be?" he asked, as he put his sunglasses on against the glare of the sun. I stepped to the right and blocked the sun with my accusing silhouette, but he kept his glasses on.

"I want the truth."

"You don't believe in it."

"You lied to me."

"No, you never asked me," he said in English now. "I don't speak English anymore because that part of me is dead."

In silence we balanced the discomfort. He was trying to admit something; I wanted to hear what it was. I pulled out the chair across from him and sat down. My need to understand was greater than the humiliation I felt. I wanted his lie to have been for a good reason: run away from something he'd done or because of some deep family shame. I also wanted an answer to a question I'd always had about his looks: was Spain an uneasy place for a black man?

"Is it something you've done?" I asked timidly.

He stared at me. I was sure I'd hit a nerve, but after a few seconds he laughed, "Why would you think that?" he said through his teeth.

He looked insulted. I felt small. I shrugged and didn't know how to answer.

"Man oh mighty, you're as bad as all the rest," he said, shaking his head. He held up his hand to wave at the full-cheeked waitress, who came over quickly. I felt ashamed of myself. He ordered another coffee, smiling at the woman, who casually brushed his cheek with the back of her hand as she left.

"Look," he said softly. "I have no connections to my past, so why dwell on it? Don't take it personally," and he held my fingers in his hand and rubbed them.

"I'm your friend," I said softly.

"That's true. It's what you let me be," he said. I didn't understand what he meant, but was relieved that he was ready to talk.

"Then tell me."

He fidgeted for a moment before wading in, slowly, in the nascent language between us. The effort of English, along with the memory of the past, seemed to harden his features.

"My mother liked to dance," he began. He waited, smirked, and continued, "but in East London, Bow, there wasn't enough dancing for her, so she went across town."

I waited. "What are you getting at?" I asked finally.

"What do you want?"

"Who raised you?"

"Mum—who lived alone with her mum, who drank too much, until she found Christ, and then my mum got an office job and moved out."

"And?"

He sighed, giving in a little. "She went out at the weekend, to the West End, Ladbroke Grove," he said, and I wondered why this detail was important, but didn't want to interrupt him now. He rubbed his fingers together. "Miriam," he said, with kindness. "Miriam met a West Indian man on the dance floor one night. He was my dad," he said flatly. "He came to our house once. I thought he was going to live with us, but he left. My mother met another man—Miguel, a Spaniard . . . that's how I ended up here." He seemed to have concluded any disclosure he felt was necessary. I waited. "There's not much to it, Em. I prefer Spain."

He picked up his espresso and tossed it back.

"But your Spanish ..." I said.

"I have a good ear."

I felt like I knew him even less than before, and yet there was a new texture to his mystery, which deepened my appreciation of him—of the phlegm in his voice, of the flaked scalp near his neck, and the small bumps there as he grinned in memory.

There were many ways one could come from an island.

"Did you know Gavin before?" I asked.

"Gavin doesn't know anyone," he answered, then lit a cigarette. I grew anxious. I knew then that I should have told Marcus what had happened between us, and that I thought Gavin was looking for him, but I don't know what stopped me. Perhaps I did not want to share Gavin.

"He's an odd one," I said. "What do you suppose he wants?"

"Probably just to get laid." He dragged on his cigarette with concentration. I felt my face turning red.

"Are you still going to Santiago next week?" I asked to change the subject.

"*Si.*"

"Why do you do that every year? You said you weren't Catholic, but maybe you are turning into—"

"I'm not."

"Why do the Camino then?"

"Because I can," he said and shook his head, becoming irritated with me.

"Do you want to return to Spanish?" I asked. He looked up at me and took his sunglasses off. His dark eyes gave nothing away except his obvious beauty. I waited while he considered my question.

"*Si, ... es mejor,*" he concluded.

"*Y que del libro?*" This return to my faulty Spanish pushed us back to a safe distance from each other again, but I wanted to clarify why he'd been reading Marcus Aurelius.

"I did get it from a pilgrim. I *can* read it." Then reverting to English once again, Marcus quoted: "*All is trite . . .*"

I leaned over and kissed his cheek. "You do paint," I said, needing to confirm one thing about him that I believed was concrete.

"Si."

I quickly stood up, waved goodbye to him, and rushed off towards the outskirts of the city. It felt as though I was leaving it, but I wasn't. I just needed a change of perspective. To see it from the position of the windmills that gave the city its power, to feel and hear the hum of something mechanical, solid, real. Marcus had barely opened up, but I had been given an entry into his story, and insight into Marcus as a man who had hardened because of his displacement.

It must have been then that I first began to actively construct another person's thoughts. I hadn't pinpointed the moment until now, as it coincides with what I have been trying to achieve with Gavin. What were Marcus's thoughts like? Were they lumbering and tottering, as those I have invented for Gavin, or were they sculpted, like the back of his head, like the curve that was made to be touched? Firm, curved thoughts, like ballads, surely. I remember his *Vacía, vacía, querida, vacía* and the *man oh mighty* of his English. As I piece together what he told me with what I know, I also must hear his thoughts.

So, it's his tempered voice that I now add to Gavin's, and my own.

Seven

Act the pact—be good. You should.

 The man wearing his striped shirt walked towards him, and while Marcus couldn't place him, something more than just the shirt made Gavin too familiar to ignore. He moved like the tottering constable in Harlseden who had once knocked him on the head with a bludgeon. There was no chance he was that policeman—that man would be eighty by now—but the steely Britishness set off a cold wave of old feelings, and these had turned him aggressive in the bar. No doubt Gavin had arrived to blame him, just like all the others. But of all the other accusers, none had seemed as personal about it as this man who had limped into town like a wounded bounty hunter.

 Marcus checked his watch. Constanza would be furious with him for being so late for their lunch date. And right now he wanted her kind of comfort. He rested his hand on the entrance gate to the Plaza de Toros and waited for Gavin to reach him.

Sleep had culled him. *Faded*, he thought, and when he touched his hair it didn't hurt. *This*, he felt as his finger twirled the scruffy fringe. He walked as steadily as his feet would allow and tried to hear the heart-racing certainty that had brought him to this city, but it was dim. Only a humiliating laughter remained, and if he listened to that he'd have nothing. He'd have to count on instinct for now and hope to draw reason alongside. Marcus had phoned and had told him to meet him at the Plaza de Toros. If Marcus had recognized him and put the pieces together, resolution might come sooner than he'd expected. He touched the pearl-handled knife in his pocket and welcomed the thought of Marcus's anger. He hurried.

Marcus stood waiting for him. As Gavin arrived, Marcus turned and silently led him towards the pens around the left side of the bullring, where he introduced him to Christophe, a man, Marcus told him, who tended bulls and knew all the foreigners in Pamplona.

"He might know the man you're looking for," Marcus said. Gavin's heart sank as he realized that the end he'd been walking towards would still be delayed, and yet he felt relieved that Marcus had not recognized him. He played along, shaking Christophe's hand. He followed Marcus and Christophe into a bull's stall.

"Come, come, you see, look here," Christophe said. Gavin hesitated, but Christophe seemed so confident that it was impossible not to listen and watch as he pulled on the leather straps of the tether and filled the water trough from the running hose.

"You can see here, these puffy sacks, like extra balls at

his arse . . ." Using the prodding stick, Christophe raised the bull's tail to expose the anus beneath it. The bull stopped feeding, shot a custodial glance to the right, and snorted, before chewing again.

"The laxatives. His shit is unpredictable."

"Hemorrhoids?" Gavin asked, as he gazed at the aubergine coloured sacks under the tail. *Fester*, he thought, and took a step back, feeling queasy. He touched the knife in his pocket again.

"Of course. They pump them full of laxatives before fights and before San Fermin. It makes them . . . unhappy. They do their job, they put on a show, and they suffer for months."

Christophe explained the stand he had taken against San Fermin. He asked Marcus if he would take part in this year's protest. Marcus grinned, shook his head, and said to Gavin, "Hippie foreigners who think they will change Spain." Gavin felt the stall shrink with the fact that he had understood the Spanish. Despite the broad, open face, Marcus was hard— his body a shield—and it had the effect of throwing him off course. He looked towards the exit. The option of talking and reasoning, which after his failure at Finisterre had seemed the only reason to continue on to Pamplona, seemed unlikely now. When Christophe went on to elaborate, telling them that most of the protesters were actually the sons and daughters of Pamplona's bankers and bureaucrats, Gavin had to swat his neck to hush the rising tide of sound. He took a step to his left.

Christophe described the protests they had been organizing against the running of the bulls through Pamplona's narrow streets. "There was a point when we thought we would free them all, but that would be useless; they'd be recaptured. I look after them as best I can," he said, explaining that his job was to clean the stalls, water and feed the few bulls who resided here in the off-season. "They're my responsibility now," he said with conviction. "This one," he said as he pulled on the leather strap, "he sees me now, I know, but in the summers he barely sees anything."

He watched Christophe's peculiar movements with the tether. "There now, that's it," he said gently to the beast. Christophe had a lulling wide-eyed manner. Talking to him would be simple. He would listen, take it all on, easily, whereas Marcus had conviction, and that had a scent, the way greed does.

Justice, he thought, to kick-start his reason. The right man had to be punished, and Gavin had to stop being controlled, stop being less than a man. He'd allowed Porter to silence him for over two decades, but there was still time. Porter was alive, the truth could still come out, justice would be served, and then it could be the *haa haaa* of his existence that would be silenced. It was a matter of finding the right way.

He noticed how Marcus patted Christophe's shoulder, his admiration of the Swiss man's faithful service to this old bull apparent. There was still an opening in the man.

"*Por qué?*" asked Marcus, eyeing Gavin quickly, then looking back at Christophe. "Why can't he see?"

"Because they put petroleum jelly in their eyes to cloud their vision."

"So the matadors can win," Marcus added in Spanish.

"So they can look like they win," concluded Christophe, as he dropped the bull's tether and moved towards the feeding trough. "This one is a farm bull now. They'll use him to calm the others they bring in from the south, spiked up for San Fermin and the next fight. He's docile compared to what he used to be. Harmless."

Gavin looked upon the bull with sympathy.

Name it. You name the date, he thought. And Christophe can vouch for me. Marcus knew that whatever it was that had brought this Englishman all this way, he hadn't done it, and he would not be trapped, not this time. Perhaps there was nothing to worry about in Gavin's presence, and that he was merely a lost soul in Pamplona, but there was something suspicious about how focused the man was on him. He'd help Gavin find a different Brit.

He felt safe here, with Christophe, who had known him for fifteen years, and would stand up for him. Marcus had learned after all these years that you needed two things in this world: a friend and the right skin colour. He'd had neither back then, but now at least he had Christophe, who would help him put this man off the scent of his tail-in-the-air track. And in a few days he'd be gone to Santiago. His timing was good, for once. Gavin would never find him in the hills of Galicia. He would not be running, but he would also not be taken easily. Not this time.

All arrivals were like this, he thought as he leaned against the wall of the stall. All the men who caused trouble—the first one, then Miguel, then the accusers, then the constables, and with the exception of Lacey—they all arrived like they wanted to give you something precious. But he was well versed in that trick by now.

He thought of the first arrival that he could remember—an early, almost black-and-white memory. The sense and nonsense of a man on a train. A man who was familiar but unknown. A black man, island man, do-it-for-yourself-and-get-away-with-it man. His father on a train platform in Bow. He remembered that the station floor was slanted. Rubbish rolled towards edges from the middle. A sheet of newspaper stuck to his trouser leg. The black man looked at him with cold-eyed amusement. My son without sun. And Miriam was coy and fawning, desperate for the black man to stay. But of course he didn't. And never again would the get-away man come to visit them. And, yes, even then, it was all his fault—this son without sun.

Now this tall white man might be looking for him, and it would start all over again, and the blame would rain and the smallness would pucker like wet paper. But Christophe was here. He had a friend.

"How long did you say you were planning to stay?" he asked Gavin, taking in the wrinkles at the man's eyes, trying to place where in the past he belonged. Gavin merely stared at him, and Marcus knew the answer was "as long as it takes." Yes, blame, like returning rain.

"I have to go and mix the feed," Christophe said. "Pull the tether out, this way, and draw him towards the trough. I'll be back," he added, pointing towards the front of the stall before he left.

Marcus stepped forward to do as he had been asked. He moved around the beast's head. He was good at getting out of the way—he had learned it best with Miguel, the man his mother had come to love after the get-away man had made it clear he would not be got. Miguel was like Christmas morning, all wishes won, until it wore off, and then he would threaten to leave them whenever things became more difficult than they would have been with his real kids and real wife in San Sebastian. He was the man Marcus once called Dad—mistake, mistake—whose other children Marcus had wanted to know because Black in Bow alone with Miriam was not. Not full.

Marcus heard Gavin move at the back of the stall, and suddenly he was tired beyond explanation. These thoughts of

Miguel and London were sparking because of Gavin's presence and he was fatigued already with the effort necessary to defend himself against any charge. Yes, he had a record. Or rather, David Williams had a record. But for fifteen years David had done nothing, because David was dead and Marcus, in his place, was clean.

But oh so fucking tired.

He remembered a feeling from boyhood, when Miguel had moved them from the East End to Notting Hill and would take Marcus out at nights with him to drink with the whores who worked above the Pakistani shop on Ladbroke Grove. Marcus had known on the first night that he met the women that he'd never feel as alone as they did. Each Friday night had been the same. He'd arrive in the shadow of the mighty Miguel and the women would flock to him, fight over him, want to touch him. He had let them stroke his head, his cheeks—they loved his cheeks—and did not try to pull away. In the kitchen-sized bar above the shop, as Miguel drank into the night with his mates and the women prepared for work, Marcus sat on the vinyl sofa, forcing himself to stay awake by doing sums in his head, needing to stay alert, because he wanted to be like Miguel more than anyone he'd ever known. Then one of the women had taught him about colours, showed him how to mix paint so that he could create all the colours he needed for his drawings. He would draw and paint into the night. One night he found himself slipping sideways and onto the shoulder of a big-breasted woman in a bright green dress. Her black legs were like shiny bollards. The woman took him by the shoulder and eased him onto her lap. The leg was softer than it looked, and he let his eyes close. The bright green dress shone on the edge of a dream. The woman had put her hand on his forehead. And kept it there for what seemed like forever.

The bull pen was getting hot. He wiped sweat from beneath his eye.

※

Gavin edged around the bull's backside towards the front of the pen. The animal's smell was peaty; its hide glossy. He wanted to see the bull's eyes—see the filmy sheen over them that Christophe had described. The blindness of running, hitting walls, slipping, sliding, and scrambling during the run— this he knew.

"Never understood what people saw in the fights," he said to Marcus as he edged towards the bull's head. He could feel a part of himself return: the easy way he had with people at work, when small talk was a way into doing business. The bull didn't look up from the water trough, but Gavin looked up at Marcus, who was holding its tether. "You go to these kinds of things?"

"Have done, but it's not my thing," Marcus said defensively.

Gavin wanted Marcus to recognize him now, to say *I know who you are and I saw what you did*, but there was nothing forthcoming.

He locked eyes with Marcus as the man dragged the tether towards the back of the bull. The bull snorted, and Gavin heard a rustling from the bull's back end. He turned to watch the shit rolling out from under its tail. The loose clumps of straw filth plopped into a heap. He needed to get out of the stall. The bull stepped back on its right hoof and snorted. Gavin jumped back and pressed himself up against the wall. Marcus dropped the tether and moved to the wall on his side, inching his way towards the exit, taking a wide berth of the animal.

But not wide enough. A skip. A buck. The hoof as fast as a shot nerve. A splash of black and a spray of dust and straw. Snorting. Then a low moan—*whoa, whoa*—that escaped from Gavin's mouth.

The blow caught Marcus in his ribs. On the ground, half in and half out of the stall, he clutched his side as the bull continued kicking and snorting.

Trapped in the corner of the stall along the barnboard panels, with splinters of wood piercing his shirt and skin, Gavin closed his eyes. The animal's huffing and snorting could not just be heard—it was felt. He opened his eyes in time to see the bull buck and strain against the tether, jerking the wooden panels all about him. The snorting and bucking reverberated in his chest, while the dirt flew up to the ceiling, and hooves danced in the air. He could see Marcus from an angle beneath the bull's torso. One high kick, the side of Marcus's leg. A contorted flank, Marcus's shoe. The bull's muscles contracted then shivered like liver.

He saw Marcus hunched over on the ground, pushing his foot against the stall and rolling completely clear, curling up, then falling flat. Passed out.

Bull flank. Wood. Hoof. Dirt. Bull and wood and straw in a dance that blocked his sight of Marcus on the other side of the stall door. He strained to see him between every flicker of bull flesh. *Help.* But no words came. He couldn't scream.

A thought came: there was more to achieve than merely relief.

As the bull's back hooves rose again, he rolled beneath them and reached the door before they fell back to the ground. As he rose from his hands and knees, the animal's rump struck him, and he tumbled face first into the dirt a few feet from Marcus. He lifted his hand out of straw-and-dung-softened gravel and pulled himself to Marcus's side. There was no movement, no sound. He touched the neck, felt only a faint pulse. He couldn't lose him. Not after coming all this way. He lifted Marcus's hand and held it, looking down along the body. A brown inky stain was spreading on the skin underneath Marcus's T-shirt. Gavin thought he could see swelling. A hematoma. He dropped the hand gently and moved to the man's head, lifted the broad shoulders, and turned Marcus fully onto his back, holding the head in his lap.

"Help me," Gavin whispered, and watched the other man's mouth for movement. Time funnelled, lost its shape, and everything before him fanned out into a flat moment of knowing absolutely nothing.

Once more he is on the ridge in the Highlands, but this time it is a moment before the onset of the screams. He is near the edge with Porter, the two of them play-wrestling, waiting for the others to reach the top. Porter's arm is wrapped around Gavin's head. The rain has stirred up mud, and he slips and slides in it like an otter at play.

"Behave," a voice thunders at them from farther down the path, where the other boys are approaching. Sir is hollering at them again. Porter releases Gavin's head, whispers, "Fucking arsehole." Sir—Mr. Douglas—bellows again from below, "You'll get confinement! Don't risk it . . . not a laughing matter . . . who do you think you are anyway? This is a privilege." Mr. Douglas, who comes to the school once a term to give the boys lessons in wilderness survival, reaches them. "Come on, that's not cooperation, is it? That ruins the mission," and Gavin notices that Sir has a hint of a lisp. He and Porter go quiet. Gavin wipes his face with his hand. The cold rain is swelling. Sir walks towards them, intimidating, pressing home his point. "Lake, you don't want your family dying of shame, now do you?" And this pricks him. Sir turns to leave them and looks out to the view of the facing Munros and greater peaks in the distance, the molars of rock and grass that are agape before them.

Porter pulls Gavin off the trail, down beside the rocks and the alpine cushion plants embedded in the cracks so that they form a screen between them and Sir.

"Scare the bastard," Porter hisses, and then whispers a plan.

They scamper around the trailing azalea and approach the edge of the ridge from the opposite direction to where Sir is gazing out as he waits for the rest of the boys. His back is to them. Scuttling steps. Then a few more. Gavin's heart is racing, not from fear, but from trying to out-think Porter, to know when the other boy will pull back and when the ruse will be up. Porter does this, tests Gavin to see if he knows exactly where the line is drawn between talk and action. Gavin watches for something in Porter's shoulder—a slight twitch—because it's here he's seen the line drawn before. Twitch equals Talk. Stillness equals Action. Porter twists his head to check behind them; in the slanted rain Gavin loses sight of the shoulder.

Marcus groaned and Gavin felt a muscle contract in his hands, the man's shoulder coming awake. Then a muscle along his back quivered against Gavin's thigh. The small tremors of a living body stirred him. For the first time in weeks he felt an easing of the tension along his neck. Being close to this man who had been there all those years ago was the opposite of seeing Porter in the hospital. The two of them together, he was sure, could make Porter pay for all he'd done. He watched as Marcus's fingers rose up and hovered, as though counting time in music, then fell back on the ground. Gavin thought that he and Marcus should have aligned back then. If only he could have gone to this boy instead of Porter, things would have turned out differently for all of them. It wasn't too late to make amends, was it? Marcus opened his eyes. *This . . .* Gavin thought with relief.

Eight

A wet groan echoed in the square of the Plazueta de San José. Gavin could hear it from the street, and followed it up the stairs to our apartment. When I heard the knock, I knew it was him. I ignored it. I wasn't sure if Marcus had heard, but his eyes flickered, and then he seemed to drift back into the state of ebbing consciousness he'd been in all day. I pulled gently at the bandages around his ribs to adjust them, as I felt him slipping away. I wanted to keep him awake and out of danger of concussion. The knock was louder the second time. Marcus opened his eyes and looked at me as if to say either let him in, or don't you dare let him in, I couldn't tell which. I chose the latter. I searched for something to distract him.

"Nobody believes the story told by this knight," I began, "because of the look on his face: he's terrified, and when people see terror like that it makes them so uncomfortable that they want to laugh. The knight continues to tell his story, but no one is convinced, including me . . . so I ditched the whole thing," I said, not letting on that, in the knight's place, Marcus had become my protagonist. He wasn't listening. The pain killers dulled his senses and consciousness. He was off again.

Another knock. I adjusted his arm to lie flat along his side. The bandages covered most of his torso, even though the doctor had said the real problem had been the broken ribs. The hemorrhaging had stopped. The bruise would heal, but Marcus would need rest, and for me that had been perversely good news, because it meant he wouldn't be taking off on his annual trek—he refused to call it a pilgrimage—to Santiago. He groaned again at the next series of knocks at the door, and opened his eyes again.

I didn't bother greeting Gavin; I swung the door open and turned without looking at him. The door handle banged against the wall, and made more noise than I had intended. Gavin followed me into Marcus's bedroom.

Marcus was gone again, but a moment later he must have sensed a new presence. He opened his eyes. Gavin moved forward, as though he would embrace him. "Be careful!" I whispered furiously, and he stopped short. I stepped back and stood in the doorway. Gavin hovered over Marcus, who was struggling to say something. I wondered then who Marcus would call in an emergency. Who did he see as closest kin? Miguel, the man he had referred to in his brief revelation to me, lived in Spain, but he was not in the picture. I was all he had, and I wanted to protect him.

I watched Gavin lean in and touch Marcus's shoulder. I angled forward to see their profiles, like priest and confessor at last rites, but it was a *contre-jour* trick of roles, and it was Gavin who spoke.

"You said something about fixing things, at the bar, do you remember that?" he asked quietly, yet with insistence. "About reason ruling it all . . . ?"

Marcus made a humming noise, which could have meant either that he didn't have the slightest idea what Gavin was referring to, or that he hadn't heard. Gavin appeared agitated. He looked like he still had something to say. But I waited, and no one spoke again. Gavin took his hand off Marcus's shoulder and we both watched Marcus's breath deepen and draw out, occasionally sputtering.

"Leave him, now." My whisper was acidic. Gavin, as deep in thought as I'd seen him before, slipped by me through the door without a gesture or nod. I was invisible. His pain was that powerful.

Nine

A single virus particle is called a virion. In and of itself it is inert, but once injected into a cell, it's very powerful. Many, many progeny ensue. The exact nature of what happens after the host is infected varies depending on the nature of the virus. In most cases, the process depends on the nature of the genome. The process for single- and double-stranded DNA, and single- and double-stranded RNA will differ. However, once the guts of the viral material are produced by the cell's machinery, everything else is automatic, no more catalysts are needed.

    This fact struck me earlier today, around noon, after having spent a few hours struggling to describe with precision exactly how Gavin and Marcus felt in one another's company, and how with the blow of a bull Gavin's desires had shifted from self-serving relief to believing that there was a way to mend the damage of the past. I had reached for Sam's virology textbook as a way to reconnect with the present, to my life with Sam here in Santiago.

    I took the textbook description to mean that a virus is merely half alive before it enters a cell. It becomes fully alive only once inside. I needed to consider this fact more deeply, and needed something to eat, but I was also late for the convent, so I grabbed a piece of bread and headed out.

I carried with me all of what Gavin felt: his guilt, an urgent need for relief and justice, and the need to enlist another's help to accomplish his desires. And once he had invaded that other life, there was no leaving it. The effects of his presence, according to the virion principle, would have been self-perpetuating. So not only did I have to look at what he felt, but I also had to track what he did with what he felt. Gavin chose to enlist Marcus in his pursuit for peace, and as a result, they both underwent an evolution of a sort. What Gavin was from, even as recently as the cliff at Finisterre—and the feeble belief that suicide would free him—was clearly no longer who he was.

And myself? I too had been affected. I had been drawn in by a romantic notion of Gavin as a charming vagabond with a past. If I insinuated myself into his life then somehow mine would take on romance too, a vicarious danger that would free me from being plain old Emily and connect me more deeply with the original Alexandra who had been too much for my mother to handle. I had played out the intrigue; I hadn't told Marcus what I knew. I was not that Emily anymore, I was doing something exotic, playing a game with danger.

I need to find out why.

I sprinted down the hill towards the convent. I didn't like the developing image of myself, and wanted to return to the present, where I know I am different.

I am.

Rather than believe my cynical interpretation of the textbook passage as a metaphor for basic human emotions—that in coupling, people are only ever truly alive by infiltrating, adapting, replicating—I choose to see my relationship with

Sam as less opportunistic. I do not have to use Sam to become alive. I love Sam because he's the first person around whom I have allowed myself to be whole.

I walked quickly through the outer edge of the old Santiago, passing a variety of people—a man and a small dog, a young couple holding hands—and I thought of another way of looking at virion particles that underscores the beauty of structure and function: the chapter stressed that viruses typically can only infect a limited number of hosts. The lock and key mechanism is the most common explanation for this range. Certain proteins on the virus particle fit only certain receptor sites on a host's cell surface. This seems to me more akin to how we love. Choice is limited, so when we find something that fits, we lock in. Sam and I fit.

I arrived at the convent to commotion. The usually silent corridors echoed with activity coming from the end of the long wood-panelled hall. I made my way slowly towards a low moan and the high-pitched scoldings of female voices. I stopped at a small desk where Sister Alicia sat, reading a paperback novel, unmoved by what sounded like a torture scene down the hall.

"*Buenos dias,*" I said, and let her know I was reporting for duty. She handed me a list of the meals to be delivered and asked if I would then sweep away the twigs and leaves that had blown into the courtyard with the strong northern winter winds. I took the list and headed towards the kitchen, but was drawn to the groans and squeals of disgust coming from the room at the end of the hall, which suddenly I identified.

I stood in the doorway. The smell was fierce. The moaning faded out and the clacking of the disgusted sisters took over. I saw Señora Ormaza's tortured face on the pillow. We locked eyes, and she appeared mortified that I had arrived just as the sisters were stripping the fouled sheets from beneath her. There was shit everywhere. On the sisters' habits, on the wall, on Señora Ormaza's hands and dressing gown. I turned quickly and hustled down to the lavatory, where I washed my hands over and over. I shuddered at the image of Señora's face, her humiliated, impotent anger. I wanted Sam, but he was due back from the conference only in the evening. I performed my duties at the convent and killed time by walking home very slowly.

Sam arrived home before dinner, from the Rethinking Aids conference in Paris. As he put his bags down and walked to the fridge to get a cold drink, he did a little dance, almost like a cha-cha.

"So, you had a good time, then."

"Don't stop questioning," he said as he grabbed a Coke. He snapped it open and took a long swig. "It applies to everything; it was the theme of the conference."

"Not even whether or not you have a talent for dance?" I sat up straight at the kitchen table and watched with a growing smile. I was on the wave of his happy body, which seemed to have regained its athlete's balance. He aimed the metal tab of the Coke can at the rubbish bin at the far end of the kitchen, missed, shrugged, and then sat with me at the table. He put down his Coke and held both of my hands in his.

"Good to have you back," I said, not knowing if he'd realize I meant that in many ways.

"I love Paris," he said, stroking my hand, and I tried to keep my heart from sinking.

"You look relaxed."

"I needed to get away." He sipped his Coke.

He described how he had realized that the pressure he'd been feeling about the grant probably tainted his understanding of his own research. It didn't seem authentic anymore, felt like he had adjusted his methods in order to justify the money. "A lab has its own rules, ritual, structure of authority, modes of behaviour. You don't have to be an anthropologist to know this. But one of the key messages at the conference was that HIV and AIDS are culturally constructed."

"What?" I asked, in my most skeptical voice.

"Not that they don't exist, just that the way they're studied—you know, *disease is rampant among black people. Monkeys + disease = Africans + disease*—it's a bogus premise. There are lots of those floating around," he concluded.

I shook my head, not totally understanding, and panicked about the virology research I would have to do to keep up, while Gavin's story and his future—how would I introduce Claire?—tugged at me more fiercely.

"I want my lab to be different," Sam said. "Open to new ideas, people . . . people make all the difference. It's good for the research to be attached to them." He lifted my hands and kissed them both.

"What do you mean?" I asked. "I thought people were biased and you had to stay clear of that."

He stood up and stared off. "Never mind," he said, and stood in front of the fridge again, opened the door, and looked inside. "Marianne agrees. She's organizing the next conference. Boston. Cambridge. That's where it is all happening." He examined a plate of roasted sardines with *cachelos* that I had prepared for myself last night but had not eaten. "For the first time, I miss America."

I wanted to remind him of his own words to me only a few months ago: that everything moves about the globe, the way creatures did, the way horses did. Viruses, theories, us. But as he shut the fridge door, dissatisfied with his options, he began again—like a child describing a fair—to talk about the conference. His questioning extended beyond science, to the misfit borders of the social and the personal. "New social groups are no longer blood related, or even living in the same city . . . or country," he said as he nibbled at the potatoes.

"All constructs can be challenged," he continued as he sat back at the table and fiddled with the Coke can. "When you believe too strongly in something it can hold you back."

"Is there something you believe in too strongly?"

He looked up at me. "Something I believe in too strongly?" Stalling. I could feel my face heating up. "Yea, maybe, that you can know how someone—"

"Are you hungry?" I said, cutting him off by standing up from the table. I didn't want to hear that there was even the smallest opening for lack of faith in us. I started to set the table for dinner and Sam changed the subject to how viruses interact differently with different animals.

I had made *caldo gallego*—a soup of turnip tops, cabbage, green beans, and pig's knuckle—a recipe that Señora Ormaza had given me weeks ago, but the soup was bland and unnecessarily gelatinous. I was not the cook that Sam was. We ate with our usual rituals of table arrangement and candlelight, but Sam put Curtis Mayfield on the CD player, which I thought was unusual. When we were finished, I sat back to allow him to clear up.

"Want to take a walk?" I asked, still needing fresh air to flush out the earlier smells from Señora Ormaza and the shit-covered sisters.

"And besides, very few animals mate for life," he said. His back was to me as he faced the sink. My heart finally sank.

"What do you mean?" I had to ask. Now I really needed a different vantage point and thought that I would go without him, run to the ruins of the San Fiz de Solovio, then on to the monastery, where sometimes you can hear the nuns singing their descant masses.

"Birds, of course, but we're nothing like birds," he said as he wiped the last plate and put it away.

"Only in that some of us mate for life."

"We don't fly . . . there's a more important difference." He turned to face me.

"So, flying and mating for life are connected?"

"Sure, if you can get away, disappear into the sky, you'd submit to a life sentence," he said, not looking at me, but slightly off to my side, into the distance.

My temperature rose like the rev of an engine. Anxiety was so obviously the evolutionary prerequisite for wings, but I stood still and rationalized, and tried to remember how much pressure he'd been under. I thought of his face as he'd watched the news reports of the tsunami, and then later after he'd had to share his lab with government technicians.

"Does Marianne believe in birds?" I tried teasing, as I watched him head to the door to put on his shoes. It was a feeble attempt at directing my feelings.

"Marianne and George have been married for a long time," he said matter-of-factly, as he loosened the laces of his walking boots and slid them on. He tied them and stood up, ready for our outing. He seemed to be lost in thought for a moment before looking at me again.

"Don't tell me, you've got a joke," I said, approaching him.

"No. No, I don't," he said flatly.

I needed to sit down; instead I followed him out the door.

I had seen Marianne from afar, entering the biochemistry building, one day after leaving Sam with lunch and treats I'd brought to the lab. At least I had assumed it was her, because

Sam had told me that she was African-American. I had watched her long legs take the stairs two at a time and thought I'd like to know her. She is an expert in retroviruses, and Sam attended the Paris conference at her invitation. Born in Virginia, Marianne's home is now in Boston, but she has arrived in Santiago like a new strain, standing out in her colourful clothes among the university population and tourists.

As we walked, I realized that Sam might want to check in on the lab, but I proceeded slowly, trying to draw out our time together. He does some of his work in the evening now, as the lab is sharing facilities with its EWARN (early warning and response network) partners, analyzing samples provided by WHO task forces in the tsunami-hit areas. They use statistical analysis and epidemiological data to monitor the spread of diseases and health "events," as the bureaucrats call them, including acute diarrhea, malaria, measles, meningitis, and malnutrition. Shigellosis. It's the beautiful name of the virus the lab has been tracking. Outbreaks of diarrheal diseases are the main threats and, as a result, the tracking of what people eat and drink has become urgent. The tsunami has jeopardized even the most basic elements of existence.

My own urgency has to do with water, but it is the water of 1999, not the tsunami. As I thought of the look on Señora Ormaza's face I wondered if perhaps I should be focusing on disease. Cholera? *Vibrio cholerae* is a bacterium, not a virus. Sam gave me cholera's Latin name as we watched news of the tidal wave's aftermath. In a cholera epidemic, he told me, the source of contamination is usually the feces of an infected person, spreading rapidly throughout areas with inadequate drinking water. Diarrhea, vomiting, and leg cramps are the symptoms, and the rapid loss of body fluids leads to dehydration and shock. Death can occur within hours. In addition to a shortage of drinking water, toxic waste and asbestos from buildings may also contaminate the water. Throughout areas of southeast Asia, agricultural land has been flooded and damaged by the salt of the ocean. Mercifully, healthy dead bodies are not producers of viruses, and decomposition does not create germs. But viruses find their way in any disaster. Mosquito-borne diseases—malaria and dengue—are possible. Piles of rubble that hold rainwater become excellent breeding ground for mosquitoes. Malaria is a wily parasite.

As we strolled to our spot near the Convento é Igrexa de San Domingos de Bonaval, I concluded that one answer to the question of what to do with what you feel is to help yourself, rather than enlist anyone else. If Gavin had been so desperate for survival and relief, he could have checked himself in somewhere, rested, taken a long hard look at himself, or joined a monastery.

"He did it, you know," Sam said with a note of pride.

"Who? What?" Had Sam read my thoughts? I was jolted back to the present.

"Mike—his little plastic purification. Sunlight in a plastic bottle. He invented it for Maasailand and it's being used in Sri Lanka now."

I nodded, and realized he was talking about his colleague from Kenya who had invented the simple system for water purification.

"Marianne wants to go, to meet him. Her HIV protocols could use some monitoring," he said as we sat on a bench behind the seminary.

"Mike doesn't experiment . . ." I said defensively, unable to relax.

"Of course not, that's the point. I'm thinking of going again too."

My cheeks burned. Two years ago in Kenya had felt like a turning point for us.

"Do you remember?" I asked him.

"What?"

"The drink?" I wanted to remind him that Kenya had been ours, that unique things had touched us both there.

"Of course I do."

It had been our last day in Kenya, in the Ngong Hills made famous by Karen Blixen's *Out of Africa*. The *I had a faaarm in Africa* hills that I had expected to be filled with safari adventure were filled with disease instead. Sam had volunteered with a heath-care NGO, and we had spent three months visiting hospices and dispensaries in the middle of nowhere. Flies swarmed over food and faces, where I was sure I could see them dropping their eggs. The sick children in the arms of their malnourished mothers had evoked flashes of memory about Gavin—his bloated face and hands that day—similar to the flashbacks of the Scottish Highland that I have been imagining for him. I was weighted down with rotting. To have called me squeamish over food, insects, and drinking water would have been an understatement. In witnessing the undernourished, I became so myself, and was told that I was anemic. I knew that my anemia was also of the soul and all that I hadn't processed about Spain. Sam by contrast had seemed capable and calm, but he had gone from asking many complex questions to posing a few simple direct queries that needed yes or no answers. I had watched as his shoulders appeared to diminish in size, the weight of all we had seen eroding his stature.

Our last visit was to a dispensary in Maasailand that treated malaria, typhoid, diarrhea, and starvation. On the way there, our driver picked up a Maasai elder, a warrior in full regalia returning to his compound. He invited us to enter the cow-dung-constructed banda of one of his son's wives. As we crouched down to enter the hut that housed the family, our eyes adjusting to the smoky darkness, I began to feel safe. Sitting on the bed made of sticks and a stretched, dried cow hide, I focused on the few things around me: the open fire in front, the leg of drying beef beside the tiny window, and, most prominently, our brightly dressed Maasai hostess on a stool, as she must have sat for many hours, tending the fire. She smiled and greeted us. We proceeded to sit in silence for what seemed a long time. Our intimacy in extremes—her extreme poverty, our great wealth—made my heart skip beats. She smiled at us, and speaking through our interpreter invited us for tea.

Using the last of her water before the following day's many-mile hike to fetch more, she washed cups slowly and meticulously. My queasiness returned, and I pushed back a flash of Gavin's leg. She prepared a sweet milky ginger tea. Sam looked at me, knowing what I was thinking about drinking it. Up to then we had both escaped stomach sickness. We took the tea and sipped.

More silence.

I began to enjoy it, but Sam was less comfortable and, in what seemed like a desperate burst of energy, launched into questions: How many live here? Where do you get your water? Where is your husband? Questions about daily life. I asked a few questions of my own but stopped pursuing the food angle when the answer to "What do you do during a drought?" was "We drink blood and milk when there's no food." I realized then that the silence was also about the people who were no longer with us. Those who had died right where I was sitting. I was in the presence of the very thing I had been pushing away.

Sam shifted on his stool. It was the first time since the focus group where we'd met that I had felt him flounder in the face of facts. I switched tack to ask what they did in the evenings. Tell stories. It was the answer that struck me most: the fact that stories and the heightened pursuit for food coexisted seamlessly. Their stories were about Maasai lives, the woman said, about ancestors and about what went on in the past.

Of course. How to fill silence? Stories. How to understand hunger? Stories. How to understand stories? Silence. The silence of survival, the quiet ticking of a life concerned chiefly with living to the next day. A simple *faarm in Aaafrica* equation. It must have been then that I became aware that the only way to deal with Gavin would be to write.

Later that afternoon, hot, exhausted, and covered in the red dust of the rift valley, we sat in the compound at base camp with our bags packed. Our driver approached and offered us drinks, and then returned with a bottle of gin and some tonic water. On his tray was another glass filled with what looked like light red wine.

"A Maasai cure for anemia," he said, handing me the glass. "White-meat blood is better for you than red-meat blood," he added, and seeing the puzzlement on my face, he said, "Chicken."

I went cold.

Sam and I sat in silence in the shade of the acacia when the driver left us to give us a moment to relax and enjoy our drinks. It was that banda silence again. Sam held his gin and tonic glass tightly and didn't take his eyes off me. I thought of the two Maasai women I had met that day. The one in the banda, her smiling face, and another, later, who was crying as she held a child in convulsions in her arms. I raised the glass of blood quickly to my lips and gulped down a very large mouthful. I winced and shuddered. I looked up at Sam, on whose face was a look of proud disbelief. He laughed and raised his gin and tonic.

"You never drank it," I now reminded him as we headed back up the hill through the cemetery. "I did." There were things about Kenya we'd never discussed—like how the trip changed both of us.

"No," he said, "that's true, and you did a good job."

"But you were the one who seemed affected by it," I said, remembering how in our Nairobi hotel that night he'd fastidiously unfolded and refolded his clothes in the suitcase.

"There was a lot to take in," he said.

"A lot of blood?"

"Don't be facetious. I mean, everything we saw felt like too much. Still does, sometimes."

I panicked and touched his strong, humble shoulder. He flinched ever so slightly. He turned and looked at me with a question as complex as a cell, dividing and multiplying behind his eyes.

"Tell me the one about the turtle and the sandwiches," I teased. He managed a weak smile but remained silent as we neared our apartment.

"Maybe it is all too much," he said.

In my struggle to rescue our connection I stopped and drew him back towards me. We stood looking at one another on the street. I kissed him gently just below his left eye. He breathed more deeply. I kissed his other, high cheekbone, then his chin, then neck. I stood pressed against him. We breathed into one another, as we had the first time we had ever kissed in London. Our breath was silent, but I heard the hoot of an owl.

"At the conference," he said suddenly, stepping back from me.

"What?" I waited, confused, abandoned.

"It's one of the things I meant, one of the ways of looking at things that hold you back . . . I was."

"Was what?" My lip started to tremble.

"I had been, at least."

"Sam, please!"

"All through Kenya, I'd been obsessed with them. The thought of them. And then you drank that . . . it threw me." He started to walk slowly.

"The thought of what?" I caught up to him.

"Needles."

"Needles?"

"The shared blood."

"Whose shared blood? The chicken's?" This was getting absurd.

He stopped and looked at me. "No, the thought of needles and the fact that a bit of blood gets passed along each time."

"What are you talking about?"

He paused, stalling again, I believed, and then looked as though he'd made up his mind to tell me something. I wasn't sure I wanted to hear it.

"I never told you."

"About what?"

"Thomas."

"Yes, you did—" I started to walk towards the apartment, relieved.

"He used."

"Used to what?" I asked, slowing down as we approached our front door.

"Used."

"What?"

"Heroin," he said as he looked for his keys. "Smack."

I stood still on the pavement as he opened the door and

entered, but he held my arm and drew me in. We walked up the stairs as he spoke.

"One day in December, just before Christmas, the police came to the house to tell us he'd overdosed. They'd found him, near death, beside a dumpster behind a Dunkin' Donuts shop."

"Near death?"

"He had a buzz cut, that guy, I remember . . ." Sam hadn't heard me, was deep in memory. "But his face was peaceful, not like a cop's. At first I thought he was selling something or from Publishers Clearing House and I was getting a prize, or he maybe he was our first Christmas caroller . . ."

"What happened?"

"Thomas spent a week in hospital over Christmas, and then he left in the middle of the night. Took off. That's the last we heard of him," he said with finality. My mind moved like molasses. By the time Sam had kicked off his shoes inside, I could speak again.

"I can't believe you never told me," I muttered, standing looking at my Converse trainers as though it had been they that had withheld something. "You never told me . . ."

"I never like to think about it . . . and I recently have . . ." He put his keys on the table and went into the kitchen. He took a glass from the shelf and ran water at the sink.

"You never told me," I said again to my left shoe and remembered the term *chasing the dragon* that he'd explained when we first met, that night in Maida Vale. He'd told me that people he'd known had smoked heroin, but I'd never suspected he meant Thomas. I looked up. He was sipping from his glass of water.

"Why now?"

"Why now?" He put his glass down and came towards me.

He held my hands. "Things I've wanted to tell you, but I didn't want to know them myself. I do now," he said.

I pulled my hands away and took my coat off. "I'm scared," I said to the chair on which I hung it. He came over to me and put his arms around me.

"How come?" he asked.

"I don't know," I shrugged and felt silly, when what I wanted to do was tell him about the vision of shit smeared on the bed linen, the headboard, the floor, the disgust on the faces of the nuns, the shit on their habits, the one fleck that had spread itself across Sister Gabriella's face as she tried to clean up Señora's shame. Poor Señora Ormaza—the shock of everything we can't control. I wanted to tell Sam that I was afraid of everything that we keep from one another, the way Marcus and I had each kept our secrets, the way this news felt like something that had infected Sam decades ago but which I had not yet factored into who he was.

And I was afraid of change. Change is the basis of what Sam knows. Scientists believe in change; whereas I believe in stories that insist the world is always fundamentally the same.

"I love you," he said, quietly, and I believed him, but I was bruised with secrets.

We kissed. Time stopped for a necessary rest.

When it regained its momentum, I was left feeling tired, and wanting to take a break from writing. I told him to wait for me in the bedroom while I turned off my computer. After doing so, I went there to find that he had fallen asleep on the bed in his clothes. I didn't want to wake him, he looked so peaceful, and so I find myself returning here, to hammer out the details of the day that began with virions. Tomorrow is Saturday, and I will put aside my work, in order to truly help myself. I'll ask Sam to take a drive with me.

Ten

Santiago de Compostela is a careful city. Like any place built on a legend, sanctified and maintained as a seat of holiness, it cannot afford extremes. The five-hundred-year-old university's student population offers it a challenge from time to time, but its character is embedded in the sixteenth century. There is an edict in the city bylaws that states that "nobody or no group of persons dare take or do any expense or uncleanness, to soil or stone or anything else in the barriers and cave and gates of the said city." As one of the three spiritual centres of Christendom, together with Rome and Jerusalem, it can't afford to be unclean.

Even the university's renowned medical tradition was founded on pilgrimage: the pharmacies of the convents that looked after pilgrims led to the creation of the Faculty of Medicine and the reputation of Santiago as the medical centre of Galicia. Sam loves this about Santiago, but there are times I feel entombed. In the almost two years that Sam and I have spent here I have never felt like I did in Pamplona, where, at least once a year, the inspiration to run with bulls is in the air like perfume. In Santiago de Compostela all roads in through the various gates of the old city lead to the Apostle St. James's sepulchre. Even on Franco Street—replete with bars and restaurants and hints of gaiety—exuberance is restrained.

Today I took the day off from writing, and Sam didn't even call the lab. We needed to get out of the city, so we decided to see Finisterre, which I'd never managed to reach in my haphazard trekking five years ago.

Although January in Galicia is not known for its good weather, today was sunny and crisp as we headed out. Sam had borrowed his colleague Paolo's beat-up blue Renault, and we drove out through the main gates of the city. We followed the rugged Costa da Morte, which has seen its share of shipwrecks in bad weather. After passing through many small fishing villages along the way, I gasped at the sight of the dramatic cliffs and the Church of Santa Maria against the horizon. We wound our way to Finisterre as the foghorn blew and frightened me. I hadn't realized the horn was a feature on this spot, and had not written it for Gavin, which bothered me and distracted me from enjoying the view. We walked the last section to the lighthouse, where the four winds lashed us as we stood watching the clouds piling up in the distance, overtaking one another like a Venetian blind unfolding over the blue sky.

"Here, take this," Sam said, picking up a weighty stone and placing it in my two hands. "That way's America," he added, pointing westward, to sea. "If I were to be a pilgrim it would have to be across there."

"Why's that?"

He shrugged. I thought of what he'd told me about Thomas yesterday. Maybe he felt he should have looked after his younger brother better. I felt uneasy again. He'd taken years to share this fact. Was it—as it had been with Marcus—because I'd never asked?

"But you never know," I said as the wind swirled gently. I hoped he'd understood that I'd meant it wasn't impossible that Thomas would come back.

He smiled. We said nothing else for a long time, and looked out before us, where there was only the sea. Finally, Sam's mood shifted and he stood straighter.

"Here," he said, coming towards me. My back was facing the cliff edge. He held out his hands, and I reached to take them. "Let's play something," he said, excitement speeding up his words.

"What?"

"Something I used to do as a kid."

"What?"

He unfurled his scarf from around his neck and made a gesture to suggest that I put it over my eyes.

"You must be joking," I said sharply.

"No, trust me; that's the whole point."

I thought of Gavin on this cliff edge, at the beginning—had my descriptions been accurate?—as he tried to make it his ending. I looked behind me, along the coast and the many ridges and levels of land.

"Why?" I asked Sam, deflating his mood slightly.

"It's fun—try it. You have to trust me."

I took the scarf from him and placed it over my eyes. He turned me around and tied it behind my head. It was tight. I could see nothing.

"We don't speak. Just touch or non-verbal sounds or vibrations," he said. My heart raced nervously.

He touched me, and his hand on my back guided me forward. I was acutely aware of the ground beneath my heels, toes, heels, and toes again. The wind was not strong, but I could smell the sea, imagined I could hear the flight of birds. Sam dropped his hand from my back. I stopped, waiting to sense and follow. I felt a tap on my left shoulder and assumed I was meant to turn left. I did and could feel Sam in front of me. I sensed I was walking directly in his footsteps. Sam turned again, this time without touching me, but he stayed close enough for me to feel him. I was enjoying my dependence on him, and the freedom from the constraints of vision. Sam did various things to guide me. At one point he sighed deeply, with a drop in tone that I knew was meant to indicate that I was to swing round and change direction. I sensed him up ahead of me.

Our game continued for another slow and erotic ten minutes, as we floated over the grassy cliff plateau. I experimented with grunting as a question, so that Sam would have to respond, and I would be comforted to know exactly where he was. He sniffed one or two directions; I brushed his chest with mine, trying to feel his intentions, knowing that the heart has claims on the direction we take. Sam did his best to encourage me and yet not give any explicit clues—to test my trust in him, in myself. We drifted apart and together again, with the cliff edge, I believed, far enough way to allow for playfulness.

The wind changed. I felt the temperature drop. My body responded instantly, as though my skin was zipping up. I tripped on a rock and plunged my hands into the long pebbly grass in front of me. Sam arrived promptly and lifted me up. He moaned a condolence and led me, again, into the wind to our right. He dropped his hand and I couldn't hear him. I stopped, sniffed the air. Salt. Chrome-smelling wind.

"Sam?"

No answer.

I spun around with my arms outstretched, hoping I would touch him. Nothing.

"Sam?!" A little louder.

I dropped to my knees and on all fours I made my way slowly in the direction I sensed him to be.

"Sam!" I cried. I tried not to become angry. I was not going to give in. I would not fail the test, but my heart was so far up in my throat I could almost taste it. I inched along over the small rocks and occasional patch of dry mud. I reached what felt like the edge of land and my outstretched hands could find nothing solid beyond. Could it be? Could he have led me here? I was disoriented and used my hands to search to the side and behind me. I tried to hold back, but suddenly I emptied sob after sob into the salt air. I curled up, my head to my knees, and cried to greet the thick pain in my chest that lodged just above my ribs, viscous and bulging forth like something I would eventually chew.

"Emily!" Sam's voice actually came as a surprise. I had so easily accepted that I had been abandoned.

"Emily . . . love . . . please . . . I'm sorry," he said anxiously.

I couldn't stop crying, as I kept my blindfolded eyes to my knees. Then I heard Sam, his sniffles and sputters. I lifted my head and removed the scarf. He was kneeling beside me, his head bowed, his arms folded. He looked up at me and shook his head.

"But you didn't cheat!" he choked.

"What?"

"You didn't cheat. I've never played it when the person didn't cheat. Thomas always did. Without fail. I just assumed . . . I'm so, so sorry."

It took me a moment to understand what had happened between us, but a slow calm flowed up from my toes, like rising pain relief. I rose to my feet. I wanted to be at home. I wanted us to make love like we had before the changes in Kenya.

When we got home, we did just that. And tonight I know that everything is going to be fine between us. I can return to my writing. In this way I am helping myself, securing the order of events and the reasoning behind all of our actions.

Eleven

Wind. Like a wail. As he stood on the barricades of Pamplona's fortress and looked out across the river to the surrounding hills, Gavin saw where the wind was harnessed, performing in the turbine generators that had three blades each the length of an eight-man scull. He remembered the rowing races he'd been to with Kate. These little details about the world out there were coming back to him now. He rubbed his ear, hearing a hum like the shared *om* of monks in meditation. He turned and walked back through the park.

It was May, he realized, as he wiped his forearm across his brow to clear the sweat. He heard sentences in the Spanish he now understood more and more of, some of them plaintive, the way his neck felt beneath the thick dry hand of early summer. The maids at La Perla had refused to clean any rooms until late in the afternoon, and everything was gritty. In the evenings he had found the light unbearably tender. Life had chosen him, and now he had to discover what he was meant to do with it.

He walked through Media Luna Park, where the cherry blossoms withered and fell, blanketing the paved paths with pink petals. Small shoots of green leaves barely poked out from branches. The lawns were dry and faded. His senses were returning.

He put the bags in his hands down, touched the phone in his pocket, and pulled it out. He dialed her number, knowing she would be at work. He flinched when he heard her voice on the answering machine.

"It's me," he said, and flinched again in shame. What was there to say? "I'm sorry . . ." he began, but all the explanations under this hot sun would be useless. What he needed to say was that he would not be worthy for her until he made amends and became the man she would want him to be. He hung up and put the phone away.

He made his way from the park, along the Arga River, towards the historic quarter. Crossing in front of the Plaza de Toros in the heat, he adjusted the bags, easing his fingers from the weight of gifts. His fingers. His arms. Shoulders. These had feeling now. Climbing the stairs to the apartment, he could feel strain in his muscles, stiffness in his bones. *Hush.* There was a quieter rushing sound now.

He stood outside the door to the apartment and braced himself. The fact that Marcus had not recognized him meant that he could choose how to proceed, but the right way included Porter being punished, so he would have to make sure that Marcus was won over. With the man's head in his hands, the sinewy frame calf-like in the straw, it had felt safe to touch the face, before he called out to Christophe again and again. By the time Christophe arrived, his fingers had felt the thick bristle growing behind Marcus's ear. The defenceless head had made him want to cry. Marcus was just like him: a man in a town, without bearings, without a tether to anything.

He could feel Porter's leash starting to loosen, and even

though Porter had been right—it was between them and the mountain—Porter was almost gone and soon it would be his alone. This thought made the hush seem louder. A hush that was just his was still a hush. If he reminded Marcus of the ridge story and stressed how violent Porter had been with all of them, things would start to be right. He would help Marcus recover, and by then his confession might not come as such a surprise. They would lead the police to where they should have gone in the first place, and he'd be able to leave Pamplona and listen for silence.

He looked at his feet and could feel them throb. Like capsules of cod liver oil at his ankle and on his big toe, the blisters were part of his returning senses. He had popped one, watched it ooze, and felt its burning, while remembering that one of the things he'd wanted from Finisterre was to feel, as Sir must have, the ripped skin and broken bones. But sensation was funnelling down from pain to pleasure and towards minute details. This was a different kind of punishment.

He had been led to the texture of things, to slivers of paper, to creases in leather like a line in a palm, to the shaving bumps on Marcus's skull. He had visited him every day since the accident, helped to make him comfortable in bed, fed him broth and bread, and watched the bumps grow red with the hair follicles pushing up beneath the skin. He hadn't recognized the form of caregiving he was performing, until yesterday, when he realized he'd observed it once before, eight years ago, when his mother had nursed Martin back to his formidable self after a heart operation. Broth and bread made a man stronger, his mother had said. As he tracked the winces and groans associated with Marcus's injury, he also looked for each groan to bring the moment when Marcus might recognize him. Every *oww* was a song about shame. But Marcus was walking again, not fit enough for work, but functioning. Gavin felt grateful for the man's strong constitution that would have also seen him through the hell of twenty-six years ago.

His relief felt like affection.

He put the designer shopping bag down and examined the indentation that the handle had made in his fingers. He felt for the knife in the deep pocket of his trousers. This too had a unique texture. He couldn't understand why he had brought it, but it gave him comfort. He stared at his hand again, curled his fingers together, and used his knuckles to knock on the apartment door.

※

Marcus rose stiffly from the bed. Run, his heart said, but his muscles were locked. He rubbed his hand over his head and felt the growing fuzz. Without even the strength to shave, he'd been at the mercy of this man who'd come again and again, his search for the Brit dropped suddenly, or now obviously concluded successfully. He couldn't be sure. Gavin had tortured him with his care, his teasing efforts to bring him back to health. There was something else to come. Had someone in England set him up? There were many things that could have been pinned on David Williams. Once you were locked up the first time, even if no convictions were ever reached—you had a page with your name on it, it seemed, for anyone to use, to tick a box, to get a raise, to settle a debt. Simply to blame, because blame was what made someone else innocent. David Williams had known this. After the first case in Scotland there had been several—a shooting, a robbery—pursued by a friend of the Scottish PC who had never believed that David was innocent. It was the thread still connecting him to Scotland. *You take the low road.* While Miguel's taunts—*nigger father, bastard liar*—had disappeared after his release from HMP Peterhead, because Miguel had disappeared with them, this thread seemed to be woven into who he was now.

He knew how these things ended up, and no matter what the charge, he would have to defend himself. For nothing. He thought of calling his mother in London to see who had been trying to reach him, but fuck it, all of it; it was nonsense, because he had done nothing but be barely alive in this town.

He held the bag of gifts that Gavin had handed him and looked into it.

"Try it," Gavin said.

Marcus took out the linen dressing gown. He put it on over his jeans and T-shirt.

"Chic," he said, holding back the flight from his voice. "Bullish . . ." he said slyly, his best acting. "Takes one to be kicked by one," he added, looking up, catching Gavin's face, which was hunting, finding, trapping. He quickly took off the robe.

"Why have you done all this?" he asked, as he took out the jar of bath salts and the two books: *The Sun Also Rises* and *The Monk*—that had been beneath the dressing gown. His glance caught the ray of sun streaming across his bed and the corner piles of clothing, tissues, glasses, and bandages, whose angles looked alive—that was a still life he'd like to paint. Someday.

"No reason," Gavin answered.

"No such thing," Marcus countered, knowing it was best to find out now just how the man would accuse him. He found himself handling the gifts as though they were evidence in his own trial. Exhibit A: last chance to cleanse; Exhibit B: books to be locked away with . . . "Not a soul in Pamplona who hasn't read this," he said, pointing to the Hemingway.

He looked up to see Gavin's serious expression. He felt himself shifting shape, the chameleon in him trying not to stand out too much. Trying to become . . . what? Whatever the man wanted. But he needed to know what that was. This game was tiresome. Whoever he was, Gavin had a reason for looking for him. If it was something he hadn't actually done, that didn't matter, it could easily be pinned on him. Miguel had done it each time an officer had appeared at their door on Ladbroke Grove. *Half-breed waster you are.*

He waited a few minutes, but he realized he would have to beg for it. He handled the fine linen dressing gown: "Man, this is 'nough-good for a nigga'" he sang. Gavin blanched, shuffled. Marcus laughed, but realized he hadn't given the right opening.

"Look," he said, finally, turning and sitting down on the bed. But, instead of asking, Who are you? And what do you want of me? he said, "Spain's a good place to unload the past," and what he meant was that in Spain he hadn't been a target, hadn't been blamed for everything that happened in proximity to him.

Gavin stepped back with a look of surprise. "You think so?" Gavin said nervously. Something shifted, and he seemed to return to the agitated man he'd been when he'd first arrived.

Marcus watched him touch his head then search in his pockets for things that jangled and crunched there. He put the dressing gown back in its bag and considered the backpack in his cupboard. He'd fill it and leave. Full-up with fed-up with the flack-that-comes-back. And back. He now was running a few days behind and might be stuck with tourists, but he would go anyway. He needed to go now more than ever, with this threat reminding him that freedom deserved a tribute.

"I'll keep it all for when I get back," he said. "Ta," tossing the books into the bag too.

"When you get back?" Gavin moved again towards the bed. Marcus breathed in, his space invaded.

"Ya, need to recuperate properly, and had a trip planned anyway."

"No," Gavin almost whispered and stepped back again. Marcus was sure he hadn't meant to be heard, so he pretended he hadn't. He turned, picked up a shirt from the chair, and tossed it into the laundry basket beside his dresser.

"Where?" Gavin asked.

"Santiago," Marcus said quickly.

"Why?"

A rap. A trap. Fight back. But there was nothing to hide. "I do one every year around this time."

"Every year?"

"It marks an anniversary," Marcus allowed. Gavin's face looked gripped with more questions as he clutched for something in his pocket.

"Walking," Marcus added.

"Pilgrimage?" Gavin asked, almost begging.

"I don't do pilgrimage. I walk," said Marcus. Run, run, said his mind.

"I could go with you," Gavin said, lowering his head as he spoke.

Marcus swallowed, and swallowed again. He touched his fractured rib, then he rubbed the soft hair on his arm and thought harder. Run. But he was so tired. Spain had been his last place on earth. But the last place had now yielded this. He would try to hold his ground. The Camino had a law unto itself. He wouldn't let this man hold him back from his life.

"Not a good idea to do it alone, not in your condition,"

Gavin added as he looked up. They locked eyes.

Marcus's hand rose to his hip. It was a familiar, ancient feeling. A snap, a tumbling. The feeling of falling through the floor. The shredding of a membrane. It was a feeling that had once been a part of surrender. He swallowed again, laughing to himself. He thought of Lacey, one of the many men who had tried to protect him in Peterhead, when the others merely wanted his black arse. Lacey was his friend and taught him how to look and act in those first few days so that he would not become prey. Lacey had touched his face. Lacey had kissed him and told him that he had been wronged, that he would be all right, that the charges would be dropped. Lacey had been a friend.

He hadn't expected this from Gavin. The man's attention was confusing. What if he had been wrong and Gavin was here only by accident, and the ministrations of the last few days had arisen out of something else?

He rubbed his hip.

It was a childhood reaction, this hand to hip. The cinema's music-hall curtains, the gilt-edged vaulted ceilings, the dark musty smell of adult knowledge—all came back with this touch of his hip. He'd been eleven at the time, just after Miguel moved them to Notting Hill, and had been helping out in a shop on Ladbroke Grove in exchange for groceries. The Pakistani grocer who'd employed him to unpack boxes had taken him to see a film on Portobello Road in the middle of the day. When the man touched Marcus's thigh there in the dark, he had felt a tingle in his groin much like this one. He had counted backwards from ten, before he put his own hand on his hip and elbowed the man's arm away, but he had kept his hand in place throughout the entire film of beds and bodies.

Six, five, four . . . two, one . . . he counted now in similar confusion. "I walk alone," he said at last, lowering his hand.

"I could tag along, see how this pilgrimage thing is done," Gavin insisted.

"I don't do pilgrimage," Marcus repeated firmly, and rubbed his hip a second time. He'd have to see what the threat was. Or if there was none, he'd have to see what the man was offering. And in Santiago he'd think again.

"Sounds like a plan," Gavin said, and he reached into his deep pockets again, lifting out some paper then replacing it. Marcus rubbed his head this time, which might have looked like he'd given in. He quickly raised his arms in a stretch that hurt his ribs, but he didn't admit to any pain.

꧁

Faded, Gavin thought of the sounds. For now.

Twelve

Spain was a good place to unload the past, Marcus had said, and perhaps he had been referring to Scotland. Had he recognized him after all? And if so, where was the fury? Was vengeance going to sneak up on him? He needed to make sure that the right man was punished. Things had to be put right. Mend what was broken: Marcus had said something of that nature in Spanish. Making amends. This warped version of a pilgrimage might be a means of doing so. Relief was still dependent on Marcus, one way or another.

Sshhhh, he said to the hum as he stood outside the refugio and watched Marcus secure their beds for the night.

He'd waited in the square outside Marcus's apartment from early in the morning, not wanting to miss his departure. By afternoon he was hot and almost asleep on the pavement. Marcus arrived down the stairs with his backpack, shot a defeated look in Gavin's direction, and motioned him back inside. Upstairs they organized what Gavin would need for the trek, with Marcus sending Gavin out to buy boots, clothing, and a backpack. They'd started walking late in the day and had covered the first ten kilometres of their journey. There was so much more, he knew, because of the bus he had caught beyond Santiago on one of the rain-soaked days. At least this section was new. He wasn't sure where he'd left the trail back in April, but was certain he wouldn't be able to recognize any of it.

Rest, he wanted: the walk out of Pamplona had been steep, but they'd left the green, rolling hills that he'd become used to and now were on more wide, arid land. He'd watched a determined Marcus labour up the trail, occasionally holding his side, shedding his backpack regularly to stretch his muscles.

Streams, hamlets, the whirring, chopping windmills on the ridge above the city—these had distracted him from the *how* of what he needed to accomplish. Now, at dusk, they had trekked only as far as Uterga and suddenly he realized that he hadn't considered what the nights would bring.

Marcus waved him in, and he entered the refugio, which had only four beds. Marcus claimed a bed in the corner, beside a lopsided window. Gavin was left with a choice. The other side of the room, or next to him? He still wasn't sure the man wouldn't wake and leave without him.

He put his backpack on the bed across from the one Marcus had chosen. He sat and released his sore feet from the new Timberland boots. He still wore the borrowed striped shirt. The brogues and trousers had been discarded in a corner of Marcus's room, the few essentials transferred to the pockets of new hiking trousers. Everything he'd left London with had now been shed. These boots seemed to hold promise. He put them back on, tied the laces, and went outside to find Marcus.

Uterga was not a real village, only a pilgrim stop with a vending machine, which he scanned for something appetizing but saw nothing. Marcus arrived at his side.

"Muruzábal is a kilometre away. It has a bar and food," Marcus said, before turning and walking, expecting to be followed.

Gavin enjoyed being led. He walked behind Marcus towards the town, and eventually into the town's bar.

Hunched-over men sat in clusters, dragging on cigarettes and sipping beer, not speaking. Dry, tinny folk songs came from speakers behind the bar. Marcus stood in front of the bartender and waited for him to look up from his newspaper.

"Estrella," he said, and looked at Gavin for his order.

He'd had only one drink—the vodka at the Mesón—since the engagement party. Since the call from Porter, the effects of alcohol had turned up the volume on the screaming, but now that Marcus was here, obliging, perhaps he was safe. He looked at Marcus's hand on the bar and examined the rough knuckles.

"Tequila," he said boldly. Marcus looked surprised. Gavin searched in his trouser pocket and slid out his last sheet of Anadin tablets. He pushed one through the foil barrier, popped it into his mouth, and bit down, chewing on the tablet before swallowing it dry. He turned back to the bar to face his shot glass of Tequila Gold, a salt shaker, and a slice of lime.

"*Una mas*," Marcus said to the bartender, ordering one for himself. Gavin thought he saw the man's hand tremble as he sprinkled the salt on the web of skin joining the thumb and forefinger of his left hand.

It was that hand, along with the face, that he had wondered about since Porter's call—there were no wrinkles on that hand. No marks of the hard labour of prison. Marcus offered the shaker to him. "No, no," he said. Marcus raised his shot glass, nodded a *salud*, downed the tequila, sucked the salt from the web of skin, and put the wedge of lime in his mouth. Gavin watched him close his eyes for the ascending buzz. Marcus kept his head bowed for a long moment and Gavin wondered whether or not he was praying.

Later in the night, still at the bar, head heavy with a tequila-lime rocking behind his eyes, Gavin focused on Marcus's arm, the colour reminding him of dampened teak, like the stain on the desk in his office. Who was now at his desk? How had his partners coped? Would they have looked for him? *Shit . . . shit . . .* he thought as he shook his head, but was startled when he looked up to see that Marcus had been staring at him. His reaction time was too slow. Their eyes locked again. He became desperate for his head to clear. *What? What?*

"Your company . . . it makes a lot, then?" Marcus asked him.

He nodded, wobbly, wondering if his thoughts had been read or if he'd spoken aloud.

"You like money," the man added.

He nodded again, but he couldn't imagine anything he'd ever really liked.

"Never had it, myself," Marcus said, then seemed embarrassed. "Man, shit, you guys have no idea," he added, trying to recover the upper hand.

Gavin adjusted his arm on the bar and realized they hadn't eaten. How capable Marcus was, he thought. And good-looking: "You could do well," he said, without thinking, finding that old bit of himself that did business.

"What? Me?"

He nodded. Marcus laughed, and his hand dropped from his chin to the bar and brushed close to Gavin's elbow. With his fingers close to the skin on Gavin's upper arm, he was swaying gently back and forth. Gavin had to hold himself still not to join in the rocking, until—accidentally or not—Marcus touched the skin above Gavin's elbow.

Shit no, Gavin reeled inside. This wasn't the unconscious Marcus, the galloping muscles in his shoulder suggesting that it was he Gavin should have befriended and not Porter. This was something else. He raised his elbow off the bar.

"I'm not used to the strong stuff," he said, nodding to the empty shot glass as he shifted, causing Marcus's hand to fall away. He picked up the plastic sheet from the bar and popped out another Aspirin.

The next morning, as he rubbed his hands quickly together to warm them, he couldn't remember how he'd managed the kilometre return to Uterga. *These*, he thought, as the warmth returned to his fingers. The air was still crisp, his ears chilled. He was careful as he picked his way down the steadily slanting path. The sign at the top of the hill had indicated the Puente de la Reina. Mud oozed through the grass and rocks. He slipped in his hurry to keep up with Marcus. Straightening up, he looked down at the medieval bridge with its arches like eyebrows mirrored in the river, the bridge a projection of light on the water, mirroring and multiplying. The arches reminded him of the exaggerated eyes of cartoon characters, one after another in a chain of twins with stunned looks. He felt the opposite: singular and matte. All he felt capable of doing was following and waiting for the right moment to beg and beg, and to find out how amends could be made.

His head was throbbing. Tequila, he remembered. He should have known better. He reached for the bottle of water in the side pack of his backpack. "Shit," he said to the air. He'd run out of Aspirin last night, and this view of the river and bridge was the *haa haaa* that kept slicing his mind. What on earth? He watched Marcus on the bridge, gazing out, drinking from his water bottle.

A phone rang. A warbling ring strained through his backpack. The annoying insect buzz intensified the throbbing at his temples. He slipped the backpack off his shoulders and slid the phone from the side pouch. The charger had worked. But now that the phone was ringing, he regretted it. He'd given in and called the hospital, and now he'd find out more than he really wanted to.

It was a London number.

"Yes," he said, expecting the voice of the palliative nurse at St. Mary's, where he'd left a message. His stomach minced in on itself. He burped the taste of breakfast ham and coffee.

"Who the hell are you?" asked a smoky voice.

"I beg your pardon?"

"I got a message from the nurse, someone trying to find out about my husband."

"Yes. Yes, I'm sorry—"

"Thought I'd see for myself."

"Just an old friend."

"Was that before or after he became a good-for-nothing bastard?" Her accent was heavy Glaswegian, and he had to strain to make out the words. "He'll die, if you must know." Her voice caught and the woman paused for a moment. "He comes up for a thought or two, mostly to ask for a fag, but then he's down again." Her voice went into a whisper: "I expect it might be as long as a month," she added, and he was sure she sounded disappointed.

"I'm sorry," he forced out. "Would you keep me informed, if anything changes?" He held his breath.

"Why's that, then? What's so special about him?"

The fleshy, blithe face of the boy Porter. The skeletal blitheness in the man on the hospital bed. Then a flash of the knife and the field mouse losing its tail. "We were children together," he said. "You have my number now. Please."

The woman agreed and sniffed again. He ended the call and touched his belly. He'd be alone with it soon. Either Porter would die and leave him with their secret, or during last rites Porter would confess to a priest. Either way, he would be alone with the grinding mill in his gut, and every decision, every certainty would be ground to dust. He had to act quickly. He looked down at Marcus on the Puente de la Reina, his body mirrored in the river below. He hurried down the slope to join him.

"You stood for a long time; I watched you," Marcus said when he reached him on the bridge.

"I was looking at the reflection," Gavin insisted, trying to sound enthusiastic. "We could cover a lot of ground this morning then take the afternoon in a taverna—talk—you've said a lot less to me now that you speak English."

Marcus smiled, despite himself.

"What do you think of while you're walking?" Gavin asked, desperate to know how to reach him. *Haa, haaaa.*

"This isn't a pilgrimage, and it's also not therapy," Marcus returned, a dimple pressing itself into his left cheek.

But Gavin was swelling with words like *mist, edge,* and *screech.* Words he would hear pronounced as a means of banishing them. When the moment was right. He found himself also wanting to tell the man about Kate, tell him then and there about what had happened after Porter's first call, and not being able to be inside her—the feeling of a curtain going down in his brain, a clamp tightening on his chest, shutting him within himself, making him singular, afloat, but full of warning.

Thirteen

On a celluloid-like loop, a scratched repetition of images jumped forward, skipped back, and looped through again. Gavin held the image there, to watch.

He and Porter are in the school dormitory late that evening, the other boys on their beds, all of them confined to the room, quarantined to silence, beyond reach of the pen and pad journalist who eagerly waits outside for the police to give him the details of the accident.

"No one saw a fucking thing, I tell ya," Porter hisses at Gavin, who is sitting with his arms hooked around his chest.

"One, maybe," Gavin says and looks about the room for the face, which now seems imagined.

"If anyone says a word, they know they'll be skinned," Porter assures him. Gavin searches the room again, and again, but the boys don't look up, no one catches his eye, no one looks familiar.

When he opened his eyes he thought he smelled toast. His father had once told him that memory smelled like toast and it wasn't worth having. As a child growing into awareness of his father's Jewish background, he'd thought there was something sinister in Martin's association, something to do with the smell of genocide, but now he wondered if his father wasn't just being literal. He sat up on the refugio bed. *This one*, he thought, to draw himself away from the memory of that other dormitory. "*Rioja*," he said aloud, practising the pronunciation in a way he'd never been able to manage when ordering that wine in London restaurants. But he had the sound of the word in his ears and before him outside. He stood and looked out the window, towards the valley's blood-red earth dotted with ordered vines like pods of roe.

He rubbed his temples. He was doing without Aspirin now, not out of choice, but because he hadn't trusted the foreign names on the packages, couldn't ask a pharmacist for what he wanted or admit to Marcus that he needed to. His head throbbed as he continued the small circles with his fingers.

More than a week had passed on the trail, and although the words had swelled up in him, he hadn't been able to say them. Each time he'd tried—"Catholics are keen on forgiveness," he'd started once—Marcus had managed to steer the topic off in another direction and he'd lose his nerve. Marcus had grown stronger and seemed in the flow of this path. Despite his injury, he took to it effortlessly, striding across the land like he owned it. He was dangerous, Gavin had thought earlier in the day as he watched the lengthening of the man's muscles, from the underarm down to the side of the back, as he bent over to sip wine from the *fuente del vino* outside of town. Gavin was next at the tap of free wine for pilgrims, but he leaned over awkwardly, almost falling, catching only a splash of wine on his tongue. The wine was foul and he was off-kilter again. He struggled to keep up with Marcus climbing the hill to this dorm. He wobbled under the weight of *what if*. Perhaps all he needed to do was protect him. Befriend him. God had ways of knowing what deeds mattered, what penance had already been paid.

He now heard voices in the other room. *Fuck*. He had nothing to share with anyone but Marcus. He rose from the bed and walked to the kitchen. Standing in the doorway he saw two men and a woman preparing food. He snuck past them and grabbed the supplies he'd bought earlier and packed away in the refrigerator. He hurried outside. The orange glow of the sunset made the castle above the town look like it was from a fairy tale.

&

"Here," Gavin said, handing him an elaborate and sloppy sandwich that Marcus thought looked like it contained a pig's worth of chorizo. Goat's cheese stuck out the sides. "You must be hungry."

"That's quite something," Marcus said and tried to sound grateful and not suspicious. Gavin sat down on the picnic bench beside him, near the fountain. They ate in silence, passing bottled water between them. Marcus tried to read the air. For over a week now, he'd been trying to understand this buzz like electricity between them, but he still didn't know what to call it.

"How are the ribs today?" Gavin asked, rubbing behind his ear, as though pain was the subject on his mind. He was often like this—absorbed in some sort of inner agony but reaching out towards Marcus as though to deflect attention away from himself.

"Better, thanks."

"I could go into town and get some more liniment for you, or we could try to see if there's a masseuse, or osteo . . . or—"

"Nope, nope . . . I'm good, thanks," Marcus said, and took it down a notch, irritated that he still didn't know how to interpret this attention, and knowing that as soon as you were indebted to someone things changed. Gavin had been trying to open him up using these small acts all week. Offering attachment. He wouldn't take that tease too seriously. He looked at the sandwich in his hand. It would be too rich for him this evening. He offered the rest to Gavin, holding it up, raising his eyebrows. Reading the air.

"You ever been in trouble with the law?" Gavin blurted out, waving away the offer of the sandwich.

Blame, like rain, returning. It had all been a trap. He'd read every signal since they'd left Pamplona all wrong. He should have trusted his first instinct. He should have bolted. He put the sandwich on the table and gulped down a mouthful of water.

In the weeks at HMP Peterhead, north of Aberdeen, there had been no juvenile section, and delinquents were mashed into cells beside men like fresh meat before dogs in a kennel. "Lacey, that's me," said the least foul of them, and Marcus had twitched with the same kind of alertness Gavin had been triggering in him all week. Something to fear. Or not. He had learned a way of compliance with older men that had allowed him to get by, but that alert feeling had turned itself on him, made him fall for its appeal. He'd been aroused, trapped, and abused as a consequence. But compared to all the others, Lacey was true to his word of friendship. Among the stench, coughing, farting, wailing of wretched men at night, there was Lacey with his photos of his daughters, his books on the Great Barrier Reef's sea creatures, and just a little kiss now and then for a frightened fourteen-year-old.

Trouble with the law? Trouble was HMP Peterhead, and law was whoever said it was so. And that trouble had begun a lot earlier than Peterhead. Even in Bow, before Miguel arrived and moved them to Ladbroke Grove. In Bow there had been the corner shop and the sweets for his mother that he'd bought, paid for, and wrapped in his shirt as a surprise, only to have them fall out on the street in front of a different shop where he was accused of stealing them, then banned from entering again. Black in Bow. Was not. Just. He'd returned home and had to draw his mother a picture for her birthday instead of wrapping the sweets in tissue and presenting them to her as he'd planned. The flack comes back. Rat. Trap.

"You enjoy that stereotype, do you?" he threw back defensively.

"No, I didn't mean it that way," Gavin corrected, and he rubbed his temples.

Marcus pulled a slice of chorizo from the sandwich and tossed it to a pigeon on the ground. In the ensuing silence, he began to feel sleepy, fatigued by the long uphill climb to this albergue and the *run, run* in his bones.

"Look, I've worked on and off in travel, hotels, bars, and I speak two languages perfectly. I know business, booze, and I make paintings. I'd like to make something of myself before it's not too late. That's me." He couldn't believe what an idiot he was to let out the bit about paintings.

Gavin appeared to relax and put the sandwich to his mouth, biting into it with relish. Marcus lifted the bread off his sandwich and stared at the meat and its greasy, nitrate pinkness staining the bread. Suddenly he felt the man's hand on his arm, tapping it. Gavin pointed at the sky, indicating the coming rain and gesturing that they should go inside, but Marcus let him get up alone and leave. He sat and waited for the rain. A drop hit his face, and he breathed deeply.

Sleep was begging for him. Each of their days had ended liked like this: exhaustion, silence, and a bit of food, but today he was more tired than he could ever remember. He bit into the sandwich, chewed slowly, then stood up and walked inside, the remaining bread and meat left on the picnic table.

※

"God, I thought you were the Germans—well, not the Germans, like in the movies—the German guy, here, with his wife. I'm Andy," said a naked, camel-haired man with a beard, as he secured the towel at his waist and walked towards Marcus and Gavin, now standing by their chosen beds. He was American, slight of build, and skittish like a chipmunk. Gavin stepped in front of Marcus to block this interruption of their privacy. A feeling of being protected made Marcus sit down on the bed.

"Looks like there are eight of us in here tonight," the American said as he held his hand out to Gavin, who took it reluctantly. Marcus rose from the bed and shook the man's hand.

"Tea?" Gavin asked Marcus in Spanish, turning his back on Andy. His face looked intent, begging for exclusive attention.

"*Si, si,*" Marcus said and nodded, understanding that Gavin was closing ranks, and feeling that protection trigger his alertness again. Gavin bent to take tea bags from his pack.

"Where you guys from?" Andy asked cheerfully.

"España," Marcus said quickly, then turned to Gavin to speak in Spanish about the weather, the food they had just eaten, and the size of the dorm beds to cement the exclusion of the American.

"It's not like some of the other albergues, the beds are bigger, more space between them, but, you know, I think this one smells a bit," Andy continued, defeating their attempt to keep him out.

Gavin retreated, nodded at Andy, and shot Marcus a pleading look. Marcus followed him into the canteen.

※

I need to get this right. There are others becoming involved. I need to describe them accurately, but make them fit. I must take the way Marcus described them to me—after it was all over—with his hyperbole and slashes of disdain, and make them relevant for Gavin. For all of us.

I am not a naturally competitive woman. I have never considered myself prone to making comparisons, to acts of one-upmanship, or feelings of inferiority. When Marcus had announced that he was in fact going on his annual walk to Santiago, I was concerned for his health, that's all. But when, on the day he was leaving, I returned from my shift at the bar and saw Gavin leaving the apartment with him, I recognized what ancient alchemists had described as bile. It was the grapefruit taste of jealousy on my tongue.

"What's going on?" I asked him there in the plazueta, knowing the answer. I stood directly between them. I wanted to draw Marcus back into our cloister of storytelling. I wanted to go back to our lives of drinking in the evenings, watching him dance with women I knew were not his equal. I wanted him to be the Spanish North African rogue I had believed him to be. I wanted everything to go back to how it had been before Gavin had arrived. And yet still there was a nagging sense of unfinished business with Gavin.

Marcus simply stated the obvious about his walk.

"And why is he going with you?"

"He can do what he wants," he said, but I caught him looking around me to see Gavin's reaction.

I stamped my foot. "You always go alone!"

And Marcus stared at me with a rising grin. I expected a rhyming chiming chastising insult then, but nothing came. "You can do what you want as well," he added, and I felt like knocking him to the ground. He touched my head and mumbled something that didn't sound at all like Spanish. I wondered what more I didn't know about him. I like to believe that it was this moment of confusion—and not the nasty, bruised part of me—that still neglected to tell him what I knew about Gavin or about the night I'd spent with him. I turned without a goodbye, walked past Gavin, and entered our building.

It was mid-May when they left, and I knew they'd be on the Camino for three to four weeks, not to mention how long they might spend in Santiago or on the additional walk to Finisterre. I saw the summer stretching out before me, tending bar at the Mesón all alone or with a new recruit hired by our optimistic manager. I was stuck. I'd considered going to Paris to be with my father—I could work in a hotel there, or study, or work in the art school, painting over their studio walls, as they did each summer, and perhaps be taught in the right school of kindness—the kindness my father had believed in, which it seemed now, as far as Gavin was concerned, I hadn't learned adequately. I could continue to invent Marcus and begin a story with him as my protagonist. But instead I quit everything and went to bed.

I pretended I wasn't hurt, just sick, but it was clear that even though I had accepted Marcus's indifference to me, I had wanted him to love me. Gavin's indifference had sparked a similar response. Marcus was an enigma, and I was not what Gavin seemed to be searching for. I was floundering with a sickening sense of exclusion.

When I was finally through with being in bed, I sought out Christophe at the Plaza de Toros, and I watched the new arrivals that had come in from the sherry estates in southern Spain, the heart of Spain's bull-rearing and fighting country. These were the *toros bravos* used in the *encierro*. They had been pampered in their rearing, selected for their combination of intelligence, strength, and aggressiveness, and given the privilege to graze in exclusive olive groves for years. The animals would not be shipped north until they reached about seven hundred kilograms. There their horns would be shaved back to a point, and they would be confined to darkness while they remembered their idyll, so that when they were released in the annual running of the bulls, they would be very, very angry.

I tried not to get in anyone's way. I watched and took in the power of the bulls' torsos. I even tried to fall in love with Christophe as I watched him from a distance. We never spoke. And my imagination failed me. But at the point where secrets and inklings converge, there's an opening to truth of a sort. The inklings line up like crumbs along a trail, and suddenly there's a story.

One afternoon, my nagging feelings took me into Marcus's room, where I stood and tried again to imagine who he was. The two paintings on his wall hung there like a clue to him. The blue and orange abstract rectangles demonstrated a deft hand with thick paint that seemed to be ladled on rather than brushed. The other one was made up of circles in various blues, orange, purple, and green. I'd never examined it closely before, but in the intersecting coronas I thought I discerned the image of a snail's face, or more precisely a snail with a human face, but I couldn't be sure. The revelation was comforting; this Marcus—a man with a profound sense of humour—was the one I'd been drawn to, despite how controlled he'd been in revealing it.

I breathed in deeply, to smell him, but there was only a neutral musk to the air. The room was in disarray, as both he and Gavin had packed there and left it strewn with the last-minute deletions from their rucksacks. I mooched about, kicking away shoes and trousers, shirts, and the underwear that had no erotic appeal. In the corner beneath Gavin's beat-up brogues, I noticed a bag with crumpled paper inside it. I bent down and picked up the bag, and took out the papers. There were three crumpled photographs and some receipts from Spanish shops. I began with the photographs. Unfolding the first was like a tingle in a numb foot. The second was more like running into a wire you'd been told was there but had never seen, its blurring effects making you look differently at air; but the third was crisp yet grim, like the taste of an unripe apple.

The first was a photo of a woman on a London bridge. The second was of boys on a football pitch, their faces confused, mutinous. And the third was a cut-out of a photo of one boy—Marcus's relative. No, Marcus. I touched my throat.

None of it made sense. I had suspected from the start that it had been Marcus that Gavin had been looking for, but this confirmation was eerie. What was his intention? I reached into the bag and pulled out the receipts. A shoe shop, an antique store, a clothing store. The antique store receipt listed a fan, and for a moment I was humbled by how expensive Gavin's gift had been, but it also listed *cuchillo*. I panicked and felt tricked. Not only might Marcus have been in danger, but I had failed to warn him when I could have.

Had I warned Marcus, they might not have set out on the journey at all. Was it my guilt that sparked my next, impossible moves, or was it something self-serving? I now had an excuse for continued involvement with them both. I packed my own bags. I don't remember what I was thinking. I only remember the compulsion, like thirst, that was leading me to save Marcus, as I believed I had to.

The details and logic of how I would find them didn't faze me. I scoured the books we had on the Camino, calculated where they might be by this time, and decided to take a coach to Leon and walk back towards them, or wait in a convenient refugio . . . or . . . I really had very little idea, but I got my gear together and set off the next day.

In the meantime, strangers have arrived, uninvited, into the space between Marcus and Gavin. These strangers are important because they disturb and distract from the inevitability of the story as it began.

And because there's Claire, against whom I now must measure my own integrity.

❧

Other pilgrims joined them in the canteen. Control and repair, Marcus thought: it was a simple recipe for how to get along in groups. He'd learned it in Bow, confirmed it in detention, practised it in jail, where he'd had no control but learned that control and freedom were easily confused. Show nothing. Choose neither side. Mirroring what people wanted to believe of themselves made them comfortable, and it was not difficult to subdue his own feelings. He'd had a lifetime of that.

He sat down at the long pine table. Curfew had passed, and the doors were being locked by Theresa, whom Marcus knew well from his annual visits. She was a tiny, middle-aged woman who now ran this refuge on her own since the death of her husband three years previously. She crossed herself when she spoke. When Marcus greeted her each year he loved to hold her clawlike, arthritic hand.

The canteen was stark: bare walls and a basic pine table and benches where Theresa served coffee and biscuits to the pilgrims. Marcus sat and gazed about the sparse room, allowing himself time to reach its only distinguishing feature: a small grey carved panel of wood that hung on the wall behind the table, depicting the death of Judas and the crucifixion of Christ. The cross and the tree were clearly out of proportion to the size of the figures, with Jesus's head at the top of the panel, the Roman soldier to his right reaching as high as his pierced hands. Mary and John the Baptist stood to the left of the cross, and on the far left of the panel, the figure of Judas was hanging from the tree. Marcus had habitually studied the carving. The heads of the figures were big, limbs dwarfed; the distorted perspective made the humans more important than crosses or trees. This year, though, he found it less than inspiring. He felt the urge to splash orange on the trunk of the tree. He looked over at Gavin, who had positioned himself on the periphery of the group, in the threadbare armchair.

Marcus adapted easily to the rules of curfew. That part of him—programmed at a young age to accept confinement—clicked into place with the tumble and clink of a padlock at the door. He watched as the pilgrims were encouraged by Theresa to commune, pray, and help themselves to her lemon biscuits. He saw Gavin take out some paper from his pocket and make a show of being absorbed in writing. Marcus took the others in: In addition to Andy, there was the German couple in their fifties, Rainer and Anya; a twenty-something American woman named Claire; Rosa, a Spanish woman in her forties who had odd, irregularly shaped hazel eyes; and a middle-aged Englishman with a salt-and-pepper beard, who seemed about to collapse with every word, seemingly growing brittle with sadness. He brought to mind other Englishmen Marcus had met in Pamplona, men on a mission to find themselves, trying to put together the pieces of a scattered jigsaw. He had seen the type in London—distinct from the working-class boys he'd known in Ladbroke Grove—boys who'd been away at school and returned with less of a silhouette. They were softer, and yet bound for brittleness and disappointment. At least when he'd been sent away it had been for punishment, not veiled as privilege. Malcolm seemed no different from those others, despite this walk, rest, meditation towards restoration. Marcus wondered if the present London would be any kinder.

"You could baptize a pygmy in that shower, is about all," Malcolm said as he sat down on the bench. Flip-flop to stay on top, Marcus thought. Try as he might, he couldn't feel sorry for this man.

"Theresa let me use hers; she prefers us," said Rosa, patting Malcolm on the forearm.

They introduced themselves to one another. Marcus nodded and said, Marco, pointing to himself. He picked up a lemon biscuit and took a bite. He refused to introduce Gavin as though they were together. Control and repair. Gavin finally said his name quietly.

Until five months ago, Andy had been a nurse in an orthopaedic ward at Boston General. He told them how he had worked night shifts, staying up listening to the breathing of relatively healthy people, compared to the breathing of those in the cancer ward down the hall. Andy fidgeted, never comfortable for long. He had started his journey, as he called it, with yoga as a way to relax, then he'd turned to meditation, to Reiki, to acupuncture, to Deepak Chopra, and finally, five months ago, he'd rediscovered his Catholicism.

"Did you know the Iglesia de San Pedro was blown up in a battle for a shoulder bone?" he offered eagerly to no one in particular.

"No, that's not the case," Rainer corrected.

Marcus began to relax. Something real would come. Whatever accusation was coming, it would be nothing new, but the measuredness he was now feeling, after the endless days of walking, had become something necessary in his life. The first time he'd done the Camino, a few years after arriving in Spain, he'd still been running. From himself. He'd been trying to shed Bow, Ladbroke Grove, and HMP Peterhead from his body. He had wanted to stride like freedom itself, to press his foot in earth and mark it with his existence. That year, the journey to Santiago had taken just over two weeks; he had walked through the night on some days. But the following year, and all of them since, had taken several more weeks. Nothing could entrap him again. He liked remembering that.

He listened as the German, conferring with his wife, Anya, clarified that Felipe II had blown up the church so that it couldn't be used against him, and that St. Andrew's shoulder bone is a myth. He watched Malcolm listening politely with his head down. Rosa wrote in her journal, and Claire, the sturdy but not cheery American brunette, sat silently, looking straight ahead.

He kept his eyes on the young, freckled face of Claire. She appeared aloof at first, but after observing her attentively he could tell that she was always tuned into the animated discussion and would become alert at odd moments. She seemed content to be alone in company, and the group let her be. He liked this about them and admired Claire, who seemed to be navigating a jagged, skinless journey. She reminded him of himself on that first journey. She held her left hand in her right, as though one side of her was on duty to comfort the other.

"Listen, I have to tell you about a man I met, from Peru, who'd come to live in Madrid, and he had a house to insure . . ." Rosa drew the group's attention away from their New Age interpretations of Camino symbolism. Marcus noticed that the odd shape of Rosa's eyes was due to semi-blindness that forced one eye to wander. An insurance broker, she was a keen observer of life's little tragedies—fires, accidents, theft over five hundred euros. She had a deep, pack-a-day speaking voice and told the story of the Peruvian man who owned a menagerie of exotic pets that lived in the house he wanted Rosa's company to insure. She had visited his home to find metre-long yellow snakes, parrots, turtles, an ocelot, and a few other South American species. The house was an exotic zoo, filthy yet magical. She knew his animals had been smuggled in illegally, but she didn't want to have to be the one to turn the creatures over to the authorities, as there was no knowing what might become of them, so she suggested to the man that they both try to sell the creatures, over time, on the black market. After he rid his house of them, she'd be able to insure it. The man dropped out of touch for a few weeks, until Rosa called him again. She asked if she could pay another visit. When she arrived she noted the smell in the house had lightened. She heard the cry of one lame cockatoo, turned to see it perched on the arm of a chair, but saw little else. Over the course of the month, the man finally told her, he had released the animals into the parks of Madrid. Rosa's face widened, her left eye drifted up towards the engraving of Jesus, and Marcus watched it twitter. She described where she imagined each creature was right now, and made much of the thought of snakes in the Parque del Buen Retiro in the centre of Madrid during the weekly promenade by the bourgeois Spanish. Reiner and Anya laughed. Andy expressed concern for the animals. Malcolm seemed annoyed at having to listen to the story itself. Claire's face grew serious. A blush striped her neck and rose to her cheek as she sipped water slowly. Marcus restrained himself from looking over at Gavin.

Repair, repair, he thought, and positioned himself between the banality of his life in Pamplona and the grave undercurrent of Gavin in the room. Normally at the Mesón, or in the streets of Pamplona with tourists or friends, he played the clown, told the stories. Bartenders were meant to make clients feel better. People expected him to listen. Blend. And draw out. But now he was too conscious of Gavin's gaze, his breathing. And he remembered that he'd touched the man's skin.

"ETA has apparently begun to target tourist areas; the authorities have been warning pilgrims," Malcolm said, initiating a new conversation.

"No, they say that, they always do, don't listen," said Rosa, trying to keep control of the conversation.

"Why not? It's perfectly plausible," said Andy.

"No," Reiner said flatly, with authority. Anya nodded knowingly.

"How can you be sure?"

Malcolm watched Reiner and Andy usurp his topic with ease; he lowered his head and listened to them discuss the strategies of terrorists and what effect targeting tourists would have on their cause. Marcus struggled to stay awake. All this talk was a distraction from the tick-tock lag in his body. He wanted to be asleep or somewhere else. He looked back at the silently ticking Claire, who was looking down into her lap, but sighing brokenly every once in a while. Finally he glanced at Gavin, who was staring into his lap at the piece of paper he had been writing on. He looked up suddenly, but Marcus quickly diverted his eyes.

"It's not so easy to kill someone, I think," Rainer said. Marcus drank his own breath, now becoming agitated. What did these people know about murder? Murder was simple. It was as easy as pointing to someone—a life could be over in one gesture. He examined Rainer's square face and dark eyes, then his wife's long fingernails, as she spoke on the psychology of murder from her work as a psychotherapist. Looking back at Gavin, Marcus felt his temperature spike. He stared at the strong nose and gently hooded blue eyes, with lashes like a giraffe's. He knew that Gavin was aware of him. He touched his hip.

"Murder's a part of human nature," Marcus said to Anya, throwing out a morsel of bait. He knew he had Gavin's attention, which was pleasurable. And nauseating.

"Oh no," Andy said, adamantly. "You can't say that . . . we're evolving out of it. The darkness is only a part of us that we have to embrace and then move away from. We have to remember our divinity . . ."

"Bollocks," Marcus said, eyeing Gavin, who looked fixedly at the paper in his lap.

As the conversation about the anthropology of murder continued—Malcolm and Rosa made small interventions—Marcus held himself in. Had Gavin been at Peterhead? Surely not. Too posh, and soft. And yet if he had been one of the other boys that Lacey had sheltered, it would explain the man's attention. Maybe Lacey was still looking out for him. Only someone associated with Lacey would be able to trace David Williams.

The group became increasingly animated in its discussion of God, nature, and the evolution of humanity. Marcus leaned against the wall under the warped-size Judas. When he looked at Claire, who remained silent, he noticed that her left hand trembled whenever she took her right hand away to lift her glass of water to her lips. She was the only one among them all who truly deserved the mercy of St. James. He watched out of the corner of his eye as Gavin carefully folded his sheet of paper, got up, and went into the dormitory. Marcus listened to the chatter. He should follow Gavin and broach the Lacey connection, he thought, but he couldn't bring himself to do it.

❧

If I can know Marcus at all, it will be through this: aligning my version of his thoughts with all that I had ignored while living in his company. I had never probed or hunted for details; I had been comfortable in my own ignorance, casting him as the mysterious Latin lover.

I remember the rain beginning an hour into my coach journey from Pamplona to Logroño—the town I'd calculated they'd be soon approaching. The bus's long wipers slapped in time with the tinny Spanish rock playing over the *Tannoy*. But I don't remember my thoughts. I must have considered what kind of danger he was in, and I must have wondered if it had been deserved, or whether, in fact, Marcus was a danger to Gavin, or even to me.

As I construct their inner lives, I wonder if it's possible for me, as a woman, to really grasp their inner reality. What am I missing? Certainly some sexual angle. What about a natural tendency towards violence or harm? I don't think so. There is something I'm tracing through them that lives in me. I must have felt that I knew Marcus, and must have believed in what I felt in order to be setting out so impossibly to try to stop Gavin from . . . what? If not physical harm, then my actions were those of a madwoman. As it was, I arrived at a pilgrim's fountain in Logroño and, while I read the pamphlets left there by pilgrims and tourists, I began to shiver uncontrollably. I read to keep still and struggled with the Spanish. As I sat on the short stone wall, I read an account of the witch hunts in Logroño during the Inquisition—the open hunting season declared on herb gatherers, midwives, widows, and spinsters. In 1483, my imagination, let alone my wanderings, would have been enough to earn me a place on a pyre. I nearly prayed. I hoped I would see Gavin and Marcus arrive at any moment, but I know now I had overshot them, and while I trembled in Logroño, Gavin was gaining purpose in the Rioja valley near Torres del Río.

✢

Stalled. The rain had moved in like sleep. Not budging. The cave was cold, and the if-if-if of the storm outside made his skin crawl. There was buzzing, there was pounding, there was wriggling—all of this inside him like a madman walking empty corridors. *God damn, God damn.* Gavin rubbed his shirt sleeve. It was the striped one again today, like a message. *Release me.*

They had left early, sneaking out of the refugio before dawn to avoid the morning blathering of Andy and the Germans. He had needed to put distance between them, but Marcus had hesitated, because he noticed that the American girl had also been awake. Gavin had worried that he might take off with her and without him, but Marcus had followed him willingly along the trail as dawn broke. Now they sheltered from the pounding rain within an enclosed overhang just off the dirt path.

Gavin took off his backpack and sat on it, watching the large drops fall to the ground. The space was cramped. He felt the man's jutting elbow, heard his wheezing. *Hear me* . . .

"I didn't think it rained so much in Spain," he said. He could feel Marcus's shoulder next to his. He made a show of looking eastward, so that his body leaned away from Marcus's.

"Here in the north, yes, pisses," Marcus answered and leaned against the opposite wall of the cave. "Why did you leave London?" he asked, simply.

Gavin looked at him, took a breath. "Don't know," and he strained to produce a that's-life-it's-tough smile that men give one another. "I needed a break," he added, and looked out into the rain. He wanted to scream Kate's name, to tell Marcus about the engagement party and the absence of a ring. While Marcus relaxed against the wall of the cave, he tried unsuccessfully to put into words what had brought him to Pamplona. He knew that confession was not enough. It had to come with the possibility of forgiveness.

"You might just have too much dosh," Marcus said after a moment of silence.

"You think so?" he almost laughed, knowing that was no longer true. "What's too much?"

"When you can stop caring."

"Caring? About money?"

"About getting it," Marcus said.

They both took a breath that might have been a laugh. The rain continued its snore. Come on, Gavin urged himself. "So, why didn't you speak English before?"

Marcus looked out towards the west.

"Emily said you were Spanish," Gavin pressed.

"I have this accent because I spent a long time in Britain—with some family and at school. I learned how to get on by sounding like this—but, *ya looka see, I cyan also sound like dis, ya hear ras hole?*" Marcus looked to see if he'd had an effect. Nothing registered on Gavin's face. Lacey would have told anyone he'd spoken to about him that David had taught him how to speak like a ras hole. "I'm not a Brit," he said. "And you can learn a lot in bed. English women like to talk ... and curse."

Gavin's expression did not change. "Where did you go to school?" he probed.

"English people always want to know that," Marcus said, annoyed now.

"Scotland?" Gavin asked, as he watched the dimple in Marcus's cheek dip.

Marcus glanced at the other man's wrist, which seemed much too fine for a Borstal boy. He thought of the Borstal's odd position at the edge of town, where the wind would whistle like a farmer for his dog, and where the other boys made it known that he was the one who'd have the most to prove. And they turned out to be right. But he didn't remember a soul. Not one god forsaken soul. He stared at the side of Gavin's face, trying to place it, but unable to turn him into anything other than every other white boy at Spiers who had turned their back on him.

He'd leave when the rain stopped. He didn't need a damn class reunion.

"You went there?" Marcus asked, referring to Spiers.

"Been there a few times, for work, and once to the Isle of Skye" Gavin said, pretending not to know what Marcus meant, and referring only to Scotland. He could see Marcus's confusion. "I was asking because you have a bit of that accent too, or maybe it's Caribbean, can't tell really," he said to change the subject.

His shoulder pressed into Marcus's with ease, sending Marcus off-kilter realizing that the Borstal link was off track. In the rise and fall of Gavin's breathing, he thought of Constanza, imagined touching her, but his body was confused, Gavin's arm warm. He sat forward and avoided another collision with it.

"Where are your parents from?" Gavin continued.

Marcus ran his hands over his face, exhausted by the uncertainty of just what was going on here. "I caused a lot of trouble for my mother, but I never deserved how I paid for it." He realized only after he had said it how strongly the image of the Borstal was with him.

It was another opening, Gavin thought. The boy and his mother shouldn't have had to pay. And if he didn't do it now, while Porter was alive, he might have to face the law alone, as Marcus had done. This was where his reason had led him. This was how a man faced up. He touched his inner thigh and tried to absorb the feeling of what was to come. He was suddenly confused by a hardness at his cock. He put his hand out from under the rock shelter and caught some rain in it. He sucked water off his palm and understood his responsibility.

Marcus watched him, in awe of the finesse in an otherwise undignified gesture. He sighed unconsciously.

"I can help you make something of yourself," Gavin said.

Marcus dug his boot into some soil near a rock at his feet.

Fourteen

At least viruses act. Do something. Most people are content to experience violence or love vicariously, rather than act. Even Sam's fellow researchers in the lab—they watch. They watch what viruses do.

Sam is asleep. I have been trying to read up on the latest virus alerts, but I can't focus. I am desperate to get back into the rhythm of my story, to find the intersecting points along the trail and to plot out the missed crossings and impossible sightings as I searched for Marcus and Gavin outside of Logroño. But the evening out with Sam has slowed me down.

We attended a faculty party hosted by Paolo, the senior professor in the virology lab. Paolo's wife is a slim Almodovar-type woman with big teeth and a raucous laugh. She was the best thing about the evening. I sat and watched her as she entertained, drawing guests together and touching their faces regularly. When she found out I was a Canadian, she asked me if I'd ever seen the northern lights; "aurora borealis," she said beautifully, touching my arm. I told her I had, as a child camping with my father in northern Ontario. The loons were warbling, the black sky weeping tears of light. I don't know how my Spanish translated.

Drawing me into a secret, she pointed out to me a roundish woman across the room. She recounted the story of the woman and her veterinarian husband, both in their forties. They had three children and had taken precautions—a vasectomy for him—not to have any more. A few months ago the woman had become pregnant. Insisting she had been faithful, the woman tried to calm her husband down. He didn't believe her, stormed out of the house and drove to his veterinary clinic, where, to the sounds of barking dogs and mewing cats, he provided himself with a sample of his ejaculation. Using the lab next to the operating room for small pets, he examined his sample under a microscope, only to discover there were motile sperm in the seminal fluid. The marriage was saved. Paolo's wife laughed. She touched my face—as if to pass the story along to me—then flitted off to talk to a graduate student from Valencia.

I introduced myself to a few people, including George, the husband of Sam's new colleague, but I had little ability with cocktail-party chat. After each introduction I found a reason to make each conversation brief. I would go to the bathroom and spend time looking in the mirror or washing my hands. I thought of Marcus, his defences dropped in the cave with Gavin, both of them aroused, and my heart beat faster, a growing fury that I couldn't explain to myself, so I washed my hands again. I returned to the party and surveyed the room.

A group of graduate students occupied the far corner, exhaling their cigarette smoke politely out the window, waving it off in the direction of the street below. They watched one another. In the middle of the room, a group of researchers, among them Sam's colleagues—some seated on leather Barcelona chairs, others standing—were deep in discussion about the latest scientific studies. As my eyes roamed over the outline of the various people, a room of mostly men, I wondered how conscious they were every day that they were engaged in a ritual observance of the very core of life. Did they take for granted that they were chronicling the invisible, or were they content with the process that was grounded in balancing equations and the comfort of numbers? My eyes moved from one to another, then another. There was Sam, his chestnut curls bouncing as he spoke about something I'm sure would have seemed dull to a casual listener, someone who didn't chronicle terrestrial minutiae.

A commotion erupted in a corner from Paolo's two boys. The eight-year-old, dressed in green velvet trousers, held a Game Boy up over his head as his younger brother pursued him in tears. The older boy wove among the legs of the researchers of the invisible, not one of them noticing the cries of the younger, until Sam looked down and held his arms out to the small five-year-old in similar trousers to his brother's. I watched Sam pick the boy up and sit with him on an armchair, talking to him in his brittle Spanish, and then I thought I heard him switch to English, but I couldn't be sure. I strained to listen:

"The duck says to the bartender, 'got any grapes?'" and I realized that Sam was telling the boy a joke, knowing that the little one didn't understand a word. I adored him for hoping that merely the phonemes of humour might work. The boy listened intently, waiting for a punchline he had no idea how to interpret.

My glance slipped towards the sofa, where someone was watching Sam as intensely as I had been. The woman was dark-skinned with black plaits falling behind a white linen headband that outlined her large, oval face, her cheekbones rising towards the white linen like a vase holding a calla lily. Her eyes were not only huge and dark, but they were focused on Sam. Something flipped below my navel, and I was suddenly hot. I had not known Marianne was beautiful. This first close-up of her was like seeing a statue I'd always heard about or seen in reproduction but never stood before, my flesh before its stone.

Sam was oblivious to any eyes but those of Paolo's son, who was now showing him a cut on his finger. Paolo's wife interrupted them with a stroke of Sam's cheek. She lifted her son into her arms, gently scolded him for being up so late, and took him into the bedroom. I made my way quickly over to Sam's side and sat on the arm of the chair. He touched my back and asked me if I was having a good time. I wanted to be at home. I didn't tell him so, but I wanted to be back here, at this desk, mapping out just where I was and how lost I had become on the Camino. I needed to get it right. The tsunami has come and gone, and I still feel as though I haven't done enough. I didn't want to be watching.

The evening wound down relatively early for Spanish events, and we waved off first, Sam a little tipsy and giggling. On our way back through the town he suggested we should wander, be like the Spanish and enjoy the night. In the winter months, Santiago is not dominated by St. James and the Camino, and the atmosphere in its Gothic streets is relatively quiet and sombre. In February, the nights belong to students. We went into the old town, to Rúa do Franco, and immediately ran into groups of undergraduates, who seemed so unbearably light that I felt foolish for my morose thoughts. I felt old. Outside one of the tavernas was a *Tunas*—a group of students in medieval dress, who go from bar to bar together to make the most of their weekend liberation from studies. They were engaged in cavalier talk about politics and culture. Sam and I chose a seat outside and listened to the debates as we drank Ribeiro. Suddenly a young man began to sing, softly. A low hum like a night creature from the Ontario woods. Then the tune developed into a Spanish chant, the melody becoming clear and ringing out so compellingly that people around him stopped to listen; they became absorbed in the music. I was not calmed, but I could see that Sam was. He sipped his wine, closed his eyes, and swayed his head. I touched his hand.

"That child was sweet," he said as he opened his eyes. I sighed and relaxed, warmed by the thought that Sam and I might one day have a child that he would soothe as he had Paolo's boy. Everything would be fine. I listened to the music, sipped from my glass, and thought of names for boys.

Sam is now in bed, and as I flip through the pages of this H5N1 report, I wonder about boys and how I would fare as the mother to a boy if I can never really know them, as I struggle to know Marcus and Gavin. Will I always be missing insight into that sexual undercurrent that drives us all, but men differently? Do I know my father?

My father is flamboyant. He is a sculptor and an aesthetic gourmand. Paris suits him, whereas my mother prefers the aesthetics of a canoe. That may or may not have contributed to why they are no longer together, but the fact is they made a daughter who would like to be in Paris. In a canoe. Paddling down the Seine at dawn might just be the perfect expression of my complete self. I have never been completely comfortable with my father's sense of adventure and his peacock excesses of colour and flair, but without them, I would not be living here in Spain.

Even so, I miss the smell of Canada.

One winter. Me. Ten years old. I was on snowshoes, walking behind my father, on the surface of the snow that covered the frozen Mazinaw Lake. The snow was like packing foam, making pop and gnaw noises as we tread towards the Bon Echo Rock, which stood before us like the jagged mouth of Satan leaning into the frozen wind. I smelled watermelon. Lovely and terrifying.

"Red rover, red rover, let Emily come over," I sang to myself, to make light of the fear. It was the chant from a game the kids played in the summer, in the hydro fields near my house. Two teams stood paces apart, in a row, hands clasped, facing one another. The first team would call someone from the other team over, inviting them to run through their chain, daring them to break through the clasped arms and hands. If they couldn't break the grasp of two hands, they had to become members of the side that had called them over, increasing the size of the team. I had been good at Red Rover, always able to charge through. Always breaking the boundary. While I sang the chant to myself on the frozen lake, I charged towards the foot of the cliffs, behind my father, who had no idea a child might not be as bold as he was. I wanted to prove him right.

When we reached the far shore, under the shadow of Satan's teeth, I was out of breath, but not afraid. Rocks bulged from beneath the ice in spots where the snow had been blown clear. Up ahead, my father had stopped on a clear patch and was staring down at something trapped in the ice. I trod quickly towards him on my snowshoes and came up beside him. I saw what he was looking at. A paw and a hairy leg. The mangled hind leg of what I knew then was a wolf. The leg was caught in a trap, and the trap was locked in the ice near a rock. The rest of the wolf was nowhere to be seen. My father sat down on the rock and stared at the leg. I watched him, to see what the appropriate reaction to the bits of carcass would be from someone who knew that life was to be lived on the edge of death. He stared for a long time. Slowly the look on his face changed from amazement to amusement, and he slipped off his backpack and opened it, looking for something. I wanted him to hurry up and relay the appropriate gestures and sounds, so that I could just make them and get away from this sight. As he took his time to find what he was looking for, the severed leg appeared to prance towards me, alive. How had it been separated from the wolf's body? Where and in what condition was the rest of the wolf? An image of the wolf's tortured face formed in my mind and stuck there.

Just as I was about to ask my father if wolves were like coyotes, whom he'd told me would chew off their own legs to escape from traps, he pulled out a sketch pad and a charcoal crayon. He slid off his thick mittens and, holding the charcoal gracefully, began to sketch the wolf leg and trap. I swallowed my question, because I knew then that the only answer to every question in the wilderness was: Take note.

My father's careful attention to violence has been my way of understanding how men act. But Sam doesn't have a lust for wilderness. He was content to be engaged at a distance in the science of the tsunami; my father would have wanted to witness the event. That's probably why he left my mother and her canoe-sized passions. He wanted the sea. A lake would not dare a tsunami.

It has been two months since the great wave struck. The outpouring of goodwill and money has been unprecedented, to the extent that some agencies have asked people to stop sending donations. Rebuilding is underway. People are recovering their lives. The water contamination and cholera outbreaks that early predictions warned of simply did not occur. Apart from this evening my handwashing has become less frequent.

One night last week, when Sam arrived home late from work, I groggily mentioned my latest visit with Señora Ormaza, who appeared to have fully recovered from her bout with diarrhea. "I was worried I would lose her," I said, trying to make conversation with him, wanting to appear awake despite the late hour.

"People are funny," he said. As he slid into bed beside me, I considered why he thought this made people funny. His touch, as he rubbed my back, made my skin tingle.

"Why?" I rolled over to face him.

"You know, it's ironic, after all the fear, all the threats of the death toll doubling with diseases following the wave, the only viruses that seem to be proliferating are computer viruses. Hackers have been targeting the donation sites." His voice slurred slightly. I thought he had drifted off to sleep, but he continued, "Viruses don't like to be predicted . . . or tracked."

"They are wild," I said, as a cadence to his idea.

"Mmm hmm," he said and his breathing deepened. He was soon asleep.

The morning after, I was at the convent, where Señora Ormaza looked and sounded robust. She asked me to sit awhile and play a board game with her. She pointed to a Spanish version of Snakes and Ladders, called, roughly translated, "The Healthy Goose." As I set it up on her bed, I told her I welcomed a chance to beat someone at a game, because I always lose to Sam, who is luckier and much quicker at strategic thinking. We chatted on and off throughout an entire game in which it seemed that she had only ladders, while I slid perpetually backwards. She asked me more questions about my *hombre*, as she called him, and I told her that I barely saw him these days, that he had been working late.

She stopped her green marker in a climb upwards and looked at me. "Maybe you need to have a real home," she said, apropos of nothing.

We continued with the game until she became tired and Sister Maria came to pray with her. I left and strolled home at twilight, knowing I had the evening to write.

I thought about when we first arrived in Santiago de Compostela and were looking for a place to live. We had wanted to stay near to the university, for Sam's sake. We drove around the area and ran across one of Santiago's few poor districts, a housing estate known as Barrio de Vite-Vista Alegre. If anything could be called a ghetto in the richness of Santiago, it was this estate, populated mostly by migrant Romany. We slowed to look. Teenagers with nothing to do and visibly distinct from their counterparts in the old town, glared at us as we drove by the apartment complex. The glares were intended to ward off intruders, protecting something they had that we didn't.

"They're hiding," Sam said as we inched forward, and only now do I wonder if he might have been relating their behaviour to Thomas's, before he disappeared. "Smack looks like a good mood from the outside," he said as we idled in front of a For Rent sign, and then he made a scoffing noise that translated as, *you'll never see me living in a place like that*. We drove on.

I became more and more anxious about being back in Spain and was hard on Sam, erratic at times, arguing with him about the smallest thing, like a rattling window in one otherwise acceptable apartment that he thought was suitable, but which felt too much like the rattling of my nerves. "It's not safe, Damn it!" I yelled after he had insisted it was the best of the lot we'd seen. Sam calmly moved on to the next place. When we finally found this apartment up high above the cathedral we were both relieved. It's a renovation of an older building and reminds me of the good things in all of the places I've ever lived: the wooden beam across the ceiling is like the one in my grandmother's house near Flinton; the view reminds me of my father's Parisian apartment in Montmartre; there are the layered generations of architecture, masonry, and pastiche design that remind me of London; the Maasai warrior dagger hanging on the wall is the one that was given to Sam upon leaving Kenya; and there is this desk—its cylindrical oak legs and the thick, smooth top make it as solid as a whole home to live within. And that is what I do. I live inside this desk and now inside the story. Sam seems to be living at the lab, so I think we are both as much at home as possible.

With Sam's late evenings I have had more time, but have felt guilty for neglecting my research. When we got home from the party tonight, I asked him if there was anything I should be brushing up on in terms of Spanish translations or other issues related to his work. He told me that he was fine, felt covered, but then handed me a journal and said that if I wanted something to study the really hot topic was the mutation of viruses that initially are transmitted only among animals but become transmitted from animal to human and then human to human. The H_5N_1 avian influenza is caused by one such virus. Until now, the virus has largely been confined to certain bird species, but that may be changing. Scientists believe the bird flu might be carried by ducks. How clever of a virus to attach itself to a species that migrates throughout the world.

What I have been able to find out from this pathology journal is that influenza viruses contain eight genes, composed of RNA and packaged loosely in protective proteins. Influenza reproduces sloppily; its genes fall apart, and it can absorb different genetic material and get mixed up in a process called reassortment. When influenza successfully infects a new species—say, pigs—it can reassort, and may switch from being an avian virus to a mammalian one. When that occurs, a human epidemic can result. The transmission cycles and the constant evolution are key to influenza's continued survival, for were it to remain identical year after year most animals would develop immunity and the flu would die out. But viruses, it seems, know how to step on.

It's odd being up this late, but the party, viruses, and my story are all roaming, unbridled, in my mind. Usually when Sam gets home at night I am asleep, because I find it difficult to write after eating. I watch some television to keep my Spanish proficiency, I read what I can tolerate of the news from the Internet, and then I go to bed. Sam slips in beside me sometimes after midnight. Some nights his skin is warm, his mouth dry, and if I do manage to speak to him his speech is so slurred with sleep that he barely answers. Or other nights his humour shines through, his tired voice making observations about my tendency to talk in my sleep. He rolls me over and kisses my collarbone, beginning at the left shoulder and moving down towards the centre of my chest, then up again towards the opposite shoulder. He is playful and gentle like a lake otter. He seeks me out to frolic with, slide into; his body lithe and firm. He is not a wolf so wild that even a trap could not contain him. When he falls asleep I am blessed with serenity.

The sky is lightening. Dawn is not yellow now, as it is in April. A February dawn in Galicia is a forsaken green, like an unfurled fern just before decay. These dawns are the end of a harsh winter.

I must get some sleep, even though Marcus and Gavin are not sleeping. No, they are wide awake. And I am in pursuit of them, walking in reverse along the Camino. In our way we all are. Stepping. On.

Fifteen

I had walked from Logroño back towards the Rioja Valley, guessing that they would be moving towards me, but that first night, as I found myself far from any town, with no idea where I'd spend the night, and having passed one lone pilgrim on a bicycle coming towards me, I quickly made an about face and returned in the blackness after midnight to Logroño, checked into a hotel, and re-examined my strategy. What had I been thinking would happen? That I'd casually come across them, warn Marcus about an inkling of danger I couldn't even articulate?

Yes.

That foolishness is only now obvious.

I stayed in Logroño for two days, checking the albergue, the refugio, and the local pensiones, and sitting in the main square, where all pilgrims inevitably show up. Provided my timing had been right. But it hadn't been. I had to rethink my plans, and found myself on a coach. I travelled into the mountainous landscape of Villafranca, and arrived in the city of Burgos, certain that they had not yet passed through. Two days in Burgos and my certainty dissolved. I lost faith in my purpose. Burgos is a big city crammed with monuments and cars. I stayed close to the cathedral, thinking they might pass by there, but then began to worry that they wouldn't make it this far at all. Gavin might have harmed Marcus and fled by now, or he could be waiting to do it in Santiago. But why? I sat in the main square and wrote a description of Marcus I thought of giving to the police. The description, I realized, was of a man who I was now seeing as a ruffian, someone who would stand out in staid, conservative Burgos, which had a reputation for being proud of Franco's reign. I decided not to approach the police. I was floundering. I had no idea what they would do or where they were, so I merely set off, in the direction of Santiago, all on my own, hoping to learn their whereabouts along the way.

The mountains challenged me. I was learning something about my body that I wasn't able to define. I stepped on. And meanwhile, so did they.

※

Constanza had desired him as though with claws, breathlessly and with certainty, and he had looked after her, but the truth was that he'd become bored with her. Marcus stood near the door of the bookstore in Burgos and watched Gavin as he talked to the voluptuous woman who ran the shop. A nicety-nice woman whose unattainability was like the ache of centuries. He overheard Gavin speaking softly, heard her name—Martina—and her perfect English as she revealed the fact that she was a descendant of Ferdinand III. Gavin seemed impressed as he leaned forward to listen. She was more his type, but then why was Gavin wasting time with him? She told him about the twelfth-century Monasterio de las Huelgas Reales. Bollocks, Marcus thought. She went on to describe in detail the final resting place of much of Castilian royalty. Marcus turned and walked out of the shop.

A few minutes later Gavin hurried out in search of him. "She's elegant," Gavin told him as they walked towards the Camino.

"Is that right?" Marcus said, sarcastically. "I don't usually stop here long. Got no time for kings and their bastards."

"What I meant was her facility with language, her culture . . . a grace—"

"Ya, I know you did." He walked faster, with quick-tempered self-contempt. Mix-the-match-that-melts-me-flat. There were still things about the connection between him and Gavin that reminded him of Lacey, but Lacey would never have fallen for show.

Gavin stopped. "We should talk . . . I've been thinking . . . ," and then he tried to catch up. "Are you trained?"

"Trained?" Marcus said over his shoulder.

"As a painter?"

Marcus turned with amazement at this man who for some reason would not be shaken. "Why are you asking me that?"

"Just wondering. When you said you wanted to do something more—"

"What's that got to do with it?" And Marcus could feel himself slowing down, despite himself, with merely the image of the sweep-wipe-dab pleasure on canvas making him weak to suggestion.

"I was thinking maybe I could help you . . . if you're good, that is, I know people, galleries . . . ," and finally Gavin could sense the hook he needed. *This*, he thought, and for a moment he felt sure he'd found the way to make it all right. "You seem to have been given the wrong end of the stick. I have friends who could invest—"

"You've seen my work." Marcus felt he'd sounded too defensive.

"Where?"

"My room," but that sounded too intimate. "Look, let's get moving. I don't like this town."

Hours later he was still moving forward, forward being enough. As they passed among the deciduous trees of a small forest, he stopped, turned and joked effortlessly with Gavin, who continued to trail behind. He pointed to the plaque that announced the jail that had held Franco's political prisoners.

"My kind of place, that," but that too was overly chummy, a territory he never let anyone into. Gavin's face was stony. Marcus turned and walked, hooked ever-so-slightly on promise.

The flatland returned. At the top of a rise he paused to take in the interminable plain. Treeless, immense, and circled above by kestrels, while in the shrubs the strong wind battled with the song of larks. He listened.

They met few others on the trail, but when they did, and they shared a travellers' data exchange, he knew these strangers thought that Gavin was his mate, and surprisingly there was pleasure in that. Friends were a marker of a man's worth. The man's attention seemed meant for a reason, to include him, and so he walked.

Brushes of broom and widowed grasses, he thought, as his feet mashed down on the terrain of the Meseta.

I need to consider what I have just written. The last paragraphs have taken me by surprise and flowed uncomfortably from my fingers. If friends are a marker of a man's worth, then what are the signposts leading to Sam? He has many colleagues, acquaintances, people he plays sports with, goes for a drink with, but he has never spoken of any of them being close. I am his best friend, which makes me proud. But perhaps a man also needs other men? When he stays late at the lab, as he does every night now, do he and Paolo take time to get to know one another?

I must find out.

Sixteen

"Paolo?" Sam said this morning, as he was leaving for the lab, in response to my question about intimate friends. "Paolo's wife must not let him talk at home, because he talks at me all day." He turned the handle on the front door, but before he left he looked back. "I think it's good for my Spanish," he said with a smile that I knew meant that I was all he needed. It soothed me. He left and I began to work. But *all day*? Does Paolo not talk as much at night?

I must return to my story.

From where I last left them, I know what the trek over the next few days must have been like for Marcus and Gavin. I had walked that terrain myself, just ahead of them, without knowing I was doing so at the time. The plains, the dull constancy of the horizon. Cloudy skies. Rain. Blazing sun. The days spun the meteorology wheel and came up with something new one after the other. The Camino itself was dull, with the don't-blink-or-you'll-miss-them villages, leading to the hopefully named Calle Mayor.

I imagine that Marcus must have taken the lead most days, when he would feel the familiar path in his legs, the long strides that might have said, *each year, there is something else that comes with this*. On other days, Gavin would have led, striding, head down, into any weather, any company, any landscape, and on these days he must have seemed like the man to follow, the fork in the road that Marcus had chosen.

❧

Despite it being the most bleak section of the Camino, the meseta—bold, big, barren—always felt like a break from the rest. Marcus enjoyed travelling across this cracked dune and its lack of colour. The emptiness of the last few days had given him dreamless nights, a plunge into sweet, meet-the-dark exhaustion. He had no craving for alcohol and had smoked only two cigarettes. Constanza was not around to sap his strength. His hair was growing fast. Even his desire to paint had weakened. These were the things that the walk always brought.

One stretch was a nasty patch. The exhaust-choked road beside them ran like a broken rail track through the think-thought verses of his mind. He had led all day, and walking on the meseta had felt like walking in a floodlit underworld. Few trees in sight. The wind a persistent howl. He touched his ribs. There was no pain or tenderness.

He looked up into the sky as he massaged the muscle of his lower back. A desperate buzzard circled. He stopped walking at the top of a hill as the sun scraped like a razor on the back of his neck. He raised his arms and stretched out the leg muscles that had pulled him up this rise to the view of León in the distance, spreading like melting blocks out onto the dry plains. Beyond it there was a severe climb, he knew, as he took in the snow-tipped Monte León and, further, the Cordillera Cantábrica.

"I can't breathe," Gavin said as he reached his side. Husking, chaffing breaths came from him and made Marcus smile, but he resisted laughter, as Gavin released his arms from his backpack and threw it on the ground.

"Bend over, breathe between your legs," he said, noticing that Gavin was jumpy again, his hand reaching behind his ear in a familiar slap at an invisible insect.

Gavin did as he suggested, and after a few moments, with the sun hissing like a spark, he sat down in the dirt, keeping his eyes on his boots, his breathing less laboured yet still gritty. "It's enough. This. I don't know if I could bear . . ."

"Bear what?"

"What I thought . . . I needed so much to—"

"It was never going to be a holiday, if that's what you mean," Marcus said quickly. Control and repair.

"Not to walk . . . To talk to you," Gavin added.

This seemed true; they had barely spoken, and what if the man had really only needed a friend all this time? Gavin slapped behind his ear again—he was that caged thing again, like he'd been in Pamplona, Marcus thought. "Let's find some shelter, sure," he said, and felt sorry for Gavin, who, sifting air, then reached out with his hand to be helped up. Marcus took the hand. Gavin rose and picked up his backpack.

Marcus thought of Constanza's hands on his thighs. He tried to keep Constanza's hands on his thighs, but they dissolved and were replaced by the corner of Gavin's mouth—a millimetre of top lip that jutted ever so slightly over the bottom. He'd noticed it early on, but now he found himself fixed on it. The man had a hold on him, protective in a way similar to Lacey, but softer, more like the Danish man in Barcelona.

Marcus had been eighteen—a riff-raff swagger of a boy who had recently run away from London and his legacy at the bulging pit of Peterhead—and was now reeling from the not-gently closed door at Miguel's home. The dad-you-can't-call-me-dad mistake that would not allow him to return to London to face his mother, and no one else would care if he did or not. But Spain could still hide him. The Danish man was older, tall, like Gavin, and had a similar urgency about him. They had explored the darkness of the Gracia quarter. The man had introduced him to Spanish cubist painters, and had told him he was in love with him. Marcus had reeled and fled, even though he had learned from Lacey that love was not as simple as the emotion he had grown up believing he would never have. He hadn't known what to do with his own feelings then, but maybe he would now.

He stood and opened his shirt to the wind, letting it caress his ribs. Suddenly a noise rose out of Gavin's backpack.

꙳

An annoying, ecstatic chirp, growing louder and louder, adding to the suffocating heat, the grating sun, the dreadful dry plain spread out in front of him. At least this noise wasn't from inside him. Gavin tried to steady his hand as he put the pack on the ground again and rummaged through it for the twittering telephone. He had turned it on again in Burgos. The message from Porter's wife had sounded urgent, and the last few days without reception had torture underscoring it, with the lack of champagne-glass signals on the phone's face making his neck sting again and again.

He looked at Marcus as he held the phone up to see where the call was from.

"It's your broker," Marcus chimed, "Sell!"

Gavin pressed the answer button. "Gavin here," he said quietly, but had to repeat himself to be heard above the whistle of the wind. He listened. He looked at the phone. His arm dropped.

That was it then.

He had failed.

He lifted the phone to his ear again. "Thanks. Yep. Goodbye." The press of a button ended the call. He thought he would lose control of his bowels. *This* . . . and he grabbed his stomach as the cramp hit him and bent over again, his hand reaching for the dry ground, the sun punishing, the wind unrelenting.

"What's up?" He heard Marcus's voice near his ear. The man was crouched beside him. Now, he thought. He could take out the knife and ask him to hold it and he could just fall on it; from here, this low, it would work. He looked up. Marcus's face looked hot with concern.

"You okay?" Marcus asked.

"Mm . . ." Gavin mumbled, nodding. *Now.* "The person I know . . . the one who was dying. He's dead."

"Sorry . . ." Marcus said. Gavin felt a hand on his back. He couldn't hear himself think for the howl of the wind. The sky was off-kilter. The sun liquid.

"Were you close?" Marcus's hand slid along his back towards the far shoulder. Gavin almost laughed. He shook his head, and there, again, was Scotland.

In a small room at the police station in Dundee he is alone with two officers with yellow teeth and tobacco breath. He has given a description. Yes, he says. Him, he says of the spongy-haired boy. Yes, a skirmish, he says, as Porter has instructed him to say. Use that word—skirmish—Porter had hissed. Porter is in a similar room down the hall and they will both finger the spongy-haired boy.

Later, in the dormitory, Gavin packs his bags because his parents are waiting to take him from this place of death, this place where delinquent boys go for rehabilitation but where there is death along the ridge of one of the highest ranges in the country and irresponsible boys are left alone with one timid junior supervisor to get them back to the school. No Department of Corrections will allow this kind of residential school to flourish, so they are transferring some of the boys and giving the better-behaved boys a reduced term.

Gavin is one of the lucky ones, especially as he has cooperated. He will go free, while he will never really be it. Not with Porter's threat that he will kill him if he says another word about the incident to anyone. No chance of that. Gavin will not talk about anything that has to do with these last months of his life. He will swallow back each syllable of the truth and it will be plunged back down his throat just as Sir plunged down the cliff. He will never speak of this event again. Never again.

Until now.

"I ran out on my fiancé," he said quietly, and he heard his own begging inflection. He didn't look up, had to keep his eyes down so that it would happen as he'd imagined it in the days tripping up to this moment.

"But that was nothing. I don't think I ever spoke a true word to her. Ever," he continued. It wasn't coming out right. He didn't mean it literally. If he continued this way he'd never get it done. Marcus deserved to hear everything, though, so he wanted to find a place to start. "I love her," he added. He felt Marcus shift, the hand fall off his back.

He looked up and stared again at the baked, risen face. How could he have damned it so easily? "Justice," Martin had said when he was released from the Borstal, "is based on witnesses not hearsay, and so you're right to tell them what you saw." Martin's justice had been just another blind bully.

He sat up straight. He closed his eyes and there it all was again.

The rain has diminished to mist. He sees the bushes rustling out of the corner of his eye, as he and Porter sneak up behind Sir. Porter moves ahead, but he stops, looks left, and thinks he spots a small head appear over the Bearberry, its dark eyes see him, this, everything. The eyes are shocked, and it's this shock that he thinks he can count on.

Now Marcus was fidgeting beside him, looking to the ground, then out to the horizon. Marcus wiped sweat from his forehead, flapped his open shirt, adjusted his collar.

"I came here to find you."

The flinch in Marcus was unmistakable. In one jerky motion Marcus got to his feet, but kept his eyes on the plain. Gavin couldn't move. Words were in his legs, his chest, his arms . . . his mouth.

"It was Porter's lead, always was. Even now . . . He was loose. Evil . . . I'd say even that. Nothing could touch him. He'd said it would just be a scare, just a little fun with Sir, that's all, the way kids strike back. Just getting even. Kids know what's fair and unfair . . . it was about that, when I look back . . . So, we decided—Porter decided—on a prank. At least I thought it was. We snuck up behind Sir on the ridge and the plan was to rush him, terrify him, make him know what it felt like, but he turned round before we got close enough, and he started to yell, we were caught out, humiliated, I stopped, but Porter, he rushed forward just as he'd said we would. I couldn't help it, felt like I was attached to him by a rope, was just drawn along behind him, didn't have the power that he had, he didn't stop, I thought he was going mad, he let go a vicious sound, like a growl, he knocked Sir to the ground, I couldn't believe how that happened, Sir was so much bigger, and I thought there was a demon in Porter, bigger than everything and everyone, and so I followed along, then he was hollering at me to come over, I tried to pull Porter away, but Sir flipped him over and started to beat Porter in the head, holding him down by the neck, punching, and it was then, just one second, as he held up his arm for one more blow that my hand stopped him, but he was off guard, and lost his balance, and he toppled over, and fell on his side, his shoulders just out over the edge. Porter sat up, and I remember thinking that his face didn't look touched even though it'd been beaten. Porter grabbed Sir's legs and pushed him over the edge. I watched. Sir bounced off the wall of the cliff below us and tumbled down, his body like a dummy, splayed and ragged, he bounced and tumbled, and screamed and screamed, over and over, lower and lower, until there was no sound."

He looked up at Marcus, the sun blinding him, the flashback glaring before him. Marcus shifted his weight, his silhouette so obviously the boy rising to the top of the ridge all those years ago. Gavin was incapable of going further, of speaking of those moments at the police station.

"You have to turn me in," was all there was left to say. A buzzard circled in the distance, spiralling in an updraft.

He watched as Marcus's hand rose and hovered near his thigh. Those fingers moved again, as he'd seen them on the ground at the bull ring, as though he were playing the keys of a piano. Two, three . . . Gavin held his breath . . . four. The hand fell to the man's side. *This* . . . and he could feel the beginning of release, but he knew there was more to come. At least now Marcus would know why he'd done it. There had been no escaping Porter. He touched his hair; it was hot from the excruciating sun. He looked out towards the yellow, unflinching plains.

"What?" Marcus barked finally, but didn't wait for the answer. He pivoted and walked off. Gavin stood up, stiffly. His knee gave in just slightly and his ankle turned.

"I'm begging you!" he hollered after the diminishing figure.

※

"Bred by liars," Miguel had said. "No, not liars, hiders. Worse. You don't know where to find the truth." Miguel had been the one to arrive at the Borstal when the police had requested all the parents on site, while his mother had stayed in Ladbroke Grove and had started to behave like her mother . . . just a nip, a sip, a snip of the heart. Miguel had dutifully shown up and had gone into a tirade about "that side of the family."

The other boys had accused him. "We saw him coming back down the ridge just as we heard the scream," one of them had said to the warden with the protruding nose hair. By the time the boys assembled at the bottom of the ridge before the bus took them back to Spiers, he had already become the prime suspect. The two older boys, who had been up ahead of him, blazing up the trail as only the most accomplished of hikers could manage—the kind of boy he had decided he would become, the kind of boy Miguel would have wanted—had somehow arrived at the bottom long before him, so when all the wagging fingers were pointed his way, his guilt, his inadequacy, his slowness, his lack of accomplishment was obvious even to him. The headmaster came to take the others back in the bus, while he and the one other black boy were taken separately, in the police wagon, back to the station. Question after question.

None of that was as bad as what had come from Miguel. Miguel had cried that first night, alone with Marcus in the boys' dorm as they waited for the police to question everyone. "What are you crying for?" he'd asked the stay-with-it-if-it's-easy Miguel, as the man rubbed a tear into his cheek.

"You can't help it, can you?" Miguel said to the shivering Marcus, who shook his head, wanting to agree with the man who was acting like a dad, but he didn't understand what he was agreeing to. Miguel began to speak in Spanish, but Marcus could understand the meaning if not the words themselves: Miguel was crying for his own son, his real son in San Sebastian, the son he was betraying by being in England with Miriam and the half-caste bastard. And Marcus knew there and then that this was the last they would see of Miguel.

Charges were laid and the only facilities for juveniles were at Peterhead, the hell of Aberdeen, and, even there, the tiny ward for juveniles was full. He waited for trial in a cell at the end of a line of steeled, raucous men—*Hey you! Chocolate arse!*—and absorbed the shit-cum-porridge smell, and sank into the mattress that was as firm as damp loo paper. Then in the canteen Lacey had said, "Ya play chess?" and looked at him like he understood what hell was.

There had been no evidence against him except the word of the other boys, so after the body was recovered the police declared the death an accident, and he was released, only to be sent to another Borstal, closer to London, for a year before he was released for good.

Now Gavin had flung him back into a moment he could almost recall, like a word waiting to be discovered by a sentence being written. He could feel the dip in temperature upon taking the final step to the top of the ridge, and he could hear something rather than see it. Voices, a rush of air. No faces in particular, just the paleness of anger. He'd turned back, down the path. The boys on their way up had rushed towards the scream, but he had been frightened by it. He had been the new boy, sorry for being there, sorry to his mother, sorry to Miguel and everyone he had continued to disappoint. He hadn't seen anything. It's what he told everyone who had asked. He hadn't seen anything.

The pin-prickle heat was making a wound. He walked. And thought of how, after he had been released from the second Borstal, Miriam had said, *You leave me too, it was you who made him leave,* as she swayed with the drink inside her. He had spent a wayward two years in London, living on the dole, shivering in a bedsit, until he'd taken a lift in the back of a friend-of-a-friend's lorry that took him across two borders, to San Sebastian. He had needed to see Miguel's face, needed to feel if it had an opening for him, but the face was bulbous, blackened, and hard like an iron pan.

"Why'd you come here, boy?" the face had hissed. Marcus had left a day later, with no answer to that question.

Now, as he edged a double-laned road outside Mansilla, only a pathetic strip of bramble protected him from the bullying lorries and the overloaded family vehicles. He spat on the ground, kicked the insulting brambles and propelled the stray stones so far that they pinged onto a car's bonnet. He didn't stop walking until the sun was low and he had trekked the last miserable kilometres to León.

When he looked back, he saw that Gavin had dragged his sorry arse along behind him, struggling with every step, his body hunched over. They entered the open square of León, and Marcus slowed in the Plaza de Santo Domingo. Gavin drew up beside him.

"Here, please," Gavin said, as he pointed to a café.

It could be here: ten . . . nine . . . eight . . . seven. . . . Marcus thought as his fingers folded in a countdown towards a fist, but he wanted to hear more, so he pulled out a chair at a table. They sat in the shade. A waiter served them, bringing coffee almost immediately.

The bells of the great cathedral of León rang out. Marcus dipped his head, waiting for them to stop. Gavin looked anxiously about the square, searching, until he seemed to pick out a particular building with elaborate balconies.

"We could stay in town . . . over there. . . . I think we could both use some comfort tonight," Gavin said, pointing to the modest, classical sign of the Husa Alfonso V. Marcus couldn't take his eyes off Gavin's reddening ears.

"You do, do you?" he replied, in as neutral a voice as he could manage . . . six . . . five . . . four . . .

Gavin looked relieved to have elicited words from him and took his wallet out of his pocket, placing it on the table like a marker.

"We could clean up, have a good meal," Gavin waited for a reaction, "and then talk more—"

"Talk? You want to talk?" He sat forward, flattened his fingers on the table, holding his hand back from the rising fury . . . three . . . two . . . one . . . that would knock the man's teeth into his guts. He felt like he himself had eaten something sharp—a mirror. No, a window shattered upon closing.

He sat still, his face giving away nothing.

"Then talk," he said.

Gavin sat back in the chair and took a sip of his coffee. "I was used by Porter," Gavin said, and Marcus watched how Gavin propped his eyelids open with his thumb and forefinger as though the lids were too heavy to stay open on their own.

"If you turn me in, it won't be Porter, it won't be everything that's right—I waited too long—but it will be close," Gavin said finally.

"Oh Christ," Marcus said. How pathetic. "And why don't you do it yourself?"

"I can't . . . I've tried. I have tried. Before I came to Spain. I couldn't. I'd been fine just not looking at it, just fine. I asked Kate to marry me, Porter called me, and then it all became too loud." Gavin started to tremble.

"Too loud?"

Gavin shook his head.

"You didn't consider telling the truth before that?"

"Porter would have killed me. You were the only witness. Porter—you saw him."

"You say Porter is dead." Marcus pumped a fist. *Rock, paper, rock, paper, rock.* "So you're free." The cage-rage memory of the Borstal came back. The longing for his mother and Miguel. But when he thought of anything else—trying to see who had been on the ridge when he arrived—he drew a smoking blank. He knew there was something behind the smoke. He just couldn't see it.

"It's a matter of principle, of honour. It's the right thing. You have to—"

"I have to do fuck all!" he hollered, and struck his fist onto the melamine tabletop. The woman at the next table shunted her chair closer to her companion's.

He stood, took a five-euro note from his pocket and threw it on the table, turned, and walked away.

Roman arches. The grand market flanked by the monasteries and palaces of those throughout history who took all they could get their hands on. León's sour-smelling alleys had a mausoleum lull. He couldn't place the stench. As he reached the cliff of the León cathedral, with its massive rose window and flying buttresses like barmy toys, he turned to see if Gavin had followed.

He had.

More tight alleys and cramped ideas, and then a high-octane road crossing. He trod across a manicured plaza garden and arrived at the Parador San Marcos. The hotel was adorned by a St. James sculpted in the saint's finest hour. With Gavin scrambling in tow several metres behind, he walked through the soaring arched entrance. A man in a pinstriped suit, mauve shirt, and a polka-dot tie on his way out of the hotel passed by him followed by a golden blonde woman in a short peach dress and mauve high heels that matched the man's shirt. Pushing through the revolving doors, Marcus didn't look back to check on Gavin, but heard the cool tones of the stocky doorman's greeting repeated a few seconds later.

At the reception desk, he asked the manager for two rooms. "The best," he specified. The thin man bristled, asking him if he had a reservation. "Of course not, we're pilgrims," he replied with the fire from his belly. When Gavin arrived beside him, Marcus stepped to the side, and nodded to them both, indicating that they should take over the details from there. He slipped off his backpack and said loudly, "The best room, I insist," before removing himself to the lobby and flopping onto a sofa.

In the plush room he felt immediately for his blistered toes—wiggling them inside his hiking boots. The crack-of-a-whip pace had hurt. He threw down his pack. As he turned to head into the bathroom, he heard a knock on the door.

"What?" he asked as he opened it to the looming, begging Gavin.

"I told the police it was you . . . your name then . . . I pointed you out and told them it was you. 'David Williams,' I said when they asked me if I was sure."

Hot ash in his throat, Marcus grabbed Gavin and shoved the bastard against the wall just inside the entrance to the room. Gavin unravelled, let it all happen.

"Fuck you!" Marcus shouted, and pushed him again, slamming his back into the wall much harder this time. Gavin came to life with the glow of reward, which enraged Marcus even more. A punch rose from his gut, up through his chest and, fuck you, his fist met Gavin's face. He heard a crunch in his fingers but felt only the burning that rose up from throat to lips. He spat.

Gavin wiped away the saliva but lowered his hand again, leaving his face exposed, inviting Marcus with his eyes to hit him again. Marcus struck hard, into his cheek. They fell towards one another, Marcus lowering a one-two punch to the kidneys, Gavin not even attempting to block. The other man's submission was so complete it exhausted Marcus, who threw another punch at the chin and fell towards him, then quickly pushed himself away.

"Fuck you!" he said again, disgusted, panting. He looked at Gavin's face and watched it swelling as the man began to sob.

"I came to tell you: I want to make it up to you."

Breathing. Listening.

"I could kill you," Marcus said and he pushed Gavin out the

door, turned, and slammed the door shut behind him. He sat down on the bed, gulping for air.

❦

He couldn't stop them, these hot tears. He ran the bath water to mask the sound of weeping. He looked at himself in the mirror and saw red becoming purple, a growing plum around his eye. He touched his nose. It might have been broken, but that didn't matter. What mattered was that there had been no blood. With this disappointment, the tears came steadily. Blood would have made a difference, would have marked him. A price would have been exacted from him. He was still not free.

Shouldn't he be locked away, cut off from everything he had once wanted? He stripped off his clothes. Shouldn't Marcus be given another chance? He sprinkled the bath lotion from the bottle provided on the shelf into the water and watched the foam rise, letting the sobs rise from his gut into his chest, through his swelling lips. He got into the tub and lay in the water, allowing the suds to take over.

Would being locked away bring back desire for everything he couldn't have? He watched his floating penis. He pictured Kate's firm breasts . . . Nothing. He turned off the water. He thought he heard sounds from Marcus's room next door. The television news was on, the volume turned up loud, and from the tone of the presenter's voice, he was announcing something dramatic. *Please.* There might be one last chance that Marcus's fury would take him to the police, or there was still the knife, but there was also a small part of him that still believed what Martin had said. He had been whisked away from the Borstal, told by his father that he was in their custody now, and after weeks of an illness that had felt like the end of his life, he had resurfaced well enough to return to studies, overseen by Martin, whom he overheard one day telling his mother that the whole incident had been cleared up now, it had all been a tragic accident.

    He pulled the plug and the bath water began to drain.

Seventeen

If the relentlessly evolving H5N1 virus becomes capable of human-to-human transmission, develops the contagious power typical of influenza, and maintains its virulence, humanity could well face a pandemic unlike any other witnessed before.

Or nothing at all could happen.

"Evolution knows how the joke ends, we don't," said Sam today, as he sipped Coke at lunch. I had surprised him at the lab with a picnic, and we sat out on the grassy hill behind the psychology building. He'd looked uncomfortable when I turned up—I suppose because the lab was so chaotic and untidy—and he was eager to get out, saying it was a lovely day and that we should take in some fresh air. It was far too hot to sit in the now burgeoning spring sun, so we found a tree and accepted its shade. I was nervous around him. I had conflicting feelings about where my tracking of Marcus and Gavin was leading me, how at that point I had not taken into account just how damaged Marcus must have been by his history. As for my role in that story: I was suspended, lost, and melting in the heat along the meseta, with neither man in sight, desperate to find them and attach myself to the intrigue I knew was going on. At lunch I didn't know how to talk to Sam. We seem to be leading separate lives.

"Have you talked to the olive vendor's son recently?" I asked.

He looked at me as though it had been an odd yet astute question. "Why do you ask?"

"Just making conversation," I said, uncomfortable with my faux pas. His face turned sad again, and I couldn't trace the reason or think of how to help.

"He's thinking of moving. With his father dead, this place doesn't tie him down. He's free . . . lucky guy," he said as he gazed out. I fidgeted. I waited for a joke that might lighten us, but it didn't come. I resorted to what I knew worked and returned to the topic of the H5N1. I wanted him to explain why nothing at all might happen. "Isn't a pandemic inevitable?" I asked as I unwrapped our sandwiches.

"Influenza is a sloppy, mutation-prone pathogen that keeps scientists from smugness," he said with certainty. I couldn't help but think of the complacency denied writers who don't know why their characters behave in certain ways. Absolute uncertainty is difficult for people like Sam. I often wonder how Gavin and Sam would have got on. Would Sam be like me, or Marcus, in the downdraft of Gavin's need? He might have paid him no attention at all. But if I look at Marcus and his hardened stoicism, I see that he and Sam might have had something in common.

I want Marcus to have seen Gavin's repentance, but is that just because of what Gavin and I share? I have to delve into the choices I made as we approached Santiago.

I was making my way. I had run into more pilgrims now, as the season picked up momentum with the gentleness of May. I had trekked with determination out of the meseta and up onto the misty mountain passes, where, out of the haze, there would emerge a figure walking slowly in front of me like a zombie from a B movie. I would offer a hello in Spanish or English, and usually overtake them, as I had a specific mission, and was not walking for contemplation.

Or so I thought. But something settled in my ankles, calves, my thighs, pushing itself up from the earth through my toes and beyond. A purposeless momentum took over slowly as I trekked along the ram's horn–shaped Cordillera Cantábrica, which curled down from Asturias. The Camino rides the back of their quartzite, schist, slate, and sandstone foothills, and the trek can feel like a hoax, like walking on the back of a prehistoric beast, getting nowhere but deeper into its skeleton. I felt bare as the weather and terrain took up their places in me. When I talked to people it seemed to be from a place between my toes. I met some who didn't care to talk at all, and we'd walk together and arrive at the next albergue and say goodnight, and never see one another again. People spoke mostly from their toes or between their teeth, I noticed, but I began to map the site of certain words. Home sat in the collarbone; bread in the cheeks; and tomorrow in the belly. I began to enjoy these little encounters, which almost took my mind off Marcus altogether, but the Cordillera Cantábrica path at times was so steep that I needed to preserve breath for the effort, and discerning the placement of words in the sternum, ear, or forehead lost all interest. Silence was a good companion. I realize now that all of that stepping on felt very much like stillness. I might even have been growing smug with contentment, feeling virtuous about my detachment.

But then I met Claire and she challenged this detachment. She stumbled towards the refugio in the village of El Ganso just before me. I had followed her for several kilometres, our paces similar as we both climbed with great effort out of Astorga. I had watched how she would stop, look down as if to watch something moving at her feet, then continue striding on without looking at the ground at all. I watched her pause on the ridge with views of Astorga and the valleys next to it. She touched her stomach, then her thighs, and I could tell that she was gauging the effects of the climb on the few extra pounds she seemed to be carrying.

She looked tired when she arrived in El Ganso, but she almost danced towards the refugio as though into its arms. There was a man there, apparently waiting for her. She took off her pack when she reached him and took out a tangle of thick elastic straps and tried to put them on the man's head, giggling in the effort and at his reluctance.

As I drew up beside them, the man took off the headband, which appeared to have a small lamp fastened to it, and he went on to discuss with her the following day's trek to the Cruz de Hierro, the iron cross that marks the highest point on the Camino. I was surprised to learn where exactly I was. I had been obliviously following the route, obsessed by my own muscles and drawn in by the landscape and the sky. I introduced myself to them both, though I had little interest in Andy, who noticed this and drifted off to let us get acquainted.

"I never realized I didn't have to be good," Claire said, startling me, after a tepid introduction and a few niceties.

"What do you mean?" I asked.

"Being good . . . it's irrelevant," she said, then looked to the ground as if in search of something to show me. When she looked up again, her face seemed younger. I had guessed her to be in her twenties, but she became childlike.

"You mean on a pilgrimage?" I wanted her to keep talking.

"Everywhere. I used to think that if I got sick, or angry, or numb... even numb... that I wouldn't be good, and that good mattered." She rubbed her foot in the ground, excited by what she'd said. I thought the earth might spark.

"Is that what you've felt, walking?"

She nodded and let out a little laugh, embarrassed at revealing herself. She picked up her heavy pack with one hand. I was astonished at her strength, as the pack seemed double the weight of mine, which I had been struggling to get on and off.

"How'd you do that?" I asked.

She didn't understand my question.

"You seem like you've done this a lot," I said, following her towards the benches next to the refugio.

"Never before. This is my first real trek, and my first ever pilgrimage. I trained to get into shape, but you can't train for the things that really happen here," she said, revealing again more than I think she realized. But I couldn't have stopped her if I'd wanted to, her revelations now flowed freely.

Claire was from Michigan, but she wanted to have been from Cape Cod.

"Provincetown. The one place I've felt free from definitions."

"Definitions?"

"About who you are or what you do," she said as we sat on the benches and ate food from our packs. With only bread and cheese left, I was hungry, but too embarrassed to ask her for one of her apples. She described her visit to Cape Cod two summers previous with a tone that was like the plea from a mermaid out of water. I was drawn to her plain-spokenness.

In Michigan her life had been all about worms. The earthworm bait market, she explained, was her territory. As she described it, I began to see worms through an unusual perspective. An industry traditionally seen as vampirous, the earthworm harvest had been an extension of her family's fertilizer business, and it was how Claire and her brother made their living. "Every night," she said with gravity, "my brother and I meet the other pickers in a park on the outskirts of the city. It's my brother who organizes, helps us strap on the tins at our ankles and adjust the beams on our miner's lamps." She talked with an earnestness that surprised me. The twentysomethings I had known were mostly cynical.

"We'd get nearly five hundred worms picked within a half an hour; the tins hold about that much," she said. On a good night of seven hours back-breaking labour, a picker could collect up to ten thousand worms and be paid twenty dollars per thousand, giving them a seasonal income of about ten thousand dollars. "I was pretty good, I have to say," she said of her summer occupation. In the winter she had worked on the administrative side of the family business, saving money to move to the East Coast. As the worm industry expanded to vermiculture in what they hoped would become the "vermillenium"—a new century of composting, biofertilizing, and the greening of the planet—her family business thrived, and she became heavily involved with the administration, and trapped inland. "It gets tedious looking down all the time," she said, and I was surprised by how simply she saw what might be missing from her life. She wanted to look out across an ocean, she said, and she had her heart set on Cape Cod. After living there for two months, returning to Michigan was a disappointment, and she resented her job, her family, the earth itself. She had left abruptly a month before, and this, her first trip outside of America, was proving to be the time of her life. She had chosen the Camino over a return visit to Provincetown because she knew from her Catholic upbringing that St. James had answers to indirect questions, like what she would do if she left her family.

I have to admit that I thought she was weird. She talked like someone who had stood back and watched us all from a different planet for years, and she was now coming to join us. I knew about Provincetown, had been there with a girlfriend once in my twenties. We had both found it beguiling. Two young adult girls at the height of their curiosity about men and sex, we didn't know what to do with the array of same-sex couples, drag queens, and transsexuals out on parade along the main street in the evenings. I was too immature then to appreciate the variety of how people love. And even at thirty when I heard that Provincetown was Claire's destination of choice, I was puzzled. I pegged her as gender-confused or sexually repressed. But I was drawn to that oddness. I wouldn't have given her a second look in my normal life, but the Camino was having its effect, and I was opening up. There was something graceful yet awkward about her that defied type or station.

When we finally joined Andy inside and said our goodnights—she going to sleep in a bunk next to his, me choosing one by the window—I began to think about my father, for some reason. I pictured Mazinaw Lake when I was a child, and the otter that he waited for every year to come back to the shore, and that stopped coming back when he returned to Paris. I wondered about the things we notice, the attention we pay, and what it says about who we are.

The next morning I made sure to rise and set off at the same time as Claire and Andy. At breakfast, Andy made coffee in the communal kitchen, and Claire had a small container of jam she shared with me for our bread. I did my best to put my original purpose back into focus. I asked them if they'd run into two men travelling together—a British man and a dark Spaniard. Claire's look of recognition at the description excited me. She had seen them, and guessed that they were either just ahead or just behind us, she couldn't be sure. It meant that I wasn't far off track. I didn't want to appear overly interested, so restricted my questions to place, date, and general well-being. Marcus was probably safe. Now all I needed to do was see for myself why I had come all this way to find them. Why had Gavin travelled with those photos?

I walked with Andy and Claire through Rabanal del Camino, up into the mountains towards La Cruz de Hierro. I was finally on the trail to Marcus and Gavin.

❧

"Your maker is not in heaven; he's in your heart," Lacey had told David Williams all those years ago, when he had finally been allowed the kisses he'd wanted. It had been the one thing that Marcus had hung onto in Spain. Every day he tried to become the words—*libre* and *nuevo*. He'd started his first Camino. Alone. But now, even though he'd left at dawn and thought he'd shaken Gavin, there he was trailing him, not like the bounty hunter Marcus had once believed him to be, but like a devoted dog.

"Marcus, please, wait," Gavin called as the terrain began to rise and Marcus was forced to slow down.

"I will murder your fucking arse," Marcus said almost casually over his shoulder. *Libre. Nuevo.* But the consequences of murder, he knew, were not for him.

"Wait, please! I know what to do." Gavin said.

Marcus slowed, despite himself. This bugger was something else.

When Gavin reached his side he seemed diminished. Damned. Marcus stopped to stare at him. He could see nothing familiar in him at all, except that he wasn't like other middle-class businessmen. The Borstal boy was in his twitching edge—that crack in his respectability.

"Please," Gavin said, catching his breath.

"What?"

"Hear me out."

"What for?"

"Because there's too much at risk now," he said, then winced as though he knew it was the wrong thing to say.

"Ya fuckin' bastard!" Marcus said, through his teeth. "You think I care about your dirty little secret and your guilty little conscience? You think I'd go to the police?" He paused. "I wouldn't give you the satisfaction."

"Look," Gavin said, "What I said, earlier, you know, about you doing it . . ." he looked down at his feet. "I know it must sound mad—"

"Fuck you."

"—but I should take my punishment."

"Then take it," Marcus growled.

"You don't understand," Gavin insisted, "punishment is just one aspect—it's right that you should be the one to turn me in." Marcus sucked his teeth and turned to leave. Gavin placed his hand on his arm to stop him. "Who'd believe me?" he asked.

"You're deluded."

"Okay, but beside that, I could help, do something for you . . . the least I could do . . . I have . . . I had . . . connections," he said finally. "You deserve to be more—"

"More like you?" The whip of the words was pleasant.

"No, more like you," Gavin said. Marcus knew there was

a trick in all of it, but the tone of voice was genuine. He kept walking up the slope.

"You know who you are. More than I ever did," Gavin continued at his back. "My friends talk around things, make jokes about everything that scares them. All sideways . . . You shouldn't have gone through all that."

Marcus nodded to himself in a *you-bet-your-sweet-arse I shouldn't have*. This white man with the world at his fingertips was begging for him. He spat at the ground beside him.

"What did you have in mind?" he asked. He wasn't sure which way revenge lay—by doing or not doing what the man begged for. *Don't you believe 'em when they say revenge is sweet*, Lacey had said. *Dig two graves if revenge is your plan.* But Lacey had died in that place of filth, had hanged himself years later. Alone. Free.

"Anything. Anything you want. I do have connections . . ."

Marcus sped up the incline to try to put some distance between them. He would get his own back, somehow.

There were more people on the trail now. Since leaving the bearded Bostonian, the Englishman, the German couple, the insurance broker, and the twitchy American, Claire—the only name he could remember—Marcus had seen them in various groupings. He had spotted the Germans in a bar in Belovado opposite the church. The man had looked up from his tapas, while his obtuse wife had sipped a beer looking unhappy. He'd nodded, and the German man had made a gesture with his hands like an apology. Later, on the meseta, along its wingless horizon, just before Gavin's obscenities, he had thought he spotted the insurance broker walking slowly with what seemed like a limp, up ahead of him.

Fucking hell. For the first time in fifteen years he welcomed an intrusion from others on this trek—anything that would give him space to decide what to do with Gavin, whether to torture, use, or simply let go. Something else had to change now, once and for all. He walked faster and focused on the stamp of the boot on the dirt path, the bend-roll-lift of the toe, the pulley motion of thigh and hamstrings.

He led the way, with Gavin still in tow, through the mist into a valley, on the heels of three pilgrims. He stopped suddenly at the sound of a male voice; then another voice—female—at an unusual volume.

"They call them the hounds of hell, so your guess is as good as mine." Her sentence, eager and light, had carried through the fog and he was sure he knew her. He walked faster. But the next sentence was from an even more familiar voice, and he stopped suddenly.

❧

It must have been a sound that was familiar and alerted me, because I turned. I ran towards him.

"What in hell?" he said to me in Spanish.

"Are you okay?" I asked.

"What are you talking about?" he spoke in English and I felt grateful.

I pulled him aside, and we sat on a rock beside the trail. I trembled, realizing as I spoke that I'd been a hostage of my imagination. But as he talked to me, I began to piece together real events. We talked and watched for Gavin down the trail. I saw nothing in the distance, because of the fog, but Marcus's attention to the path made me nervous. Gavin might appear at any moment. Marcus described how Gavin had come to confess and be turned in. As he described the ordeal of his incarceration, I thought I saw a head bobbing through the fog in the distance. I wanted to lurch at it, tear at it for what it had done. I now understood why Marcus had hidden his past from me and my heart broke for him. I also understood why Gavin must have rejected me. I was not the one he needed. But now that I was with them both again, my part in their stories seemed to be reinstated. Marcus needed his friend back, and Gavin seemed more desperate and needy than I'd originally thought. It sickens me, now, thinking about how that might have spurred me on.

As I listened, the bobbing speck went in and out of sight, and grew bigger and wider each time it reappeared. As his body cleared a path through the fog, and as details—his limp, the lanky legs and noble shoulders—became sharper, I hated him. But like the first moment when I'd seen him at the fountain, something about him was still familiar. I looked up ahead of us on the trail to where Claire and Andy had stopped for a break on the hill. The fog up ahead seemed even more dense, and I could barely discern their outlines.

"Don't mention a word," Marcus warned harshly, following my gaze. "To anyone," he added. I promised him I wouldn't.

"I've overreacted in coming after you," I told him.

"What, did you think he'd kill me?"

"Maybe. How would I know?"

"And what would you do about it?"

"Warn you . . ."

He smirked in that *vacía, vacía* way he had and I remembered what he'd said when I'd accused him of reading my notebook. *That's what you think of me?* This look was similar.

"Better warn him; he's the one in danger now," Marcus said. I didn't believe Marcus could really harm anyone, but I could sense an undercurrent in him. And now that I knew how his life had been ruined, it was even more impossible for me to tell him about the night with Gavin.

When Gavin arrived beside us, I saw that there was something between the two that was bigger than their history. They were like brothers who shared a family secret. Gavin stopped next to me, but his energy was directed entirely at Marcus, who shunned and yet demanded it as he shifted back and forth and looked about him as though for something to pick up and hurl. I saw the bruises on Gavin's face and now felt a little wary of Marcus.

I made uneasy small talk, and if Gavin was shocked to see me, he didn't let on. I thought of the fan he'd given me, which I'd left behind in my room. I was still willing to believe the gesture had meant something, despite his needs, and it was hard to ignore the fact that, like me, he had been trying very hard. He asked me how I'd made it to this precise spot on the Camino and found them. I kept steely for Marcus's sake, and told him that Marcus and I had always had a sixth sense with one another. But it was the two of them, now, that seemed to share a bond. We were an awkward trio as we started off again up the hill to meet Andy and Claire.

". . . that's what's so great about it. Foncebadón doesn't live up to the image of satanic dingoes." We heard Claire's voice through the fog, and then her giggle.

"She's something," Marcus whispered to me in Spanish.

"Why do you say so?"

"Finding herself."

"How do you know?" I was confused now.

"By her voice. It's changed . . . she's had a shag," he said, breaking into English and speeding up.

"How could you possibly know that?" I asked pursuing him. Like an idiot, I was trying too hard again, so I slowed my pace.

"Hello," he announced quietly, yet with enthusiasm. Andy stopped and turned. Claire caught her words and ceased her story.

"Hi, hi, how's it going?" Andy asked eagerly.

Marcus nodded at him. When he looked over at Claire he didn't seem surprised to see her approach with arms to hug him. Gavin hung back lurking along the side of the path that edged the valley. We both watched. An alpine chough swept down just to my left, its vivid yellow bill piercing the mist that seemed more dense over the valley.

"Let's go," Andy called out, and I followed them, leaving Gavin to lag behind. I was disoriented. My Pamplona life seemed insignificant here, and yet it was the reason I had come. I walked well back from Marcus, Claire, and Andy, listening and watching.

They spoke only sporadically before climbing steeply uphill again. At the top of the rise they stopped, waited for me to catch up, and Gavin did his best to keep right behind me. Now I could hear the Río Meruelo far below, just beyond where we trod, and the steep ascent explained why walking was so difficult. We passed a heavily guarded military station on the hill and reached a sign that pointed out the elevation—1,517 metres, the highest point on the Camino. I was struck by how ordinary the spot felt.

"Let's sit. It will rise," Claire said to the group, referring to the fog.

I was envious of her; she wasn't someone who waited for approval before making decisions. She knew what she wanted. She pulled Andy towards her and led us all to a cluster of rocks off the path. She sat down, Marcus sat to her left, and Andy to his left. I waited, wanting to see what Gavin would do when he arrived. He looked at Marcus as if to ask him to make room for him, but Marcus turned his back and gave all of his attention to Claire. Gavin sat down on Andy's left, and I beside Gavin, at the end of the line.

"We saw a wolf," Andy said to Gavin, and he went on to describe their last few days in the Cordillera Cantábrica. Gavin looked irritated.

"It's not common, except deeper in the woods, but this was a lone wolf. Off track, or maybe mad." Andy began to describe other sights along the journey. He spoke with self-consciousness, a little out of his depth in the realm of the ritualistic, Celtic-based spirituality of the Camino, while Claire, on the far side of the line, spoke freely to Marcus. I watched and listened to them both, my attention divided like a spy's.

"I find by this point in the trip I'm always just starting to feel free. How about you?" Marcus said to Claire. I resented the way he was sharing his private annual ritual as though she alone would understand. The way he had turned towards Claire, blocked out Andy, Gavin, and me from the conversation. I leaned forward, catching sight of Claire's face, and from her expression I could tell she knew he was asking more than a simple question. Her brow creased. I wondered what Marcus wanted from her or if he was making this show of attention to keep Gavin out.

He rested his elbow on his knee and his head in his hand. "Something's changed," he said to her in the voice he used for women.

She seemed to have prepared for a different question: "I like the sea—I've decided to live near the sea, so walking towards it makes sense."

Walking towards the sea did make sense, to me as well. I felt stupid for not having known this, and it might have been then that I unknowingly chose the way things would end. Marcus drew her out, and she described growing up on the outskirts of Detroit. She told him how much she'd wanted to escape but that her family depended on her.

Marcus muttered something that sounded like "Guilty conscience," then looked over his shoulder at Gavin, who saw him, and seemed to say in return that he would take whatever Marcus was dishing out. "I understand," Marcus said, turning back to Claire, sincerely now. He listened as she talked about the fact that she had spent the first few months of her life in an incubator and how she wondered if this hadn't set the stage for her life. Her work within the family business had isolated her from everything the daytime had to offer. She had worked at night since graduating from high school but didn't want to do that anymore. She was planning a move to Cape Cod, where she could feel more real.

I listened, leaning either back or forward in order to hear more clearly, but I was also aware of the conversation going on between Gavin and Andy. I saw that Gavin too was straining to hear what was going on between Marcus and the girl.

All of us tuned in and out of one another's conversation. I heard Andy tell Gavin about the abandoned village of Foncebadón and the ghost dogs there. Some pilgrims had even come prepared with Dog Dazers after reading an account of a pilgrim attacked by Foncebadón's wild dogs. He spoke about the pile of stones at the Cruz de Hierro that marks the pass over Monte Irago and the border between Maragatería and El Bierzo. Constructed slowly over the ages, the pile was built by pilgrims carrying stones—*murias*—and leaving them there to calm the mountain gods and ask for safe passage through the mountains before moving on towards Santiago. I watched Gavin become restless as Andy recited facts and trivia.

I remembered the ruins at the end of a tortuous climb, where we had arrived to rubble, a mound of tossed-aside belongings. Everyone had brought something to discard. The pile was the most intimate rubbish site in the world. I had watched as Claire deposited something I couldn't make out, over on the far side of the pile. I could tell that what she'd placed there had meant a lot, as she did it so gently, the way one might set down glass. I had been tempted to go over and see, but I was challenged by what to leave there myself. This hadn't been what I had come for. I searched in my backpack and then it occurred to me. It had to be that—the one thing that I'd brought that had meant anything—my notebook, with scribbles of stories about Marcus and Gavin in it. I had placed it gently in among the necklaces, the shoes, the T-shirts, and the stones.

Marcus shifted and caught my eye. We both saw Gavin fidget, with Andy's pedantry grating on him. Andy's account of a mystery like Foncebadón was like someone rhyming off a shopping list. He did his best to keep the intrigue—telling us that some former pilgrims had attempted to revive the ghost town, noting that the church was one of the few buildings that hadn't fallen down—but it was tasteless, and Gavin leaned farther forward, hoping to be closer to Marcus, and catching Claire's description of the witches of Galicia.

"In the highest mountains, the witches incant and cast spells," she said in a tone that reminded me of bedtime stories my mother had told me as a child. Her eyes became wide, and she seemed constantly on the verge of smiling. She took something out of her backpack, then held up a water bottle full of a brown liquid.

"Here, taste this," she said, opening it and passing it to Marcus. "*Orujo*," she added. Marcus sipped.

"Liquor, sugar, lemon peel, and coffee beans. The man who

made it for us was called Jesus—really he was." Marcus took another sip then handed the bottle back to her, ignoring Andy, who had turned towards them hoping to be passed the bottle.

Andy turned back to Gavin and continued, "At the iron cross, I placed my stone to the side, so as not to make the pile higher, but to make it wider, you know..."

As Andy spoke in a dull drone about altitude, Claire spoke of getting high on the magic of witches. As he spoke of the other precious objects at the Cruz de Hierro, she described how in a small village she'd helped a man lift heavy sacks of grain off his cart. The man had been surprised at her strength, but she'd felt nothing of the weight, being used to hard work. The man had thanked her by giving her some of his homemade cheese. I examined her face carefully to see if she was conscious of the effect she was having, drawing us all in with her naïve charm. But she was free of craft or design, and believed in every word she said.

Marcus looked again at me, then at Gavin, who had leaned forward onto his knees, no longer even pretending to listen to Andy. I wondered again who I should have been to make an impression on him, and why I had never been part of his salvation. Claire apparently was of interest; I was not.

Andy was oblivious to the interplay around him, and continued to describe the iron cross itself, which was erected in order to make the pagan tradition more palpable to the Catholic Church. I watched Gavin look at Claire's face, and I believed he was taking in the freckled skin, full lips, and the flush that streaked her cheeks. "And he gave me more of the quenmada," she said, naming the *orujo* potion. She gazed out into the valley, and I tried to find what she was seeing there.

Gavin stood up and seated himself on her other side, leaving Andy by himself to take in the panorama and make whatever he would of it. The fog had begun to roll back, permitting a view of the stone monastery of Campludo perched on the river before us. Gavin said nothing to her, but looked relieved to be away from Andy. He rummaged in his backpack, took out a pear and handed it to Claire, and continued to search in his pack. He brought out an antique, pearl-handled knife. He took the pear back from Claire and carefully cut a slice from it, offering it to her with a nod and a shy smile.

"Your eye," she said, noticing the bruise from Marcus's fist.
"I hit a door," he said, touching his face.

Marcus glared at him, but turned back to Claire and joked with her about witches and her own night work. As I listened to her describe her earthworm life in Michigan, I felt its simplicity.

We five accidental pilgrims sat like this as the fog cleared over the valley. The yellow-billed chough performed its acrobatics high above and behind us. Andy and I were set apart from the others by the space that Gavin had vacated. Marcus, Claire, and Gavin had banded together, like the three monkeys of no evil.

I recognized a new triangle forming that didn't include me.
I must have decided to force its shape.

Here, at the highest point in the narrative structured by the pilgrimage to St. James himself, a reader might expect something to change for Gavin Lake or for me. But, no.

Every story takes its own time.
Another step.

Eighteen

When a wolf gets caught in a leghold trap it will likely struggle in a frenzy, mutilating itself, dislocating joints, breaking teeth, chewing the leg or paw in an attempt to break free. If it succeeds, death will surely come from infection, starvation, or predation because of its weakness. *A wild thing is a sad thing,* I remember my dad saying, looking dolefully over the wolf leg we had come upon that day snowshoeing on Mazinaw Lake. He said it as though he had foreseen his own future. They may be sad, but wild things face an honest struggle. The more limited among us are caught anyway.

It is Saturday. May envelopes us like silk on skin, and I am able to sit outside most afternoons with my laptop, on our tiny balcony. I left the narrative alone for over two weeks, stranding the five unlikely pilgrims at the highest point on the Camino de Santiago. We've been suspended for this long, because, until today, it has been impossible to venture back in time. I have been in a trap.

I've spent these weeks continuing my research into viruses in order to understand. Everything. Sam's research is making slow progress, while I am running on the spot over a virus's mutation. While he has received accolades for the paper he gave in Paris, and while his lab has received more funding from the Spanish National Research Council, my own progress has been negligible, and I miss the urgency I felt. About everything.

No one talks about the tsunami anymore. The online charities have closed, the threat of rampant disease has been averted, and, in the world of virology, at least, the focus has shifted to the H_5N_1 virus and its potential threat to humans. Sam has little time for my questions on this area of virology, as retroviruses are different. His is viral research in the slow lane of the perfect experiment: the preparation of the cells in microtiter plates, the dilution of virus stocks; the incubation; collection of cells, transference and, finally, the careful, objective and dispassionate observation. The opposite of the tsunami's urgency.

About three weeks ago, he had been staying late regularly at the lab and came home sleepy, slurred, and then would sleep in late the next morning. I had put it down to the demands of reporting to the funding bodies and the urgency to show progress. Something. I would welcome him into bed in the small hours of the morning, his body hot and limp with fatigue, smelling faintly of smoke and must—the mouldy fragrance of growing cultures I associated with his lab. He was of course too tired to make love, and disquietingly disinclined to talk. In the morning I would wake to find him in the same position as he'd arrived a few hours before. I'd creep out of bed gently, not opening the shutters in our loft bedroom as the city went about its business of accommodating the rush of Easter pilgrims eager to experience St. James in the calendar's holiest of weeks.

Easter would have been a perfect time to get to the climax of my story, to uncover how my actions five years before might have had any redeeming consequences, but I couldn't write. The city itself distracted me, and Sam's emotional distance made me feel as if I was dangling on my own in mid-air, watching all the activity below. Even as I was stuck without vision, Santiago de Compostela was being reborn, as it is each April. The process begins with the Semana Santa procession, which starts at the cathedral and ends at Conxo's parish church of Nuestra Señora de la Merced. Eight robed and red-sashed priests lift onto their shoulders a carved mahogany pedestal, adorned with a pyre-like assortment of fresh-cut flowers that reach up to the nailed feet of the life-size Jesus on the cross, his wounds weeping, his ribs and pelvic bones peeling out the agony of flesh. Pilgrims gaze silently, feeling something more profound about this effigy than any other they've experienced on the long road to Santiago. I watched these processions in aggravation; why wasn't Sam with me to make our usual cynical observations about these rituals?

April was also the beginning of fiestas and other celebrations—this year, The Day of the Tree and Water commemorated World Tree Day in Eugenio Granell Park, where children planted 150 trees; the eleventh annual architecture prize was announced in the first week; and the book fair opened in the Alameda Park in the second half of the month with much ado over the announcement of the literature prizes. But I was unable to celebrate anything.

My night-life bled into my day-life, my story unwritten and my life disconnected, telling me something about the here and now. Claire kept creeping into my thoughts, even though I could not write her. I needed her way of looking at things. And if friends are indeed a marker of who a person is, where were mine? Where were the Claires in my life?

I began to make more frequent visits to the convent. Señora Ormaza had fully recovered from her flu, but had been weakened considerably. She had developed a blockage in her colon and had needed a colostomy. I was now assigned to the regular checking and changing of the good Señora's colostomy pouch.

She didn't like the change in our relationship at first, and I felt punished for this new, unwanted intimacy.

"And your man . . . you making him happy?" she asked with a sharp edge to her Spanish.

"*Que?*" I asked, put off, as I peeled the small plastic sac away from the skin on her right side.

"You know, women must play. Men like if you play," she said, and I couldn't believe this was the same sage Señora I had known for over a year. I put her attitude down to discomfort and took care to clean the skin around the stoma then fit a new, clean bag to her tube. But her remark stayed with me, and I thought of the day at Finisterre and the game Sam had played, which Thomas would have understood but I didn't. Perhaps I had been letting him down.

I was even more restless at home, poring over virology articles and thinking of tricks with the Latin words that I might play with Sam when he got home. One Wednesday evening, when I could no longer bear to read another virology Web site, I took myself to Pub Momo, as the English-speakers in town call it. The interior of Momo a Rúa imitates a street, so the April inside was as warm, treed, and bustling as the April outside. I made my way to a blue slatted-wood chair in the main room rather than continue out to the garden, which had attracted most of the other clientele. I was aware of the music from the band, Jazzen Cuentro, but wasn't in the mood for it. I ordered a mojito and watched three fair-haired men play billiards. I stared as the tall player's fingers curled over the cue, and followed the flick of his wrist that resulted in the pocketing of a ball. I wondered if I should ask him to teach me to play, if this was a game Sam might want me to join him in. I knew Sam came here sometimes with colleagues for a game. I raised my eyes and looked at the man. He had a football player's build, broad shoulders, and thick neck. And, now, with the beginnings of a smile, his face began to look familiar. In the slow dawning of his name, rose a parallel chill.

"George," I said in shock, standing up and walking like a robot towards him. George looked over at me and his hesitant smile said, who on earth are you?

"We met at a party," I said, feeling diminutive next to him.

He stared; memory or judgment flashed across his face, then he nodded. "I thought you were out with Marianne and Sam," he said, matter-of-factly. The flash in his eyes now made sense.

"No, no . . ." I stuttered, nodded back in an attempt to reassure both of us, and returned to my table. My mojito went down with one suck on the straw. I left soon after.

When Sam got home a few hours later, he was again the tired, floppy version of himself that I'd welcomed to bed consistently over the preceding weeks. "How was work?" I asked, facing the wall, as he kissed my ear. My back was not rigid enough to form the wall I had willed it to become.

"I'm beat," he said, and within seconds he was sound asleep.

The next morning I got up and—with very little sleep stored in my muscles—felt achy. Sam slept on. I decided to take a swim in the university pool, which I'd started to frequent in my efforts to motivate myself to write. The pool always helped to balance my system. The way the delicate sac of a fish provides it buoyancy, my swim bladder allowed me clarity. When I swam, I imagined myself in Mazinaw Lake, in the cool, deep waters beneath the cliff face. The only discomfort in the pool was its thick chlorination. My eyes would sting if I tried to open them.

That morning I decided to buy goggles from the small boutique at the pool reception. I was eager now for my Mazinaw fins, and the way being with my father had made me swim so effortlessly. One year he had paddled beside me in the canoe as I swam across the lake from the cliffs to my grandfather's cottage. In the pool I wanted to feel the ease of that stroke, which would tell me I still had some control.

I put the new goggles on as I stood in the fast lane at the pool, breathing in deeply to fill my imaginary swim bladder. The first length was a breeze, and a marvel, my breathing regulated, the blue-tiled pool floor starkly vivid. I was in my stroke by the second length, but I was no longer concentrating. I was looking at the water that came towards me, pressing into my goggles, forcing me to examine it. Close up, it appeared pristine, almost sparkling in its purity. If I focused farther ahead of me, though, I saw what seemed like an underwater atmosphere—particles like floating light in an underwater film. The particles fell slowly through the water like viscous dust motes in a suddenly disturbed attic. I swam, amazed with sight, until my mind clicked in and began to query my dust-in-water hypothesis. As I examined the consistency of the motes, my stroke slowed. In a near deadman's float, I watched a few larger motes float away and sink before me, drifting towards the slow lane, where other swimmers created less of a wake. I put my feet to the pool floor and stood up, suddenly off guard, and with one gulp I swallowed a mouthful of chlorinated water. As I walked to the edge of the pool, my goggles now pushed up on my forehead, I tried to control my repulsion. What I had thought was water dust was, in fact, flecks of spit from other swimmers, or even mucous and other body fluids.

I got out. I took a shower.

Instead of going home I stopped at a small restaurant and forced myself to think about food. I wanted something comforting, like a North American breakfast. Eggs. I wasn't truly hungry, I simply needed something to nibble on as parallel action to the gnawing inside me. I sat at a table for four, near the door. I was the only person in the restaurant, but by the time the waiter in the standard burgundy shirt and black trousers came from behind the cash register and sauntered over empty-handed, I had formulated the Spanish that would describe the perfect breakfast. But he didn't allow me a chance to speak, and he rambled on about the fact that I had sat down at a table for four. He pointed to a table set for two at a far corner. I made a show of looking about the empty restaurant. Then in English I said, "Oh, come on," not realizing my tone until it was too late. The man scowled and straightened. "Señora," he said simply, and opened his palm to point his hand in a gracious manner towards the other table. I resisted initially but gathered my gym bag and jean jacket and, with spite in my shoulders, moved tables. We had chosen our weapons. When I ordered I was demanding and difficult, asking for eggs with meat, a fried breakfast I knew would be scoffed at and rejected as impossible. When his insolent silence filled the room I capitulated and ordered a tortilla and a coffee.

My double espresso arrived half full. The *tortilla de patatas* came suspiciously quickly, and the waiter had a pleasant courtesy that wasn't always offered in Santiago de Compostela. I took a forkful of tortilla. It tasted very good. After three or four mouthfuls, I looked over at the waiter, who had kept his eyes on me. I looked back to my meager meal—the bill for which would result in a very small gratuity for him—and began to feel queasy. As I chewed on the egg and potato combination, the obvious occurred to me: the man had spit in my food before serving it. Of course. I had heard of it happening in restaurants, and certainly at the Mesón we had joked about what the waiters might do to drinks. Now I was sucking and chomping on this man's saliva. My fork hit the plate loudly. I paid the bill, leaving him more than double what he might have expected from the happiest of customers, and left quickly.

I remained agitated for several days, but the passing of time dislodged my ability to mention to Sam that I'd seen George at Pub Momo. I soon lost sight of George as the source of my mood. I decided that Sam and I needed to do something together that didn't involve sleep or food. I had seen an announcement for an art exhibition at the Centro Galego de Arte Contemporánea featuring international artists. I'd heard of one of the artists—a British man named Isaac Julien—from my father, who had mentioned him the last time we spoke by phone. I wanted to see what my father currently thought of as impressive, and I wanted Sam to be there with me.

The work was a video installation based on a poem. The colours of the film were saturated and tropical, oddly like camouflage. A black man stood in a cyan sea. In the images that swirled in and out of the frame, there were lost things—articles of clothing, discarded belongings. The man was rootless, his skin as boldly defined against the surf as a ship. I could see why my father had liked it—and it reminded me of Marcus and my writing. Marcus needed revenge. I wanted it for him. The supersaturated, unsettling colours of the video were just what it felt like to be in his company.

"I don't get it," Sam said, as he turned to me. He sounded

distinctly foreign in the gallery's atrium. I bristled, but reminded myself that Sam was a scientist, and that was surely one of the reasons I loved him. My dad would have rambled on about form, about light and references to the films of Buñuel or the paintings of Chagall, and I would have felt challenged. "Good colours, I guess. Kinda like a moving postcard," he added. "Did you know that guinea pigs are the one species that became larger after domestication? Cows, pigs, sheep—all smaller. Think about it—wild rats need to have bigger brains in order to be pets . . ."

I looked back at the video to see what could possibly have sparked this non-sequitur. Just as I had felt something about Marcus, I guessed that the work had led Sam to a connection with his own research.

"The colours are sexy," he said, and I was thrown again, back into the moment with him. "Reminds me of you," he concluded and hugged me hard, my face in his neck, my eyelashes licking the skin behind his ear. Sam was a beautiful relief.

When we let go of one another, I patted his arm and entwined mine in his as we walked towards the exit.

"You're an unlikely art lover," said a female voice to my left. My hand twitched on Sam's arm.

"Hey," Sam said as he stopped and turned. He dropped my arm and turned towards Marianne. My eye caught George's round face. He was a few steps behind his wife, emerging from the coat vestibule with a small leather bag. He held my gaze for as long as was socially acceptable without acknowledgement, and then we both turned towards our partners, who had already begun to exchange opinions on the exhibition.

The conversation took place, but I was not inside it. I was circling around the four of us, my awareness like a camera, zooming in on Sam's mouth, then Marianne's eyes, George's hands reaching to rub his wife's shoulder as if to draw her back to him. And I caught myself in a tight frame, beside Sam, slouching for attention like a hungry pet.

It was in the moment that I caught a metallic smell coming from Sam's arms that I also learned through the faint soundtrack of conversation that Marianne had been tired, had been working long hours, not getting enough sleep.

My breath felt like glass.

When George finally wrapped his arm around Marianne's shoulder and raised his other hand to us to signal their departure, I was relieved. During the drive home, over dinner of leftovers and cheap wine, in the bathroom while we were both brushing our teeth, and still, later, in bed as Sam leaned over to kiss my forehead, I was unable to ask him why. Instead, I churned *why* until it creamed and thickened between us and kept us from touching, from looking directly into one another's face, and from speaking about anything of importance.

The heaviness lasted three days before Sam casually looked up from his coffee at breakfast and said: "There's another HIV conference in July I want to go to. Marianne's organizing it."

Particles stilled their microscopic movement. I couldn't feel the broad thump of my heart, and I couldn't respond in any way except to say, "Oh, good," and then get up from the table.

"It's only a few days in Barcelona, I won't be far . . ." Sam said, watching me as I put on my shoes and headed outside.

"Of course," I said, "I'm just going for a walk . . . lots of work on my mind . . ." By the time I reached the cinema down the hill, where a Spanish-dubbed version of *House of Flying Daggers* was playing, I could feel my heart again. I made the decision while staring at the woman in the movie poster: a fine-boned, almond-eyed beauty dressed in embroidered pink with dragoned-printed gold inlay; her forehead was marked by a red diamond, and jewels from a crown dangled before it like a child's mobile. She wielded a sword of machete proportions. This woman knew both vengeance and forbearance. My writing had so far helped me learn that where you were from didn't matter and what you felt was not enough to move you forward. Claire had helped me learn that I should have been looking differently at the things going on around me, as this was ultimately what distinguished our behaviour in those final moments that summer of 1999. I needed to see differently now.

I decided I would meet with Marianne.

It took me a few days to pluck up the courage, but I retrieved her number from the university listings, set up the rendezvous with the pretense of becoming better acquainted, and yesterday walked into the university canteen to honour it. The banality of the surroundings, the less-than-cinematic splendour of the setting, deflated me. I looked about, realizing the other mistake I'd made was not to have arrived early to be the one sitting and waiting, composed and ready. Marianne was at a table near the coffee machine, preoccupied with notes on the table in front of her. I floundered before committing to approach. She looked up when I reached the table. Her smile disarmed the defences I had been marshalling in the previous days—including the image of the Chinese woman with a sword and a diamond tattoo.

"Hey, Emily, sit, or do you want to grab a coffee first? The machine's there."

I shook my head and waved my hand in an *I-don't-need-any* way, trying to remain in control.

"It's taken me months to stop watering it down," she added as though we might share an aversion to strong Spanish coffee.

I sat.

The first thing I took in was her hair: I inhaled jasmine from the long, coiffed locks, more brown than black, each one rising out from the white headband like tamed serpents in her army of nature's gifts. Time slowed, and when I tried to speak, to say something trivial to break the ice that I felt encasing me, I faltered and my eyes moved lower. Her brow. Shining skin. Smooth. Tawny, like plumage. Perhaps his lips had started their forage there, a gentle probing at the silky door to her mind. Her thin eyebrows curved only slightly, following the line of her wide, intelligent eyes. She was looking about the canteen as she spoke. I watched her eyes move unselfconsciously over a female student at the next table. She looked back at me and asked me how I liked it here in Santiago. I nodded to indicate *fine enough*. Breath glass. Saliva glass. She stopped talking and looked down at her coffee. My eyes moved to her cheek. I imagined his lips there. In successive, framed visual bites I surveyed her: the line of her jaw, neat, neither rounded nor square; her neck, smooth with the exception of two thin lines like wisdom rings on a tree. Her shoulder was covered, but veering out from the neckline of her scooped T-shirt was a collarbone so delicate yet prominent that it defined her. I felt myself wanting to run my fingers along the ridge of smooth skin that led to the breast plate and lower, towards the cleavage (the darker skin there like chocolate) that stopped at the neckline of her shirt. I wanted to follow the dark fold that would lead me towards her ribs, her belly. Beyond. I needed to possess her.

As my eyes moved back to hers, I remembered a moment from my early adolescence. Winter in Flinton. My parents had decided we were to spend Christmas at my grandfather's cottage. It was December 21—I remember, because my father had made a big deal about it being the shortest day of the year. This was also the day my father and mother had an annual argument over religion, my mother's United Church upbringing making no allowances for my father's Catholic mysticism or reverence for First Nations beliefs or pagan rituals. How best to serve the soul was the theme of the argument: by ruling it or setting it free?

I left the cabin with my snowshoes in hand. I walked along the frozen shore until I reached woods and an untrod path through birch trees that whispered an invitation. I was perspiring, my clothes felt heavy. I tired quickly but kept up a pace for no other reason than it produced a swooshing rhythm in the silence that otherwise overwhelmed the woods. When I stopped in a clearing, the silence echoed. It was exhilarating. I was making tracks in virgin territory. The sun was winter-weak but, reflected in the snow, it was dazzling. I knelt down on a raised mound, turned, and released myself into powdery snow, falling backwards onto its cold cushion. I stared up at the blue sky and the clouds that passed as though the earth were turning at an accelerated speed. My face felt the faint heat of the sun. The air seemed to house only the sound and steam of my breath. I lay like that for a long time, until I became thirsty. I scooped up a handful of snow and dolloped it onto my tongue. I lay back down and was lost to silence.

Suddenly, I heard something behind me. I went stiff with fear, straining to hear more, but nothing. I turned my head to the right slowly and tilted it back so that the snow reached my forehead.

Its eyes. Its careful, calculating eyes.

People say deer look innocent, but I disagree. This animal was staring with nostrils flared, its mandible rigid and set in a scowl. No one has ever spoken of deer growling, but I could have sworn I heard it emit a low rumble. I examined the protrusions of muscle below its neck shaped almost like a collarbone. We watched one another. The moment I swallowed was as though it had heard me, or had been tracing me and felt the movement of saliva from my tongue to my throat. Its ears pricked up and it bounded off.

I focused back on Marianne's plum-coloured lips. She was telling me how lucky she felt to be working on the projects she'd been seconded to in Spain, even though at times she missed the United States in a way she had never thought possible or particularly healthy.

"We're lucky to have you too," I said, surprising myself, realizing that what the deer had given me that day in my teens had been a moment I could own, even as my parents were losing each other. I had rejected my role as solder in their relationship.

"Sam's a marvel at his work," she said.

"He loves it," I acknowledged. I looked again at her collarbone, imagining kissing it the way Sam might have, forcing myself to imagine embracing her, and recognizing what I already knew: that someone is never wholly ours alone. Marcus, Gavin, Claire. I wanted to know what changed about love if sex was no longer exclusive the way it seemed was true now for me and Sam. I wanted to weave something out of the broken tendrils of trust. I held myself still in my chair.

After exchanging a few female perspectives on the nature of what men need and how we must not forget to praise them, I could disguise my fidgeting no longer. I told her I had to get home, where I hoped my writing would begin to flow again. She wished me luck and kissed both of my cheeks in the European way. I left her as I had found her, poring over the notes on the table, her mind clicking like a combination lock.

Nineteen

Marianne's curved, dipping collarbone has led me back to the shape of the winding Cordillera Cantábrica mountains. I can almost feel them now in my legs, as I remember that part of the trek and how it contributed to the end. I remind myself that Marcus was vengeful, but he was also stonewalled. If I'd thought it would release Marcus and also save Gavin, I might have gone to the police myself, but nothing was clear. I could turn back, catch a bus to Pamplona, but life there felt less vital than what was taking place on the Camino. Why not keep walking? I asked myself. Walking towards the sea makes sense, as Claire had said. And she kept my attention, not only because Marcus approved of her, but because I felt I might learn things from her.

I followed them; I watched.

ॐ

"Careful not to confuse this with what you deserve," Marcus said, as Gavin, breathing heavily with the punishment of the steep climb, passed him. "Bastard." *Control*, Marcus thought.

He was sorry he knew anything. He wished it hadn't been this man who had betrayed him; it had been easier to despise a pack of same-faced boys and an ugly system. He was not capable of either killing him or giving him what he wanted. This trek was supposed to mark an anniversary of freedom, but Marcus felt more trapped than ever. He picked up his pace; there was no way he was going to let himself be overtaken.

Gavin felt Marcus behind him. The rising mist made him want to cry. He had to keep walking because something was taking place. The valley to his left was wide and lush, but the mist seemed to be getting thicker. He was walking into clouds like someone already dead. Maybe he had died, he thought, or at least all this walking had been the equivalent of death and he no longer had to enlist Marcus to help him. What was there now? Ancients had walked in search of redemption, and so could he. He suddenly suspected that his old companion, Hope, might be lurking between the steps he took.

"You ever go to church?" he turned and asked Marcus, who was almost at his side now.

"Fuck no," Marcus said, the mention of it ringing out a familiar irritation linked to his mother. His mother's discovery of Christ had been yet another of his faults. The O-Lord-take-away-the-sins-of-my-son echoes had kept him away from London. "A priest would be happy to hear you out, if confession's on your mind," he said to Gavin, as he dropped back, deflated.

"It's not just for that," Gavin said, over his shoulder. This sudden inkling was more subtle than the hope of the past; more like the pressing up of a new shoot through the earth he trampled.

"The soul's not worth much on the FT-SE index," Marcus

said, wanting to twist any screw to torture the other.

Gavin flinched. "Please, I've been trying to tell you . . ." He stopped and turned, forcing Marcus to stop. "I could pay for art school," he said looking at the face, now quite accustomed to this adult version but surprised at how little it moved him anymore. Marcus was a man whose life he could not carry, although he knew he would not be able to do anything else but try until they exchanged something. "I could get you a job, or you can have everything I have left." He paused and they looked at one another.

Marcus felt mist on his face but refused to acknowledge anything pleasant. This little trade Gavin was offering made him sick. He held himself in; he had to keep walking. He had to arrive in Santiago. He had to know something more.

"You hold onto your shares and bonds; you'll need them in hell." He took a quick look into Gavin's eyes before pushing past him.

Gavin wondered how to tell him that hell was over for him now, and no matter where he ended up, nothing was as bad as where he'd been. Suddenly Andy called out from farther up, telling them that there was a plateau just beyond the peak and they didn't have much higher to climb. Gavin looked ahead and put everything he had into his legs as he hoisted himself up the slope.

⚜

I remember the effect of the mountains, and I want to get it right—for Gavin. Because it might have been there that something changed for him. I walked behind the group and on occasion even lost them, but I would catch up by evening. If I'd been there, closer, perhaps I would have witnessed a shift, something I hadn't detected going on in him, and I might not have acted as I did later, and the outcome would have been completely different.

Along this portion of the trail, the heights would have sustained him. The sky, the fog, the views, and now the lurking, gentle dusk, as they climbed out of a river valley from El Acebo to Molinaseca, would have had their effect on him. The curves, the ups and downs, the tiny hamlets, all would move him. He would sense a rising in tandem with the landscape, and would even have regretted not staying longer near the Cruz de Hierro, which had separated the straggly peaks of Galicia to the right and the scorching meseta to the left, where he had begged for Marcus's mercy. This new perspective might also have included Claire, as it had for me. If Marcus was not going to turn him in, then Claire might have seemed like someone who might point the way to relief. She was, after all, the only one of us on a true pilgrimage.

❧

Fog. Gavin tried to keep sight of her backpack just ahead of him as it drifted in and out of view. Marcus, now farther ahead, might as well have been on a different mountain. It was strangely comforting to be alone with the ghost pack. Gavin sped up, the backpack coming into view, then her head, her arms, her sturdy legs in khaki shorts.

"You need your miner's hat," he shouted into the fog. She slowed and looked back at him, but kept walking.

"Too late for that."

"What do you mean?"

"I hadn't brought anything to leave up there. I didn't realize people left personal things—did you see?" she said, referring to the iron cross at the Cruz de Hierro. Claire stopped and turned towards him. "There were stones, but also other stuff, I couldn't believe—how personal . . . stained handkerchiefs; there was a porcelain doll with winking eyelids. Andy saw two bras, and lots of books . . . I saw the *Collected Works of Emily Brontë* . . . a full pack of Gitanes with a rubber band around it and a condom tucked into the rubber band."

He remembered things, yes, but had paid no attention, certain that the items had been mere rubbish. She'd known they were more than that.

"So I left my picker's light, which I brought to use as a flashlight. I hope no one takes it. It's in perfectly good shape."

He saw himself on the street, a child of eight or nine, with others in Golders Green, laughing, playing with a flashlight . . . signalling on-off-on-off to confuse oncoming cars. When neighbours had complained, Martin said nothing to Gavin, but talked over his head to his mother, "What are kids doing with flashlights, anyway? Too damn spoiled." Privilege and flashlights had become entwined.

Nothing he'd known in the past could be counted on now.

℘

The fog had lifted. The dusk grew deeper, the sky rusty. I caught up to the group, which had slowed, Claire now walking beside Gavin. Ahead of them, Marcus and Andy were waiting for us.

"We should stop for the night. There's lots more traffic now. Tourists," Andy said as we all gathered.

"And we are . . . ?" Marcus asked.

"Pilgrims," Andy said, and I saw Marcus bristle. "Did you see that couple who passed us? They had no packs; they're Spanish, walking for a day or two, no more." Andy sounded almost panicked.

"Is there a refugio coming up?" he asked Marcus, who looked tired. Rage is tiring. Meanwhile Gavin opened his mouth wide and shifted his jaw back and forth, as though feeling the still tender bruise.

"There is, just up there. Riego de Ambros," Marcus said flatly over his shoulder as he walked away.

Gavin looked about to chase after him.

"Claire was thinking of sleeping out in the open air," I said, jumping in to divert Gavin, planning to follow Marcus myself, in the hope of getting time alone with him.

"Yes, that's true," Claire said, looking at me as though I'd revealed something she hadn't intended to share with everyone. I launched into plans.

"It's high up; the night is clear..." I said to her, in a coach's voice, as though all she needed was some encouragement, but I was really looking over her shoulder at Gavin.

No one was quick to a decision. We had become dependent on Marcus as the experienced trekker, and as we hesitated the light all but faded. I thought of heading to the refugio by myself, but I saw Marcus returning down the path.

"It's full," Marcus reported. "I'm bunking down over there," he added. "The next refugio is too far in the dark, in these hills." He walked off to the edge of the valley, where he took off his pack and sat down on it.

"I didn't bring gear for that," I said, now balking at my own suggestion. I had expected that they would sleep outdoors and I would take a bunk next to Marcus. "Claire!" I called her over to confer on God knows what. I was stalling. How could I make everything work the way I felt it should—Gavin getting a bit of Claire's clarity, Marcus being supported by his friend?

"You can use my tent if you want. I really don't mind the

open air," Claire offered kindly, and I was humbled.

"I think he likes you." What was I doing?

"What?" She looked confused.

"Gavin . . . he nearly said as much, really, yesterday. I think you've had an effect on him."

She looked at me as though I'd lost my mind, and perhaps I had. I was trying to use her to rescue Gavin so that Marcus could rescue me and make me feel less ridiculous about this journey. I wanted Marcus to talk to me like he had at home.

"Really." I ignored the rising feeling of self-loathing.

"Here," Claire said as she untied the tent and bedroll from her pack. "I can share with Andy." She was running through the previous two days in her mind, to see if what I said could possibly be true. Satisfied that I'd had an influence, I took the tent and headed towards the edge, and Marcus.

"You go ahead," he said when I showed him what I'd procured for us. "I like the open air. Prefer to be alone up here . . ."

A lump rose in my throat. I wandered back over towards the others.

"Thanks, but we'll be fine," Gavin said as he took the groundsheet from Andy. I wondered who this "we" was, until I saw him heading for Marcus, who was spreading his jacket on the ground. When Gavin reached him, he held out the tarpaulin like an apology. Marcus took the edge without looking at him and together they unfolded the groundsheet. Gavin stretched out its corners and sat down.

I stood stupidly not knowing where or if I fit. I took Claire's tent back to her and told her I wouldn't need it. I didn't know exactly what I would do, but I kept walking in the dark, which seemed to slide like mud down the side of a mountain. The sound of the wind and the creatures rustling made me mad with fear. I found a rock that looked like it might protect me, so

I curled up beside it and felt the warmth it had retained from the sun. I took clothes from my pack and covered myself in them. The rock stayed warm while I tried to place the sounds from below in the valley. As it cooled off I realized the night was passing and that sleep was not possible. I don't remember what I thought about as I waited for the sun to rise, or if I wondered what the others were doing. My fear didn't allow me the luxury of my imagination. I held close to the rock and I believe I might have cried for my mother.

When dawn came I kept going, trying to stay ahead of the others, and only now can I imagine how little it might have mattered to them.

❧

He watched the sky. He could smell the earth, and he was terrified that he was nearly alive again. He listened. A river below in the valley. Stars appeared, but he had trouble tracing them. His eyelids felt heavy. He might sleep now.

A rustling nearby startled him. He turned quickly on his side and had barely enough time to make out the figure that loomed above him before the awkward, freckled woman dropped to her knees beside him. He sat up quickly and faced her. She closed her eyes, as though waiting for him to do something. Hold her, kiss her.

"I don't know," he whispered, and hoped she understood. Claire opened her eyes and gave him a look that could have meant anything from *I don't mind* to *this is not what you think*. "What?" he asked quietly. She touched his face with her hands, then stood up and went back across the wild thyme to her tent.

He looked towards where Marcus lay and thought he could

see his thick silhouette sitting up.

"You like them with a little flesh," Marcus jeered.

Gavin closed his eyes. How could he explain to him how meaningless flesh was?

"It's like for you, I guess . . . not hard to get someone . . . the right one, that's different, you know?" He paused. "Someone . . . appropriate." He thought of someone from long ago—Amira, her name a prayer and her body beautiful, but just not a match.

"You fucker," Marcus said as he stood up. "You know fuck all about me, so don't you dare compare us. You know what appropriate is in jail?" He grabbed the edge of the tarpaulin and heaved it, pulling it out from under Gavin, rolling him over onto the ground. "Appropriate is a hole. A hole just tight enough, doesn't matter where . . ." He crumpled up the tarpaulin and tossed it down on the ground beside Gavin, who had rolled onto his back. Marcus picked up his pack and moved away into the darkness.

Gavin stretched out his legs and stared upwards.

The darkness was complete.

The usual rumble of panic lay near, but he didn't pay attention. He lay, watching the stars, the long night, and he struggled with the noises coming from all directions. He followed them, then lost them. A flapping sound he traced to something inside his own head. He had missed an opportunity back at the iron cross. Something else should have happened by now. He pulled an edge of the groundsheet beneath his head and rested on his side, until a thought made him sit up. He drew his backpack towards him and opened it. He fished out the pearl-handled knife. Rising to his feet, he fingered the handle, rubbing his thumb along its length.

He stood up stealthily and climbed up through the leafless shrubs and their golden-yellow flowers to the edge of the hillside.

He flung the knife with all his might into the black Spanish night. It disappeared somewhere on the hillside well above the river. He tried to sense some reaction within him. He strained to feel meaning in what he'd just done. The knife had not been left at an altar. And the moment had not been witnessed by anyone. It had not been brave like Claire's shedding of her torch, or her tender act of submission in front of him, but it had been a small gesture. Of something. He returned to the tarp, spread it out, and lay back down.

Twenty

I had put distance between myself and the others, and I tried not to think about them. I concentrated on the walk itself and found that it calmed and kept me from sulking. I decided I'd see it through until Santiago.

I had many second thoughts along the way. Once, as I was making my way up a steep hill towards the hamlet of La Faba, it began to rain and I slid down the muddy trail into the path of oncoming cattle. I had to roll out of the way to avoid being trampled. But I loved the views, the conical, thatched-roofed *pallozas* dotting the rolling hills, the white broom, laburnum and gorse, the small cones of excavated earth that marked the entrance to a large rodent's burrow. It was a chance for me to take in the wild Spain, and I made mental notes of images and locutions I would use to describe things. Without knowing I would have a story to write, I was preparing myself, forming descriptions of smells, sounds, and textures. Yet I was entirely unaware that I was missing important developments in the episode I had set in motion.

"Pulpo," Andy said. Gavin watched as Claire took in the Spanish word for octopus, saying it to herself and smiling as though she'd learned the name of a newborn. *Ready*, he thought—a word suited to Claire, who had continued to walk in his company as though her gesture towards him had been no embarrassment, only a prong in the fork with which she was devouring what life was offering.

"There's an excellent octopus house in Melide, it says here," Andy said, closing his guidebook. He looked over at Gavin, who had stood to the side to let them discuss the evening's options. The skittish man disliked him now too, the more Claire walked beside him, the more they talked to one another. Claire had suggested they take a vow of silence after Melide as a way of easing tensions. Andy didn't hate him the way Marcus did, charging on up ahead while Gavin had kept back, relying on Claire for comfort. No, Andy's hatred was of the subtle competitiveness found in the faces of business colleagues and competitors alike. That *haaaa haaa* of a contest he would never return to. He would use his colleagues as bridges to help Marcus, but he would never again be swallowed up into their world.

"I wonder if we'll see Emily there," Claire said to him, before she started off.

"Emily?" Gavin had to force himself to sound concerned.

"Yes," she said over her shoulder. "I'm worried we haven't seen her yet. She left in the dark that night. That was five days ago—I hope she's okay."

"She's too intense," Andy said from behind him. Gavin couldn't help but wonder about the pot and the kettle and yet he had to agree with him.

Claire stopped and turned around, frowning. Gavin became fixed on the especially large freckle just to the left of the pleat in her top lip. This freckle kept her from being attractive, he thought.

"I'll look out for her, and maybe ask around. She might need company," Claire asserted before continuing towards the village. Gavin watched their evening shadows stretch like stilt walkers, and the trail between their legs become an impossible tightrope.

❧

Marcus was out in front, trying to get clear of the others, but Andy had caught up within a few metres of him. In the depth of this eucalyptus forest, he felt drugged. Camphorated. Capitulated. He had discovered in the last few days that he was not a man to be fed on vengeance, and so the tedium of walking was all that was left now. He spotted carcasses by the roadside—chickens and possibly a pig—and admired the dry, meaningless bones. At least it had been quiet. Gavin and Claire followed several hundred metres behind them, observing the silence they had avowed and kept since leaving Melide two days previously.

Claire, on her knees, on the tarpaulin. Ever since then the centre of gravity seemed to have shifted to her. Marcus had to admit to himself that there was a part of him that missed Gavin's attention.

"In the Middle Ages the town was a ceremonial stop for pilgrims," Andy said as he came abreast of him. Fucking hell. "Lavacolla was for cleanliness," Andy continued, reading from the guidebook, "The pilgrims would clean themselves before continuing on the last few hours to Santiago. Likely their first wash since the beginning of the Camino, in the small river at Lavacolla (which means "'wash scrotum'"), called Lavamentula (which means "'wash phallus'"), they would wash their private parts before presenting themselves to St. James."

Dear Jesus. After all these years of being someone who walked for his own sake, he had become one of them, one of the feeble-of-faith pilgrims who had smack-packed into the Mesón and had no clue why they were there, except that there was something at the end, something different. In the mountains he'd felt the teasing reappearance of his annual sense of freedom, but now he was rat-trapped in his own missing faith-in-nothing. No thing.

Andy led them clear of the eucalyptus forest. Farmland appeared, and in the distance new housing developments on the periphery of Santiago.

And a runway. The noise of an Iberia flight in steep ascent blasted him like a spray of insults. Marcus remembered the usual feeling of annoyance at seeing this airport, but this year there was a new runway squeezing the Camino. Fucking joke. The Camino was letting him down. The Spanish pilgrims behind them now were backpack free, the kind whose taste of a pilgrimage would take a total of two days, unburdened, as their packs would be transported from Melide by taxi and would be waiting for them at the five-star Hostal de los Reyes. Bull. Shit.

He sped up and passed Andy, moving across the edge of the runway to a wooded ravine. He marched towards the village of San Palo. The luscious mountains were gone along with his tolerance for anything other than the end of the route.

"How far to Lavacolla?" Andy asked. Marcus counted to five.

"Almost there," he said, and turned to see that Andy had stopped to take something out of his backpack. Would he place this under a flight path and hope to be seen from the air? Fuck.

Fuck. Fuck. Andy drew a stone out of the pack with great care, holding it like an egg, or a crystal.

"I'll wash this there too," Andy said, rubbing the odd-shaped stone.

"You were meant to leave stones at that pile or along the road. It's yourself that you offer to St. James," Marcus barked at the man's supermarket, grab-bag spirituality.

"This is precious," was Andy's only response. He drew closed the strings of the pack, flung the flap over, and lifted it onto his back.

Lavamentula was dry.

Marcus watched as Andy walked up and down the banks of nothing. A little farther along, the river did run in trickles, but the water was polluted, piddling like leaking sewage. Marcus walked into the small bar in Lavacolla. Pil. Grims. He sat at the bar, and a few minutes later Claire, Gavin, and Andy followed, after they'd given up the idea of a wash. Claire and Andy joked about how filthy the pilgrims must have been to greet their saint in the days before hot showers. Marcus bit his bottom lip, forcing his teeth deep into the flesh, gnawing the lip back and forth. Grim. He sipped a beer and kept his back to them. Claire and Gavin had given up silence and were making plans for the best way to enter Santiago. He listened, head lowered, as Gavin's voice squeaked the squawk of hope he'd heard all through the mountains, before the crowds at Ponferrada and the choke-joke crassness of this path.

"I didn't think I'd feel anything," Gavin said to Claire. The murderer was thinking about his feelings. Murder was only this, Marcus thought. Feelings for yourself gone too far.

"But maybe that's not the point," Claire shot back quickly at

Gavin, "it's all about what you come across, don't you think?" she said, still with the dappled tone that Marcus admired. He looked over at them and saw Gavin's face as he listened to Claire. The look there was like that of a man in love with his post-op nurse. He turned back to his beer.

He could take a coach back to Pamplona and skip Santiago altogether, or he could run now, see if the end made any difference, then leave Spain altogether. Time was precious in these last kilometres. He'd have to decide if he would do the man's bidding and turn him in. Had turning him in not also meant doing his bidding he might have chosen it, but the man's bidding was just what Miguel would have expected of him, and he'd be buggered if he would let them be right. There had to be something else.

"The tradition is to run to the end," Claire said from the table, but when he turned to her, he quickly realized she had been addressing Gavin and not answering his thoughts.

"Ahh," Gavin said, not looking up at him. "Not sure that suits me," he added, glancing at Claire.

"I never thought I'd want to, but there's something about rushing towards a beautiful ending that makes sense." She looked down into her lap. She was not being coy, Marcus felt. She too wanted something. Else.

"It's about ten kilometres!" Andy protested. "And hilly."

Marcus watched Gavin for his response. The man's firm features had been made even more so from the Camino. He was trimmer, and although he still limped, he was more solid than when he had left Pamplona.

"You also said something about a pig-herd girl whose pig snouts had turned into gold," Gavin said, labouring to speak in a light tone.

"Everyone we spoke to was a tourist," Claire said, looking up. "This is from the history of pilgrims." Her voice was self-assured, her eyes certain. There was a burst of commotion from the tourist pilgrims in the bar, getting up, gathering their things, and moving on, wanting to make it to the cathedral by evening.

Gavin looked at Marcus. Claire looked from one to the other, and then turned to Andy, who seemed absorbed in his book of miracles. Seconds passed.

"Let's run," Gavin said finally, still with his eyes on Marcus. Claire let out a little yelp and gathered up her things.

Marcus had a choice then: he could disappear once again from his life, or he could see what else there was to happen. He had to finish. Something. He chose to keep walking.

*

Where do you get to in the end, Gavin wondered, catching his breath, his hands on his waist. Santiago de Compostela? Santiago felt like it would be a line crossed over into a whole new way of caring for life. Would he get that far? He stood at the top of Monte del Gozo. Mount of Joy. Of course. Claire had primed him that this was where pilgrims got their first rapturous view of Santiago's cathedral spires. What he saw was suburbs: bungalow bunkers, like the Lego he had played with as a child; an aloof plaza, self-service canteens, sad shops with bagpipe music ringing out from their tannoys. He eased the cramp in his side by bending over, his face to his knees, his pack feeling like it would pitch him forward. Straightening up, he looked back to see if he could spot the others anywhere in the distance. As Claire raced towards him, he wondered if perhaps he should have shared this mount of sorrow with Marcus.

Claire stopped a few feet away, caught her breath, and surveyed the dreadful horizon before them.

"Wait . . . look," she shouted, and waved him over. She was pointing, and he followed her fleshy finger but saw nothing but the finger itself. He traced back up the arm, to her wrist—thick as dough, freckled—to her hefty biceps. *Here.* He walked to where she was standing. She dropped her finger with a sigh and moved to stand behind him, positioning his head to see through the copse below so that he might focus on, in the distance—them. The spires of the Cathedral of Santiago de Compostela, rising humbly out of the surrounding rubble. "Ahh," he said, and suddenly missed Kate. How was Claire so effortless? He searched again for Marcus, but he was nowhere in sight.

"It's about an hour away," Claire said, as she turned him back to face her. He stared at the freckle above her lip. "I think we should keep running." She turned on her heel and was off.

He would wait for Marcus in Santiago. He followed Claire. Not running. Walking with a crisp click. *Onward.*

Twenty-One

I didn't gasp, the way I imagined a good pilgrim, like Claire, would. I entered the cathedral from the Plaza del Obradoiro, climbing up the imposing double staircase to the dramatic baroque façade. I looked at the carved saints and gargoyles the way one does a family tree, wondering which branch might be the one you really sprang from. Where was the joker, the outcast? I searched for my father here, but saw only why he had abandoned his Catholicism. It was like the theme park where my grandfather had once taken me. I squeezed past the pilgrims and other worshippers and sped through each of the cathedral's important stations.

At the Pórtico de la Gloria I thought about how Claire would feel after over four weeks and the 770 kilometres she'd travelled to get here. Following the established ritual, she would touch her right hand to the middle of the central column of the Tree of Jesse, to give thanks for her safe arrival. Moving to the back of the pillar, she would face the small bust of Maestro Mateo, architect of the magnificent Pórtico de la Gloria, and she would butt her head up against his three times, in devout pilgrim fashion, in order to be bestowed with the blessings of his genius.

I walked quickly towards the altar, but looking up, I finally did gasp, at the huge, vacant angels like obscene dolls hanging from the ceiling of the nave. I proceeded to the high altar, and still higher, up the narrow staircase that led to the thirteenth-century jewelled statue of St. James.

St. James had his back to me. Appropriately.

I deserved that snub. I patted the cold, jewelled-inlay shoulder, forgiving it, and retreated down the stairs.

I left the cathedral through the same doors I had entered, squeezing past more and more incoming worshippers. I took up a strategic point so that I wouldn't miss Gavin and Marcus when they arrived, but by the time they did—and I watched them from across the square—I knew I would be unable to be a part of what had passed between them in my absence. I inquired at the tourist centre for an albergue and found one at the edge of town, near the Seminario Menor. Once settled on my bunk, I began a new notebook.

୬

A church. Simply that. Ornate and venerated. But still a church. He thought of his mother for the first time in months. His mother's Catholic church, his father's lost Judaism. His sister, whom he rarely saw, had married a Protestant. And he felt nothing. Still. He touched his hair. Longer, more grey. It tingled at the forehead line. Porter reappeared, a surprise after a week of his absence. Had he been given last rites? Gavin made a sign of the cross as he remembered his mother doing at the engagement party. She had stood before the cake and presents and crossed herself as though they themselves had been a miracle. His mother would now be crossing herself at the sight of men with his colour of eyes. He stopped those thoughts.

He skulked around the walls of the cathedral, watching the crush of pilgrims. There was Andy, with his radiant imposter's face. Gavin lowered his head and turned quickly in the opposite direction. He looked up again near the far end of the plaza. The rounded head and the frizzy curls near the column belonged to Marcus. *There.* That had been the reason he was here. And now all he had was this weariness in his legs that seemed to be enough.

Marcus stood still, looking up. Gavin crossed the plaza and stopped by his side. He followed Marcus's gaze skyward.

"I don't like spires," Marcus said, simply, but that simplicity was a lie, Gavin knew now.

"You going in?" Gavin asked.

"Nope."

"You come all this way and don't go in?"

"Yep."

Gavin looked up again at the spires, then back at Marcus. Look, look, he wanted to say. At me. I'm not the same.

※

The early summer evening was confusing—a darkening or a lightening? The sun hung low, hovering, and as he walked away from the cathedral the day felt as though it could be endless, with this back and forth of options and what nows. Would he regain from Gavin anything to do with a life that could have gone a thousand ways? Would he have been better off not having been sent to Peterhead? Not having felt close to hell, not having been sheltered by Lacey, not having smelled the mint—distinctly so, and the smell he associated with Aberdeen even now—that he'd inhaled on the day he had been let out? Without all of that, would he even be in Spain now? He thought of his mother and her friends who told him when he was finally free that the buses were a good place to make a steady living. The buses? Nothing could be regained from Gavin. The only question left was whether or not he could let Gavin walk away from sin.

He turned and confirmed that, yes, he was there, his puppy shadow, following him through the back streets of the tourist quarter. He pulled out a chair at a table in a café that was shaded by the grand church. Gavin followed, pulled out the other chair, and sat down.

How was a man meant to pay for all he'd caused since the day he was born? In the mountains it had been easier to play what he knew against what he felt, but now Marcus was in a free fall.

"So, you're turning yourself in now," he said, bluntly.

Gavin looked at him with his familiar, imploring expression.

"What? Changed your mind? Not guilty now? All sins redeemed for taking a walk?" Even this little bit of torture felt tedious. Gavin's hand trembled as he sipped his coffee. Before Marcus could speak again, Andy and Claire arrived at their table.

"Here you are . . . Did you get stamped at the pilgrim's office, your compostela?" asked Andy. "Our name will be read out at tomorrow's pilgrim's mass." Andy was beaming.

"No, no," Gavin mumbled, and looked to him for help, but Marcus kept his eyes on Claire.

"We're going to continue to Land's End, tomorrow," Andy added, and Claire nodded in agreement.

Marcus grunted, shaking his head, then downing the last of his coffee. He stared at Gavin.

"I think I'm done," Gavin said, staring back.

"It's supposed to be the most beautiful part," Claire insisted. Marcus felt her effort to disguise interest in him.

"I don't think so," Gavin said. Claire was visibly disappointed. "But let's eat together at least," he offered. She brightened.

Andy looked at his watch. "If we're in the first ten to arrive by seven o'clock at the Parador, we eat for free. Five-star! Because it was built as a hospital for pilgrims, they still feed ten of us at every meal. We have to line up," he explained.

"Not on your fucking life." Marcus spat the words.

"Let's just go to the restaurant. I'll buy." Gavin's voice was anxious, high-pitched like a terrier's.

"Good," Marcus said, and slapped his hand on the table. He stood up and led the way through Santiago's small streets, back towards the Plaza del Obradoiro and to the Parador's restaurant.

They sat at a linen-covered oak table, and waiters fussed around Gavin; Marcus marvelled at the way they knew that he was the one with the money. He devoured food deliberately: the roasted sardines, the boiled pig's knuckle and turnip tips, the lobster, the cheese with quince jelly, and finally the *tarta de Santiago*. When he looked up he saw that none of the others had eaten much, and no one caught his eye. Gavin hadn't touched the glass of expensive Albariño white. Silence had overtaken Andy.

"What's up with you?" Claire asked Andy.

"It's extravagant," he said. "Not what pilgrims would eat. A true pilgrim would have settled for scraps from the back door."

Marcus could hear the ticking detonator of his rage.

"I think we stay here the night," he said, turning to Gavin, who made no response but looked like an ill child, responsible for nothing. Marcus wiped his mouth. Andy gazed into his plate. Claire looked at each of them and a smile blossomed on her face.

"I get it," she said, putting her knife and fork together on her plate and nodding. "This is what's supposed to happen. I get it."

"What?" Andy asked, looking at her.

"We can't change, just like that. It's not automatic," and she looked at Marcus as though he would know what she was talking about.

"No, but—" Andy protested.

"No, we understand the motion; that's in our muscles now," she said, staring at Marcus. "It's like change is there, if we want to take it." She took her napkin off her lap and folded it over the plate.

Marcus rubbed the curls on his head with his hand; he was touched by Claire's reasoning. He waited for her to grip her right wrist in her left hand, but she didn't. Whether or not she had been sleeping with Andy, or wanted Gavin, the fact was that the woman had matured.

"I'll pay for a room, if you want one," Gavin said to her.

She hesitated and considered. "I don't think so. There's the albergue outside of town that will do me fine. But will you come to Finisterre?"

"No, no, I don't think so," he answered. He glanced over at Marcus, who sat steady, his smirk-lurking face staring straight ahead.

"If you change your mind, meet us at eight, at the Seminario Menor?" Claire offered. "Or at the beginning of the trail?"

Gavin nodded at the scraps on his plate.

❧

It was backwards, all of this. The faint *ahh* that an answer could be found. With Marcus, or somewhere else—in the church that hadn't moved him, or the movement still in his legs, as Claire had said. Finisterre had been where all of this had started, and maybe he would have been better off ending it there months ago, when there had been a single moment of certainty. After that it was farce, but, for a moment, he had known. Something.

❧

He was relieved to be rid of Andy and Claire, knowing he'd never see them again. He watched Gavin enter his room down the hall and then shut the door of his own luxurious suite. He threw his things on the floor and caught his reflection in the long mirror beside the broad cherrywood dresser with enough drawers to contain a pilgrim's life. Shit, man: the black forest of his head, thick and darker, and yet with grey streaks. Black ferns and sprigs of wild grass. Curls would sprout next, and he knew of the straight-frizzy-dizzy future if he let it grow. But he was attracted to the man in the mirror with the dark primeval helm.

He was tired. He stripped to his undershorts and got into the king-size bed. He was relieved the day was over so that he could find the self that he knew—the Marcus who had lived emotionally unscathed these past fifteen years in Spain. Something needed to count for something. And account for something. He would change his life. He pulled the duvet to his chin and closed his eyes. If he returned to London, he could stay with his mother on Ladbroke Grove, and start again; or there was Madrid, or Barcelona. It was clear that Pamplona was now his past.

He turned on his side, and suddenly there was a knock at the door. He ignored it, but the knocking persisted. He got out of bed and opened the door to Gavin's passive blue eyes. They were not searching as they'd been in Pamplona. No, this man was a pilgrim who had walked his walk and now was only waiting for the moment of pardon.

"What do you want?" Marcus asked.

A long silence snaked along the corridor before Gavin asked, "What will you do now?"

"Don't know." Marcus shifted the weight on his feet and felt suddenly cold with the draft from the hallway. He turned his back on Gavin and entered the room, leaving the door open, allowing the lost dog to follow him in if it wanted.

"More to the point, what will you do now?" he asked over his shoulder.

"I want to go home, but I can't," Gavin said, but when Marcus turned around Gavin looked embarrassed. "I have to ask you, one last time, if you'll go with me to the police, or if not, what it is that I can do to help you . . . to make it all go away."

He could feel the coursing of blood towards his face. "To make it all go away? For you to tick off a little box in your conscience?"

"No . . ." Gavin said, shaking his head, but Marcus knew that there was nothing else for either of them to do. He sat down on the bed to stop himself from flying at the man's throat. He took a deep breath. Gavin walked to the bed and stood in front of him.

"Why me?" Marcus asked, looking into his hands. Gavin was silent, trying to understand the question. "Why did you pick me? Of all the boys at that school, why pick me to accuse?" He suddenly realized that all along this had been the real question of his life.

"I thought you'd seen us."

Marcus shook his head, then looked up at him. "No, you must have known that when no one accused you immediately . . . so why me?"

For a moment Gavin looked as though he'd gone back to Scotland.

"Your face . . . it had something special that drew me in. And I was scared," Gavin said, so clearly that it couldn't have been misunderstood, so that when Marcus finally registered that all these years had been a result of this man's cowering awe, he couldn't hold himself back.

He bolted from the bed and flung himself at the bastard. He rammed Gavin's chest with his shoulder; they shot against the far wall. He punched the kidneys, the belly, then reached up and struck Gavin's face. Gavin tried to push him off, turning away, but Marcus forced him back towards the bed, where he threw him down on the mattress and straddled him.

His panting was wheezy as he raised his hand and slapped Gavin's face, once, with one hand, one cheek, then the other hand, the other cheek. He slid his hands into the waistband of his underpants to slide them off, but Gavin struggled beneath him so he pulled them down with one hand, while holding Gavin down with the other. With his underwear around his ankles, he grabbed Gavin, picked him up, turned him, and tossed him back, face down on the bed. He grabbed the hands and drew them around the back, clasping them in arrest at the base of the spine. He struggled with his free hand to pull down

Gavin's trousers, tearing at the clasp and pulling.

Down.

Help.

How? Marcus cried, to himself, enlisting the mercy of his mother's god. When the trousers and underpants were down far enough to expose Gavin's arse, he spat and prepared himself. For this.

It would make the difference he'd needed his entire life. He took his cock in his hand. He tried to make it hard. This. Would make. A difference. Tears began to stream from his eyes. They splashed on Gavin's skin. Back. Hip. Buttocks. He had trouble seeing straight, his eyes streaming, spit drooling. He took his soft cock and moved it closer. But he couldn't see. He couldn't see.

How.

He pushed the clasped hands away and got off.

"I'll do it," he said through a sob. "I'll turn you in."

Gavin's mouth was full of blood; he had bit down hard on his tongue just before Marcus had released him. He scrambled to sit up, holding both hands over his mouth.

Marcus saw blood trickling through the fingers as he pulled up his underwear.

"Uhh," Gavin muttered, releasing his hands and holding out his bloodied tongue. He cupped his mouth again. Marcus stared at the blood on the man's chin. Time fanned out, and he was caught out, not knowing how to react. Gavin looked at him, but was it with gratitude? Marcus sat down beside him on the bed.

Happiness is a warm gun, Marcus thought, unsure of why such lyrics would come to him at a moment like this. He leaned over and grabbed the back of Gavin's head, drawing him forward, their faces almost touching, the pull and the resistance making them both tremble. He touched the blood on Gavin's lip with the tip of his finger. They both straightened up and retreated, but quickly, as though remembering something, moved in close again. It was Gavin, now, who pushed Marcus onto his back.

It could not have all come to this, for this.

Marcus tore open the striped shirt, exposing Gavin's chest, and Gavin lay on top of him.

Soft skin, hard pecs . . . ribs beneath his ribs.

Their hips, legs, just to the side of one another's.

For the first time in months having to will away the savage stiffness between his legs.

Breath was heavy; movement was nil.

Was he to feel relieved? How was relief possible from something that had, over the years, grafted on like a new skin? He held his breath.

Marcus smelled lavender at Gavin's neck. He tried not to move. Gavin let out his breath and nestled his head in the hollow between Marcus's head and shoulder. Marcus moved his hand gracefully from the bed to Gavin's forehead, where it lay still for what seemed like forever.

Twenty-Two

The origin of viruses is obscure. Some scientists believe that the mammoth capacity and variety of self-replication among these particles reflects their evolution from original life, before the appearance of double-stranded DNA. Or viruses may be the degenerate descendants of parasites, which may have been so successful at exploiting their hosts that their laziness became an advantage. Whatever their origin, viruses are successful. And fierce.

I read this. It must be true. Putting to paper the intertwined fates of Gavin and Marcus makes me feel that there are still things I don't know about my own relationships.

I've stopped asking Sam about the complexities of the structure and function of viruses, why their shape determines their viability and their ferocity. My research is solitary now. He works harder, talks less, and sleeps a lot. I am closer to understanding Gavin, Marcus, and myself that summer.

But I am losing Sam.

I feel lonely.

I tried to engage him differently the other day. "Knock, knock," I said as I stood at the door to his study.

He smiled, while still looking at the screen of his computer.

"Who's there?"

"Control freak—now you say: control freak who?" I said quickly.

He paused. He was good; he didn't say anything, he had understood the joke immediately, faster than I had when it had been tried on me years ago.

"You're pathetic," he said with a smile.

"I bet Thomas didn't like knock-knock—"

"Stop," he said, cutting me off and looking back at the computer screen. "Don't."

"What?" I asked, but knew I was trespassing. Research was serious. Unlike me, Sam had things to do that were more important than counting loss.

"Leave it."

I backed away silently, but he looked up briefly to tell me that he had to go out and might be home late.

He is becoming immune to me.

During the day, when I'm alone writing, I tackle the problems of the universe: the intricate challenges of space and time that I construct for my own purposes. My imagination controls time. I can be in my past, Gavin's, or Marcus's. I can stop time or accelerate it. I can think in words that don't exist, or hear a sound that no one else has ever heard. Nothing enters unbidden, and play protects my tranquility.

My evenings are routine, broken up between slow nibbling at the stove and a visit to Señora Ormaza, who has acquiesced to her colostomy bag, and with whom I play cards. But even that tranquility has been stolen from me.

"Here," I said to her a couple of nights ago, tired of our regular game of *Mus*—a Basque passion, which uses a forty-card deck without eights and nines—which she had taught me months ago. I shuffled the cards and asked her to pick one. She did, I put it in with the pack, counted the numbers and the options, having to modify what Sam had taught me to suit the forty- and not fifty-two-card deck. I was able to look deft under her bewildered gaze. I liked that.

"It was the caballo de copas?" I asked, feeling smug that what Sam had taught me was foolproof, even in this *baraja* of cups and swords rather than hearts and diamonds.

"What? Hey! You!" Señora stammered, with half delight, half disdain.

"What?" I asked, confused by the disdain. "Didn't you like that?"

"Na, na . . . where did you learn that?"

"Sam—he's a master at card tricks."

"He tricks you?"

My stomach rose and rolled. "Just playing," I muttered and shuffled the deck.

"He tricks you!" she said again, and I began to perspire. I quickly reshuffled the deck and dealt her a hand of solitaire, but when she looked down for a moment to adjust her colostomy bag, I held back two cards from the deck, sliding them into my pocket. It was small satisfaction for unwieldy, misplaced motives. I left, saying a tiny *buenas noches* beneath my breath.

My night territory is all that I cannot control. I push away each thought that leads to pain—the barbs of feeling that arrive like the tips of tiny weapons. Nothing is happening. Nothing. It's a rallying call of what's left of my certainty. All that's left unscathed by wildness.

Twenty-Three

I have to make it all stand still long enough for me to see. It can't go wobbling off course now. Not as it's almost clear: Marcus in bed with him, as I had been—both of us in the glow of the warm gun of . . . what? Of what? I must look to one other key moment, which involves these tricks. Of perception. Of belonging. I have to make something of the pattern that now extends to Claire.

She arrived, along with Andy, at the albergue a few hours after me. I jumped off the top bunk bed in the brightest corner of the dorm to greet them, and Claire seemed relieved—and even happy—to see me. After assuring her that I was fine, I immediately asked after Marcus. When I heard about the luxurious choice of hotels, I felt even more confused by him, and what he might be doing. She told me of the tentative plan with Gavin to meet in the morning. I went to bed thinking, planning. I would propose my idea for us to leave Pamplona and move to Barcelona, which would have opportunities for us both. I barely slept.

Claire and Andy were in the flimsy bunk beds next to me, and it must have been about two in the morning that I heard them arguing in whispers beside me. Both of them lay on their backs and spoke to the air. I tuned into Andy in the bunk below Claire calling her a fake. I had difficulty following his argument, until I realized he was referring to her attention to Gavin and was accusing her of falling for his looks. I hadn't realized until then that the small seed I had planted in her had grown to this.

"Fuck off," Claire said softly to the cracked ceiling. "You have no right."

They went silent and I assumed they stewed in their anger, but they probably slept. Andy's alarm watch beeped annoyingly a few hours later. He packed up and told Claire he was leaving and asked if she was joining him.

"Go on," she said quietly.

I finally dozed off in the small dawn, and woke with a start just after eight. Claire's bunk was empty. I had missed her. I rushed to get dressed, leaving the dorm and searching for her in the few nearby cafés, until I thought more strategically and headed to the edge of town. I spotted her sitting under a eucalyptus tree in the grassy square that led towards the Camino at the end of Rúa das Hortas. The small poison I'd let drip was potent. She was waiting for Gavin. As I approached, I noticed that the eucalyptus wept its sticky gum just above the spot where her head rested against its knobby bark.

"You're here," I said, pathetically. She didn't admit that she was waiting for him, but this spot was not accidental. The tree's full branches and sprawling bow sheltered her and seemed like the perfect place for the opening of a love story.

"Watching the birds," she said.

I couldn't help but think how eucalyptus trees were known to be lethal to birds, their sticky gum liable to clog a bird's throat and kill it, but I went along with her.

"I'm going to see if I can find Marcus," I said. "Will you wait?"

"Yeah, sure," she said. I knew she was thinking that waiting suited her well. I headed up the street towards the cathedral.

※

He was roused by a shiver. Then another. And another. His eyelids opened. He couldn't stop shaking. It was early morning, the light still crouching beyond the hills. He raised himself up on his hands but was trembling so hard he fell back down on top of the duvet. *Here*, and he tried to remember the how and what of here. And before here. Sitting up quickly, he saw the dried blood on his hand and the fabric. He swiveled towards the window. Marcus. *There.* Marcus was at the edge of the king-size bed, on top of the duvet, but he had pulled the corner up and had cocooned his torso. Gavin's eyes shot down his own body. Buttonholes on his shirt had been ripped open, his trousers kicked off, his underpants in place. He looked at his belly and the crinkled red patches of rubbed skin near his nipple. He had slept on Marcus, whose breath had smelled like egg. His skin had pressed on bone. The bone belonged to a man who had spared him from something he deserved but could not have survived. He stood up, trying to hide the trembling, trying to make his bones stop rattling. It could not have all come to this.

He listened, inside. It was not screaming now; it was like the clanging of cast-iron pans. An alarm. Marcus stirred, and Gavin held his breath, watching the man's deep breaths, the peaceful look on his face.

His legs shook as he tried to stand up from the bed. He held on and said *hush* to the metal clanging. How was he to be saved? He thought of his mother and father, the proud look on their faces at the engagement party. He knew that connection to another person was a right path—his trembling told him so—but not this kind of intimacy. No matter what he thought he could do for this man whose head he had stroked and begged for at the bull ring, no matter what could be set right, this ambush by male love was not what he had come all this way for. The walking, the mountains in his legs now, the *next, next, next* of each glimpse of horizon. Surely this was not how it all ended.

His lips began to quiver and he was afraid of the noises escaping through them. He looked about the room and saw his trousers and boots on the floor. He tiptoed towards them, spotting a T-shirt sticking out of Marcus's pack. He grabbed it, stripped off his shirt, slid into his jeans and the new T-shirt, and checked to make sure his credit card was still in his back pocket. As each hand grabbed a boot, they shook so violently that the caked red mud flaked off and dusted the floor. He crept to the door. Tucking the right boot under his arm, he turned the handle and stepped into the lit corridor. He wouldn't look back. The bruised sides, aching kidneys, the sting still on his cheeks; and more, the creases on his skin, the red blotches near his thigh, the gentle ache he felt in his pelvis. If he saw Marcus awake, he would be forced to admit that these were real. It had not happened. This was not the release he needed. The door clicked shut louder than he'd intended, but he scurried away.

He was packless, jacketless, and dishevelled again, much like the Gavin I'd first met. He was wandering along the street behind the cathedral, headed somewhere and yet lost. Again.

I called to him but he didn't hear me at first. After the second call he stopped and turned. When he saw me he paused, but then continued walking.

"Wait!" I shouted. When I reached him he slowed. "What's going on?"

"Nothing, nothing is going on," he stressed.

"Where's Marcus?" Something was wrong.

"He's gone," Gavin said, walking faster.

"What?" I stopped and watched him walk off, the lumbering, tottering back and forth of trouble.

"Wait!" I called again. I stopped him by tugging on the back of his T-shirt. "Where?"

His face said he hadn't planned on me. It was puffy and streaked along the cheeks in red splotches. His eye was swollen.

"He's going back, home," he said. "He's had enough." As though that was all I needed, he started walking again.

Had he hurt Marcus?

"What did he say?" I asked, before following Gavin again. "What did he say?" I repeated.

Gavin hesitated, stopped, and looked at me. "He told me if I saw you to tell you that you should go with him, meet him at the coach station this morning." This might have been true, but I couldn't be sure. There was a difference between this man and the desperate man in Pamplona. Not merely the random raw materials; this man had finally made a choice.

"He was asking about me?"

He seemed surprised. "It was you who left us, remember." He squinted. "I think he missed you."

I almost laughed. "Don't be ridiculous."

"He thought you'd say that," he said. The implications of

his statement disconcerted me, but I didn't know how to ask him more.

"Where are you going?" I asked instead, trying to sound tough, for Marcus's sake, but also not ready to let him go. If I believed him then that Marcus was going home, it was because I wanted to, not because I trusted him. The wildness within him still drew me and I convinced myself that if I lost track of Gavin, no matter what he'd done, he'd have got away with it and Marcus would have lost.

He shrugged.

"Walking towards water makes sense," I said, echoing Claire, but dizzy with my creative power. "You should finish the Camino, to Finisterre. You're almost there."

Gavin's face twisted in a look between anger and pain.

"What?" I asked.

"I started there," he said thickly.

"You did?" I was confused, but on a roll, and still blindly trying to save something or someone. "All the more reason—it'll be different. You'll see. Water will give you perspective, and besides Claire is waiting for us. She knows . . . she knows lots of things; it doesn't seem like it, but she does," and I knew from the change in his face that he'd felt this too. "You have nothing to lose. Why not?" I pressed. He couldn't argue with me. I started to walk and gestured that he should follow. And with some sense of satisfaction, I was aware that he was behind me.

Claire was sitting up straight, meerkat-like, waiting for us under the tree. "Where's your pack?" she asked Gavin as she stood up with hers.

"Don't need it," he said, and she looked at him, believing him, the fact of his shedding it giving him even more appeal.

In silence we continued past the large yellow scallop marking the trail's return. Claire led, while Gavin was between us.

I watched him up ahead as he touched his forehead several times, wiping away sweat as we crossed the bridge at Ponte Sarela and forded a stream. The trail was moist; the earth slumped underfoot, and we walked on, and on, until the oak was usurped by the predominant eucalyptus and the light turned flaxen.

Several hours out of Santiago, the Camino changed—looking more savage, as though revealing its pagan roots. Purpose was falling away from my boots with each step, and I began to feel guilty for my meddling, while still uncertain what to do about Gavin. Would Marcus want me to turn him in? Did I want him to be turned in, or did I think he deserved forgiveness and had decided Claire would offer it? I asked Claire to walk beside me, coming up with questions that I thought would engage her, things she knew about the Camino from her research.

"For people of ancient times," she said as she swung her arms over her head, releasing a kink, "the Costa da Morte was the end of explored land, the final stretch mapped by the Milky Way." I saw the muscles in her arms contract and bulge, and it crossed my mind that she could probably beat Gavin at any fight. "It's where the Christian and the pagan met—the Holy Christ had come after the cult of the Virgin who arrived there in a stone boat," she added.

There it was again, her utter credulity coupled with a kind of animal simplicity. I wondered if this was the formula for integrity. She told me that this was the Sarela River that would lead us to Negreira. "For whom the bell tolls," she said, and I remembered that it was the town in the novel. There was something too obviously ominous in those words, which I chose to ignore.

We covered a substantial distance that day—the eighteen kilometres from Ponte Sarela to Negreira. The walk was silent, amber, and always on the verge of forking. Simple equilibrium might give way, or it might not. Gavin was steady, walking ahead of us both, and it felt like we were in his downdraft.

At the entrance to the Negreira refugio, a group of cheery pilgrims had gathered, waiting for the doors to open. Gavin stopped to let us catch up. "Let's keep walking; we can get there," he demanded, but Claire said she was tired and didn't want to rush. Gavin watched her walk towards the building. But Claire stopped short when she saw Andy standing near the door, talking to a woman wearing a multicoloured Mexican headscarf.

I arrived beside her and stood as she considered what to do.

"Do you like him?" I asked her.

"Andy? No—"

"Gavin," I corrected, cutting her off, and she looked at me gratefully, as though I'd granted her a wish she'd kept secret until now. I was sickened by myself. She merely smiled and continued towards the doors that were now being opened.

As Andy picked up his pack, he spotted Claire, put his head down, and entered quickly, taking up a bunk in the far corner. Gavin followed us in and chose the bed nearest the door. I put my pack down next to Claire's and went over to him.

"Is there more you want to tell me?" I asked.

"No," he said and rubbed his upper arm. He seemed unconcerned about what I knew or did with it, and this denial of any power on my part must have kept me hooked. He disappeared into the canteen without me. I went back to my cot and took out my notebook.

I must have been the first among us to wake. I lay silently in bed, listening to the birdsong that started up at the first glow of dawn. I heard the woman who Andy had talked to get up and leave first, before the sun was up. Andy was next, hastily setting off shortly after dawn clearly intending to catch up with her. Gavin rose just after him. I heard him speaking to the American pilgrim who had slept in the bed next to him. The man had noticed how cold Gavin was and offered him his jean jacket, insisting that he had no need for it now that the spring had truly arrived. I heard Gavin thank the wide-mouthed man and proceed to wear the jacket as though it had been tailored for him.

In the morning sun outside the albergue, he was finally warm enough to take the jacket off. "You have this way of standing that reminds me of a cousin, but I haven't seen him in a long time," Claire said, barely loud enough for Gavin to hear, and I wondered if she had wanted him to. Did he remind her of a childhood crush? Perhaps she wondered what her parents would think of this man: too handsome for you, might be on her mother's face even as she complained about his less than perfect teeth; too hoity-toity her father might think as he shook Gavin's smooth soft hand. Claire smiled at Gavin as he tied the jacket around his waist.

"Look, let's get going. We need to get going," Gavin said.

And so we did, Gavin now carrying the borrowed jacket of the tall American, who, unlike me, was just able to let things go.

༄

Would the end make a difference? Now that he'd offered up his guilt to Marcus, perhaps the end of the earth would work for him. He had begun to let go of all that had kept him believing that he was different from any other pilgrim. He had nothing else. Even so. What if *purpose* didn't need to have a purpose, if *intent* was just to make *intend*, so the verb could exist? He felt around in his pockets and touched the credit card. *This* and the clothes on his back were all he had left. And even the card had been rejected the previous day. What if hope was merely the movement of his legs? His ribs, shoulders, and back—all ached from the blows. He focused on his legs and briefly he believed in himself. The terrain became mountainous, and below him was a grand river—Claire had called it the Xallas. The sky seemed important. And colours. Yellow wild-flowers. Yellow. He needed colour. And the feel of the earth beneath his boots. Had they cremated Porter or was his body now moistening in the earth, ready for worms? Porter had said to him in the hospital that to get what you wanted someone else had to suffer. But he had defied Porter. He was not acting like that kind of man. He had done what being a man had demanded of him. Marcus had made him suffer, enough, and if he hadn't in fact seen the fall, then Marcus had nothing to add to corroborate Gavin's confession regarding Sir's death. What was important was that the nightmare flashes had stopped, and Gavin was approaching something now that felt like grace. He would disappear altogether from the world he'd been a part of. A man speaks words, makes gestures, performs actions, his father would have said, only to be witnessed. *Watch me . . .*

※

In the modest canteen that evening, I sat at the end of the bench, by myself, but I watched them. Claire wasn't even attractive, I thought. We were served garlic soup and hard white bread. Simple. And, for Gavin, appropriate for the *not yet* he still must have felt. I watched him watch her. She appeared to drift off. He sipped his soup. She gazed away.

"Where are you?" he asked quietly.

"Sorry. Michigan . . ." she muttered.

"What about it?" he asked, with genuine interest.

"When I was a kid," she said mischievously, "I used to think my parents sold the worms as food. Worm soup." She paused. I saw him lean in. "I was sure of it, and I kept looking in all the food my mother made to find traces, and many things looked like they could have been worms, but my mother denied it every time. I could never get my head around pea soup, sure it was a trick," and she shook her head and dipped the spoon into her bowl, bringing soup to her mouth.

I watched as he looked and saw the little girl in her. Beautiful.

Twenty-Four

I used to think that my mother's conflict with my father's nature was rooted in her family history and all those trees planted by my grandfather—her certainty that stability was sacred and that a tree was rooted, not wild. Roots were preferable to perpetual motion. But year by year I have recognized her certainty for the terror it really is. The rich yet febrile texture of conviction itself. The way a child needs his invisible friend. And, like a child, my mother found it difficult to see outside herself. Maybe my father was always away, but she was always tied up in her relationship with conviction, as though cuckolding him with something with which he could never compete. He was locked out. No wonder he had to run.

Sam has begun to remind me of my mother—his conviction in his research. It's being shut out that I mind the most. That snowy Christmas morning many years ago, my father had yelled "Why is it always about you?" to my mother as I had been putting on my snowshoes. Sam's viruses, Sam's sleepiness. And Sam's nights? I want him to include me. He must tell me himself. He must.

Sam.

Marianne has the strong neck of a deer.

Twenty-Five

A beach. Claire had said all morning how she'd wanted this beach. "Sardinero," she'd repeated to me, as we walked along beside each other; Gavin now trailed us, almost dawdling, as though his urgency had been only to be out of Santiago.

"Did you bring a bathing suit?" I asked, imagining she'd want to show off to Gavin.

"I haven't worn a bathing suit in years," she said and touched her belly unconsciously.

"Hurry," I called back to Gavin. "It's the sea!" I said as though I had created it myself. Through the break between the stunted trees and shrubs ahead, I could see the curling surf hit the sand. I resisted the sense that I was becoming loathsome.

❧

He arrived behind Claire on the beach, the sea before him unimpressive and anticlimactic after the first sighting from atop the cliff. *This?* The cove was stark and bare, wisps of wild grass, bramble. *This?* He looked at her and the smile on her face. His heart sank again but he tried to believe in what had brought him here.

"Let's rent a boat," Claire suggested.

"You're kidding," he blurted, hugging his arms around himself, suddenly cold in the barrenness of the place.

"Come on, it will be great," she said and touched his arm. He watched her go about the work of talking to a man on the beach, who directed her to the marina. He stood in the sand, away from Emily, who dipped her toes in and wandered aimlessly back and forth along the shore. A family on the beach was having a picnic. Fishermen near the dock were unpacking, coming in with the day's catch. He spotted other boats beyond the cove, all apparently headed back to the marina, and he looked up to the sky, wondering if they knew something that wasn't yet apparent. A man and woman in a rowboat floundered with oars and ropes close to the shore. He watched them all with his life in his throat. All the walking, talking, gauging—it had to lead to something. His throat tightened. He swallowed. Now. Now. Now. He walked to the shore and took his boots and socks off. The water was cold. He withstood the freezing on his ankle, hoping it would rise and cool the inkling of sound rising up through his chest, which would bring him nowhere. Once more.

The wind rose in a huff. A grey cumulus passed just to the edge of the sun. Pewter. He was relieved he was still feeling colours. Other, white clouds were accumulating just above the horizon.

⁂

Claire had done everything, arranged the boat and paid for it. I'd followed her over to the pier to see if I could help, but she seemed proficient enough in Spanish to understand the owner's instructions. She asked me to join them, but I hesitated. This was an opportunity for things to unfold without me. I wanted to let it go, but it was my epic now. I looked over to Gavin, who was standing on the beach. I thought about what he'd said about Marcus missing me. He was full of twists; I couldn't understand why he had said that, let alone why my presence always seemed so insignificant to him.

※

He surveyed the bay and chose a destination. Beyond the rocks to the left of the bay the sea appeared to flatten again, a suggestion of a cove on the other side. He imagined himself drifting there, waiting for the something that he felt would surely come. He felt he would reach something new, if only the sky would stay full. If only the cloud that was now pressed up against the sun wouldn't pass over it. If only the wind continued to speak for him.

※

The three of us stood on the pier, as the owner of the boat held it for us to get in. Gavin got in first, then looked surprised as I put my pack in, preparing to put a foot into the salt-eaten wooden rowboat.

"You too?" he asked, and I pulled my foot back and stood on the pier.

The owner of the boat moaned and said something under his breath, looked up at the sky and said something else related to the clouds.

"What?" I asked Gavin.

Gavin looked at Claire, who giggled nervously. An itchy flush rose in my face, like a growing rash.

"You weren't so reluctant that night in Pamplona!" I blurted. I was losing my grip.

His face went sour.

"Please, Claire," he said, and tapped the seat beside him. But her intuition wouldn't let her get in.

"What's going on?" she asked.

"He's probably afraid I'll tell you about his performance." I didn't know what was happening in me. "But don't worry, he'll buy you lovely little gifts to make up for it." The outbursts of vileness were uncontrollable, the story was writing itself. "Not to mention another little issue, but maybe he thinks he's not a murderer now." Even as I said it I felt that I knew nothing that was true, and saw, once again, the venom of trying too hard. He looked at me with wide eyes, but I kept a face that said that what I knew was dangerous for him. I couldn't be sure of anything, and yet I'd spoken words that formed an angle that would become solid, not just air, not just thought, but a hardening of syllables into a so-called truth. Claire looked as though I'd hit her. The owner of the boat swore and asked us to hurry up. I stepped into the boat, while Gavin looked pleadingly at Claire. I sat down, with everything hard and hardening.

Twenty-Six

A story told properly has a satisfying, cathartic ending, but the truth is that I am having trouble finishing this tale. Not only is it obvious how my behaviour contributed to what eventually happened—why did I get in that boat?—but I have lost hold of the past, of the ability to put myself back with Gavin and Claire. The proper narration for those last events has been interrupted by the present. Fury won't let me speak.

Sam didn't come home two nights ago.

"Where have you been?" I could barely get the words out, my mouth heavy with the night's calamity of curses and wailing.

I had paced; I had vomited; I had slept and dreamed of raccoons. The morning had found me numb. I uncurled from my fiddlehead position and sat up on the sofa as I heard the door latch open. I watched as Sam slipped off his trainers without untying them. I noticed the tips of the nylon and rubber shoes, which looked like they'd been singed by fire or blackened by powder. Out of sync with the moment, I found myself thinking of the qualities of rubber that allow it to keep its form and support a car or truck at high speed and yet melt to liquid at a specific temperature. By the time I refocused on the room, Sam had disappeared into the bedroom. I stood up and followed his tracks—the leather bookbag on the floor in the hallway, his jacket flung on the chair, a sheet of scrunched paper, which I stooped to recover from the floor. I flattened it out. Foreign handwriting: an address and directions. It was an address near the barrio, the gypsy tenement.

It must be difficult for Marianne and George to live there, I thought with clarity. The area was rough, but then again very close to the labs. And George, he seems so suburban, in that square-jawed, large-appliance way. I recrumpled the paper, dropped it back on the floor, and tiptoed into the bedroom, where Sam was already asleep on the bed. An odd smell surrounded him: a smoky, metallic odour that wasn't like the smell from a bar, but more like the smell of burned eggs. I imagined their breakfast and wondered how long George had been gone and whether he was in the States or somewhere else in Europe. I searched my image of Marianne from that day at the cafeteria: her poised neck, her collarbone, the curve of her breast. I wished I hadn't stopped there, that I'd made it to the delicate fingers that were yellowed with nicotine from the cigarettes she must smoke.

"Sam," I said, but he had fallen asleep. I wanted to tell him that I was ready to hear what there was to hear. I wanted to let him know I would love her too. It would be okay. I understood. But he was long gone and far away.

This morning he woke before me, so exhausted was I by the previous night's railings, and he was gone by the time I opened my eyes. I tried to phone him at the lab, but it rang without stop. His mobile phone rang, like humiliating laughter, from inside the pocket of his trousers on the floor.

During the week we first met, in London, I had watched

Sam sleep. After the touch and lick, the nibble and slap of our abandoned lovemaking, he would doze off and his breath would narrow in his throat like breeze through a shutter. I watched him because I really couldn't believe in him yet. I was so astonished by the ease between us and the rightness of his body that I had to stay awake to make sure it was real. I couldn't believe his face, hands, the way his curls grazed his temples when he laughed. I was gazing him into existence, like something I'd invented. Everything he was and said confirmed what I unconsciously understood about the world—that it was perfectly formed, like him—and anything that baffled me could easily be conquered with an explanation.

But now his sleep has a gnawing quality, an animal disquiet. Or like the hum of a machine in need of repair. Computer viruses can be detected and blocked. I wonder about a firewall for the heart.

I will talk to him tonight.

The moon is a smirk. The stars are embarrassed to shine. He still hasn't come home. I cross the Plaza del Obradoiro towards the cathedral and I give St. James a big *fuck you* under my breath. This route to the university lab is not direct; it meanders past the old town and old thoughts and old ways of worship, old heartaches of the individuals who have crossed this square in their last gasps of faith. The plaza is full of tourists out in the moist June air, under a sky that refuses to go black in these long days towards the solstice, and that grates with an eternal drone. If I make my way slowly up towards the university, perhaps he will appear, full of haste and explanation of how absorbing the new project is, how nearly on the brink they are of a cure for . . . something.

My mind runs through other explanations on his behalf: I didn't call because I thought you'd be asleep, you seemed so tired this morning; my watch stopped; I lost all track of time; George came and Marianne and I went out with him for a drink; we thought you'd be working.

But these thoughts make me an even bigger fool.

I reach the humanities building at the edge of campus. The Department of Contemporary and American History is housed in such an overtly dignified building that I feel sorry for her, and for her country that must continually prove itself. There is a wheezing that I realize comes from me. It reminds me of my mother, her difficulty with breathing in the damp, mouldy air of her house in Tweed. Marianne, I am convinced, is fit, her lungs pristine, her flank and thighs in the movement of love like an unbridled galloping horse.

As I approach the medical sciences building I know there's a part of me that wants to stand in awe at the university's illustrious history. I am indignant on its behalf, certain of what's taking place at my destination. Here is an institution founded on the care of the mind and the soul, and here am I, pursuing tainted flesh. But all I want to be is included.

There are few people about—medical students working late—but I want one of them to tell me that what has happened can be reversed; that what is wild can be tamed, that flesh can be forgotten, that spit does not leave a trace.

I enter the building as a student leaves it, climb the stairs to the second floor, and push through the doors of the microbiology department as I have done many times, this time without the picnic lunch or token gift from the market. I smell a hint of sweet smoke. I prepare myself. For the candlelight, for the other smells I hadn't anticipated until now. When I imagined this it was all about what I would see. The other senses hadn't figured.

The parasitology lab. There is a light.
I turn the handle.
The click causes movement inside. Bodies.
I look for flesh.
My first glimpse is a coat. It's June—a coat?
A coat. A leg.

I see a leg. But there's smoke in the room and everything is so unexpected that my eyes feel tricked. A candle is burning on the desk.

He is lying on her and it's her jeans I see. Jeans and a coat. Opening away from her small body. Smaller than I remember. And he is there on her—or rather, beside her as though fallen there, and something in his hand is burning.

She is the one who sits up and pushes him off, and I can see.

She is small and bleached blonde. Hair spaghettied over her face. She sees me, but doesn't. Sees the presence of me, the threat of me, the I-caught-you of me, but doesn't know me. She tries to stand.

"*Mierda . . . mierda*," she says and now I see this something in Sam's hand as he rolls onto his back on the desk and almost off the edge. It's a toilet roll and some foil. *Chasing the dragon*—it comes to mind again out of the past, from the bed in Maida Vale where he had explained what the words meant, and my heart vaults and my eyes burn. The bleached blonde rises. Not Marianne. Not anyone. Just a small young body with a face older than time. Her voice is fuck-fucking in Spanish "*Coño . . . Coño.*" Her eyelids droop. She stands. Wobbles. Collapses to the floor. Sam is on his back. The bare toilet roll drops from his hand. *Chasing the dragon . . .* and the candle falls off the desk. He turns over on his side, the burned foil slips from his other hand, his body curls into the interminable question of Thomas.

My throat is choked with the impossible. His curls. His

curls drip off the corner of the desk. Hopeless. Like the algae on a drowned vessel.

The smell of igniting paper distracts me from replaying fully the moment on the hill when he told me the truth about Thomas, or the moment in Kenya, when he had watched the sick boy and thought that everything was perhaps too much. I should have known that all this was possible. I rush to the desk, and I stamp out the fire that has flared up among the paper where the candle fell. I pick up the square of foil. Charred. Sticky. I sniff it—its pungency is not unappealing. I stand beside Sam and watch him inhale and exhale the same spittle of drool over and over again.

I take his head in my two hands.

"What? What?" he slurs, defensively. He isn't able to open his eyes, but I think he believes they are. "It's just a joke, for fuck sake. You can't take a joke," and I think of the trick of following him blindly on the cliff at Land's End, and I let his head drop against the desk, step over the makeshift pipe of foil and tube, and leave the paper smouldering. I don't turn back to see what the bleached blonde is doing.

Twenty-Seven

Leg-hold traps are lethal to both the wild and the tame alike.

    I am in the Hotel As Artes on Travesía de dos Puertas near the cathedral, where I walked to last night after I packed up a few essential belongings from our apartment and dragged them down the hill, through the moonless streets of the old town, past the cathedral, towards the Carballeira de Santa Susana. I went up to the top of the Carballeira and down the stairs facing the main campus of the university. I sat in the concave compostela-shaped portico watching the back of the statue of Figueroa holding out his testament of gratitude. Enclosed within the compostela I felt safe for a few minutes but then I worried I'd eventually be seen by one of Sam's colleagues, so I got up and headed back to the cathedral, the still bustling Plaza del Obradoiro, and I found the hotel. I thought that tourists might make me feel less abandoned. My room is well appointed, almost luxurious. From its window I can see the back of the cathedral. The view makes the structure look odd. Merely stone. Irrelevant.

    There is nowhere to walk that doesn't feel like a lie. I will gather myself, make the necessary arrangements, and head back to Canada. My mother will be happy to have me.

But first I need a conversation.

We meet in the same place as the first time, but today there are very few students, and the offerings are restricted to a vending machine's wrapped ready-mades and machine espresso. And, this time, I am first to arrive.

"Hi, Hi, I must be late, sorry," she says, as she pulls out the chair and sits. She looks at me like a person who knows more than she should.

We sit silently for a few moments.

"How long has he been doing it?" I ask.

"Not long, I don't think, just recently," she says, not bothering with the pretense of segue.

"Did he tell you?" I sneak a look at her collarbone.

"He was acting strange; I asked him," she says, and then I am jealous, because she at least hasn't been blind. I feel stupid, ignorant of everything real, so consumed with my role as a secondary character that I have been left out of my own story.

"You weren't going to tell me."

"I didn't think it was my place."

I remember my promise to be willing to love her. But I'm not interested in love. I look at her hand instead of her neck. I see, of course, there is no evidence of nicotine staining. Why had that story been so easy to imagine? That story was easier than this. What is this? This is beyond me.

"I don't think it's gone so far that it's an addiction," she says, way ahead of me.

"How do you know?"

"Because the effects of prolonged use of heroin make you a captive for life. Intravenous heroin peaks in the blood in less than a minute, crosses the blood-brain barrier within seconds, and most of it is absorbed into the brain. If that rush is something you start to love, you're dead."

I was astonished by her. "How long then?"

"I don't know, but not that long."

And as I try to replay his absences, step back to see the storyline I have been neglecting, I feel some relief, as a part of me knows it's true. Not long. But why?

"And one thing's for sure, it's better that it's smoke and not needles. The risk from dirty needles—HIV, Hep C—a nightmare," she says in her scientist's voice, and oh how camp I feel viruses are, how utterly over the top. "Mainlining is nasty," she adds, and I want to know how she knows this, and how everyone else speaks of danger like it's merely the troublesome relative.

"I thought it was you," I say, trying to be as dangerous as the world seems at this moment. Her face freezes, then a slow quizzical smile appears, and I feel more ridiculous than before.

I think of Marcus, of the Marcus that is suspended in my narrative, walking or hitching back to Pamplona, to . . . what? And suddenly I think of what I might do before I return to Canada. Something I have to do. Now, as Marianne is about to speak—I don't want to her to ruin my brainwave—I pre-empt her, "It would have been easier, that's all. I wouldn't have had to leave."

"Why leave?"

"He's a liar."

"He needs you now."

"I'm not his mother."

"You're hurt."

"Don't tell me what I am."

She's chastened, but she's right about hurt. I would never tell her that, and would never let her know that I want to put my lips to her shoulder and to taste the skin at her bones and sinews because that's where I thought he'd been all this time.

"Did you know he was taking art appreciation classes?" she asks with an apologetic tone.

"Sam?"

"I encouraged him, thought he'd feel better. He's a bit intimidated by you."

It takes a moment to comprehend what she's saying: she encourages him; I intimidate him. I start to feel hot.

"It's not me who knows . . . it's my dad . . ." and I stop because I hear my own intimidation expressed. But classes? I could have joined him.

"The grant was more than he could handle," she says, and this I can relate to.

"I know, but I've been trying to make things easier . . ."

She looks at me and blinks at the irrelevance of what I've just said. I tear open a packet of sugar and empty it in a line across the tabletop. By the time I realize that this looks like something I hadn't intended, it's too late and she has taken it in, looked away, and smiled. I am a fool.

"He told me about his dad, you know." She pauses while I clean up the sugar and I wonder just how much he has confided in her. "The story of what he said just before Sam moved away from the States . . ." she pauses again, looking at me as though I know what she's referring to. I am even more of a fool. I don't respond; I let her tell me about my own lover.

"I'm sure you know . . ."

"No."

She looks uncomfortable, adjusts her bra strap, and tosses a braid over her shoulder. "That his father said to him that he could just as well leave, that all he had lived for had been gone for some time, in the other son, so what did it matter. He had nothing; Sam could leave and it would make no difference." She flips another lock over her shoulder. "I think his research is about making a difference, but the work itself doesn't matter. It's his brother."

Living for two, as Señora Ormaza had said, and for a few glib seconds I am glad that the good Señora is wrong. He hasn't been living for two. He has been guilty of barely living at all.

"Who are you to tell me that?" I ask, annoyed that I only saw viruses. I am sorry the moment my words come out.

She starts to pack up her things. This is not what I expected, and my imagination has trouble working this fast. The vein in Marianne's deer-neck is beating out the patter of her heart right under my eyes. She and Sam, their research, the certainty of proof—while my proof has been false all these years. Now I see the fallacy of my binary opposition: Tame and wild are not opposed, only relative, one to the other. Sam needs to be set free as much as my father did.

"I'm sorry," I admit.

She gives me an it's-okay nod.

Now what? We both wait. But before I can come up with anything I am back with Marcus, wondering how to write the defeat he feels. Wondering how far off the truth I've been in his story, how much of him I have left out, the way I've missed parts of Sam.

And what about Marianne and what I am constructing now?

The story I'm telling this second?

And this one now?

And even now?

Marianne sees me drifting off. I think of something to connect to her, and the obvious question rises.

"But where were you that night? When George was in the bar?" I ask, remembering the look on George's face when he saw me.

She swallows and looks away and then back. "I used you and Sam as an excuse," she says boldly, as though she's been preparing to tell me, or someone, about this for some time and now her conscience is clear. "I saw someone else, a man in town, just once, and nothing happened, but I was tempted, and I didn't tell George. It was wrong, so I ended it there and then. It was nothing. Absolutely nothing." I can feel that American certainty, that direct and knowing conviction of rightness and wrongness in her voice, and I'm amazed by all that we don't know about one another.

Twenty-Eight

The end of June. In two days it will be the first of July. Oh Canada. I never fail to mark my country's birthday wherever I find myself on that day. It's usually not a grand gesture, merely a bit of song in my head, but this year I hear big, angry chords. I don't know who I am.

Two days ago I would never have consented to what is about to take place. Now I am more clear-minded, have slept enough for a season, and, as I walk up the hill towards our apartment, I am calm.

I stand at the door and scrape it with my fingernails, a gentle scratching rather than a knock. He knows this sound, the pet wanting in—it's a game we play. But as soon as it's done, I regret it, not wanting him to think we are on normal ground. There is no normal now.

His face is sallow, his hair like limp, wilted salad. I can't grasp exactly what I need from this meeting. A nod towards what's real—which I don't think I'm going to get.

"Come in, please," he says as he reaches for my shoulders, but I hold myself stiff. How many liars does it take to screw in a light bulb? None. "Light bulb? What light bulb? I don't see any light bulb?"

I make my way to the kitchen and sit at what is usually his chair at the table. I have decided that he must do all the talking. Any words I have left are for this notebook. He sits across from me and I notice that there is a streak of pink across his cheeks. He looks unusually young.

"You have every right to hate me."

Oh, please. I hadn't anticipated self-pity.

"How long?" I ask.

"After Christmas, I guess." I'm relieved he isn't going to play the game of pretending not to understand me.

Then a date stands out: December 26; the day of the tsunami; the day I started to write Gavin's story. And twenty years since anyone had seen Thomas.

But what was our rush? Nothing lasts longer than ruins.

"With who?"

"A student."

And I don't ask if it's the bleached blonde because I know at least not to expect the logical with smack. But I still need to pay lip service to reason: "Why?"

I don't expect him to speak; he would want me to have known the answer, would be insulted that it hadn't immediately made perfect sense. But he surprises me.

"Experimenting, I guess, just to see what was possible."

"Don't you have enough of that to do at work?" I clip.

He looks down, accused, but seems to want to make me see. "I never accepted it . . ."

"Accepted what?"

"That if he wasn't around, he was really gone."

I know he means Thomas, but I don't want riddles. "That was obvious."

"And so I wanted to see. I didn't have any idea what he

might have been going through, or how it would have affected him. I was never going to know. So it was like having a conversation with him," he says, but his face grows red as though he's boiling with anger.

"But you had so much to do!" I'm stuck on my own story of him from the past few weeks, unable to take in just how much he had been obsessed with Thomas. I'm not defusing his anger but making it worse, and I don't care. Now we both have it.

"All that time," he starts, thinks, then begins again, "with my mother sitting waiting at the window, by the phone . . . And he was out there having the ride of his life," he says, and looks up and me, and I'm terrified, because he's telling me that what he's been doing has been the ride of his life.

"But you had so much to do," I repeat again, like a broken talking doll whose string has been pulled loose. Because I had so much to do, surely we both had so much to do not to go off experimenting, after the news of limbs and heads stuck in Asian trees. I want to remind him that it was I who drank the blood in Kenya, not him. I was the one taking risks, while he didn't need to.

"I felt like a fraud," he says, and I know that I have struggled to see happiness awake in him but he hasn't allowed himself to be happy.

"This research was real. He isn't necessarily dead," he says, calmly. "I'm here, after all." He sounds lucid. I offer no response. "He might surface," he adds.

I have not been paying enough attention. I hadn't realized that in the six months since the tsunami he had been clinging to life by holding a severed arm. I look around our apartment: the shambles of his last few days alone—peaks of rubble formed from our seismic shift. There is nothing of me here, even though my desk, my books, everything but my laptop and clothing is as I left it. I feel sick with responsibility and resentment.

"It's not something I need," he says in a liar's wobbly pitch. Was it always this? Has everything been at a cliff edge in the weak hands of trust? I wonder what it is that I have been trying to save in him. In myself. I think of Gavin, and the creeping feeling of what he and I have in common makes me shudder.

"I've stopped. We'll take a trip. It'll be like it was," Sam says. And like it was suddenly becomes as much a fairy tale as once upon a time, and I see that all along he hasn't been optimistic, he's been in denial. Tame and scared appear to be the same.

I look at him. He looks diminished as he slouches at the table.

"I tried everything," I say, indignant. My tone affects him.

"You did what?" he asks, sitting up straight.

"Tried. Everything."

He shakes his head and I can see he is becoming angry again, at me this time.

"What?" I ask, defensively. He can barely sit still now. His lips press tight.

"You moralize," he spits out.

Stung, I bolt up from the table.

"You're always controlling it, even in English."

"It?"

"You, me, everything." His lip starts to quiver as though this is hard for him to say, and all I can think of is how in Kenya he had rested his forehead on my shoulder at the sight of the dying child. How was I to keep the *too much* out of our lives? Damn him. Damn them all.

I stand, pick up my bag, and hit my toe on the table leg in the process. I don't let on how much it hurts. He doesn't attempt to stop me. I hobble out of the apartment.

Twenty-Nine

Alpha males are alpha only with the permission of their pack, the docile willingness of the weaker. But alpha is a relative term, not a permanent state. Gavin and Marcus alternated being in control. I had followed Gavin willingly, because he had been like a photograph of Yves Klein that my father had shown me as a child: the artist is caught in a moment of flight from a building in a Paris suburb, a cyclist casually passing by. I had become obsessed with the man's graceful plunge, because all along it had been my own. But Gavin got in that boat because of me. And for years I have been dodging my responsibility, hiding behind Sam, needing his stillness to make me feel safe.

But stillness is not real.

I arrived very early in the morning at the convent to let them know I would no longer be helping out. One of the sisters greeted me at the door, then as others appeared I felt ashamed that I was leaving them, and for a moment I wondered if somewhere along the road I had missed a calling to be one of them. I considered leaving without a goodbye, but Sister Marguerite spotted me and waved a cheery *buenos dias*, motioning me over.

"Señora is sleeping," she whispered, as though we were in danger of waking her in the room down the hall.

"I'm leaving," I returned in a whisper.

"OK, then, see you tomorrow. God bless."

I didn't have the heart to tell her that I'd meant permanently. It was a familiar cowardice. *You moralize*, Sam had said. But I was not a sister.

I walked swiftly but quietly up to the doorway of Señora Ormaza's room. The familiar sour smell topped up my guilt. I tiptoed to her bed and stood by her, watching her sleep. Her mouth was open. I watched spittle slide towards her chin. She had sensed something wrong in my relationship with Sam all along, but I had thought of her as an old woman—so what did she know about my love? Now I wished she'd wake up so I could talk to her and ask her what else she knew. I wanted her to point me in the right direction from here.

He was wrong. It wasn't what he thought. Moralizing was merely protest at all I didn't understand, everything that flees from me and keeps me out. I just wanted to stay. Within. The same impulse that drove me to the mad moment on the boat.

But what Sam has been engaging in is beyond me, even now.

I touched Señora on the forehead and held my fingertips lightly there. Her skin was not very warm. I rubbed it gently. She was unmoved.

"*Socorro*," I whispered, but I knew she wasn't the one who could help.

Not every trek has a destination. I walked backwards along the Camino from Santiago for a day, not knowing where else to go, and fed up with the whole notion of ahead or onward. I tried to get back into my story, to feel it, and tell it the way that it had really happened, but more and more I felt like it was nothing but shams and lies. As I retraced the path, I barely remembered having once been on the trail. In Lavacolla I wished that the river had not now vanished altogether, because I needed to cleanse all I had seen in the parasitology lab from my body. I kept seeing the image of Sam's arm hanging off the desk. I loved him.

I took a coach to Pamplona and arrived where my Spanish journey had begun. I will stay here until I can arrange a flight back to Canada. Everything in reverse. My mother says she will wire me the funds. My father can't be reached.

Pamplona hasn't changed much in five years, except for the currency—the euro that has made life so expensive—and the shrunken-expanded world of the Internet and cheap flights throughout Europe. I have made a point of keeping my mobile phone switched off for this reason. I want time to rewind. And I don't want to speak to Sam.

I feel the absence of Marcus sharply here. He had been my best friend for the two years I lived with him and worked at the bar. I knew I would not find him here, but I wondered if there might be more that I could find out about him.

The owner of the Mesón bar has let me stay upstairs in the maid's room—a single bed, a sink, a bare, hanging light bulb that accuses me of disbelief. I am cradled in the smoke, shouts, and laughter of the activities below. I am their conscience. Yesterday Christophe was in the bar. I was sure he wouldn't have recognized me as I sat in the corner looking at travel brochures with flights to Montreal, but I felt I knew him. His countenance was the same as it had been five years ago, even though his face was darker, his arms stronger, his hair even blonder. I wasn't inclined to reconnect with him, but my curiosity about Marcus was stronger than my indifference to someone I'd once regarded as arrogant.

I was wrong about him too. Christophe remembered me with grace and warmth. He described the changes in Pamplona as being much more drastic than I had noticed, and complained about the same tourist euro that I had thought would have improved the city.

"No," he said gravely, yet with a smile, as though he had a secret weapon that would defeat the foe at the gates, "the tourists who come here might as well go to Brighton for all they care it's Spain. Bulls will attract the basic, if you know what I mean." He lost his smile for a moment, "Sometimes, I'm shocked." He went on to describe the growth of what had merely been an idea when I had lived in Pamplona: he had organized the Running of the Nudes to protest against the use of bulls in the San Fermin festivities, and the run had become an annual event, had grown beyond his projections, and was now alerting the outside world to the horrors of bullfighting.

The first run had been a three-man show, as Christophe and two Danish tourists had run naked well ahead of the release of the first bulls. But he had felt that by running on the first day of San Fermin, both nude and red-neckerchiefed men were perceived as one and the same, and the protest lost its impact. The following year Christophe decided they should run a few days before San Fermin.

"I thought if people saw how stupid it looked to run a beast of any nature they'd be less inclined to force the bulls," he said still smiling. "It worked only to make them think, not to stop them." The year before last, nearly a hundred people joined in; last year, nearly three hundred; this year could be as big as five hundred, if PETA organizes it as they have promised. "We have people from England, Scandinavia—and Canada," he added with a wink. But I have no intention of stripping bare and running through Pamplona, no matter how good the cause.

The human run will take place on July 5, three days' time and two days ahead of San Fermin, but Christophe is still fighting the city officials who are refusing to allow full nudity, making the protest illegal for the first time. PETA has begun negotiations with legislators, proposing to legitimize the run by agreeing to the city's demand for clothing.

He described how he thought it was easy to change things, if you kept time in perspective and remembered how relatively slowly the universe expands. Five years ago, when Gavin first came to see him tending bulls at the *correo*, Christophe believed all he really needed to do was keep the animals from suffering. Now he wanted to stop the whole thing altogether and was convinced it was just a matter of time before that happened. That's when he asked me about Marcus and what had become of him.

"You two were a good pair," he said, surprising me. We talked about how the summer of 1999 affected Marcus, and between us we have pieced together much more about the man. I can better imagine him that morning.

❧

The morning after. A shock set in, sharp-bending his fading dream so fast that his eyes shot open and he had to remember that he was in the Parador beside Santiago's cathedral. He heard bells ringing out from the cathedral and rolled over and looked beside him, the ruffled duvet, the blood, and the evidence of flight. He ignored it. For now. He rubbed his hands over his face, then over his head. A pelt. The new hair there felt like the hide of a small hair-raised-stand-back dog. He felt as if he had overindulged in weed or drink. But he was calm. All that had passed between him and Gavin along the way had come to this. He would try to make sense of it. He touched his chest and remembered the feeling of the other man's weight on him. He rubbed his belly. Hungry.

The rest of the luxurious room came into focus. Marcus stood up and looked out the tiny square window and could see the empty cloister gardens. He rubbed his hair again. Better not to think yet about the previous night. The ledger was more balanced now and something had been released. He got dressed.

In the corridor he stopped at Gavin's door and knocked. And knocked again. No sound came from inside. He headed outside.

Plaza del Obradoiro was in the shadow of the church and as busy as a late-night city. He spotted blue sky beyond the square and headed towards it. As he walked he saw the cobble-gobbled streets differently. The centuries of stone were shadowed by God's house. Rúa do Villar, Rúa do Cuba. He passed tourist shops with pilgrim souvenirs and could enjoy again the metaphor of the scallop shell—its grooves representing the many paths that lead to one place. He stood at the window of a bookshop and read a reproduction scroll of a twelfth-century tract by Aimeri Picaud. It warned pilgrims of the murderous nature of the Basques and the Navarres, who rob pilgrims and ride them like beasts before killing them, and cautioned against the Castilians, who are vicious and evil. The

Galicians, it stated, were irascible, and most like the French. This Santiago was familiar. He strolled on.

He'd always liked Santiago's walls—tall, stone, with vines and grass sprouting like rebellion up through the ancient mortar, and these had inspired his best paintings. The variations on the crucifixion, the stalwart saints, and the dizzying stained glass had always felt like the dirty secrets of priests. The crypts, the altars, the angels the size of whales—these he could do without. He wandered further, soaking in the feeling of the stone, but he couldn't completely recapture his usual peace. He headed back towards the Parador.

As he approached the Praza da Quintana behind the cathedral he heard the tune of "Dream a Little Dream" played on an electric guitar echoing out beyond the square into the streets. He hadn't seen a jazz busker here before, so he eagerly climbed the stairs towards the plaza. A man was seated near the cathedral shop, guitar on his lap, a small amplifier at his feet, and sweet sounds of syncopated riffs coming from it. But Marcus was rattled when he arrived up close. The musician was thin and tall, his black suit jacket hanging loosely on him. He wore an old panama hat and, most striking, a woollen black ski-mask over his face. His exposed eyes were closed as he dreamed a little dream, and in his mouth he sucked on a pair of exaggerated plastic crimson lips. A mockery of Al Jolson in blackface. Marcus sought out the man's hands, but knew already. White hands strummed the instrument delicately as the tune changed to "Cheek to Cheek." Marcus felt hair rise on the back of his neck. He'd let down his guard for a brief moment, but now, he was reminded. This he understood. This criminal-clown-jazzman was his shadow on this continent. He turned suddenly and walked back to the Parador.

He wandered. Calm, calm, the ancient hospital tried to tell him. The high-walled courtyards and arches of the Parador had been built to lift the soul. Shaded not only from the sun, it was also sheltered from the cathedral itself. The thick walls would protect him; the day had yet to become anything. He knocked once more on that other door before returning to his room.

He waited.

Everything came back: the flack; the flip-flop of know-not-know; the hint of faith that things would change; the blame. Everything came back, so surely Gavin would too. But everything had also told him to expect the opposite of what you thought. He wasn't anxious, wasn't cheated, wasn't even angry. When Gavin didn't return after an hour and the Parador's cleaners knocked at the door, he collected his belongings, walked through the old town, up a hill of new buildings and ugly, scallop-less architecture, and made his way to the Santiago bus station.

⋄

When I finally returned to the apartment I'd shared with Marcus in Pamplona—after the crowd that gathered on the beach and the owner of the boat and the police, after all of it—I walked, now with my own limp, up the stairs. I felt a crawling, furrowing resonance to the air around me. I opened the door and could only make it all into a joke.

"My dinner ready? Hell of a day at the office," I said in the direction of his room as I threw my pack down on the floor. He came out into the living room, stood still, and looked at me for what seemed like a long time. Then I limped quickly to him and threw my arms and legs around him. He lifted me up like a child, and for a deceptive second I was home.

"Your face," he said, and touched the cuts and bruises there.

We talked in English into the early hours of the next day. He told me his everything; I told him mine—but after I managed to extract a few details about his last night with Gavin, it felt beside the point to reveal the events of my liaison with Gavin in Pamplona. Instead I underscored my story with the irony that it had been me who, in the end, had been held at a station and questioned by the police. The irony and this new language between us invigorated our exchange but reduced what was left of any sexual charge I had ever felt with him. And gradually, through the night, I forgave him for having kept so much of his history from me for so long. By the end of our recounting of our time over the month, I felt I had to write again, and was determined to write Gavin and get him out of both of our systems.

Marcus and I spent the day in our separate beds. I believed this was how it might be again, that he and I would live like this forever, two parts of the same confused entity, together but separate from hereon in. I would write; Marcus would be Marcus.

But change is the only thing that's certain.

He resumed his ways, calling on old lovers and seeing one, then another the next night, and another. But the women had no effect on his sadness. Everything about our apartment was infected somehow by the presence and absence of Gavin. One morning, a week after my return, once the click of the door and the tap of stilettos down the stairs signalled that Constanza had left, I got up from my bed and entered Marcus's room.

I went to the bed, which smelled of grapefruit and fish. He was naked, his arm draped over his eyes. I pulled the sheet over him before I sat down on the mattress. His hair still surprised me. I would never get used to it. It spiked up on the top of his head and matted at the back.

"What will you do now?"

He looked at the ceiling as if hearing something.

"It's too old here," he concluded. I knew exactly what he meant but I didn't want to acknowledge that he might be thinking of leaving.

"Did you see them push the teacher?" I asked, flatly, realizing that I hadn't fully grasped it from his telling. He shrugged and shook his head at the same time, clarifying nothing.

"Where would you go?"

"Somewhere newer. The States . . ." He sat up and adjusted the pillows to support his back. "Or Canada!" he added with enthusiasm, and for a moment the flattery convinced me. I imagined us living together in Montreal, though I could imagine him better in New York.

"Everything that's there comes here eventually," I said, trying to beat him at his own reasoning.

"But as Eurotrash."

"Trash is trash," I trumped. I kissed his forehead and left his room. I was lost. If he left, I'd have to leave too, and my options were just as they are now: Canada, to live with my mother before finding a proper job and acknowledging my failure as a writer, or Paris, with my dad and his new wife, where I would feel like a burden.

Marcus went out that morning to visit Christophe. It was that day, Christophe told me, that the idea of the naked human run had surfaced. Marcus visited the Plaza de Toros and sat with Christophe as he tended the bulls. San Fermin was a few weeks away. I imagine that Marcus watched the bull and felt, over and over again the kick it had given him. He would have forced himself to feel it, as though it was something he deserved time and again, and something he needed to face up to. He would have remembered the look of brute necessity on Gavin's face moments before the blow, and might have had an intimation of the nature of their entanglement. As he discussed the torment of the bulls with Christophe, Marcus casually suggested to his Swiss friend that they should run in San Fermin, but that they should take the place of the bulls and chase the *divinos*—the expert runners who stay surprisingly ahead of the bulls—and end up in the corral faced with the next great matador.

"That's it! We're the bulls. We feel the bull," Christophe said and proceeded to brainstorm the first protest that would eventually burgeon into what he was hoping would become the largest animal rights event in Europe.

Marcus furrowed his brow, disappointed at being taken so literally, and nodded at Christophe's optimism—or naivety. He too knew change took a long time.

The next day he was packed and sitting at our kitchen table in a bright orange T-shirt when I woke and shuffled to the toilet. I pretended not to see him, but on the way I noticed that his hair was styled to accentuate its new length, and that a few of his most valued objects were missing from the hall table. I sat on the toilet for a long time, imagining that I would postpone goodbye forever if I didn't come out. Finally I gave in and shuffled into the kitchen and sat down.

"You should write something that means something to you. Don't pose," he said, almost cruelly.

"Oh, ya? And what will you do that means something?" I shot back. He looked wounded and I felt wretched. "Are you taking those, then?" I pointed back into his room towards his paintings on the wall.

He shook his head. "I'll do more."

"So, America, then?" I asked.

"Nope." I wanted him to stay the Spanish Lothario I had met. I didn't want nope and yep coming from him.

"Where, then?"

"London, first, to see *mi madre*, then . . . I've been thinking about Cuba. Use my Spanish."

I felt a wave of love for him that nearly tipped me off my chair.

He stood up and lifted his pack from the floor. I started to perspire. He walked to the door and turned to wait for me to come to him for the ritual friendly goodbye that would be our last.

I stood and limped my way to him. I was ungraceful, still in pain from my bruises. I held his head and ran my fingers through the thick black wires of his hair and pulled his face forward as I'd been wanting to do for two years.

Our tongues met.

The taste of his saliva was strange but not unfamiliar—a warm recognition that felt both right and wrong all at once. He pulled away and looked at me.

"Too bad that didn't come sooner," he said, looking serious. I didn't know whether or not to laugh. Or be cross. He was teasing me.

He turned away. "Look me up," he said in Spanish as he headed down the stairs.

I stayed, fidgeting and thirsty, in Pamplona for another six weeks. I nursed my leg and my scrapes with arnica. I spent the rest of my time at the bar, working again, saving my tips, and in the daytime I read. It was during those next few weeks that stories began to circulate, in snippets, Chinese whispers of events passed from pilgrim to pilgrim. My name was attached to them as was Marcus's. The story of Gavin had gone from news to lore. That was enough. I left. I stopped in London on my way back to Canada to look for Marcus but I never found him. I didn't realize then that the first kiss I had with Sam was not dissimilar to the one I had shared with Marcus.

I miss him.

Thirty

Today I worked with Christophe as a way of getting my mind off, among other things, the conversation with my mother I had last night. Christophe is struggling to maintain his vision of the Naked Human Race in the face of the bullying—there's no more apt a word—from the city bureaucrats. PETA has secured the permit based on a compromise: no full frontal nudity. He's despondent, so my work has helped him, and it has kept me grounded. He hasn't told his friends and fellow nudists from last year what has happened, hoping, I think, that they will not be discouraged and leave. I have turned on my phone and have been helping secure campsites for the participants. There have been further complications for the event, with the threat that the bull run will be cancelled due not to protest but to the viral outbreak of Bluetongue disease in the south of Spain. Restrictions on the transport of bulls to uninfected areas might mean that for the first time since 1591 San Fermin will be called off. But Christophe believes the Spanish officials will turn a blind eye and allow the pedigree bulls entry. Bureaucrats are good at hedging, he said, and the protest will be stronger if the bull run proceeds.

I called my mother last night to check on the funds, and I'm still unsettled by our conversation.

"Maybe you should live in Montreal," she said when I opened up the topic of what to do next.

"Why do you say that?" I asked.

"Lovely men," she said. I hated her on Sam's behalf.

"And why would anyone in Montreal be better than Spain?" I asked sarcastically.

"My experience, that's all."

"But Dad is from France, not Quebec."

"Oh God, not him."

"What do you mean 'not him'?"

"A man I met before your father . . . I wanted to marry him."

"What?"

"We were in love, but my parents didn't approve. He was Lebanese. They were old-fashioned and wouldn't let me see him. They liked your father, though, but I was still in love with him all those years. Emil—you were named after him, but your father didn't know that then."

What? I asked silently. "What do you mean 'all those years'?"

"Through our marriage . . . it was why your father left."

My skull felt as if it would crack open. My father had left because my mother had loved Emil who was not an Emily, but the love of her life? All these years I had believed that my mother's mewing had been a result of her loss of my father, and that somehow it had been my fault. But no, it had been because of my namesake.

"What happened to Emil?"

"He got married, but we write now and then."

They wrote 'now and then'? Now? And then?

"Gotta go, Mom. I'll let you know when I'm leaving here."

How much more of my own life didn't I know? I didn't have the wherewithal to pursue this question. Christophe called me right after I hung up and, thankfully, has kept me busy on the phone.

The number of people needing campsites is higher than we expected. I've found a few farmers as far as Estella who are willing to let some of the visitors stay, for a very small fee. One farmer said he'd take fifty, for which I'm sure he'd need a permit, but I didn't mention it, knowing that San Fermin is Pamplona's one chance each year for fast cash. There are still many runners without accommodation—they are competing with the tourists who have come to watch El Encierro. I am humbled by Christophe's determination to accommodate everyone. I feel capable only of distraction. I need to get away from Spain altogether, but my heart won't let me leave yet.

Christophe took me to see the recent bull imports for the Encierro. These are old and ill. They snort listlessly. He assured me that the prized bulls in transit from the south are fiercely superior, and that by Thursday these will have been so prodded and electroshocked that they will make a good show through the streets for tourists and locals alike who need to shore up their manhood.

Run, baby, run.

Marta is from Denmark. She looks roughly my age, but is very unlike me. Tall, lithe, and muscular, her face is angular, her jaw is strong, and she has thin but perfectly formed lips that need no lipstick to be seductive. Her eyes are blue and her hair is almost white, either bleached from the sun or prematurely grey, it's hard to say. She came to see me in the tiny room above the Mesón, which has become my coffin. I return here each evening to merely sit and stare and listen to the noise from the bar below. I push each thought of Sam away.

Marta needed a room, and Christophe wondered if we might share mine, not realizing how tiny it really is. It looks bigger now only because I've stuffed all my belongings into the modest wardrobe. There is nothing to stop the smoke from the bar seeping in through the cracks and spaces in the floorboards, so everything in this room is tinged yellow. I thought I should at least be willing to help, so I invited Marta to visit me here, to see for herself.

She was scantily clothed, her spaghetti string top revealing a tanned and toned belly that shamed my own pink flabbiness. She wore a cotton miniskirt and flat sandals. She stepped into the room. I stepped back, but hit the bed. She kissed me on both cheeks. Christophe had asked me not to tell her about the ban on frontal nudity, as she'd been one of the first runners, and was dedicated to the idea of authentic protest. With her perfect English, I found many other things to discuss: the nationalities of the protesters, their projected numbers, the scorching temperatures. She had encouraged hundreds of people to come to Pamplona; I wanted to preserve her excitement, which was contagious, although I felt humbled by her conviction to the cause, to any cause. When she assumed that I would be running, I had to clarify that I felt too old and flabby to strip bare in front of a whole city and TV cameras from around the world.

"Nonsense," she said with a smile, "that's the whole point. We're not models . . . and I am much older than you," she concluded.

I waved the comment away, and told her of my fear of forty, now that I was on the other side of thirty-five. She stared at me and then laughed.

"I'm forty-nine," she said simply. My shock shut me up, and she proceeded to tell me about her two teenage children, their father, who died three years before from cancer, and the fact that six months ago she had been diagnosed with Epstein-Barr.

"Sleeping eighteen hours a day keeps you youthful, I think not." Her eyes twinkled. Mono, I thought. I had an association with Epstein-Barr that came from childhood . . . *don't kiss him, you'll get mono* . . . and remembered it as the kissing disease of glandular fever that made you sleep all the time. I thought of Señora Ormaza, whom I'd left sleeping in Santiago. I realized suddenly that I'd never known the good Señora's age, but that she couldn't have been more than seventy. Or could she?

My phone rang. I answered it in confusion.

It was Marianne.

"I've been trying to call you for days," Marianne started in response to my silence. "Where are you now? How are you doing?" I shivered at the thought that something had happened to Sam. I waited.

"I wanted to let you know: Sam's clean. He's checked into a clinic; he doesn't need it physically, it's only because he knows . . ." her voice trailed off, "that it would make a difference to you."

Marta saw the look on my face and made gestures indicating she would leave. I held my hand up to stop her, shook my head.

"I want to talk to him," I said into the phone, and wondered what had changed my mind. It was something I hadn't wanted to admit yet.

"I'll tell him to call you. Tomorrow, probably," Marianne said.

"OK," I said and hung up.

Marta looked questioningly at me.

"I'm confused," I said simply. I must have looked upset, because she moved in to hug me. There was no space left in the room to step back, so I let her.

"Look, you come out for some food," she said as she released me. "I'll sleep there." She pointed to the corner under the window. My shoulders tensed.

"No, no, it's too uncomfortable!" I said. "I'll help you find another place."

"Don't be silly," she said, and there I was, silly and lost, with the feeling that I wouldn't be able to breathe if she were so close.

"I'll get some foam, make a mattress, it's not a problem." It's not a problem, I told myself, but my self wasn't listening.

"It's not that . . . it's just that I have someone coming, here." I heard myself release a desperate little whimper.

"Oh, when?"

"Soon," I said, stalling.

"I could stay until he comes. He, right?" And she smiled. "Is he the one Christophe told me about? The black man who liked you?"

"What?"

"I met him, years ago, and asked after him today, but Christophe said you'd both left, but that you've come back."

"No, he and I weren't—"

"He was lovely. Christophe said you never gave him a chance. You shut him out . . ."

"I shut who out?"

"That man you lived with back then."

"What on earth are you talking about?"

"Sorry, I didn't mean to interfere," she said, as I flattened my back against the wall.

I thought about Marcus's comment after our kiss. Had he once wanted to kiss me? I blocked him?

"How did Christophe know that?"

"Your man told him."

"He's not my man!" I yelled, and suddenly felt itchy, like the world was made of wool. I remembered that Marcus had said, *It's what you let me be*, when I'd said we were friends.

Marta nodded, indicating she understood, but neither of us knew where to go from there. I was searching for a way to understand how all the details were so disorganized, the events so out of order and unbelievable.

"Good, then there's someone else," she said, generously.

That was all it took. My face felt as though it had burst open. "You're not running nude! What on earth do you think you're playing at! They won't let you, they banned it, and he didn't tell you, don't you see? How stupid can you be!" And I kicked the bed with my foot, then picked up the edge of it, trying to overturn it. I would have thrown it out the window had it not been too heavy to lift. I wept.

Marta came up behind me, put her arms around me, and drew me to her. The sobs kept coming. "I got it all wrong," I blubbered. I thought of Emil, my mother's lover. I had spent a lifetime trying to keep my parents together and alive, equally balanced, in me. But they were just individuals who needed the love they sought in the places they sought it. By feeling responsible for everyone's life, I had been missing out on my own.

"It's not your fault," she said, and as I cried into her hair, tears and snot flowing and blending, I wondered how she could know that. "Whatever it is, it's all right," she added, though. I doubted that Christophe would forgive me for telling her about the nudity ban. But she hadn't flinched. Why didn't someone with all of Marta's troubles think that things were all too much, as Sam had? I hadn't asked for her help, but here she was offering and I wanted to accept it. Sam had been right: I have been editorializing, not helping, and, still, trying too hard.

Marta released me and stood, holding my face in her hands. I stopped crying, feeling strangely relieved that things might never line up again. It's not just about how you feel, or where you look, as I'd learned from Claire, but it was also about why you act. The lonely-creature-based reasons for what we do, or what we fail to see. I hadn't believed in myself.

I lacked Marta's gratitude.

I had turned my sense of exclusion into a career. But Gavin and I had only tricked ourselves into believing we didn't belong. I had to give him at least the humility I wanted for myself. Who was I to say what was wild and what tame? I felt the thin boundary that separates us all. And suddenly I knew how to tell the end of Gavin's story.

Thirty-One

Claire stood, dumbfounded on the pier as Gavin said, "Get in, please," once again. I held onto my bench in the bow of the rowboat, as the waves began to rock it. Men on the pier around Claire spoke quickly, and I understood that there was debate about the boat, some saying it wasn't seaworthy, others tut-tutting the owner for charging the tourists too much to hire it. Claire shook her head, and I knew that the word "murderer" was rattling around in it, like something chipped from innocence. The Galician men continued their discussion, using the old boat as an excuse to redress old scores, grievances, and shared calamities. The owner of the boat had begun to swear and to tell us that if we were going we had to go now, as he wanted his boat back in before the weather changed.

"No, no, you go without me," Claire said. "I . . . I've changed my mind."

"I'm not going without you," Gavin said, and stood up in the boat, about to get out.

"No, you should." I had tried to make it sound like a threat, but I knew he had never seen me as one. I softened and added, "Please," and touched his thigh. He stopped and looked at me.

"I have nothing to say," he said.

I panicked. I had not been alone with him since that night at his hotel, and there was a part of me still desperate to erase that image of myself. I wanted to find out why he could ignore me so easily. I wanted to talk about Marcus and who he really was, and to tell him about my own good intentions towards both of them, but I was unable to say any of that.

"Nothing about Marcus? Nothing about what I'm to do with that information?" I said instead, again with a threat in my tone.

We were caught. Both of us had sought to steal a shred of authenticity. He looked up at the sky. The mountain of white cumulus had darkened, but was not blocking the sun, which had reached an angle of intent, downwards, towards the horizon. He sat back down.

"Wait for me, please. There," he said to Claire.

He began to row. I held onto the sides of the small fishing vessel, and felt nervous, but the gentle lean of the sun seemed to make the water welcoming.

"Where to?" I asked, trying to sound cheery. He looked back at me, pausing his effortful rowing.

"This wasn't my idea," he said scornfully.

I looked in the direction we were headed and saw a bay around a point where the water looked more calm, and where I might finally be able to talk and to make up for my fumblings. I pointed, he looked towards it, then headed us in that direction.

When we reached the point, the wind's surprise show of force blew the boat close to the rocks, and Gavin had to pick up the pace. The wind persisted and was much stronger than it had first let on. We made little progress in rounding the point, and the boat crept closer towards the jagged black rock to the right. The volcanic rock was gorged with holes from the sea's tantrums over eons. I could see mussels and tiny shell-life that clung to the rock in refuge. Gavin rowed harder, and it felt like he'd suddenly discovered his strength. I wondered if he had any thought for Marcus then, Marcus's strength, Marcus's ability with his body. He might have been thinking that only real freedom would do now.

I held on tighter as the waves made it more difficult to get around the point.

"Throw out that rope," Gavin called to me, indicating with his chin the stern line near my left hand.

"To where?" I yelled back at him, anxiously.

"Its loop—let it catch on the point of the rock, on the end there." The waves were rolling in and pushing us towards the rock as he spoke. I looked out to sea and then back at the rock. The salt in the air was the perfume of wishes. I brushed sand from my hands, and remember noticing briefly the dirt beneath my nails. I took the looped rope and steadied myself as I stood, preparing to toss it out. I hesitated, wondering why securing the boat to the rock would be the right thing to do just now. Wasn't the rock something we should be trying to move away from? Gavin had seemed certain, so I threw the end of the rope, and in the instant I let go of it:

"No! Not there!" he called.

I slipped.

※

A skipped-frame flicker of a body flashed before his eyes. Her, the rope, her body, pulled forward, twisted in an impossible way at the bow, her hands holding on, one leg over the edge, the other unnaturally wrenched inside the boat, until the next wave brought the vessel careening onto rock, squeezing her torso against it, and then, in and out with the to and fro of the sea: crush, release, crush, release. He watched. He was aware of her voice, the screaming and the pain. He watched until the end of time. When time restarted he felt the now, now, now of his heart. He lunged forward and threw himself between the rock and the boat so that it would not play out its rhythmic battering of her body.

He felt the crush of the port side of the tiny vessel. But more, he felt the jagged rock with its tiny volcanic spikes. Sliding down the rock, he thought he heard tearing, an elaborate ripping of cloth, skin, flesh. His head sank below the surface of the water, farther, farther. Now more tearing. Like drilling, a tingling flow. As he opened his eyes, he could make out a watery blur of her leg beside him, and saw that on her fall forward, after the rope had slipped from her hands, she had stepped into the loop of the stern rope, become trapped, and her body was wrenched between rock and boat. He struggled to right himself, but his feet were pinned above him, his boot lodged somewhere solid. His childhood trainers flashed into mind. Too big, laces loose and the *you'll trip on those, darling* soft voice of his mother. In and out of those trainers his feet would slip, until one day they didn't and his mother hugged him and told him he'd grown up. He had wiggled out of her arms. Now he wiggled and twisted and tried to release the tightly laced Timberland from the rock.

His knife. The pearl-handled one he had flung into the night. If only he had the knife. He tried to grab the keel of the boat, but it slipped out and away, then glided back towards him as though in revenge, knocking him against the rock. His breath was running out. He looked to her leg and watched as she wriggled it loose, little by little, her hand pushing at the boat and then against the rock, her agony apparent. All that was needed was one more thrust against the boat and she might wrench herself free. He thought he saw a purple line growing down her calf towards the ankle—a line that snaked around the ankle and led him to the moment he had sensed was coming. In a *now, now* burst of certainty he heaved his head up and knocked his shoulder against the keel with all his might. The boat moved, but before he had the chance to check her position, it swung back and knocked his head. The water seeped in.

He had no capacity for irony, even though he knew that the end of the earth was a few kilometres away. But he was allowed a final gasp of insight: he had acted in the moment. He had helped her, and had not been shell-shocked in the face of necessity. Action was the question and the answer. After all, he had not actually pushed Sir. He had technically only been a witness, not a murderer, yet he had never acted on what he knew was right. He had blamed. He had chosen guilt and numbness, remaining smug in all the unbelonging he'd felt since he was a child. And he had pursued others for relief. The opposite of what it meant to be a man. He knew now, with the impossible wisdom of death, that it was simple. As he sank away from life, and his head battered the rock and lost its capacity for pain, he knew that rather than have engaged in the long prevaricating somnambulism of his adult life, all that had been required was for him to have done. Something. Purely, and without motive.

For someone else.

Thirty-Two

A bang. A crack. A whistle. No high-tech rockets. They will come in two days time, announcing the start of El Encierro. Today we have Christophe's homemade explosives sounding off the start of the Human Race. These rockets whiz and fizzle, mocking the real ones, as the runners will mock bulls.

Hundreds of people have come. Christophe would not have been able to predict these numbers even a few days ago, but his surprise has given him the graciousness of a host at his first party. He has swallowed his pride at the compromise of half-nudity offered by PETA to the city officials, and he greets the various animal rights groups and eager individuals with enthusiasm.

I watch.

In two days' time the bulls of San Fermin will bring out a display of men of all shapes and sizes defining masculinity. They will dress in white with red neckerchiefs and waistbands, some still drunk from the night before, and stand in wait for the first call of the festival to run the 848 metres to the *corrida*. The tension in the air will be thick, the testosterone nearly liquid.

Today, however, men, women, and children are having protest slogans painted on their chests, bottoms, and arms. They too wear the red neckerchiefs of San Fermin, but little else. A woman wearing only a thong is having an N painted on one butt cheek and an O on the other. A young mother, holding a toddler in diapers and also wearing bull horns, stands beside her husband. Both are in their underwear and red neckerchiefs, the man holding a sign that reads: *Stoppt den graussemen Stierkampf!* Another sign, painted on a white sheet and held up in front of the naked breasts of three blonde women reads: *!No a las corridas de toros!* Still others—a man in a small thong with Vegans Make the Best Lovers painted on his chest—prepare themselves for the run. An elderly couple in red sashes that barely cover their genitals hold a sign that reads, Join the Human Race. Some people remain completely clothed, watching, like me.

The drumming is infectious. I can feel it in my throat and down through my chest as the musicians warm up. It's carnival.

The press of bodies feels dangerous. I think of the Bluetongue virus and what Sam would have to say about the unlikelihood of it being a real threat to Pamplona's livestock. But everything is possible. Today's heat, the live nakedness, the drums, make the tsunami feel so very far away, but its urgency, the day that began under water, has had its consequences. My story is finished, and yet I had no idea it would take me where I am now. I have been following my thoughts towards an inevitable collision, and I spent the morning in an Internet café.

From what I can understand of the data posted on a new Web site I discovered, viruses mutate in one of two ways: either a slow, low-key change that usually results in a minor public-health problem; or a fast, highly important genetic transformation that is cause for great social alarm. The big leap, called a genetic reassortment, occurs when one type of virus swaps genes with a related virus. That way it gains characteristics that it did not have before, becoming able, for instance, to leap to other species, become more virulent or contagious. If I consider Gavin's guilt in these terms, I think it has brought me closer to knowing who I have been.

There are many ways of being in prison. Gavin saved my life, in perhaps more ways than one.

A papier mâché bull head, carefully constructed and lifelike, passes before me. The bull is wearing sunglasses. A list on the bull's naked human arse reads: No Laxatives, No Shaving, No Vaseline, in commiseration with what the bulls of San Fermin are subjected to. The Vaseline that blurs their vision—along with the blinding Spanish sun after being kept in dark cellars before the run—causes them to slip and slide over cobblestones and into the high walls of the narrow streets. This bull wants none of that. A woman in her sixties, wearing only panties, follows behind the bull. Her drooping breasts are like two ripe figs. On the back of her panties is a delicately painted sign: Granny for the Human Race.

The drumbeat gets louder.

More and more people crowd in at the starting point outside the corral at Santo Domingo, and I am in awe of the mass of humanity before me. In this tiny space between the high walls there is only room for something like madness. Does madness breed in a cage?

I am hot.

And jiggling inside.

"You're not stripped," I hear over my shoulder. "Come, I will paint you."

I turn around to see Marta, completely naked, with a set of

horns on a strap around her head. The painted sheet she is carrying says something in Danish on one side. I can't read the English on the side she wraps around her. She ties it over her breasts and under her arms, and then picks up the small paint tin and brush at her feet. She looks tired, but I know that she slept many hours last night, because I let her stay with me in the tiny room above the Mesón. She started on the floor, but in the middle of the night, sleepless myself, I got up and led her to the tiny, rickety bed, which we shared, and where we both slept like pups in a lair.

"Come, you need green," she says with authority. A tall blond man in a thong nudges her by accident as he passes through the crowd. She eyes him quickly then turns back to me with a smile.

"No, no, I don't think so." I have to speak more loudly as the drumming is taking over. "I was just helping out," I say, feeling silly in this heat, where nakedness is simply common sense.

"You disappoint me," Marta says, loud and clear, and I shrink. Of course I do. I am neither wild nor free. "I thought you'd be one of us—the two or three—who are going to defy this ridiculous statute of covering up. It's the whole point. It was why I came. Otherwise, it's senseless. Just like PETA—a childish game," she continues, and I feel even smaller, humiliated by my passivity.

Another rocket goes up. A middle-aged man with a potbelly ties a red scarf around his neck and strips off his trousers. I notice the dwarfed sac in his underpants, overwhelmed by the rippling belly that falls to shade it.

"We'll run, not march, the ones who join me. We'll cut along the sides," she points towards the walls, "and go in front, when we get the signal—the next rocket to go up." Marta turns, interrupted by another woman wrapped in a sheet. I watch them walk off and wonder why I've never joined in. Why would one choose to write life rather than live it? I am not a real writer anyway, just someone posing on the outside and looking in.

I feel a vibration in my pocket. It's my mobile.

I press the green button.

It's Sam.

"Hello? Hello?"

I hear him, barely, as the wavering pauses and the static obscure any clear connection. I make my way through the crowd, towards the front, my fingers covering my left ear as I press the phone to my right. His voice sharp and rapid-firing. He doesn't mention that night. He says that he's going to come here, to take me back with him to Santiago, look after me for a change, and prove to me that the world has not passed from him, not yet. He wants therapy and flying lessons. As the static takes over and the sound of drums and trumpets takes up a place in my chest, I realize he sounds different. Taller. Is it possible that it's not all too much? He promises me a change. He sees now. It's been long enough, he says.

Poor Thomas, I think. Really alone now.

The connection goes dead.

I am being pushed and shoved by the half-naked bodies of the Human Race. I put the phone back in my pocket. I take off my T-shirt and toss it on the ground, where it gets trampled on by the marchers anxious to begin.

Up on my toes, I peer over breasts, heads, horns, and placards, looking for Marta, trying to discern if there is Danish on any of the sheets I can see.

I slip out of my sandals. I am even shorter.

I reach a corner with a bench and stand on it to look out

above the crowd to see if I can spot her. I undo the clasp of my trousers and then the zip. I slip them off. Sudden, loud laughter nearby startles me, and for a moment I think it's directed at me, at my short and flabby body, pocked with scars, thighs like orange peel. But I don't care. I don't have to moralize. I don't have to describe the laugh; I can just listen.

I step down from the bench, leaving my trousers there. In my bra and panties I again press past the bodies that are no longer naked enough for me. Then I see her. Marta and other women are wrapped in sheets that read JOIN THE HUMAN RACE. They are making their way to the head of the crowd. A tall, skinny man, a red cloth wrapped at his waist, follows them.

"Marta!" I shout, but of course she doesn't hear me. I have to press my way past too many people, and I begin to worry I won't make it to her before she starts. A muscular man with horns and red underpants puts a placard in my hand, but I hand it back with a *"gracias"* that sounds angry, but I don't mean it to be. I just need to get to Marta.

The tempo of drums and horns increases; start-time is near. I reach my hand around to my back and unclasp my bra, which releases my breasts like seeds from their husk. I feel the heat of the sun's rays as though they are aimed at my breasts alone. Not since I was a teenager at Mazinaw Lake, on the cliff face where I would escape to examine my slow accomplishments as a woman, have my breasts been directly exposed to the sunlight. The heat blurs my mind, and I try to form the story of this, to see how it fits with Gavin's.

I want Marcus to have a better story.

But all stories are slipping away, and I am an unworthy scribe. Loose ends are bad form. Characters must resolve their arcs; there must be closure and resolution. The truth is I don't know what happened to Claire.

But there is Marta.

The rocket goes off. She drops her sheet, as do the other two women and the man. They run in front of the rest of the crowd, who are marching, holding back. Too clothed.

I slip out of my underpants.

I run.

When I reach the man, who is slower than the three women, I reduce my pace to his. Looking down, I see that his penis is large, and I find myself examining it for colour and shape, for comparison. I speed up. I pass Marta and the two women, and suddenly I'm in front of the pack.

Sam sounded taller. Can people still grow after the age of thirty?

I wonder, do I need Sam?

I can't save him.

Maybe I don't need Sam. I slow down, and then veer to the left. My elbow grazes the steep wall of the Cuesta de Santo Domingo. Marta passes me with the two other women right behind her. I am back beside the man with the large penis. Maybe I don't need Sam; I am my own alpha, after all.

As the man and I cut sharply left, onto the Mercaderes, we try to catch up to Marta and the women, who are now at the town hall. I feel a tingle in my nipple. Sun and motion. And I think, no, I do need Sam. I couldn't do this alone. I don't want immunity.

I want to be changed.

A sharp right turn and I hear the babble of the crowd and whistles, their surprise at our defiance. The man's arm rams into mine; his turn is not sharp enough. I pick up speed to put distance between us. As I enter the Calle Estafeta I know I have only four hundred more metres of a straight run. I catch up to the women. Two of them are breathing heavily while Marta is soaring like a gazelle. Shoulder to shoulder, she and I curve left through the *callejón*, the narrow tunnel leading into the bullring.

I brush arms with Marta, then to my right feel the man, and hear the women just behind me.

Here we are.

As we enter the bullring to the sound of nothing—no crowd, no cheering—we slow, and I try to remember what's true, and what it is that I will tell Sam. But standing in the centre of the bullring, bent over, holding my side, and containing laughter that is rising along with Marta's, I realize how our stories are mixed up with one another's. It was Gavin's story, then it was mine, and now it's yours. Our need brings language. Bleeding, silver voices.

Marta's laughter bursts forth and inhabits me, and the others also start to convulse with it. It is the laughter that accompanies knowledge; the long, slow flame that launches a story. As the sounds of the Human Race approach the bullring, I swallow the necessity to pronounce our success to Marta. We acknowledge our act in silence, and the rocket that rises up over the Calle Estafeta confirms the uselessness of a sentence.

We laugh.

Her voice is mine.

My tongue is hers.

And look.

My spit has the taste of you.

Acknowledgements

Many books and people have inspired this work.

I am indebted to Anne Carson's "Anthropology of Water" in *Plainwater*, for first thoughts about the Camino. The following books provided guidance and insight: Alison Raju, *The Way of St. James*; Davies and Cole, *Walking the Camino de Santiago*; Tim Moore, *Spanish Steps*; and Jared Diamond, *Guns, Germs and Steel*. Helen Humphreys' *Wild Dogs* and Fides Krucker's *Yours to Break* confirmed my hunch about the blurred line between wild and tame. Grace Cavalieri's poem "Day of the Dead" in *Only the Sea Keeps: Poetry of the Tsunami* made me ask "if we who are alive really live," and inspired phrases on language and blood.

Thanks to Roma Backhouse for correspondence from the Camino; to Susan Shipton for Mazinaw Lake; to Mike Meegan for Kenya; to Laurel Sherret for legal research into juvenile penal institutions in the UK; to Carolina Aivars, Liam Needs, and Alex Needs for Spanish phrases; to Melissa Grunberger for story insight; to David Godwin for belief in me; and to Stephanie Young for faithful feedback, enthusiasm, and "the tape."

This book would not have been possible without the patience and determination of Iris Tupholme, who thankfully never let up in her conviction that there was more for me to explore. Jennifer Lambert's astute and creative encouragement helped me to take it farther, and Attila Berki's precise editorial eye was invaluable. Thanks to Noelle Zitzer, Allegra Robinson, and everyone involved in the process at HarperCollins.